W9-AVI-158

ALTERED STATES

Sci-fi and Fantasy
Stories About Change

A Main Street Rag
Short Fiction Anthology

Edited by
Amy Locklin

MINT HILL BOOKS
MAIN STREET RAG PUBLISHING COMPANY
CHARLOTTE, NORTH CAROLINA

Acknowledgments:

> *The Southern Review*: "If You Must Know" (as "Honeydew")
> *Barrelhouse*: "My Mantle"
> *2004 Robert Olen Butler Prize Stories* (Del Sol Press, 2005): "My
>   Polish Widower"
> *The Marlboro Review*: "Paris Street"
> *Salvage*: *Literature and Art for the Capital Region* [of New York
> State]: "Once I Was a Gravedigger"

Library of Congress Control Number: 2011935281

ISBN: 978-1-59948-313-9

Produced in the United States of America

Mint Hill Books
Main Street Rag Publishing Company
PO Box 690100
Charlotte, NC 28227
www.MAINSTREETRAG.COM

Contents

Introduction

Change defines us. Time ticks another moment lost thrusting us forward even when we would prefer to look back. Some folks call for change; some become lost within it; some seek control, some abandon, some denial, and some merely witness, when facing it; some have adapted to change in the distant past.

Science fiction and fantasy genres dramatize the human response to change with heightened symbolic meaning. In this way they are most like poetry. When experiencing realism we can feel comfortable in a literal reading, even when a narrative overflows with metaphors and subtext that warn us against such complacency. In contrast, fantastic genres force us to feel discomfort, to see the unfamiliar in the previously familiar. Things are not as they appear, or not only as they appear.

The stories in this collection will make every reader a detective. The process of discovery will please, not just for glimmers of truth perceived, but also for the artistic choices made, at times subtle, flamboyant, risky, mysterious, and outright funny.

I became interested in seeing a theme of change represented in sci-fi and fantasy short fiction in part because of popular debates concerning politics, psychology, socioeconomics, and the environment. Many fights are more about keeping things the same than about finding the best answer and too often in real life the anxiety of influence trumps making necessary change. I had long known the power of fantastic literature to address those realms of experience we deny, for instance the power of dreams. Dreams can exert an influence over us whether we remember them or not. Fantastic literature forces us to remember.

The thirty sci-fi and fantasy stories in *Altered States* will push our understanding of human nature and change to surprising new levels. Organized in five subsections, "On Reality," "On Place," "On Family," "On Romance," and "On the Body," the short stories here speak to each other and challenge our definitions of these essential categories of experience.

Amy Locklin, Editor

On Reality

GREEN GROW THE LILACS

Larry Lefkowitz

'Green Grow the Lilacs', the phrase unaccountably jumped into Brendon's mind, as Giselle turned, smoothly but unmistakably, into a lilac bush. A white lilac bush, not unfittingly, he thought as his second thought, Giselle having always favored white. His third thought (his having absorbed the reality by now) was: what happened?—or rather, What/how did this happen?

It was likely connected with Thelp, his and Giselle's host and guide on a tour of the creature's planetoid. He and Giselle were galaxy tax collector and galaxy tax assessor, respectively; they had come to the planetoid to inventory Thelp's taxable property and tax it on behalf of the galaxy. "A pittance," he had explained to Thelp over dinner, and so Thelp had seemed to consider it at the time—but how to explain flowering Giselle? How indeed. Cellular transubstantiation skills on the part of Thelp was Brendon's first thought, but he surmised that it was equally possible that Thelp might have employed ultra-penetrating mind-illusion control. A control so powerful that even Brendon's surmising that it was an illusion might not be enough to break through its concomitant mind-block. He chastised himself for engaging in such speculations, however brief, given Gizelle's predicament. Although she was not always the most companionable of partners, her professional ability merited her his commiseration.

He did not commiserate long—comforting Giselle by petting her bark, let alone her flowers did not seem right, somehow. Nor even bestowing a reassuring pat on the large blue cephalic flower that, Brendon discerned, crowned the lilac bush in front of him and at the same time separated it from any known variety. He did have the presence of mind, however, to impart, "Giselle, I'll get back to you soon as I can. Don't mo—," he stopped himself, not sure Giselle could hear. Yet he felt that she probably could, Giselle had always possessed a certain utilitarian intuition.

His seeming lack of empathy came as a surprise to him. But then he was an optimist, and besides, as a tax inspector, he had seen a lot of things on a lot of planets around a lot of stars. And at 210, he, Brendon Bolingate, was at a somewhat jaded age. On one hand, Brendon was your stereotyped galaxy tax collector who had made his way up from planetary and regional stages to the galaxy classification level, by dint of an almost laser-like memory of the voluminous galaxy tax code combined with a certain withering glance which put collectees on the requisite defensive. Added to which was a certain mannered charm that often was effective with recalcitrant taxpayers when joined to actual, or implied, threats of punishment under the code.

His partner, Giselle, possessed the sharp, if somewhat actuarial, mind necessary for tax assessing. Her only prepossessing physical feature was her fulgurant blue hair, which often served to cause her assessees to dub her 'Giselle with the dark blue hair' after the words of the popular song, an assumed familiarity that failed to soften her assessments. For these she favored a blue laser-scripter, and there were those who thought the choice of color a purposeful sobering response to any actual or potential distracters on the subject of her hair coloration. She favored matching blue toe- and finger- nail shading, using a lacquer she had found at a bargain-sale (on which planet Brendon couldn't recall), whose aroma was too tart for his taste, though it possessed a certain musk-like substratum whose sensuality stimulated him, usually for naught as far as Giselle was concerned. He had once supplemented the lacquer with a bit of aphrodisiac from the moon of Atrana (the extolled 'Attranan attar of ecstacy') but Giselle had been so uncharacteristically aggressive as a result, and worse (from Brendon's measured viewpoint) so uncharacteristically feminine, that he rued the night he had added it. A post-coital realization (and apparently some chemical verification) on Giselle's part as to the cause of her uncharacteristic responses, led to a month long super-bitchiness from her that cured Brendon forever of tampering with anything of Giselle's.

"Thelp," Brendon shouted, suspecting the rascal was about somewhere surely spying on his reaction. Maybe that explained his own attempt at sangfroid. Panicking would play into Thelp's hands, or rather, prehensiles. Thelp could grasp forcefully, as he had learned on that first de rigueur digit grasp. Thelp's failure to respond caused Brendon to remove his verbal gloves. "Thelp, I'll triple your taxes," he shouted.

A slight waver in a crimson bush some multi-meters away showed he had calculated correctly. An orange-brown eight-digited "hand" rose above the crimson, followed promptly by the rest of Thelp, where had stood the bush.

Brendon was perspiring now. The playful, genial Thelp of the night before when he had hosted him and Giselle upon their arrival (the rascal paying particular attention to him, less gracious to Giselle, perhaps because he, Brendon, had the tax clout as tax collector)—the quondamly Puckish Thelp, now seemed sinister in the light of day. Not in the way he stood, his attitude relaxed, but in the power he obviously exerted over Giselle. In his sixty years of tax collecting, Brendon had seen a lot of tax dodges, but nothing quite like this. He hesitated between a threatening approach and a cajoling one. Better to play it cagey, he cautioned himself. Trying to control his voice, he approached Thelp and stood, arms folded, glowering.

"Enjoy your walk?" Thelp inquired in that mellifluous voice of his. There was something alienating about Thelp even in a galaxy where 'alienation' was of necessity common, and which concept Brendon had to work against mentally invoking on meeting new 'variations' of intelligent life, since a form might possess mind-reading skills. A proper initial mind-set was crucial to tax collecting success.

Brendon forced back his anger. "Giselle … had an accident."

Thelp's features transformed themselves so rapidly into a surprised and then sympathetic mien that Brendon thought for a moment, but only for a moment, that Thelp may not have had anything to do with Giselle's transformation. "Really?" expressed Thelp.

There was something in this 'really' that disabused Brendon of his momentary absolution. But what was at work here—artifice or caprice—or both? Brendon felt himself losing patience, the quintessential Earth trait, responsible for 'the patience of Earth' as ironic metaphor for impatience used throughout the galaxy.

"Giselle has been turned into a plant," Brendon said evenly, carefully choosing the passive form.

Thelp caught it immediately. "It must have been something she ate."

Brendon almost smiled, before catching himself. If Giselle had been less of a tart-tongued colleague (and more often a willing, if somewhat mechanical, sex-partner), he wouldn't have even thought of smiling. Still, to get a replacement for her would require a lot of time and bureaucratic effort, not to speak of personal breaking-in. "We only ate at your place," Brended reminded Thelp, loosing patience.

"On second thought, not something she ate—since you are not a plant," Thelp pointed out helpfully.

Controlling himself, Brendon replied evenly, "I remind you that the penalty for obstruction of a galaxy tax collector, not to speak of harming same, is severe. Incidentally, toying with the tax appraiser is also forbidden."

"Perhaps if my assessment were less…" Thelp lay down to concretize his message.

Brendon was on him in an instant. It was forbidden to use violence to enforce tax collection, but Brendon was seeking more than taxes now. He was seeking Giselle. In any event, the galaxy judicial apparatus was far away. He threw Thelp to the ground on his back, then held him there by dint of his boot on the latter's throat, a very sensitive spot for Thelp's indigenomorphology, but not a totally inapposite move since if Thelp ever got his prehensiles on Brendon in anger, he wouldn't have a chance. Thelp began to gag immediately, and turn beige, his prehensiles thrashing about in panic.

Brendon eased the pressure. "If I finish you, your property escheats to the galaxy, and it will be sold off. I'll handle the sale myself. Transform Giselle back and I'll knockoff five percent from her assessment. Giselle will be angry, but I'm not such a stickler. Agreed?"

Thelp made a sound incapable of being interpreted as assent or dissent. Yet it sounded as if it had assent possibilities.

"Well …?" asked Brendon, relaxing the pressure slightly.

"You are most gracious," Thelp gasped. "Also most earth-like. I agree."

"You can change her back?"

What passed for smile appeared on Thelp's features. "Of course. At least I hope so."

You bastard, thought Brendon, hoping he was being playful and not truthful. "Let's go."

Thelp skipped along ahead of Brendon and waited next to still flowering Giselle until Brendon, heavier, arrived.

"Well ..." menaced Brendon.

"You're sure?" asked Thelp. "I sensed last night that—"

"What's that!?" glared Brendon.

"That you and I might be—compatible. That with no third party to interfere or to tell the tale ... to suggest that a bribe was at work ..."

Brendon felt himself reddening. He was engulfed with a realization that Thelp hadn't read the situation altogether wrong. He started to perspire. The tax code did not cover a situation like this. He looked at Giselle and back at Thelp. Those prehensiles were capable of affording infinite pleasure, if used skilfully, he mused.

Was it his imagination or did Giselle's branches sway ever so slightly? Perhaps she was angry.

He looked at Thelp, who stood, prehensiles on hips, watching him carefully. He looked back at Giselle. He sniffed Giselle, trying to recall if he had ever told her that since a child he was stimulated in an almost aphrodisiac way by the aroma of lilac.

THE GUIDE

Eva Langston

Friday evening I was feeling especially low, so I drove to Wal-Mart and bought a shovel. It felt good to have a purpose. I am buying a shovel, I thought. For what purpose? To dig a hole.

I came home with my new shovel and went out into the small backyard that I share with my downstairs neighbor, Gloria, a fifty-something-year-old school librarian. Gloria never uses the back yard, so I didn't think she'd mind if I dug a hole in it. Outside, it was getting dark, and the nighttime cold stung my cheeks. I stuck my shovel into the hard dirt and jumped on it, feeling the satisfying sink as it crunched into the ground.

I dug until my hands developed blisters and the t-shirt under my jacket was damp with sweat. I piled the dirt near the fence, away from the hole. My plan was to make the hole big enough to sit in. I would sit for awhile, enjoying the feeling of being inside the ground, surrounded by the earth. I would scrape at the sides of the hole, letting the dirt jam up underneath my fingernails. Then I would get out, take a shower, and go to bed.

Digging took a lot longer than I expected. When I had finally made the hole big enough to sit in, I let the shovel drop from my throbbing fingers, and I practically threw myself in.

Then a strange thing happened. I just kept falling. For awhile I fell in darkness and silence, too surprised to scream. When I finally stopped falling, I found myself standing, in broad daylight, on a busy street corner. There was a small park behind me, and across the street marched a row of cheerful-looking brick houses. I knew at once I had fallen into an alternate reality because the cars looked strange, and the traffic lights changed from purple to orange to blue.

Almost as soon as I landed, a man came up to me. He held a small book, and his thumb was stuck inside it to hold his place. "Hi," he said. "Are you," he opened the book and consulted the page, "Emma?"

"Maybe. Maybe not." I looked at him suspiciously. My name is Mary Beth, but I don't like giving personal information to strangers.

"Hmm." He smiled. "Are you here to meet someone, by any chance? I'm Hadley."

I looked at him carefully. He was about my age—mid-thirties—and normal looking: brown hair, receding just a little, and brown eyes that were small and close together. I would not go so far as to say that he was attractive. His nose looked like a large blob of play dough pressed onto the middle of his face, and his eyebrows were overgrown. His lips were thin, and his teeth, though straight, were too small for his mouth. He seemed friendly, though, and harmless.

He looked at me expectantly, smiling all the while, and I shook my head. "No. I'm not here to meet anyone. I'm not really sure why I'm here."

"You're not sure? Did you follow your guide?"

"Guide?" I said. "No. I fell through a hole, and now I think I'm in an alternate reality."

I expected Hadley to think I was joking, or crazy, but instead he nodded sympathetically. "That sounds upsetting." He led me into the park and motioned for me to sit down on a bench that faced the street corner where we had been standing. "But I suppose anything is possible. What does your guide say?"

"What do you mean?"

Hadley held up the little book, with his thumb still stuck inside. "Your life guide," he said.

"Wait—what? Let me see." I reached over and grabbed the book out of his hand. The cover was made of soft, flexible leather, and it had his name printed in gold on the front: Hadley Stevens. Inside, it was labeled with tabs, like an old-fashioned address book. Each tab had a number: seven through eighty-nine. I started to flip it open, but Hadley snatched the book away from me.

"What are you doing? You can't read other people's guides!" A sharp line appeared between his close-set eyes. He tucked the book into his shirt pocket and held his hand over it for a moment.

"Your life came with instructions?" I asked.

"Sure. Didn't yours?"

"No. I thought the whole point of life is that it doesn't."

The crinkle between Hadley's eyes deepened. "But how do you know what to do?"

I shrugged, feeling grumpy. "I have to figure it out myself."

"Everyone in your world must do this?" he asked.

"Yep."

This seemed unfathomable to poor Hadley Stevens. His mouth opened and then closed, then opened again. "But what if you do the wrong thing?" he asked. "What if you accidentally mess up?"

"Oh," I said. "That happens all the time. Believe me."

"Wow." Hadley shook his head. "I can't imagine."

"What about here? Aren't there some people who don't follow their instructions and mess everything up?"

"Now and then," Hadley said. "Someone might misread their directions. But it's rare. And no one goes against their guides. That would be like buying a computer and purposefully setting it up incorrectly. Why would you do that?"

"That's different," I said, but I could tell Hadley didn't think so.

He leaned forward, watching someone cross the intersection to the street corner where we had been standing. It was a man, and Hadley sighed and leaned back against the park bench.

"So your guide told you to come here today?" I asked. "And meet a girl named Emma?"

Hadley nodded. He pulled his book out of his pocket and thumbed the tab labeled with a thirty-six. He read it silently then looked up at me. "Yes," he said. "This street corner. Meet a woman named Emma who is going to be important in my life."

"And will her guide tell her to come here so she can meet a man named Hadley who's going to be important in her life?"

"Something like that," Hadley said. "It may not tell her why, but it will tell her to come here." He was beginning to sound annoyed, and he stared at the street corner, lifting his eyes up for a moment as if expecting another woman to fall from the sky.

"What if she doesn't follow her instructions?" I asked.

"Why would she do that?"

"I don't know. Never mind."

Hadley didn't say anything.

I sat next to him, thinking for awhile. In a way, I wished I had instructions for my life. Especially at this point. I was at a dead end, and there didn't seem to be anywhere to go but down. The more I thought about it, though, the more I wondered if it would have made a difference. Even if I'd had a guide, I probably wouldn't have followed it. I was always doing things I knew I shouldn't do. Even with a really great manual, I probably would have ended up in the same crap-hole life I was in now.

"Well, Hadley, I hope she comes," I said loudly, patting his knee. He frowned at me. He probably wanted me to go away so he could concentrate on waiting for his precious Emma, the goody-goody who followed all of her life instructions.

If I'd had a set of life instructions, what would they have been? Marry Greg, they probably would have told me, instead of ruining things with him. It sure would have been nice to have that information at the time. I didn't realize I loved him until it was too late.

Maybe if I'd had life instructions, I wouldn't be living alone, drinking too much, and working a low-paying job that I hate. Maybe a guide would have told me how to prevent becoming estranged from my family, how to make good friends, how to keep from racking up a credit card debt so massive I'd never pay it off in my lifetime.

I turned to Hadley. "You've followed every instruction?" I asked. "Down to the t?"

"Yes," he said.

I wanted to smack him, the smug bastard.

And that's when I got one of my sick little ideas, the kind that twists into my stomach and makes me feel like I have to shit. It's the same feeling I had when I decided to sleep with my friend Donna's husband. The same feeling I had when I got cute little Jen fired by telling my boss she was stealing office supplies. That sick-happy-guilty-excited feeling of doing something I know I shouldn't.

"Hadley," I said, reaching out and grabbing his arm. "You said Emma, right?"

"I did." He turned and looked at me.

"My name's Emily," I lied. "But my family calls me Emma."

Hadley's eyes grew wide, and I thought I saw a twitch of disappointment in his lips.

"Really?" he said. "Why didn't you tell me before?"

I shrugged. "I don't know. It didn't occur to me because I don't normally introduce myself as Emma."

"Hmm," Hadley said. "So you might be…"

"The woman who's going to be important in your life," I finished for him. I put my hand on his knee again and squeezed. "What do you think about that?"

Hadley looked down at my hand; it seemed to make him uncomfortable. I just laughed. Being bad can be quite energizing, at least at first. When I started sleeping with Donna's husband, I went to the gym every day and got in really great shape. Of course, when Donna found out and the whole thing became a shit-show, I stayed at home sleeping and drinking and gaining all the weight back.

But I wasn't thinking about that now. This was the beginning, the exhilaration of the free-fall. I scooted closer to Hadley. "Come on," I said. "We don't need to stay here anymore. You've found what you were looking for."

I stood up and offered him my hand. "Why don't you show me around?"

Hadley frowned, pressing his thin lips together for a moment. "I don't know," he said. "Maybe I should stay here a little longer, just to make sure. It said name, not nickname. What if there's someone whose real name is Emma who I'm supposed to meet?"

"It's getting dark," I said. The sky was a deeper shade of blue, and a ghostly crescent moon had appeared. "What time were you supposed to meet her?"

"It just said afternoon."

"Well…" I lifted my arms in an exaggerated shrug. "Here I came, falling out of the afternoon sky. You can't argue with the guide."

I reached for his hand again, and this time he let me pull him to standing. "Should we walk through the park?" I asked.

Hadley took one glance at the street corner, and then he looked at me, a determined smile on his pitiful face. "Sure," he said. "I'll show you the Flying Cat Fountain."

"Sounds great." I hooked my arm through the crook of his elbow. It was only then that I noticed my fingernails were black with dirt.

The alternate reality world was really very much like my own. The differences were small: the traffic light colors, the strange playground equipment, the way people threw matchsticks instead of pennies into the fountain for good luck. And the flying cat—a mythical beast sort of like our Pegasus. I wondered if I was going to stay here forever, or if I'd wake up eventually and find myself at home in bed. I expected to be more anxious about my unknown future, but I was amazingly relaxed. Besides, what did I have back home except for a new shovel and a bottle of vodka in the freezer?

"I'm hungry," I told Hadley after awhile. "Does your instruction book tell you when to eat, too?"

Hadley laughed. "No, no. The guide isn't that specific."

"So you do get to make some decisions on your own."

Hadley took me to a little Italian place within walking distance: not what I would have picked, but I was too hungry to be choosy. Over mediocre wine and salads of iceberg and tomatoes, Hadley told me about himself. He loved dogs and tennis, he said, and he was a dentist.

"So you spend a lot of time in people's mouths?" I waved a bread stick at him, trying to flirt. "You know, I might be due for a check-up." I smiled at him before chomping seductively on my bread stick.

"Well," he said. "You really should go every six months. You might have a cavity you're not even aware of. And it's important to have your bite calibrated. Years of mastication can wear down the enamel and cause pain if everything doesn't fit together properly."

"Mmm," I said, nodding and chewing. "Mastication, huh?" He was right, though. That's why I didn't like going to the dentist. They always managed to find a cavity somewhere in my back molars, and filling them in hurt, no matter how much they numbed me.

By the time our entrees came, we had finished the bottle of wine, and I took it upon myself to order another. "So," I said, twirling my fork in my pasta, "why do you think I'm going to be important in your life?"

"I don't know," Hadley said. "I have to admit when I read that…I thought maybe Emma was going to be my wife."

"Wait. Doesn't your guide tell you? Can't you look and see what it says regarding marriage on down the line?"

"No. The instructions appear as you reach the point in which you need them. That's why you have to check your guide a couple times a day to see if anything new has appeared."

"Interesting." Suddenly I was worried. Would "ditch the fake Emma," appear in Hadley's little book?

"Speaking of which." Hadley put down his fork and pulled the book out of his shirt pocket. He flipped it open. "Nope," he said. "Nothing yet."

After the second bottle of wine, I was feeling philosophical and tried to engage Hadley in a discussion of free will. "I find it so interesting," I said, slapping my hand on the red and white checkered table cloth, "that you insist everyone here always follows their instructions. I mean, don't you think, sometimes, people don't want to do what their little book tells them? Or that maybe they want to see what will happen if they don't follow the directions? Isn't that human nature?"

"Maybe where you come from." Hadley hadn't drunk nearly as much wine as I had, and he was sitting up straight, looking rather prim. "Here, we know that following the guide will lead us to our optimal life experience. Why would we want to go against that and live a sub-par life?"

I laughed. I was feeling a bit giddy.

"Why would we purposefully take a road that leads to unhappiness when the road to happiness is available?"

"Because," I said, "at least then the unhappiness is yours. You chose it."

Hadley shook his head. "I don't think I understand you."

I drained my wine glass and smiled, hoping my teeth weren't stained red. "Tell me, Hadley," I said. "Are you happy right now?"

"Of course."

"And you think that if you ever went against the guide, you would be unhappy?"

"Yes." He pinched at a crumb from the table cloth and dropped it into the bread basket.

"But you never have?" I asked.

"Never. And never will."

I pressed my lips together and held back a giggle.

The waiter delivered the check, and Hadley looked at me, concerned. "I wish I knew," he said, "whether you're important because I'm going to marry you, or learn something from you, or whether I'm supposed to help you get back to wherever you came from." He pulled his book out of his pocket and consulted it again. He sighed, and dropped it back into his pocket. "It is frustrating when the guide is silent. I'm not sure what to do now."

And then I couldn't help it. I laughed out loud.

"What?" he asked.

"You didn't follow the guide," I said. "My name's not Emma. You didn't follow your instructions!"

Hadley stared at me for a split second, rage gathering around his eyes. Then he jumped from his seat and sprinted for the door.

I got up and followed him.

Hadley burst out into the dark street, and I heard the waiter yelling from inside the restaurant. Hadley took off running, and I followed, my drunken blood pumping hard, and my head spinning.

We ran down the sidewalk and through the park. The streetlights were on now, and the park was bathed in an eerie light. "Where are you going?" I shouted, panting for breath.

"Back to the intersection! She might still be there."

I chased after him, holding one hand over my cramping side. Luckily, he wasn't moving too quickly.

When we reached the intersection, the light had just turned blue, and all the cars were stopped. No one stood on the corner, and Hadley whirled around to face me, his eyes wild. "What's wrong with you?" he shouted. "Why did you do this to me?"

"It's not that big of a deal."

"Yes it is. Now I didn't meet Emma, and I don't know what to do next. What if I've messed up my entire life? And hers?"

"Worst case scenario," I said, out of breath, "you don't get your optimal life or whatever. But I'm sure everything will be okay. I'm sure your life will still be okay."

"Okay?" he said. "I don't want okay. Maybe that's good enough for you, but it's not good enough for me."

"Believe me," I said. "My life is not even okay at this point."

Hadley ripped the book from his pocket and flipped it open with a trembling hand. "What?" he said, "so you just want to make everyone else unhappy like you?" He waved the book at me. "Nothing," he said. "I have no idea where to go from here!"

"Welcome to my world." And suddenly, my head felt clear. As if, at that very moment, all the drunkenness had been sucked out of my ears. Maybe, somewhere inside me, I did know where to go.

I turned around and began to walk.

"Wait!" Hadley called after me. "What are you doing?"

"Walking," I shouted.

"Where?"

"I'm going to go until I get tired, and then I'm going to stop."

It felt good to have a plan.

I walked through the park, past the Flying Cat Fountain. I picked up a matchstick from the ground and threw it into the water. I wished that cute little Jen would get a better job and that Donna and Mike would stop fighting. I even wished that Hadley would get some instructions from his stupid guide.

I kept walking, through a small downtown area of banks and office buildings. I saw my dark reflection in the mirrored windows and admired my stride: long legs marching, arms swinging. Next I walked through a run-down neighborhood with sagging houses and teenagers roaming the streets. They nodded their heads at me and said "Was down?"

Eventually the houses got nicer, with fresh coats of paint and wreaths of vegetables on the doors. After awhile, the houses were set back from the road and hidden behind giant hedges and massive trees. I walked right out of the city limits and kept on going alongside the divided highway, passing an occasional trailer or dilapidated farmhouse.

I didn't feel tired, and my feet didn't hurt, and I might have kept on walking forever if I hadn't noticed the ladder. It was a ladder made of rope, and it hung from a very tall tree on the side of the highway. I looked up, wondering if there was a tree house, but in the darkness, all I could see were naked branches. Still, the ladder intrigued me, and I walked over to it, put my foot into the first rung, and began to climb.

The rope wobbled and hit against the trunk of the tree, but I made it up into the first set of branches. That's where the rope ladder ended—I saw where it had been knotted—but I decided to keep climbing. I climbed and climbed, reaching blindly for the next branch, pulling myself up. It was dark outside, and after awhile, I realized that I couldn't actually see anything. I was climbing in the pitch black, doing everything by feel. And that's when I realized I could no longer feel the rough tree bark against my hands. I reached out and felt a wall of crumbling dirt. I smelled the dank, mineral odor of packed earth.

I stood up, and I was in my backyard, inside my hole. I climbed out and stood for a moment in the nighttime cold, looking into it. There was something shining in the moonlight, down at the bottom of the hole, and I got on my knees and reached in to retrieve it. It was a small, leather-covered book with my name, Mary Beth Hutchins, engraved on the front in gold, curly letters. There were tabs on the side, and I opened to tab thirty-four. The page was blank. I flipped through the rest of the book—past and future—but there were no instructions, only empty space.

I took the book and walked up the back steps to my apartment. Inside, I sat at the kitchen table and thought for a moment, staring at my dirty fingernails. Then I picked up a pen, opened the book to tab thirty-four, and wrote, "Dig a hole." I put a big check next to it. "Did that," I said. I'd dug a lot of holes.

I tapped the pen against the table for a moment, and then I began to write again. "Plant something in it." I snapped the book closed.

In the morning I woke up with a purpose: go to Wal-Mart, back to the Garden Section, and buy a tree or a shrub. Something to fill the hole. I put on my shoes and socks, but before I left the apartment, I opened my laptop and went to the online yellow pages. I wasn't all that surprised to find a dentist named Dr. Hadley Stevens. His office was all the way across town, but I wrote down the number on a sticky pad. On Monday I'd call and make an appointment for a check-up.

LIVING THE DREAM

Terresa Haskew

I didn't think so much about it when I pedaled home after work in the inky, achy darkness and found my bicycle had gotten there ahead of me. My metallic-blue ten-speed was leaning at the bottom of the stoop. Someone was playing mind games with me. Maybe my little brother, Carl.

He'd made off with my bike before, as a joke. That middle school mentality! But if that was true, what was this thing I had taken off on? This bike sure looked like mine, the one Dad gave me on my thirteenth birthday. Same size and color, same scratches. Okay, now that I was taking a closer look I could see that the seat was wrong. Maybe less worn and torn. Fewer memories? And fewer scrapes on the fenders. Well, someone was gonna be pissed.

Now I'd have to bring it back, back to whoever owned it when I wrenched it off the broken fence in front of Greenwald's Grocery. My mother didn't like me to work the closing shift anyway, a girl riding home alone late in the dark. But the money from Greenwald's was critical; Dad's life insurance barely kept a roof over our heads. He used to tell me, "Rachel, if you can dream it, you can live it." Well, that hadn't worked for him, because I knew we were his dream. But I bought into it anyway, bought myself a prom dress of gossamer white silk, and earned my own spending money. I often rode home with a plastic sack swinging from my handlebars, full of Mr. G's generosity. Yeah, Mom would be tonight's second pissed person when I told her I had to get this bike back to the store, then turn around and study for the last of my finals.

Dropping the ride beside my own, I started up the steps to the stoop. The wrought iron rail was cold in my hand, and the way was dark. No one thought to leave on a light. I was only slightly out of breath from the pedaling, but I suddenly seemed to have little energy. The steps were steep, sweating cement secreting a limestone scent, and those steps were as familiar as my own face. Yes, this freckled reflection was firmly fixed in my mind from all the mooning in the mirror over my handsome neighbor, Sam. I used to pile my auburn hair on top of my head and parade before the dresser, imagining myself gowned like an angel for prom, Sam waiting at the door with an armful of pink roses. He actually asked me last week!

I knew there couldn't be more than three, maybe four risers to reach the stoop. In the gloom I could make out our address on the weathered siding, 127. I guess too many hours on Greenwald's gray linoleum had taken a toll, because the top of the stairs was just too far away. I had to sit on the slick steps to rest. Sore toes wiggled inside my dingy white Nikes, flexing to the cadence of crickets echoing in my ears.

I didn't think so much about it when I pedaled home after work in the inky, achy darkness and found my bicycle had gotten there ahead of me. Seems I recalled this happening before, though the fatigue of 60 hour work weeks at the Herald was enough to dumb me down. It was the job I had always wanted. Funny thing. The Herald headquarters was located where Greenwald's store used to be, right on the corner of Beale and Spring. Though the newspaper's new building covered nearly the whole block, the old mangled fence still stood beneath a gnarled oak. The site held a pervasive odor of burning rubber and exhaust fumes. Someone had erected one of those annoying white crosses, draped with a shawl of faded pink flowers. It was still a good place to park a bike.

I had hurried home, pedaling fast despite the long day. Racing under the street lamps, my marquee-cut engagement ring caught the occasional ray, flashing tiny bursts like Northern Lights. I nearly hit the curb, staring star-struck at Sam's ring. When he said "Let's do it, Rachel!" he was my proof that dreams really do come true. If you want something bad enough, you can make it happen. Our wedding was a month away. When I slowed to a stop, I saw my bike, again already waiting at the front of my house. Wasn't Carl too old to play jokes on me?

The front door opened as I stomped down the kickstand of someone else's Schwinn. I looked up to the silhouette of my mother, backlit by the golden glow of our living room light. She hadn't aged a day, it seemed. I hoped to inherit her perpetuity.

"I lived through another night!" I called, waiting to hear her relief at my arrival, wanting to hear her familiar voice. The outline of her tilted head said she was listening, but wasn't sure what she'd heard. I called again as I started up the steps, but the door closed.

I didn't think so much about it when I pedaled home in the inky, achy darkness and found my bicycle had gotten there ahead of me. Seems I was always slow these days, slow enough for the bike to beat me home. I couldn't quite remember where I'd been, but the seat beneath me felt familiar and the destination right. Drifted leaves crackled under my wheels. The pedals arced over and over beneath my feet, an automaton hurling me homeward. My hips hurt at the peak of each rotation, a geriatric groan of bones. Chill wind blew a strand of hair across my mouth; I glanced down to hook it out, was dismayed to find it not grayed, auburn still shone in the artificial light. With ribs heaving, I coughed up something copper, knew there was no time to rest. Sam would be waiting for his medicine, for his sip of water from the yellow Tupperware tumbler, for me to button up his plaid pajamas, pull the comforting quilt over his sunken chest, just the way he liked it.

I laid the borrowed bike at the foot of the steps, and paused to study my own ten-speed. Blue paint was eroded and stained the color of rust. My handlebars were twisted, the front tire bent forever out of round. I touched the black rubber handle, and fear rose in my throat at the sight of my hands. Fingers lay smooth and slim across the grips, without the warp of age. There was no display of veins on the backs of my hands, which I had imagined hovering over Sam's furrowed brow. Looking down at my shoes, those same worn Nikes, I realized they were caked with something like mud, or was it dried blood?

With my foot on the first step, I heard a distant voice, low and familiar. Just down the sidewalk, beyond the pool of poor sodium light, a man stood, tall and straight. Though I could not see his face, I knew him immediately. He told me the dream was done, it was time to come home.

DAUGHTER-OF-THE-TIDES

Vivian Faith Prescott

I'm sitting on a log watching the tide come in. I've got about another hour, so there's enough time to tell you a story. It starts like this: When I was a teenager, I was impatient and I couldn't wait for the berries to ripen, so maybe it was the blueberry leaves I ate. I loved to pick the blossoms off and eat them; I ate the leaves too. But I suspect it might have been the spruce tips, those unripe needles hanging off the end of the spruce branches that I picked sooner than nature intended. I know, I know. I've heard the story: Raven turns himself into a spruce needle and falls into a young woman's drinking cup and she becomes pregnant with him. Raven did that so he could get inside the Head-Man's house and steal the sun, moon and stars and bring daylight to mankind. Maybe that's how it happened; but somehow, I found myself pregnant at fifteen years old.

My friends swirled a ring attached to a string in the air around my belly. Someone said, if the string moved in a circle, it meant I'd have a girl; back and forth meant I'd have a boy. I watched the power in my swollen belly sway the string back and forth and they shrieked, "It's a boy! It's a boy!"

I said, "I think it's a girl." At that age, I was already aware that tricks lurked in sweaty basketball players' jerseys and on the backseat of a Plymouth Fury. I rubbed my belly. "You are a girl," I said to my swollen mound. At Doc Rutherford's office, he listened to the heartbeat: rapid and strong. He claimed the fast heart beat indicated it was probably a boy. I said, "No, it's a girl." It was.

When I held Chloe for the first time, she opened her eyes and looked up at me as if to ask her mother-child if I was, in fact, her mother. "Whose daughter shall I say that I am?" she asked. I told her that, like me, she's a child of seafoam and a child of Raven. When Chloe was six months old, I let her feel the cold sea water, let her clasp bull kelp in her hands, put it in her mouth and taste it. I pointed out the killer whale pod hanging out in front of town; I told her how to talk respectful to them. I set Chloe in the dirt and let her taste rocks. She tasted the saltwater and the earth, taking it inside her.

As Chloe grew, she showed amazing feats: she read at three years old; she loved conversations with elders; she could make her own blueberry pancakes in the shapes of dinosaurs when she was only four. Often, she'd tell me things only grownups could know, like how slack tide happens when the direction of the tidal current reverses.

Chloe loved to swing from tree branches, ride her bike, and camp outside all summer, living like a typical Alaskan child. But she knew and I knew that she was far from typical. Her Grandma said I should've made Chloe wear dresses and more pink, but we live in Southeastern Alaska on an island and it's cold here year round. Grandma Jean thought the lack of dresses and exposure to the color pink made Chloe want to kiss girls instead of boys. But my raven-child likes the color black, I argued: all ravens do. I was always defending Chloe's sense of freedom and exploration. "She's of a curious nature," I said.

Eventually, though, Chloe's dreams outgrew the four walls of my house and the island we live on. She was ready, much too soon, to leave my nest. So, I let her go—she doesn't really fit in with the people who live on this island, anyway—the people who find it intellectually stimulating to peel the labels off their beer bottles every Friday night. "Go," I told her, "Jesus wasn't welcome in his hometown either."

So, Chloe left on the blue-canoe—our ferry—and sailed "Down South." I didn't hear from her for a while, but one day she called me and told me she was working with head trauma patients in Seattle. "They throw shit at you," she laughed. "And they swear all the time and they bite you, but I get to hold their hands. And I tell them that I can see their spirit; I know who they really are. It calms them." I held the phone and sighed knowing she gets the cosmic joke too.

Chloe wandered from Raven's territory into Coyote's and, after Coyote mentored her a while, she called me and said she missed the water and wanted to come back home. So, I paid for a ticket and she rode the blue-canoe back home again. Chloe walked up the ferry ramp with a shaved head; what was left of her long dark hair was dyed pink. I felt her pink prickled head. "Indian war paint," she told me, laughing.

Chloe explained to me that Isaac Asimov, Rumi, Sherman Alexie, and Kurt Vonnegut traveled with her in her backpack. At home, she pulled out her carving tools, long underwear, and address books crammed with the names of fellow tricksters she'd met along the way. She had journals overflowing with handwritten notes and poems—lots of poems.

After a while, Chloe's hair grew out, and she started wearing her traditional dress: Carhartts and a long-sleeve thermal t-shirt. She lugged her backpack around town, telling everyone her stories while she whittled on yellow cedar, carving feast dishes and dance masks. She read her poems in coffee shops, to elders, to kids and friends, and to her university instructors. The local university was so impressed that they wanted Chloe to read her poems at the November ceremony to celebrate Indians. She told me, "Gee, we Indians get a whole month to be remembered." Chloe figured they wanted her to be their token Indian.

So, tonight, I went to hear her read her poems, thinking I'd be the only one clapping with my feet. I was watching the crowd when she was reading one of her poems—the one about being a civilized Indian. I saw she was making the crowd squirm, their Indian expectations withered. She's too pale. She's too literate. She's too young. She's not an elder.

Chloe read her poems: one about being a snail; one about killer whales; another about working in the fish cannery; and one about being, or not really being, an American. As she was reading her not-really-being poem, she paused, then tried reading again, but her voice faltered; in fact, it kind of squawked. Her eyes fluttered and she looked out at the audience and smiled. I almost jumped from my seat and ran up on the stage, but I couldn't stop staring at her.

Her long black hair fell forward into her face and when she raised her head, a beak had grown from where her mouth once was. Her dark eyes were small and round and the hair around her face turned to slick black feathers. The force of a hundred gasps in the room—mine included—created a draft that raised her up off the floor. Chloe flew up through the smoke hole and out into the sky. Afterwards, her poems fluttered from the podium, falling like alder leaves to the floor.

I ran outside after my changeling, leaving the spectators' mouths gaping open, choking down their golden orbs, stories they didn't quite understand. I knew it would take a while for their brains to untwist their long-held worldviews; to adjust to such trickery where women shape-shift into birds, windows into smoke holes and philosophies into poems. I left them wondering whose daughter she really was.

Outside, I followed the shadow of her wings down the road to the beach. She circled over the beach and landed on a yellow cedar log—the type of log killer whales are made of. I didn't approach her, but I was thinking of Chloe's birth, how her dark and watchful eyes looked up at me. She sat on the log picking off broken limpets and dried seaweed. I waited as the tide swirled and spiraled around the log, coaxing it from the sand. The log rolled trying to gain its balance atop the water, unsure whether or not it was a log or a war canoe. And with the She-Raven on its back, the log floated out beyond the islands. I watched until the log got smaller and smaller until it was no more.

Now, you have the story, for what it is. As you can tell, indigenous people are Chekhov-like: our stories don't necessarily end when or where you want them to end. Sometimes, Raven is still the trickster, waiting with us to see where things go, how they end up. So, imagine yourself here with me. I pick off some spruce tips and share them with you. We sit down on a rock near the tideline. We take off our shoes and socks and put our feet in the cold water. We chew on tart spruce tips and watch the tide swirl around a patch of bull kelp. We watch. I'm unshaken and at the same time I'm amused because I know Raven will be back someday; maybe, when the north wind blows; maybe, when the tide comes wandering back; maybe, when a pod of killer whales swim near shore, or maybe, as soon as I tell you this next story:

One day Raven was bored and turned himself into a woman. He thought to himself, whose daughter shall I say I am? Raven wanted to be a high cast person, so when he saw Sitter-on-a-High-Cliff, a Seagull-Head-Man perched high up on a rock, he decided to be Sitter-on-a-High-Cliff's daughter.

After Raven made his transformation, She-Raven went out in her canoe and saw a pod of killer whales swimming towards her. They approached her and at once saw she was beautiful. Pierced below her lip was an abalone shell labret, the sign of a high-cast person. She-Raven pointed to the Seagull Head-Man on the cliff and said, "I'm Sitter-on-a-

High-Cliff's daughter." So, one of the Killer Whale men asked her to be his wife; She-Raven agreed and married him.

She-Raven went to live with the Killer Whale People in their village. They assumed she was a high-cast person because of her father Sitter-on-a-High-Cliff. But after She-Raven had been living with them a short while, all the grease and fat they'd stored began to disappear. The Killer Whale People found themselves having to hunt more often. Their food never seemed to last long; they didn't know what was happening.

Some time later, Killer-Whale-Head-Man checked a box of grease and found She-Raven's abalone shell labret inside the box—it had fallen off. The Killer-Whale-Head-Man questioned She-Raven, but she explained, "So that's where my labret went. I was wondering what happened to it. Whenever it wants, my labret flies off my lip and wanders around. It goes wherever it wants." The Killer Whale People believed She-Raven and she got away with stealing their food for a very long time.

A WOMAN OF LETTERS

Lauren Yaffe

A was telling us about her retreat. "...It was in upstate New York," she said. "One of those places where you remove your shoes and no one locks their doors. In fact, the doors have no locks. I was assured I wouldn't be disturbed down at the lake house—too cold for the other guests this time of year—but no sooner had I settled down to work than there was a knock on my door. A man with large handsome eyes and a stylish haircut, mid-30s. He introduced himself as Max, said he was staying in the room next to mine and asked if I would join him for tea. I politely declined. I was there to write. I didn't want to whittle my time away being friendly.

"But later, when I walked up the hill to the main house for dinner, I sat at Max's table. He asked about my work and I told him I was writing a novel about Brazilian Indians. Max studied me intently, then explained that he was working with Brazilian Indians to save the rain forest and had, that very day, been in contact with a Brazilian witch doctor. Max, too, was writing—a play about healing based on his experience of dying in a car crash and hearing the voice of the Divine. When he came back to life, he knew he must write a play. He hadn't been able to work on it lately though, he said, because he wasn't living spiritually enough.

"'You don't need to be spiritual to write,' I told him. 'Use your imagination. We can't all be witch doctors or possessed by spirits.'

"'Only a special few,' he said.

"Max had heard the voice of the Divine one other time, after one girlfriend left him then the next turned out to be crazy and he had a nervous breakdown. Some guy took him in, cooked for him, listened to him, but he still felt crazy. Max suspected he wasn't healing because the guy's upstairs neighbor had killed himself and no one had burned sage to purge the bad spirits. Then he finds—in the apartment he was staying in—a book of spells, satanic paraphernalia. He was living with a satan worshipper. The voice of the Divine told him to leave.

"'Did the guy harm you, really?' I asked.

"'Evil forces exert pressure on you,' Max replied. Voices told him to do destructive things; he had to always be careful not to obey.

"'We all have destructive thoughts,' I said."

Now D., who liked to be the authority, interrupted A., "Oh, I get it. The guy's loony-tunes."

G., her voice quavery, cut in: "Because he had a nervous breakdown, you assume that he's crazy?"

"Either that or he's from California," D. replied.

E. & F., who always followed D., joined in, "Come on! Burning sage...the voice of the Divine...witch doctors," said one. "Destructive voices!" added the other.

G. asked, "And you wouldn't think twice about living where someone had killed himself?"

"Nothing a scrub brush and a little ammonia can't fix," D. said, laughing devilishly.

"I'm not finished," A. said. "So Max left L.A.—"

"Aha!" D. said.

"—and moved to New York, and in with a new girlfriend. (Her place had feng shui.) She was very maternal, always getting on him to take care of himself. She had insisted he go away to cleanse his aura and shakras, which was how he'd ended up at the lake house at this place in upstate New York. Max had spent the day speaking on the astral plane with the witch doctor but felt no better. The healing he had to do was all internal, he said. No one could see the problems or the work. He was all alone.

"As Max and I were leaving the dining hall, a woman in a white sari and turban invited us to a group meditation for world peace—"

"Hold on!" D. interrupted. "This doesn't sound like any writer's retreat I know."

"I never said it was a writer's retreat, did I? It was a yoga center... ashram, actually."

"So you think knowing it was an ashram colors how we hear the story?"

"Doesn't it?" A. asked. "Anyway…I returned to my room to write while Max went to the group meditation. Some time after midnight, he knocked on my door, distraught. At the meditation, demons had flocked around him. One came out of the floor and tried to wrap itself around his leg. 'Most people have to look left or right,' he said, 'but I have to look on three levels. Sometimes I have to jump or dodge.'

"'As long as you can function,' I said. Max gave me a desperate look. 'You'll feel better after a good night's sleep,' I said, closing my door.

"Max asked, through the closed door, if I wanted to fool around.

"'No thanks,' I said.

"'Then how about this?' he proposed. 'You write a sex scene: a man and a woman…at a kind of hotel…empty but for the two of them. They take a roll on each bed, in each of the nine rooms.'

"'YOU write it!' I burst out, then immediately regretted it. Now Max would be imagining us having sex in each of the nine rooms of the lake house. I tried to sleep but my stomach was tight. I wondered how I might barricade my door. I'm such a hypocrite, I thought. I say everyone has destructive thoughts but when someone admits to having them, I deem him dangerous. But I couldn't stop myself.

"I waited till all was quiet then tiptoed out. I got as far as the porch, where my shoes were, when Max appeared. 'Where are you going?'

"'To make a phone call,' I replied. 'I don't talk to people astrally.'

"I scrambled up the icy hill to the main house. No one was awake. I had no idea which rooms were occupied or by whom, but I found an open door. Thankfully, the room was empty. I lay in the bed with my coat on, peering out the window into the dark. Since Max traveled on the astral plane, perhaps he could find me anywhere. I thought I could see spirits on the lawn."

"Okay," G. said, her voice no longer quavery, "he definitely sounds schizophrenic. But the way D. put it was so dismissive. It's sad! Two girlfriends kicked him out, probably the satan worshipper as well—we don't know—and possibly his current girlfriend. Her wanting him to take care of himself was obviously an attempt to get him back on his meds."

"G., you would sympathize with the guy if he stabbed you!" D. roared. "Schizophrenic, crazy, whatever...why talk to the nut?"

Some of the others jumped in. "He started out sympathetic," said one. "He was fascinating." "He was troubled."

"I think," said D., "that A. here was being too curious, as usual. Or avoiding writing. Or Max turned her on."

A. made a face.

Now O. came between G. and D. "Maybe talking to Max was a mistake but it ended up saving A. Talking to him felt unsafe but knowing nothing about him actually was."

H., the history and anthropology buff (who looked the part with his pipe and jacket), said, "We don't know that Max was dangerous. He didn't go after A. when she left the lake house, did he? He tried not to obey his destructive voices—"

"—But what if he wasn't always successful?" O. asked. "And even if he wasn't a physical danger, psychic threats are real. Max said so himself about the satan worshipper."

"So he was hounded by demons?" H. said. "In some cultures, Max would be considered a shaman. If we placed him, say, in Bali or Brazil, he might look quite normal. He had visions? So did Ghandi. Hell, Jesus thought he was God. And a lot of people believe him—still! He heard voices? Don't we all? Like part of you wanting something another part knows you shouldn't have."

J., always the joker, said, "Anyone who's tried to diet knows those two voices well."

The women chorused, "Here, here!"

"The ancient Greeks," H. added, "believed these voices were the Gods speaking."

"They were trying to diet, too?" J. quipped.

H. continued, "Max believed in spirits. You could say that of anyone who believes in God. Is everyone who believes in the immeasurable— ghosts, aliens, spirits of dead loved ones, superstitions—crazy? It would be easier to say that our storyteller, A., is crazy, shutting herself away from the world, listening to characters' voices in her head."

E., who had been mainly silent, now spoke, "I believe A. does have some demons to exorcise."

"Well, I did feel harmed by Max," A. said. "Psychically invaded. And yes, to get him out of my system, to work out the experience, I wrote, I told this story. I did try to be objective."

"You manipulated us. You withheld the information about the ashram."

"A writer selects some details, omits others."

"Max isn't here to defend himself. For all we know, you're an unreliable narrator," E. suggested, "obsessed with Max."

L.Y. finally spoke: "Then call me crazy," she said, since by now you may have realized that all these voices were in her head, but everyone immediately dismissed her.

Except X., whose opinion was unknown. Y. yawned and asked what was for dessert. One would think that Z. would end with the kernel of truth to make everyone hum with understanding but with all the arguing, Z. was snoring soundly away.

A STITCH IN TIME

Tim Goldstone

Before he went travelling he'd looked it up under the constantly flickering strip light in the little rural library back in Lampeter, mid-Wales—Datura: a plant, having long trumpet-shaped flowers yielding a powerful narcotic. Dangerous hallucinogen inducing disorientation of time and vision.

But Tug has no idea how long he's spent studying what's going on here—an hour, a few months, the length of a glance: the fit bronzed local men who appear to spend all day collecting blood in plastic bin-bags and showing it off to the disheveled traveller girls living on the beach, making them scream. By late afternoon they normally have at least two full bin-bags each that swish and gulp around inside. You can't drag them. The slightest tear accelerates sickeningly. You have to be strong—the weight of those things: the distance you have to walk with them.

Then they have to carry them up the wide white marble steps of the hospital: towards the two neon signs that are a tired pink in the sunlight—alternately flashing their message: Blood. Blood. Someone told him they get ten thousand liras for each bag and that's enough for a great night out in that part of southern Italy, past Brindisi, into the deep south. The bags slush about and shift their weight unexpectedly and there's that warm, nauseating smell. The hospital accepts only full bin-bags.

The first time, Tug had eaten three of the bitter, creamy white flowers. Now he needed a lot more. He'd been warned there was a tipping point.

That night the same young men go back to the beach and smoke Nazionali cigarettes under a thatched outdoor bar and show off their muscles and laugh and joke and drink with traveller girls hanging from their biceps.

They're joking now—as they watch the old men who try to do the same thing, who come out at night to wander the beach, who constantly stoop to squeeze blood from the smaller stones. After enormous effort and pain they have nothing. They use ordinary brown paper bags—it really is that hopeless. Every now and then though one of them will find some: and a few tiny droplets will fall into the crumpled bag after all that horrible straining of the fist and heart, and what's still left of the muscles clinging to the sinews of the inner forearm, expecting support from ligaments and tendons that have lost all elasticity. Often the fingers will have to be prised open, re-cracking old fractures on the locked knuckles, until the stone drops to the ground.

Tug notices one of the old men is staggering badly in the wet sand by the edge of the sea and the young men have stopped laughing. They become quiet and some of them squeeze their eyes tight shut each time the man takes a step. The girls become uncomfortable and begin to drift away up the beach.

Tug watches them go. One of them turns on her heel and takes a few tentative steps back towards him—

She is smiling sparingly, waving a finger in admonishment. 'Tug eating too much flowers' she says, and runs to catch up with her friends. Tug hasn't a clue whether she's there or not.

B ack in Lampeter he found Carys, with her hair dyed blond and pink. When the marijuana ran out he showed her you could smoke foxglove leaves. Carys developed irregular heartbeats and the cough that sounded like wet plates being stacked.

Ignoring the acrid black smoke, they burnt, twisted, knotted dangling plastic bags they'd tied to a disused light-fitting in the front upstairs bedroom so that the flaming plastic dripped through the dark like fireworks with a zzzip zzzip noise down on to the wooden floorboards— branding them in the semi-derelict stone cottage buried deep in the Welsh countryside, squatting in the summer heat.

Febrile in the protection of thick, musty overcoats they'd found under the stairs, they took it in turns to hack a steep single-file path right up the through the ripping undergrowth that kept re-closing behind their backs and over their heads. When they realized they weren't climbing anymore they frenziedly slashed out a clearing in the heart of the garden where once there must have been a small terrace that caught the sun, with a view over the idyllic valley, and they made enough room to lie down on dusty rugs they carried up from the cottage.

The garden reared up around where they lay, besieging them on all sides with towering, swaying, humming walls of brambles, blackthorn, huge nettles, dog roses clawing the air as they're choked by flowering bindweed.

A surround sound buzzing as flying, chasing, raging insects shoot by them, too shivery-close for comfort. Tug watches Carys's pupils darting at incredible speed as she tries to follow them all: she says she's seeing trails in the air—and they laugh and sweat runs down into their eyes and stunned in the heat they watch their lives begin to melt around them. Tug peers back down to the cottage. A soldier just returned, walks up the path after years overseas serving with Queen Victoria's imperial battalions, sits outside on the stone step. He is showing off his redcoat to his parents. He is proud of its faded red. His father says he preferred it new and bright. His mother strokes the palms of her son's hands tracing the contours of the burn scars from where his Martini-Henry rifle overheated during constant firing all through that scorching, terrifying afternoon, six thousand miles away from the cheering crowds that sent them off. Tug sees the soldier's young wife peering from an upstairs window with the secret inside her not yet showing. She catches Tug's eye, shrinks back into the bedroom's shadows where Tug can make out through a powdery greyness the thin red lines appearing on her white, blue-veined wrists, and the razor falling through the air.

To accommodate the foxglove leaves, the screen had been pushed a long way down into the water pipe's chillum. But now it was jammed and blocked so he needed to raise the screen. 'Your fingers are thinner than mine' he says to Carys. He eases the snugly fitting chimney out of the hole in the cork and hands it to her.

'Oh God,' she says, 'I can't drink the water again it's disgusting.'

'We're not going to,' Tug says.

'What are you doing?' she says.

'Can you get the screen out? Your fingers are thinner than mine.'

'Oh,' she says—and looks down surprised to see the chillum cradled in the palm of her hand. It moves slightly as Tug watches it. She has something to say: wants to be able to get clean—her cuts and scratches and bites are going bad. Wants to settle down just for a while in glowing lovey-dovey homey wifey plain simple clear-eyed life with maybe a couple of children who'll wear faded grey overalls with tanned little arms sticking out and healthy bare feet and sticking up hair. They'll hurt themselves playing too roughly while Tug's at work earning real money somewhere for the sake of the family; and she'll grab them and drag them into the kitchen by the scruffs of their collars—where she's been baking something and she'll hug them and pat them and give them some special biscuits she's made along with the pie so as not to waste anything. Tug will suddenly arrive home from work and they'll all go and sit together on the big soft enveloping sofa with the huge arms that the children ride as though they're on horses and watch the television and cats will come and curl up on their laps and Tug will say 'Are you sure they're all ours?' and their spaniel will trot in wearily, stinking, and lie down across Carys and Tug's feet, yipping and snorting as it dozes.

Tug didn't like that. Tug notices Carys is all out of breath now, and for the first time sees the dark patches under her eyes. He tries to imagine all she's been talking about but watches his thoughts hit the inside of his skull and fall back. He is sickened. The green bulwark engulfing them starts to pulsate. 'We can walk to that lake' he says.

'Yes' she says.

'Yes' he says.

Calm settles again like dust. The cottage is empty.

The very last of the moisture was being enticed out of the marsh. There is a breeze that makes the reeds rasp thirstily, and that brings the smell of baking mud, and the sounds of small, darting birds. The bare soles of Carys's wet feet make soft slaps as she pads along the abandoned wooden jetty, each footprint evaporating before the next one is made. Sagging planks moan and sigh. Underneath her the water is lapping and kissing at unsafe supports. Carried from the other side of the lake: the buzz of a trail bike; a chainsaw's drone.

Under the childishly yellow sun and big blue dome of sky Tug and Carys are dangling their legs over the end of the jetty. He stares into the water—remembering cutting himself in the hospital in Italy so he could put his blood in a saucer so the fleas would feed from there and not him. It didn't work. They'd had to put a stitch in him. It worked itself loose within minutes.

'This is nice' Carys says, and begins to cough up a few tiny red droplets. She leans on Tug, her hair falling over his arm and he feels her warm ribs against him.

He corrugates their reflections on the cool surface of the lake, and when the picture returns Tug is alone. He walks back up the beach towards the hospital for help. He has no idea whether it's there or not. The two signs flash Blood Blood. A bugler boy watches him pass by in a cart. The wooden wheels on the rutted track mean Tug with his bandaged hands is being shaken as though he were a rag doll.

NIGHT IS NEARLY DONE

Adam McOmber

W hen no bear was in the fighting ring, the metal collar lay in the dust—a black shackle, shot with rivets, fitted with an adjustable hinge. Patrons were invited to examine the collar before the fight, and men like my father spent time listening to the satisfying snick of the latch and discussing the finer points of its construction. He threatened to put the thing around my own neck on more than one occasion, and the other men laughed as I scrambled away. My father dragged me to the fights every week—drunk and loud— singing the common songs and calling out the names of the bears to the darkened houses along the way. Sackerson, the blind—eyes put out with a searing brand. Whiting and Stone, the twins. And behemoth, Harry Hunks, called a god in fur for his ability to take the head off a large dog with one good swipe of his paw. The bears were chained outside the city in a gray piece of fallow known as the Gardens where a circle of raised wooden benches formed the arena, and make-shift vendor tents sold everything from salted meat to tattered sex magazines. Girls from long ago posed in those pages, chins jutting and hands on hips, skin faded to a viral green. Sometimes I pretended they could look at us, just as we could look at them, and I wondered what they must make of such pale and shambling wrecks.

My father made me ride his shoulders on our passage through the city, and one day I fell because he lurched so madly and cut my cheek on a sharp rock. He dragged me all the way to the Gardens like that, and

I stood on our usual bench to watch the fights, blood running down my face. A woman sitting near us said, "Don't let Sackerson smell you. He'll pull his chain right out of the ground." She took off her nylon stockings and told me to tie them good and tight around my neck to stop the blood. That was also the day I met Hounds, the bear-keeper's son, and I have the woman's stockings to thank for that.

I'd seen him before, of course—everyone who went to the Gardens had. He worked for his father and was usually too busy emptying barrels and carrying heavy pieces of cage to bother with talking to anyone, especially someone like me—the half-grown son of a Munsen Man. Women were never shy about sliding their hands over Hounds' shoulders as he passed through the crowd, and though he didn't seem to mind the attention, the most they ever got in return was a smile. Men liked him too and were quick with a drunken joke, which Hounds only sometimes rewarded with a chuckle. Hounds was not his Christian name, of course. I never found out if he had one of those, though it was rumored that the bear-keeper himself was Christian, as he'd once thrown a man out of the Gardens for wearing a hand painted shirt that read, "I Am the Doorway," and afterward paced the length of the park, saying if anyone wanted to fuck with him or the Lord, then they'd have the bears to deal with. Pierced through Hounds' left eyebrow was a piece of metal shaped like a tiny flower—a shining daisy—and before I met him, I spent hours contemplating that bit of jewelry.

"Fancy collar you got there, kid," he said when he saw the woman's stockings. I was standing near a tent outside the arena, and my hand went to the stockings around my neck. I fingered the toe as I said, "I had a cut. A lady told me this would stop the blood."

Hounds shook his head. "She might have been nuts," he said. "Lots of people here are."

"I don't—"

"Might as well take 'em off."

I couldn't tear the stockings off quickly enough.

"You come here to watch this sick show?" Hounds asked.

"My dad makes me," I said. "I hate to see it." For a moment, I worried that I'd offended him—the Gardens was, after all, his own family's livelihood, but then I saw he was testing me. "Hate to see the bears get hurt," I added. "And the dogs for that matter. But mostly the bears. They're—I don't know—beautiful."

He spit a wad of phlegm. "You think Harry Hunks is beautiful?"

"In his way," I said.

Hounds pushed his finger against the metal daisy in his eyebrow. "Nobody uses words like 'beautiful' anymore," he said. "But it's good. Really good. My plan is to make all these pieces of shit remember words like that—even if I have to pry their mouths open and dump the words down their throats."

Then his father was calling, and before I could ask what he meant, Hounds took his leave with only a nod.

When we got home, my older sister, June, told my father he was reckless for dragging me through the city with a cut on my face. She'd had a fear of disease since our own mother's death and asked if my father had seen the old woman down the street with the egg-sized cyst on her neck. "How do you think she'll breathe when that thing gets too big? How will she swallow?" June said. My father told her that if she didn't quit nagging he'd come after her. Once he'd actually grabbed June and stuck his hand between her legs, but she'd fought him off, and later that night, heated an iron and put it against his bare thigh while he slept. He still had a mark that looked something like a red finger pointing toward his penis, and he'd tried to punish her for what she'd done, but June was fast.

Father finally got tired of hearing her complaints and went out to comb the yard for artifacts. This was his job as a Munsen Man—making collections for the mayor, inventorying objects that no long had a use. When June and I were alone in the kitchen, I said, "I met someone today." Her frown was like Mother's—wrinkling her otherwise perfect brow, dipping the edges of colorless lips. I loved June for that frown. She was like Mother's mirror.

"Who did you meet, Freddy?"

"The bear-keeper's son," I said, "called Hounds."

"That's not a name."

I shrugged. "It's what he calls himself. And he's handsome, June."

She closed her eyes, which meant she wanted to picture him. "Handsome how?"

"Big," I said, "with a clean face."

"Does he have hair that grows from his nose or ears?"

"No," I said.

"What about his tongue?" she asked.

"No one grows hair on a tongue, June."

"Some do," she said. "The sick."

"Hounds isn't sick," I said. "You'd like him."

She opened her eyes. "That doesn't really matter, does it, Freddy? I'll never meet him, so why do you even bother to talk to me like that?"

"You could go out," I said. "I could take you to the Gardens. We wouldn't have to look at the bears."

She turned her back on me and began cutting some wrinkled vegetable I assumed would be part of our dinner. "You actually think I'd step foot in that place?" she said, chopping faster. "Freddy, just because you have a crush on the bear-keeper's son doesn't mean I have to go ogle him. Don't let Mayor Munson find out you have thoughts like that either or he'll have you burned."

"Shut up," I said.

"It's true," she said.

And I was the one to grow silent because I knew that it was.

June played a game with me in the evening hours after dinner had been eaten, and Father went out to pace the yard again and search for artifacts. She'd cover my eyes and ask me to remember what was in the room I'd been looking at only a moment before. "Black stove," I'd say from her darkness. "Coal bucket. Wooden table. Chairs. Picture of a man with a donkey."

"Is that all?" she'd say.

"That's all."

"Did you see Mother standing there?"

"Of course not, June."

"Then you aren't looking hard enough, Freddy," she'd say.

That's how she acted too. Like we weren't all alone in the house with Father. Like Mother was still around to hold us. June had a closer bond with Mother because she was older and had more time to talk to her before she died, though there were things about my bond with Mother she didn't know—couldn't know, in fact.

"How much of Mother do you remember?" June asked.

"Really nothing," I said. "Just her face."

That was a lie told for June's benefit—to protect her. What I actually remembered, in vivid detail, was the way Mother died. As June told it, she'd expired from an unnamed disease, and I suppose it might have looked like that to someone who found her lying on the floor, but I saw what actually happened.

I couldn't have been older than four or five, sitting on a pillow in my crib. Mother was on the floor, long dress tangled about her legs, hands kneading her gut like she was in pain. June was at the market, and Father was at work. Mother called out the names of objects, most of which I didn't recognize—electric razor, tissue paper, light bulb, filing cabinet.

Her hair was wet, and her face was wet, not from sickness but from fear. She wrapped her fingers around the bars of my crib and pulled herself up so she was kneeling. "Keyboard," she whispered, "lava lamp, high-heeled shoe." She put her hand through the bars and grasped my leg, squeezing too tightly.

Then she started to cough, hard enough to shake me.

That's when the walls and floor began to darken, like she was dislodging shadows from her lungs.

We weren't alone once she started coughing. There were figures in the walls and in the floor—men in fine suits and women in skirts, watching us. I'd seen people like these in the old magazines—business people, mother called them. I've considered whether these business people might have been the creation of a mind too young to cope with a mother's dying. But I don't think I made them up. There were bodies in the half-light, leaning in to get a better look.

One of them even seemed to show concern, coming close to the crib where I sat, and though I couldn't see a face, I knew she was a woman from her shape. She cared about me, was frightened for me. Then Mother was dead, her nose pressed flat against the floor like a nail not yet driven. The figures were gone too. And I was left.

Ethelsgate, one of the eleven gates of the city, led to the Gardens and looked like a fish's mouth, paint peeling from stone, forming what appeared to be scales. A portcullis had been retracted into the arch years before and was too rusted to descend. On either side of the gate's mouth was an eye-like window where my father said uniformed guards had once stood watch—not that he really knew. But as a Munsen Man, he was prone to making things up. Munsen Men, by definition, have answers. They know about artifacts. But when Father had been born, things were pretty much the same as they were when I was born. Time, as June said, was a river, damned. Everyone in the city had the same experience of the city. Nothing truly changed.

Father carried an artifact in the pocket of his stained work pants—a piece of yellow plastic shaped to look like a pencil. Mother had called this a mechanical pencil, which I'd misheard as maniacal pencil—a more apt description of something Father would own. When he pressed the hard pink eraser, a sliver of new lead was born from the maniacal pencil's tip, and he would make notes on alley walls—stars and crosses and little lightning bolts. I asked him once what those things meant, and he told me to hold my tongue.

Our mayor had run on a ticket of reform. Munsen wore fine suits and used classic rhetorical hand gestures to emphasize his words. He said soon the city gates would all be open—and held a fist above his palm to make it true. The fallows, he said, would be cleanly restructured—hands clasped gently in front of his chest. Every house would have electricity—palms open. Even the fallows would have electricity—palms still open. There would be no lack of food—hands prone and folded. The sick would be healed—fingers splayed and held high. And we would all learn the truth of our existence—a closed fist. "Our dreadful night is nearly done, my fellows," Munsen intoned with his fingers lightly steepled, and everyone cheered for him in the same way they cheered for a public burning.

Father, half-crazed and drunk, had inexplicably become an emissary of Munsen's reform. He traveled the city in an orange horse cart, collecting. June would sometimes retrieve the objects from the cart after Father had fallen asleep and try to teach me lessons. We sat at the kitchen table, the surface of which was warped like water's waves, and she'd put her cool fingers over mine and say, "Freddy, this is important. Mother taught me, and she would have wanted you to know too. We have to remember the names of our objects. This is a thimble, used for protection during sewing. And this one is called a paper's clip, for binding surplus. And this one," June held up the flat chunk of plastic with numbered buttons on its surface, "was once a piece of a telephone, I think. For talking. Using networks of the air."

I turned the fragment of telephone over and looked at it, then put the thimble on top like a small hat. "Why don't we use these things anymore, June?"

She paused, looking as if the pink eraser of Father's maniacal pencil was at work behind her eyes. "I never got around to asking Mother," she said. "I assumed she'd always be there for questions."

"June, I'm sorry," I said.

She turned her face from mine, touching her eyes. "No, I'm sorry," she said. "I was older. I should have known about dying."

After the day he talked to me about the stockings, Hounds and I started meeting at the water barrel near the salted meat tent. We pretended to meet accidentally. He drank from a rusty ladle then offered water to me, and though the water was fouled, I drank. He said he didn't mind my presence because, "We both got shit for fathers." He also said I was a good at listening, as most people who got shit for fathers were.

When there was no work for him, we'd leave the Gardens and lay in an open field to the west, far enough away so that the cheering crowd sounded like wind. On the horizon stood four buildings, colored the same dirty white as the sky. Their shattered windows looked like toothy mouths, and on the one closest to me, I could read a name stamped out in large blue letters: Sanaco 1—a name that meant nothing, though it must have meant a great deal once to have been written so large. The other buildings, I assumed, were connected to the first, making them Sanaco 2, 3, and 4. These buildings were not part of our city—they were in the fallows, the spoiled land that Mayor Munsen promised to reclaim and secure. Hounds said the buildings had once been offices where people worked, and I told him about thimbles and paper's clips and telephones of the air. He said all those things had been used in the offices once, and when I asked him how he knew, he said, "I went over there awhile back because I was sick of my dad's shit and wanted to get away."

"What did you see, Hounds?" I said, propping myself up on my elbow to look into his black eyes and watch the muted afternoon light glint off his metal daisy.

"Everything," he said. "Piles and piles of everything."

"Artifacts?"

"Unnamed stuff," he said.

"I bet my ma could have named those things," I said. "She knew all the names. Better than any Munsen Man. You want to go back to Sanaco, Hounds? Maybe look around together? I can tell you if I recognize anything."

He shook his head. "Not the kind of place I'd go twice, Freddy. There was something wrong."

"Like how?"

"The air inside was funny, even though the sun was coming in through the broken windows. It was like the night had swollen up behind the day, you know what I mean? Like when you can see sickness under someone's skin. I kept feeling like I was going to fall down a hole, but there weren't any holes. I had to steady myself, hold onto the wall—only the wall felt soft like my hand might run right through it—like a hand runs through water. When Mayor Munsen says night is nearly done, I know that isn't true. Night is hiding under everything."

"Was anybody inside Sanaco?" I said, not sure why I asked. "Does anyone live there?"

He didn't answer for a long time, then said, "I think maybe. But it wasn't the kind of somebody that you or I could talk to."

Mostly Hounds wanted to discuss his father's Gardens, saying that bear baiting was the sort of fucked-up thing that only human beings could invent. "When this place belongs to me," Hounds said, "and it's all gonna belong to me one day, I'll turn it into a park. Someplace with paths in the greenery where people can walk around decent-like and think, without all this shitting noise. In the middle of it, maybe I'll dig a big lake and put up a goddamned statue and write all the bears' names on its chest—Sackerson, Whiting and Stone, and fucking Harry Hunks. I'll even write the names of the ones that died if I can remember. There used to be one called Tangle Root, you know—got her guts torn out by a monster dog. And I won't say that nobody was blind nor twins nor god of the stupid bears."

"How'd the bears get those names anyway?" I asked.

"My old man found them in some book," he said. "A fucked up book of theatrical plays."

I didn't know what a theatrical play was, and Hounds told me it was a sort of thing where people pretended they had lives that made sense. They acted out characters who moved along the line of a story. He said people didn't put on theatricals anymore because no one believed that life had a proper story. "They'd rather see a bear bite a fucking dog in the ass," he scoffed. "And that's not a plot, Freddy. No fucking plot at all."

Bear baiting worked like this—a bear was chained to a stake in the middle of the gravel circle, then two dogs were set loose upon it. Only two at first, to make the fight fair. The bear tried to stand, swinging and roaring at the dogs whose jaws dripped foam as they bit the bears and dodged the massive paws until everyone on the raised benches had nearly fallen down from cheering. Once in a while, a third dog was released if the bear seemed to be too much in control. By the end of a fight, both bear and dog alike were wet with blood—fur standing in matted spikes, blood running from mouths and noses. The bears made such impotent and furious sounds that I often had to cover my ears, and the dogs could sound even worse. I never knew a dog could scream until I went to the Gardens.

Sackerson was a favorite. He was blind and he'd lost both his ears to the dogs. People cheered for him, emphasizing the three syllables of his name. SACK—ER—SON. Eventually the chant would sound like, "Sack her son," and then "Sack red sun," and finally when they were drunk enough, "Sacred Son." After the man in the hand-made shirt got kicked out of the Gardens, people would yell, "I Am the Doorway! I Am the Doorway!" when the keepers led Sackerson into the arena.

Stone was no longer the precise twin of Whiting. He had a gash running the length of his muzzle that actually split this nose in two. People called him split-snout, and painted him as evil because of his deformity. Whiting, the other brown bear, was thought to be an angel among bears, though I'd once seen her get one of the dogs in her mouth and tear clean through its neck. The dog's head fell into the dust with a sickening thump and the crowd went mad. At any rate, the two were said to balance each other, just as good and bad made balance in the city. I didn't believe this. They were both only bears, thoughtless and full of fear. The city was like that too—thoughtless and full of fear.

Harry Hunks was the last of the four, called a god in fur because of his enormous girth and also for the fact that he didn't really look like a bear at all, especially when he was standing on his back legs. He looked like man in a costume—even his eyes looked like a man's eyes, like he was staring right at you through a hairy mask, trying to send some sign. On special weekends, men like my father would pay an extra fee to approach Harry's chain and hold it while he was safely restrained at the other end. When these men went to work the next day, they'd talk about holding that chain, how they thought old Hairy was just about to take a swipe at them with one of his deadly paws. They'd seen a look in his filthy eye but had stood their ground. They all agreed they were brave to do a thing like that.

I saw a hundred awful things at the Gardens: A dog carrying its own leg in its mouth, tendons dangling. Another with its jaws locked around the swinging arm of a bear, flung this way and that, until its back was broken, humped like a house's roof. There was a bear with its needle black claw shoved straight through a dog's eye, and another that lay on its back, defeated, while a dog reached into its mouth to tear out its tongue, like it was some delicacy.

A little girl once ran into the arena to put a stop to one of the fights. Just before the bear, Stone I think, caught her up, Hounds' father hit her with a metal pole, knocking her back and into the dust. I think her head got cracked open, and the dogs licked up the blood.

No one ever won at the fights. Winning wasn't the point. Only losses were scooped from the arena, and that's the way people liked it.

Hounds told me his secret about the bears as we lay on our backs in the fallows one day, ringed by the pale offices of Sanaco which seemed, that afternoon, to be pillars, supporting the darkening sky. I was rambling about some rumors I'd heard about Mayor Munsen. People loved to gossip about him, especially at the Gardens. They were saying he hadn't been born in the city at all—that he really didn't even know that much about our city. He came from a place where classic hand gestures weren't uncommon and everyone wore suits like he wore. Some people were even saying that Mayor Munsen wasn't supposed to be in our city. His coming was against the rules, though when asked what rules they were speaking of, they said they didn't know.

Hounds seemed distant, staring off into the trees around Sanaco, and just when I started talking about going against the rules, he broke in with his secret. I didn't believe him at first, but the more he talked, the more I realized he wasn't joking. "I'm gonna let 'em all go," he said.

I was in the process of drinking up the weedy smell of him, so I was slow to respond. "Let what go?" I said.

"The bears," he replied, "all the bears."

I propped myself up, looking into his face. The bluish sun glinted off his silver daisy. "Your dad would kill you, Hounds."

"I don't think so," he said. "The old man won't have a chance."

The breeze seemed colder then, and I felt suddenly exposed there in the grass. The fallows were dangerous—a ruthless place, not meant for conversation or love. There were people who sometimes hunted there or came to do other things not legal within the walls of the city. Normally, I felt protected when I was with Hounds, but at that moment I understood he was not there to protect me. He was there to consider his plans. The sky was a watchful thing, and so was Sanaco.

"You're going to let them run off at night?" I asked.

"No," he said, "during one of the fights. I already figured out a way to fix the collar, the rest will just be a matter of opening cages."

I looked down the length of him, my gaze settling on the scuffed wooden heels of his boots that he often used as hammers to drive cage stakes into the ground

"They'll hurt people," I said.

"Don't all these people deserve to be hurt, Fred? Haven't the bears been hurt so much we can't even look at them anymore?"

I didn't know the answer to that, so instead I pictured the crowd— all those mismatched faces, the jumble of salvaged clothes. I pictured them running from Sackerson, from Harry Hunks and the twins. "Your dad will just get more bears," I said.

"He can't," Hounds said. "The man who got these for us died. There's no one else who even knows where there are wild bears anymore. Hopefully, they'll kill my old man first."

"You mean that, Hounds?"

He acted like he didn't hear. "I don't want you to get hurt though," he said. "I'll signal to you somehow, let you know to get away. I'll touch this—" Hounds put his finger on the daisy above his eyebrow. "You can take your father with you if you want."

"I don't know," I said.

"This'll fix things. You'll see. Or at least it'll fix this one thing—the Gardens."

His revelation made me strangely bold. Death hung around us. In my mind, the crowd was already being torn apart, and I reached out and put my hand on Hounds' smooth forearm. His skin was warm. I could feel his blood beating beneath the skin as I slid my hand down his arm in a kind of caress.

A lake of ice spread beneath his gaze, and then carefully, delicately almost, Hounds pulled his arm away.

"Oh, sorry," I said. "Sorry, Hounds. I was just feeling scared is all."

He stood and dusted his jeans, an action which seemed to take forever. "You just surprised me is all, Fred," he said. "Munsen said all of your kind were gone. Just goes to show, Munsen doesn't know shit. Probably queer himself with all those gestures." But Hounds didn't look like he was actually concerned with Mayor Munsen. His eyes seemed furious enough to catch the grass on fire.

"Well, anyway," he said. "I'll let you know, Fred."

"Okay," I said. "Okay, Hounds. I'm sorry again."

"People touch me," he shrugged. "They always do, and I never know why. I just thought you were different."

Maybe June's change of heart came from the fact that Mayor Munsen had announced his intention to tour the Gardens as part of his promised Investigations and Reforms Program. The language he used in his speech concerning the bears—"Social diseases like this one must be cured before the curtain of night can be lifted"—certainly appealed to my sister. After that speech, she'd hung Munsen posters around the house, crude drawings of the Mayor demonstrating his rhetorical gestures. Or maybe her change of heart came from the new artifact Father had found—the one that had quite literally fallen into June's lap and that she considered to be a sign from Mother. He'd brought the item home from one of his clean-up excursions, wrapped in a cloth as if it were a delicate animal. He stood at the kitchen table, gloating like a child until June finally reached up and pulled the end of the cloth, causing the object to fall into the lap of her white dress. It appeared to be a transparent rubber breathing mask with two silver filters meant to siphon air and an elastic strap so it could be worn. June drew a quick breath when she saw the thing, and Father yelled for her to give it back, that he'd found it and it belonged to him, but he didn't dare reach into the lap of June's dress to grab it—I think he was actually afraid she'd brand him again, maybe this time not going as low as his thigh.

June snatched the object and held it to her face, breathing deeply. "Oh Freddy," she said, her voice muffled. "Isn't this wonderful? I can go out without getting sick."

I tried to smile for her, as my father threw up his hands and roared, stomping out into the yard again. Later, June told me she'd be coming to the fights with us on the day that Mayor Munsen was to scheduled to visit. She wanted to speak to him about reform, to hear more about the improvements he intended—and perhaps to volunteer her services now that she could move freely about the city. "Mother believed in change," June said, "and the mayor reminds me so much of Mother. Freddy, there's just some funny part of me that believes things like this—" she held up the rubber mask, "aren't accidents."

I thought only of the shadows Mother had coughed up before she died. Some part of me also believed there were no accidents, though I wouldn't have called it "funny." No, not funny at all.

A cold fear spiked my gut as I watched June descend the stairs on the day of the fights, her long white dress brushing the toes of her rubber boots, and the mask glittering like a jewel over her mouth and nose. She looked like a girl from one of the old magazines. Her eyes were so lovely that, despite my fear, I was struggling to make a name for their color. The only thing I came up with was not so much a name but a picture—the bluish-pink of the sky when the sun first touched it—when night was done, as Munsen would say.

"June, please don't do this. You can't come," I said, an argument I'd already attempted.

She narrowed her eyes. "You always wanted me to get out of the house, Freddy, and now that I'm finally coming, you say that I can't? You need to be more consistent, or you'll go mad like Father."

"But something's going to happen at the Gardens, June, sometime soon," I said, "and I don't want—"

At that point, my father came into the foyer, loud in his boots, and stared at June, pointing his maniacal pencil at her. "You're still wearing my property, cunt!" he said.

June smiled at him through the clear rubber of the mask, "That's right, Daddy. But it's my property now. And if you shut up about it, I'll sing your bear songs with you on the way to the big show. How about that?"

Strangely, this seemed to placate him, and we became an odd procession, passing under Ethelsgate, singing together about Sackerson the blind and Harry Hunks the marauding god while my father made triangles in the air with his pencil, as if directing a marching band.

The Gardens was packed that day, and I only got glimpses of Munsen—dark in his suit, white hair rippling back from his brow in an elegant display of political polish. He was oddly more present than the regular crowd, not just because of his physical prowess—broad shoulders and long arms—but because of something that bordered on spiritual enlightenment. He made his famous rhetorical gestures as he passed through the crowds, speaking to what he called his "citizens." Even in that drunken turmoil, Munsen held sway, believing so firmly in order that everyone around him could momentarily believe in it too. A fight broke out between two filth-covered men, and Munsen simply walked over to them, put his hands out, and asked them to be brothers, which, amazingly, caused them to stop.

June nearly swooned. "He's going to surprise us," she said. "He'll show us how to change. Maybe even today."

The bear scheduled to compete was Harry Hunks, which made sense. Only the biggest and the best for Mayor Munsen. God of the people should meet god of the bears. When the keeper's men led Harry forth, my gut turned cold. One of his paws was the size of my head, and one of his black eyes was the size of my open mouth. A cloud of flies traveled with Harry, and he swung his big head from left to right, trying to knock them away. The men held him in temporary pole-harnesses while Hounds worked to fasten the collar, at its maximum extension, around the bear's thick neck, and when he was done, he turned and found me in the crowd. My father and I always sat in the same spot, low and to the left, for better view of the ring. Blood sometimes fell on us like rain. Hounds did not nod or gesture, only glared at me, as if remembering my touch. His daisy ring glittered like a mechanical third eye, and I was seized by fear.

"Is that the one you like?" June said, the sound of her voice reverberating in the rubber mask. "He is attractive."

This was the day. Of course, it was. Munsen was here. The crowd was larger. This was the best day to let them go.

"June," I yelled above the cheers, grabbing her hand, "We have to go."

She craned her neck, searching for Munsen, stopping only long enough to say, "Don't be stupid. I haven't had my chance to talk to him yet. I want to wait until he sees the fight."

"There isn't going to be a fight," I yelled, pulling at her.

She looked like she was about to ask what I meant when someone close to us, a woman holding a jaundiced baby, started to scream. I turned quickly enough to see blind Sackerson rise from the crowd, nostrils flaring, jaws agape. His eyes were nothing but two slits in his skull. Sackerson stood on his hind legs and roared, and at first people seemed unable to comprehend what was happening. This was Sackerson, after all. Sacred Son. They'd watched him week after week from afar, and yet now he stood among them, close enough to smell his barn rot and see the shining insects crawling in his hair. "Fucking shit," my father yelled, standing from the bench and dropping the maniacal pencil.

Sackerson reached forward with one big paw, taking a chunk out of the screaming woman's face. The bloody hole seemed a second mouth, also screaming. Amazingly she held onto the baby, crushing it to her chest as she backed away. I finally managed to pull June out of her seat. Her body had gone stiff. "Freddy," she said, "what—"

"Don't talk," I yelled. "No time. We have to get out before the rest of them come."

And then we both saw Munsen himself, pushed by the swell of the crowd into the arena where Stone, newly escaped from his cage, towered. The bear swayed and Munsen swayed. Then in a single smooth motion, Stone took Munsen's lower jaw off his face, and Munsen was suddenly a fountain of his own blood, his orating hands limp at his sides, his fine suit a sluiceway. He remained silently staring at us all for a moment, and then a sound rose from the exposed hole of his throat, louder than all the other screams in the crowd put together, increasing to a final inhuman volume. It was such a frightening noise that even Stone was momentarily stunned. Munsen's body had become a siren, transmitting a final message of sorrowful regret. He wasn't from the city. He didn't belong in the city. And then Stone was on him, tearing.

"Run," I yelled to June before I saw the crowd had already swept her away. I panicked, fighting bodies to look for her. And finally, I saw. June had been pushed from the arena and was running across the fallows toward the four white office buildings that stood in a half-circle, faster than I'd ever seen her run, white dress raised above her knees, hair snapping against the wind. She was closely pursued by the vast form of Hairy Hunks, his oceans of flesh rising and falling as he bounded, front legs leaving the ground, then back legs, roaring at June in excitement. Half the metal collar still dangled from his neck.

Without pause, I scooped up Father's maniacal pencil because it was the only thing within reach that might be useful as a weapon, and as the crowd fell apart, I raced after her. June was already slamming through the glass bank of doors on Sanaco 1 at the far end of the fallows. Harry Hunks shattered the glass as he shoved his body through the entrance, and a lifetime seemed to pass as I ran, moving across the fallows—heal pounding after heal, breath scorching my chest. Screams rose from the Gardens behind me, but Sanaco 1 was silent—cracked walls and broken windows, blue letters hanging from the side. I hoped this place was not Jane's tomb. I had time to wonder about my father. Had he been killed? And Hounds—where had he gone after he'd set loose the bears? Then I was at the broken door, refusing to slow as I crossed the threshold.

It's hard to find the language to explain what I found in the lobby. Spaces in the city were built on a human scale for humble acts of living. The largest room I'd ever been in was the dining hall at a local restaurant called the Horn, but that was dwarfed by Sanaco's lobby. At first, the space struck me as not a room at all, but a new kind of outdoors. There was no end—just a cold sprawl of gray tile, buckled in places from what looked like old flood damage. Plants had broken through the floor, long weedy growths that had turned pale from lack of sun, like bare appendages, reaching for an object that was no longer there. Water stains ran down the walls, and great banks of lights had fallen from the ceiling, shattering to pieces among the plants. A mechanical staircase rose from the center of the lobby, leading up to what appeared to be a second level with a floor of frosted glass. And when I looked at the staircase, I thought *escalator*, though I'd certainly never heard that word before. At a different moment, this kind of word salvage would have driven me mad. Was I to be nothing more than a Munsen Man one day? How did I know the names of objects? Had Mother filled my head with names before I could even speak and now they bubbled up from the cracks of my subconscious?

"Escalator!" I yelled at the metal staircase, though I'd intended to call my sister's name. Neither June nor the Harry Hunks was in the lobby. The place was silent. And then from down a long, broken hall behind the escalator, the echo of footfalls—not like Father's or June's but hard and sharp, something with a heal. A woman appeared in the distance, and I nearly forgot why I was in Sanaco 1—the desperate situation June was in. The woman's black hair was folded into a careful shape, and she wore a pair of clear plastic eyeglasses that reminded me of June's breathing mask. Her suit was of the same quality as Munsen's, undamaged and whole, and instead of looking at me, she read through a thick sheaf of papers as she walked, as though she weren't afraid of tripping over the debris or plant-life in the lobby. As though those ruined things weren't even there.

"Mamma," I said, because that's who it was—it was my mother walking toward me, yet somehow death had changed her—had made her clean. "Where's June?" I yelled, feeling an emotion almost like joy.

Mother looked up sharply, surprised by my voice, and though she was still some distance away, she said, "I'm sorry?"

She didn't recognize me.

That was clear.

"What happened?" I said, running toward her—and when I got close enough—when she saw my face—a wave of what looked like nausea passed over her, turning her features pale. Her make-up looked garish on her whitening skin. "How did you get in here?" she said quietly.

"I'm looking for June," I said. "June came here."

The name of her daughter seemed to mean nothing to her. She sifted through her papers, reading until she found the right one. She read it twice, lips moving, before saying, "June was killed by a bear."

My throat was tight. "Where?" I said, looking again at the emptiness of the lobby.

She read further. "The Gardens," she said, "near where she was seated with her father and her brother. Her brother held her head while she died—" Mother looked up slowly. "Freddy?"

"Of course I'm Freddy! Don't you remember? What happened, Mamma?"

Her hand went to her face, exploring the ridge of her eyebrow, her mouth. "They used my image," she said softly, more to herself than to me. "They thought it would be amusing."

"What does amusing mean?" I said, growing more angry now, thinking of June alone somewhere in the awful white monster of a building—alone and afraid, pursued by Harry Hunks.

Mother—except she wasn't mother—the woman put her papers on the floor and got to her knee in front of me, looking seriously at my face. "My name is Rebecca Stroughton," she said. "What was your mother's name?"

"Her name was Mother," I said, feeling sick with confusion. "Your name is Mother."

She closed her eyes. "And what is your surname, Freddy? What name do we share?"

I didn't know what a surname was, so I didn't answer. Instead, I scanned the room again, wondering if June had somehow made it up the silver escalator. "I was at the Gardens," I said, carefully, "and Hounds set loose the bears, and one of them killed Munsen while one of them went after June—"

The mayor's name seemed to register. "Munsen caused this?" she said.

"The mayor."

"He isn't a mayor. He's just a man who never wanted to play properly."

"Play what?"

Rebecca Stroughton looked like her whole face was breaking. "I sat with you when she died—the woman who looked like me. I sat with you and I even cried for you, and everyone thought it was funny that I could cry over something like that. But you were so small there in your crib—so real. And you had to see her die like that, so you would form a certain bond with your sister. That was the reasoning, as much as there's a reason for anything. Someone thought it was a good idea. 'Let's see how he grows up if it happens like this.' That was how someone decided to play."

"Stop saying 'play'!" I yelled, backing away from her. "What does play mean?"

Rebecca Stroughton reached out, but I didn't want to be touched. And then, from some distant corner of Sanaco 1, I heard June. She was screaming. Then came a roar from Harry Hunks. The world, which had been sinking quickly into shadow, slammed back into place.

"Freddy, don't!" yelled the woman with the Mother face. "There's no one up there." But I ran from her, up the escalator, taking two metal stairs at a time, following the sound of June's voice.

I'm not sure when I gave up looking. It's strange to think that a place could be so big. So many empty rooms. No artifacts. Nothing to name. Big enough to lose a sister. Even big enough to lose the god of the bears. I've tried telling myself that June's screams, the ones I heard so clearly when I stood in the lobby with Rebecca Stroughton, might have been old echoes, ghosts of sound. But even ghosts are too much to ask for in a place like this. I stopped looking and clicked the pink eraser of my father's pencil, releasing lead from the tip. I found a good long space of wall, one without many water stains, and I began to write, hoping that one day someone from the city would find it—maybe even Hounds would find it if he realized what he did was wrong, if he came looking. Maybe he'll read this and know something of what happened. How June got lost. How I got lost. I think the lead in the pencil is running out though. I've clicked the eraser one too many times. I should stop writing, but I'm afraid because I'm almost certain that when I stop, Rebecca Stroughton will be right. That's why her mother-face nearly broke with sadness. She knew how it played out. It was clear to her. There isn't anyone up here but me. And when I stop writing, there won't be anyone at all.

On Place

WELCOME TO CRAZYTOWN, MARTIN BUEHL

Brian Leung

Somewhere in the backcountry there had been fires. As his pen hovered over the silent auction form Martin Buehl recalled worrying over the idea of all those lost trees and the irony of how the smoke candied the evening breeze. Events had moved so fast since the distant orange glow he watched from his window a month earlier. Now, he looked at the three men and one woman bidding against him, all of whom seemed far more certain than he, but wearing awful suits, and shaggy, cowlicky haircuts. The big clock on the wall thunked forward. Just seven minutes left to submit his bid. The woman with choppy blonde hair which looked like a helmet bolted to her skull glared and pointed to her watch. They were waiting on him. "Mr. Buehl?" his host asked from the podium. "Difficulties?"

He shook his head and forced a smile. The banquet staff was removing the wreckage of squab and wild rice and just starting to bring out coffee and tiramisu. Buehl hoped the room, filled with 150 people, would focus on their dessert rather than him. None of this had gone as he thought it would. He had something to get off his chest, but what could he afford, he wondered. What could he sacrifice for the chance to tell everyone just what he thought?

A month earlier he could not have predicted this. For the first time, his love of mail had gotten him into trouble. On that night, his home shut up tight, he retired to his favorite activity as he did at the end of each day, the very end, just before he wound the alarm clock and clicked off the thin brass lamp above his headboard. Buehl read his mail, relished it, the canceled stamps, the thrill of seeing Martin Buehl printed on an envelope. His name in circulation, traveling, the idea of it!

The bills and advertisements he took care of immediately, but actual correspondence was his nightcap. At work, like everyone else, he dealt with compounding email, grammatically horrifying and fractured missives that made him feel like his computer was the bottom half of a just-turned hourglass, but at home he used his whalebone letter opener far more often than a keyboard.

The only actual piece of correspondence that night was a letter from the president of his alma mater. It was typed on a finely printed red letterhead. Buehl felt the paper between his fingers, no texture at all, which was a disappointment. So many people had given up on cotton bond. Plus, a tree was too noble a thing to reduce to a sheet of paper. He shook his head and turned to the content which was composed in a brief but personal style.

Dear Martin Buehl:

On behalf of Eubanks College allow me to congratulate you on your accomplished career. We have taken note of your exceptional success and would like to invite you here to accept our Distinguished Alumni Award during our annual luncheon banquet. Should you be so inclined, please contact the number listed below.

Yours,

Stacia Hammertan
President, Eubanks College

In the morning, he eagerly dialed the number which gave him a recorded list of options. "If you are calling for Mallory University, press 1. If you are calling for Jordan County Technical College, press 2. If you are calling for Eubanks... ." He pressed. Another recorded voice asked him to wait a moment and immediately switched to an instrumental version of "His Eye Is on the Sparrow." Buehl examined himself in the dressing mirror, tightening the belt of his robe and standing erect as possible. Though gray at the temples, it seemed to him he was too young to be receiving such an award. These kinds of things were handed out to bent-over old men and women with white hair and barely audible voices.

A woman's voice came on the line. "I'm sorry to keep you waiting."

"Hello," he said, surprised by the eagerness in his voice, "I'm Martin Buehl, and I've been given this number to RSVP, as it were, to receive the Distinguished Alumni award."

At first, the woman seemed distracted by the chatter going on behind her, but then she settled in. "Ah yes, Mr. Buehl, I have you right here. Congratulations on your nomination for this wonderful honor. Eubanks College thinks quite highly of you. And I'm sure you have fond memories of your college days."

She had a cheery, intimate voice that put him at ease immediately. He sat on the edge of his bed, straightening his robe over his lap. "Absolutely," he said. "Eubanks was a lovely place to study. Brick and Ivy everywhere. And our awful basketball team that we couldn't get enough of."

"And your degree, Mr. Buehl, that has been an irreplaceable asset in your life I'm sure. Without Eubanks College where would you be?"

He hadn't thought about it much, but it was a fair point and it seemed the least he could do was reciprocate the college's generosity. "Definitely. I owe everything to my education," he said.

"Well, Mr. Buehl, Eubanks appreciates alumni like you who understand the value of their degree and who have given back to the college that gave them so much. You can understand why Eubanks holds you in such high esteem."

On that point he paused. The truth was, since he graduated, he'd never really given much thought to Eubanks or his college days. And it certainly never occurred to him to "give back." "To be honest," he said sheepishly, "I haven't really kept up with the college at all."

The woman was silent just long enough that he felt judgment coming and a rash of embarrassment rising to his cheeks. But when the reply came, the woman's voice was reassuring. "We all have such regrets, Mr. Buehl, believe me. And most of us never remedy it. I'm sure if you had it to do all over again, you'd find a way to thank Eubanks College for its foundational role in your success."

He thought of all the letters he'd gotten over the years from the alumni association asking in dribs and drabs for donations toward the general alumni fund and special projects like equipment for the new Computer

Science program. He'd never responded to a single request, which now, with this Distinguished Alumni award, made him feel guilty.

"You're one of the lucky ones, Mr. Buehl," the woman continued. "Eubanks College has plucked you out of obscurity to nominate you as a Distinguished Alumni. How does that make you feel? I can't imagine what an honor like that must be worth to a person."

"It's stunning, actually. I've never won anything, and truthfully I don't feel all that accomplished. I have my own business, true, but it's small. Well, just large enough to keep me in headaches." He had seventeen employees and a satisfactory income, a life which he'd never thought of as notable until that moment. His career was built around business stationary, brochures, and other such products. All day long he took "emergency" phone and email orders. He wondered how some of those people stayed afloat. He could never run things so shoddily, he often told himself. Some of his employees called him a soft touch for making up for his client's disorganization, and he knew they snickered about him behind his back. But it paid off in a thriving business and maybe that's why he was getting this call from Eubanks College.

"Distinguished Alumni," the woman said. "The title fits you like a glove, Mr. Buehl. And it's so touching to hear you talk about how Eubanks College gave you your start. You wear your gratitude on your sleeve."

"Believe me," he said, "I couldn't be more grateful."

"That's good to hear, Mr. Buehl. You do sound grateful. And on that point I'd like to mention that it's tradition for a nominee to make a donation when he or she receives their award. In light of your expressed appreciation for how the college has transformed your life, what might we put you down for?"

He was caught short, his mind instantly reviewing the path of the conversation. How did it get from "congratulations" to a dollar sign, he wondered.

"Of course, Mr. Buehl, no donation is required for your nomination. You'll still get to enjoy the trip and the alumni awards banquet. Eubanks College will take good care of you whether you donate or not."

"No, no" he said, embarrassed at the surely noticeable delay in his response. "I can give something." At least there'd be a plaque he could hang just outside his office door that would let everyone know there was value in the way he ran things. Perhaps the school would even send some business his way. He tallied up an estimate of the flight and hotel and the banquet and there was value in the opportunity to walk the campus grounds again, perhaps poke his head into his favorite lecture hall with its oak paneling and stained glass windows. And in the memory of the red and blue dappling that covered him during the drone of Statistics 312, he made his offer.

"I'll enter that now," the woman said. "A representative will contact you shortly in regard to travel arrangements. Again, congratulations."

"One thing, Miss… ." He realized he didn't recall her name or she hadn't given it.

"Miss Peterson."

"If I might suggest, the college should use cotton bond for correspondence."

"I'll surely forward that note, Mr. Buehl."

He believed her. "Thank you Miss Peterson. It will be lovely to meet you at the banquet."

"Unfortunately, Mr. Buehl, I won't be there. I'm just the recruiter. But really, best of luck and congratulations." And though he wasn't sure, in the split second before she hung up, he heard the electronic echo of her last word, as if there were a half dozen of her repeating the same thing.

B uehl had not anticipated that his award would be connected to a silent auction, but at least his trajectory was steep and fast. Now it wasn't really a question about whether he would bid, nor what the first number would be. He'd already written a 1. But the amount of zeros to follow was more of a concern. What was enough to either lose face with or win without excess? The latter would buy him the opportunity to tell this room full of people a thing or two about Eubanks College. At his table the others were plunging their forks into desserts and sipping coffee, trying, he could tell, not to look at him as he considered his bid. They were so busy not looking at him that the collective energy of the effort weighed on him more than if they had just outright stared.

The strategy, Buehl thought, was to write a number high enough that it could plausibly win and yet not so low that he would embarrass himself if he lost. And there was still a chance he could come out of this with a few orders if he played his cards right. He searched for distraction, pinching the off-white bid sheet between his thumb and forefinger. They had not skimped on that at least. Near where his plate had been the tablecloth was blotched with gravy in an amoeba-like pattern that reminded him of the view from the plane. They had flown over the forest fire aftermath, miles of charred landscape spread beneath him looking as if someone had emptied out a giant can of blackish paint. He hated the idea of all those lost trees, thousands of deaths. A culled cotton field felt like potential, but a forest of trees ravaged by fire, or worse, clearcut, was a travesty. That was one thing he appreciated about going to school at Eubanks, how over the years they found ways to build around the trees. More so than the buildings themselves, it was these proud little groves that gave a permanent feeling to the school. On the plane he had relaxed into the memory of the campus, pictured a kind of homecoming, balloons and banners, a band maybe that would greet him with the school song. He recalled this favorite view through the tall beveled windows of the cafeteria, a large triangle lawn punctuated by marvelous oaks at each point.

Now, Buehl looked at the state of his bid—1. He wrote 0 next to it, which wasn't as painful a start as he thought. 0 was easy to write. He jotted down four more, and even though the five circles bumped up against the one, without a comma and decimal point it was a meaningless number. He held in a chuckle and looked up at the president of the college who was killing time at the podium by telling a dusty story about the Eubanks College Bluejay having its foam beak torn off at a pep rally. Four minutes remaining until the close of the silent auction. He knew he'd have to turn in a plausible bid, but looked again at his figure—100000—just to appreciate its abstractness. A bit of punctuation would make the difference between a mortgage and an after dinner mint.

There had been other alumni awards given out during the evening, Distinguished Creative Accomplishment, Distinguished Patent, and Distinguished Service to Society among them. Buehl watched as each person walked to the stage to receive their award. Above each head he imagined a pulsing green dollar sign that sputtered out when they shook hands with the President of the college. At least they'd gotten their awards outright. For Martin Buehl and four others, the Distinguished Alumni Award was to be won in silent auction. When they told him, he thought not to bid, but then, they were already into him for the initial donation and a banquet room full of people would see him bow out. Not to mention he'd told his employees about his pending distinction, though there was danger of coming home an outright loser. All five bidders would still receive an award but they'd be ranked. Premier Distinguished Alumni, Second Distinguished Alumni, and so on.

Besides, the real opportunity to bail out came shortly after he got off the plane. The man who picked him up at the airport looked collegial enough, white shirt and red tie with an aggressively short haircut. But he was not an alumni himself and didn't seem to know much about Eubanks College. "I'm just a temp," he said. When they neared town Buehl asked his host if he wouldn't mind driving by the campus if it was on the way. The man shrugged his shoulders. "Sure," he said. "But if you ask me it's not much to look at." Buehl was astounded. He hadn't been an attentive alumnus over the years, but he did have fond memories of the campus. Even in winter it was a beautiful place. He recalled how after a good snow the brick walkway leading from the main gate became a striking red ribbon.

"There you go," the driver said, pointing to a four story mirrored building. "Eubanks College."

"No, I meant the main campus," Buehl said, supposing the building was some sort of unfortunate annex or office space for Administration.

The man looked confused. As they rounded the corner he pointed to the top of the building where Eubanks College was spelled out in large red block letters.

"That can't be," Buehl said, but he chose not to press the matter with the young man who didn't seem to know much. It occurred to him that they hadn't passed the town square or the domed courthouse, so this building had to be somewhere on the edge of town.

At the hotel, he asked the desk clerk if she knew where the Eubanks campus was. "Sure," the woman said pulling at the cuffs of her blue jacket. Buehl was relieved at the certainty of her tone. "You can't miss it. About a mile from here. Tall glass building with big red letters."

"Yes I know that one," Buehl said, "but I mean the main campus."

The woman looked at him with about the same confusion as the driver. "Oh," she said. "Red bricks and all that?"

"Yes, yes. That's it."

"They turned that into a mall several years ago."

Now Buehl was the one registering confusion. "A mall?"

"Not the good kind," she said. "Lots of antiques and overpriced coffee. Real foo foo stuff people from out of town can afford." She brought three fingers to her lips as if it just occurred to her the man she was speaking to wasn't local. "Anyway," she said, pulling out an illustrated map. "It's about fifteen minutes walk from here." She circled the caricatured campus clocktower looming impossibly out of scale.

Buehl turned. The driver was just outside the hotel, tie loosened and dangling. He was leaning on a pillar, talking to the valet, a young woman who seemed inclined to respond only with giggles. I could turn around and go home now, Buehl thought. But before he could complete the idea, the young woman spoke. "Oh, Mr. Buehl," she said. "I forgot. We have a letter for you."

"A letter?"

She held out his room key and a white envelope with the familiar red print of the Eubanks College letterhead. Inside, the paper was of a dense cotton bond and slightly crosshatched so that the print seemed to undulate from the page. It was a letter of welcome from the president of college with an updated itinerary attached. Beneath her signature was a handwritten P.S.

"Since the above itineraries were set I have arranged to individually walk several of our distinguished visitors through the college facility. We will send a car around to pick you up at 10:30. And we've arranged a special little surprise at the luncheon banquet."

Buehl ran his finger across the letter. The texture and weight of the paper comforted him, and he thought he might express to the president his displeasure as to the disposition of the original campus. He looked again at the driver outside who had settled into an even closer conversation with the giggly valet. He would stay to accept his award.

The president finished her mascot anecdote and Buehl knew he needed to come to a decision about the silent auction. That he would submit the bid was certain, that he would not embarrass himself was equally secure, but whether or not he cared to win was another matter. His degree really had lead to the eventual success of his business, and he hadn't donated a nickel to the university since commencement where the lieutenant governor herself addressed the graduates. "Remember," she had said, "Your education is priceless." And now, Buehl was being asked to controvert that statement.

That morning, as she walked Buehl through the new glass-box campus, Stacia Hammerstan made a not-so-subtle pitch for the new direction of the college. "We've gone entirely low-residency, Mr. Buehl," she said. She wore a white pant suit with a gold E-shaped broach on the lapel of her jacket. "Virtually all of our learning is off site, which has really liberated the college."

Buehl noted that there were indeed few college-aged people wandering about the halls and that the lights were off in most of the classrooms, though the offices themselves seemed to be well-staffed and humming with activity. "It just doesn't feel like college," Beuhl said. "At least you could've stayed in the old campus."

Hammerstan laughed politely. "Virtually everyone says that at first, Mr. Buehl. Believe me, you are not alone." She placed her hand on his back and lightly turned him down a bright hallway lined with framed renderings of concept architecture. "A university has to be competitive," Hammerstan continued. "Eubanks underwent an intense self-review some years back and we learned two very important facts. Students are a huge expense in the traditional campus setting. And when they become alumni, they don't give back the way they used to."

Buehl thought about his own lack of interest in Eubanks since he graduated and he wondered if this smartly dressed woman with her thin, pulled back hair was directing her comments at him, if maybe she'd seen some sort of file on his lack of generosity to his alma mater. Plus there was something about her voice, a deep subtle wheeze that registered in her vowels. "You said there were two facts," he said, hoping to change the focus of her explanation.

"Indeed," Hammerstan continued matter-of-factly. "Not to sound crass, but the review taught us the main business of the modern university must center around raising funds. The onsite student body is an expensive distraction in light of that fact. So we changed our business model, consolidated our infrastructure and as you can see we're doing quite nicely."

They arrived at the end of hallway at a set of opaque glass doors, the pair splitting platinum lettering into TECHN-OLOGY. "I'm afraid I have to leave you here," Hammerstan said. "I've another guest to walk through campus. I've been giving tours virtually all morning." She opened one of the doors and gestured Buehl inside. There was a thin hum in the large room which was filled with double-wide monitors and a bank of blinking computer equipment.

A well-tanned man with spikey black hair and narrow-lensed glasses emerged from a side office. Hammerstan introduced Buehl as a Distinguished Alumni nominee and the man nodded smartly as if a baton had been exchanged. "Been expecting you," he said, offering a hand. Buehl reciprocated. The man's grip was firm and warm. There was something trustworthy about a handshake like that, Buehl thought. And anyway, he wasn't interested in hearing anymore of the president's theories on the purposes of the modern university.

When Hammerstan exited, Buehl's new host shook his head. "This place is too much sometimes," the man said. He walked Buehl through large computer-filled classrooms where for a few weeks a year, in rotating sessions, different kinds of courses in Programming, Architecture, and Design were taught in rotation. He explained how students did most of the coursework online and came to campus for personal evaluation. "Got to show your work," the man laughed, wiggling an index finger as if it were the punctuation mark to an inside joke.

"I hate to be critical," Buehl said as they ended their tour. "But it all seems pretty sterile."

The man threw his arms up. "You won't get an argument here. I'm just a cog." He laughed again and patted a machine winking yellow and green. "A chip, I mean." The man summoned Buehl into his office with a quick wave, as if speaking the words "I want to show you something," would break a rule. "Give you a peek at what they're launching next year." The man sat at his computer and brought up a website that looked like an aerial view of a small town. As he brought the image closer it became clear that the buildings were computer generated and not well-detailed. "This is the new Eubanks College," the man said.

Buehl leaned closer. "They're building all that?"

"Not hardly," the man said. "This is a virtual campus. Avatars and the whole shebang. They're still working on it. Eventually all these buildings are going to be filled out and they'll name buildings after people."

"For a price," Buehl said.

The man tapped his nose and looked Buehl straight in the eye. He clicked down to ground level and through a kind of jittery three dimensional tour. From this perspective a number of the buildings reminded Buehl of the drawings he'd seen in the hallway. "And the best part is," the man continued, "they can just add a building anytime they like. This campus has as much acreage as they want. Students will even access their courses by clicking on one of the buildings."

The man began to zoom out again when something caught Buehl's eye on the periphery, hundreds of red and purple sperm swimming upward at the monitor's edge. "What's that?" he asked, pointing.

The man smiled. "A little inside joke." He zoomed back in. "The programmers are going to remove it before launch." As the image grew larger the sperm turned out to be balloons rising from two ground level boxes, each undulating column framing a wide banner fluttering in a virtual breeze. Buehl read the message.

WELCOME TO CRAZYTOWN,

Welcome to Crazytown, Martin Buehl

(Your name here!)

"Guess they were feeling a bit punchy that day," the man said. "They think the whole thing is pretty F'ed up, to be honest. But it's amazing how much fiction people are willing to build into their lives just to feel better about themselves."

Buehl stood straight, imagining his own name on the banner. "But what kind of person would pay to have their name put on a building that doesn't exist?"

"I think it's pretty nuts too, Mr. Buehl," the man said. "But to be fair, if we can see it, it exists. It's like a taxidermied daydream."

"Maybe so," Buehl conceded, "but virtual is just another way of saying 'not quite.'"

The man threw his hands up in mock surrender. "I agree, but like I tell people, I'm just the messenger." He panned away from the welcome banner to a wide view of the artificial campus, each building colored in shades of blue, green, yellow and red.

"Has it occurred to anyone," Buehl asked, "how ironic it is that you use an actual building to wring donations out of people?" A lime hued triangular structure on the monitor caught his eye. It was crosshatched in a way that made him think that if it were actually built it would be constructed of clear glass like the entrance to the Louvre, he thought. Buehl caught himself in the split second of beginning a thought on how impressive it would be to have one's name on a building like that. But he brought himself up quickly and turned to the man. "And this is good for the college how?"

"I know. Pretty off the wall. There's nothing as simple as the Looking Glass anymore." The man nodded with resigned apology. "But I have to hand it to Stan. He's really turned things around financially in the last ten years."

"Stan?" Buehl asked.

The man's eyes widened. "Habit," he said. "I'm sorry. I meant President Hammerstan."

"Stacia Hammerstan?"

The man leaned forward slowly as if to indicate the weight and finality of his next words. "She's Stacia *now*."

The "little surprise" mentioned in Stacia Hammerstan's letter when Buehl checked into the hotel turned out to be the silent auction, though she had one other important announcement. "While we're waiting on Mr. Buehl, perhaps now is the time to mention a brand new initiative." She paused and raised her chin, looking down at Buehl at the same time as if to check his progress. "Beginning next year Eubanks will begin enrolling virtual students and in two years, conferring virtual degrees. Our graduation rates will soar." The exclamation in her voice commanded appreciative oohs. "Time is passing, Mr. Buehl," she said, turning the attention of the entire room. He was reluctant to bid, but then again, a winning amount would give him a chance to stand up and tell everyone just what he thought about the new college. With less than a minute to turn in his bid, Buehl looked around the banquet hall full of alumni and their spouses, most of them full of smiles. "Are you going to make it, Mr. Buehl?" Stacia Hammerstan asked from the podium. He nodded affirmatively and turned his attention to his own table where his fellow Distinguished Alumni bidders waited for him. As he looked at their anxious faces, it occurred to Buehl that the squab had been the most tangible part of the trip. We've been lunching in Crazytown, he thought. It was a convenient place, somewhere where a person could call into existence a building, or an award, or an education and there it was because you said so. You didn't have to believe it as long as it was paid for.

A recorded snare drum indicated the last thirty seconds of the silent auction. All eyes were on Buehl. He looked up at Stacia Hammerstan whose white suit gleamed excessively under the rows of stage lights. She held out her hand and wiggled her fingers, coaxing his bid, which made him feel a mouse click away from streaming balloons and a welcome banner with his name on it. As is, the bid read 100000, which was not a dollar or one hundred thousand dollars or anything. Whether I win or not, Buehl thought, I'm going home empty handed. He completed his bid and stood, walking quickly to the stage where Stacia Hammerstan's hand remained eagerly outstretched. Before handing it over, he raised the folded card in the air. "This is the winner," he announced to the room, eager to hear how the president would read aloud $0,1,0.000,0, and explain how his bid was worthless, virtually. As he returned to the table, he thought about the blue mailbox with a red flag at the end of his driveway, hoping it was full.

RODENT TOWN

Craig O'Hara

S omewhere on the western edge of the great grass desert that covers a large portion of the country, sits a tiny village where burrowing rodents vastly outnumber the villagers. The people in the village have turned this to their advantage by creating a roadside attraction featuring these creatures. In the local dialect, the attraction is known as The Eight-Thousand Pound King of the Rodents and his Subjects Who Revere Him. It's translated for tourists as simply Rodent Town.

Situated a few thousand meters from the village, Rodent Town is a large dusty outdoor area sealed off from the outside by a seven-foot-high makeshift plywood and corrugated tin fence. The attraction is nearly twice the size of the village, and the entrance fees charged to tourists who stop on their way to or from the large national parks and nature preserves to the south provide the villagers with most of their income.

The main focus of the attraction, the King of the Rodents, is actually a huge concrete rendering situated near the back of Rodent Town. A villager created it years ago, and it looks like it has never been repainted or even cleaned. It's the tallest construction for a hundred miles in any direction and seems to look out over the rodent town, the nearby café and gift store, the village, and the flat brown plains that reach out to form a tight seal against the pale sky at the horizon. The brown-painted pelt and white belly are peeling and one can see the rough cement and aggregate beneath. It is billed, on road signs and advertisements, as the world's largest rodent, an eight thousand pound behemoth of a burrowing mammal. Most tourists, expecting a living creature, see the statue and are amused by the charade; a few feel as if they've been deceived. Nearly everyone who stops to see the attraction on their way somewhere else gets their picture taken with the King of the Rodents, and most find these photos later while going through film of their trip, having entirely forgotten their detour through Rodent Town.

The King's subjects are live rodents that run free throughout the fenced-in area. Their holes dot the desiccated landscape, creating a hazard for any tourist who doesn't watch her step. Their excrement—tiny, green, sun-dried pellets—is everywhere. The rest of the animals—large peacocks that howl in the early morning, coyotes pacing back and forth, small wild cats, and large non-flying birds—are kept in small circular cages made of scrap chain-link fence. The cages are much too small for these creatures and they behave badly in their captivity, gnawing on their own extremities and rubbing hair or feathers from their backs and sides on the fence. The sight of these animals in their circular cells depresses many visitors and sometimes traumatizes their children.

Despite the steady income Rodent Town provides for the village, older residents have come to despise the tourists. But the younger locals who work as ticket-takers at the attraction behave with a strange kind of awe when dealing with visitors. These local teenagers invite young tourists, often students from the cities who are on holiday, to join them in drinking a locally brewed alcohol made from wild grasses. Many accept the invitation, and at night dozens of party bonfires dot the otherwise empty, iron-flat landscape.

The young people drink the local brew and barbecue wild rodents from outside the attraction under a huge and oppressive covering of brightly lit stars. Because the area has no electrical service, these stars are the only lights in the night and so take on even greater luminosity. The young locals ask the tourists about the cities and towns where they live, the universities and colleges where they study. Places the locals have never seen and have trouble even imagining. The answers often baffle and scare them.

As the night closes down on these groups of young revelers, and they become drunk on the grass-brew, fights break out. Because there are large numbers of people involved, and because the local brew is so hideously potent and often tainted with strange chemical residues from the salvaged auto parts used to distill it, these brawls become huge rolling battles sweeping across the plains, engulfing adjacent parties and growing larger as they move across the landscape like nocturnal dust storms. These battles plough on for miles into the empty darkness with people being punched and stomped, hit with rocks and flying bottles, and being thrown into the bonfires or into wet mud flats left over from the ponds that form during the rainy season.

The fights often take their combatants far from the village and the looming concrete image of the King of the Rodents, carrying the young tourists into places that they had no idea even existed and young local villagers farther from their tiny homes than they have ever been. And the pale dawn light creeping across the plains often finds the local youngsters as far from their village as they are ever likely to go.

A VERY OLD STORY

Mark Pearson

The allegory lumbered out of the Olangassi River south of the Hazmat County line just after noon according to witnesses gathered on the banks for a fishing expedition. It rose out of the mud, stinking of decay, switching its tail, and climbed onto the bank where it paused, appearing to plot its next move. Strands of vegetable matter dangled from its enormous teeth like ropes of oversized dental floss. "What the?" Weeb Delmar said. "That thing looks ancient, prehistoric," Ace Handly said. Bo Gillis dropped his Shakespeare and took a few steps back, his heels slipping and sucking at the slick mud. "Easy, old fella," he said. Weeb would be listed as victim number one: white male, age 49, glasses, seized by the leg and shaken until dead, the first in a series of tragic victims that day. He tried to run, but the monstrous thing lurched at him, according to reports filed by Ace and Bo, whose recollections were skewed beyond recognition by a rapid and incomprehensible infusion of facts, editorial indiscretions and unadulterated adrenaline.

"It was definitely red," Ace said.

"Kind of oily looking," Bo said. "Had a multi-colored sheen to it, as if it was veiled."

"Mostly red," Ace put in.

They both agreed it appeared slippery, hard to read its intentions. "It looked one way, then went the other way," Bo said.

Sweating and cursing, they sprinted up the bank while the allegory thrashed Weeb, their old high school chum and regular fishing partner of thirty-plus years. When Weeb's pathetic and heart-sickening cries died to a whimper, and then silence, the thing leapt up the bank as if it was swimming across the land, switching its tail, and moving its stubby arms in a surprisingly rapid synchronized motion. "It flowed," Bo said.

"Before we knew what happened, we were wrapped up in its tail," Bo said.

The two men stumbled into a swampy thicket, complicating forward movement in the entangled plot. They ran on and on, tripping over stumps and roots, plunging neck deep into murky water. Eventually, after circling for hours, lost, they found Weeb's pickup, lying on its side with a massive dent running from front to back fender where the tail had apparently struck. Footprints straddled a rut where the creature's tail had dragged. After all the action, they were thankful for a slow part. They managed to pry open a door and make a call to police on their CBs.

Gus Haller, veteran reporter at the Times-Merchant, monitoring the police radio, picked up the call and broke for the door. Born and raised in Hazmat, except for the four years he spent at the university studying journalism, and knowing the county roads as well as any native, Haller arrived at the scene moments before the Hazmat County Police Department.

The witnesses, dazed and babbling, were glad to see another human being.

"Now that's a story for you. Now that's a story," they said.

"Not a story you want to mess with," Ace said. "It'll eat you alive."

"It's one monstrous story," Bo said, shaking his head, his words heart-felt and overflowing with remorse.

Haller was a man for a story, and he knew this one was much more than your average story; it had implications: he suspected an allegory. He'd spent twenty-five years chasing the big one. News was in his blood. He loved the pressure of the deadline. It was pure adrenaline: clock ticking, his foot tapping, his fingers flying over the keyboard as he stitched the facts together. Before they switched over to computers, he loved the clacking of the old typewriters. The sound was real, letters ringing out as they hit the page. The newsroom was his home. He'd run through two marriages because he loved the late shift. His second wife cried: "Put me to bed, not the damn paper."

"Don't let it get away," the witnesses called after Haller as he headed into the swamp. He followed the trail down the road, but at the point where the footprints diverged from the road and entered a stretch of forest that gave way to water, he lost it. A few hundred yards later, he picked it up again. This time they crossed the highway. A pickup truck lay smoldering in the ditch where it landed after swerving to avoid it. Haller called in the accident, helped a young couple climb from the wreckage of their truck.

"Did you see which way it went?" Haller said.

"Follow the signs," the boy said. "They're easy to read."

"Don't be so sure," Haller said.

"We didn't want no part of that thing," the girl said, her eyes wide in disbelief. "I kept thinking it was like, like, like I don't know what to compare it to; it's not so simple; it went on forever, extended across the road and into the trees. I never met anything like it before."

Haller set off again in pursuit of the allegory. The tracks approached a remote Air Force base, but they veered sharply before entering; it was probably deterred by the sound of screaming jets, and headed into the depths of the swamp. The last print he saw was a deep impression in the rotting, stinking earth that sank into a small lake filled with cypress trees, mosquito larvae, and blue oily swirls on the water's surface. It stank, something big had disturbed the black fossil muck, stirred and released putrid swamp gas. Mosquitoes swarmed him, covering him in a hazy gray blanket, shortening his fact-finding mission and driving him slapping, and itching to his car. He left reluctantly, knowing he was on the trail of the biggest, ugliest allegory to come out of those parts.

He later picked up a paper trail at the HCPD, but lost it when the files were transferred to the state police. He was left with second-rate photocopies of records that described the size and depth of the footprints. This is where his troubles began. He wrote up a story for the Times-Merchant, using direct quotes of the eyewitnesses. The story at first tore through the community with sensational speed, but was later met with great skepticism. The letters-to-the-editor section was filled with voices crying for Haller's resignation for liberal stretching of the truth. The dispute originated with the witnesses, who after some deliberation and consultation of various zoological reference books and authorities, claimed what they saw was in fact a crocodile. Haller, for his part, maintained it was an allegory. He presented Polaroid pictures of Weeb Delmar's truck and made reference to the damage to his own career and reputation. "Allegorical beyond a doubt," he said. Witnesses Bo and Ace, fearing ridicule, clammed up, refusing follow-up interviews from all news sources.

"Allegories ain't common in this part of the country," Ace claimed.

"There's nothing but allegory in this part of the country," Haller said.

"That's blasphemy," they gasped. "We're word-fearing, literal-minded folk. We won't heed none of your fancified interpitations."

Later, overtaken by an uncharacteristic fit of curiosity, Ace accidentally picked up a Thesaurus, mistaking it for a dictionary, in his search for a definition of an allegory, hoping for a picture next to the word.

"This ain't no time to be reading about dinosaurs," Bo said, and slapped the book out of his hand. "That newsman is ridiculing our country."

"We need a parade," Ace said. "To demonstrate our pride and patriotism. Nobody's going to run down our country."

They purchased a permit, and rallied the town for a patriotic demonstration. Experts were called to testify. They claimed Haller was zoologically misinformed, pathological, a confirmed liberal, who needed to be confined to the greater northeast.

Doubts undermined Sam Haller and his story. Its authenticity was questioned. Dispersions were cast on his reputation. He scrambled to prove the allegory's existence while his detractors remained smug in the knowledge that time deteriorates original copies of official records and memory with indiscriminate abandon. He was left with smudged carbon copies in a manila folder, and the determination that truth would have its day. Gus Haller took it hard, a veteran newsman who prided himself on his news gathering skills. He'd built his career on accuracy, integrity and the tireless verification of the facts.

A spokesman for the State Department of Documentation said all available information pertaining to said allegory would be released in a timely fashion. He claimed to have official estimates of the allegory's length, its verifiable beginning, middle and end in addition to an archeologist's report that said: "These things existed here at one time." He also testified to its bite strength. An unnamed source claimed this allegory to be "nothing new. It shows up every four years or so, every time that politician runs for office, and leaves in its wake a long list of those tragically maimed trying to drag it into the light of day. It's the same old tired story," he said. "People around here with a little common sense know enough to leave it alone."

Haller took heart in the testimony of one of the archeologists, a professor at his own beloved alma mater, and was convinced he had evidence of a genuine living literary artifact. He called the New Critics Archaeology Association and pleaded for help.

"Is it a poem?" they said.

"No," he said. "It's much bigger, unwieldy, definitely a story."

"Can't help you," they said and hung up.

"Wait, wait," he cried. "It could be an epic poem." But it was too late. The line was dead.

The Times-Merchant, unable to substantiate the allegory after it disappeared into the swamp, was forced to print a retraction, admitting the photocopies of police records were not verifiably authentic. Haller was demoted to obit man, doing rewrites and research in the morgue, the final resting place of old stories in the newsroom. It was all he could take. Twenty-five years at the paper and this is the way they treated him? He accepted a buyout from the parent company and took early retirement.

It was a standard retirement party. His only joy came from knowing how much time he would have to pursue the truth. They brought out a cake and gave him a box that he unwrapped to find a clock, a reminder of the deadlines he'd spent his career chasing. It's not the end, he kept telling himself. My time will come. They'll see.

Haller, more determined than ever after retirement, his spirit not quite broken, traveled the swamps in an airboat leased with the shrinking remains of his retirement funds, parking it for long stretches to wander the dismal wetlands on foot, searching for traces of the allegory in an attempt to resurrect his ruined career. He spent nights sweating in a tent that reminded him of boyhood camping expeditions—only then the tent smelled of canvas, not nylon. Those were good memories and the longer he spent on the allegory's trail, the more recollections like that bubbled up out of the depths of his mind. He felt himself coming back to life and he hadn't realized the torpor twenty-five years of the same job had left him in. He was shaking it off now, and he felt the old enthusiasm for chasing a story, the butterflies in his stomach—the way it used to be when he first started in the business, before twenty-five years of rewrites and sewer board meetings took so much out of him.

There was nothing better than following a story, and this was a big one, an elusive one like all the great ones; it's sheer size was impressive; it had sustained itself far beyond the length of the average story. It inspired visions of a Pulitzer Prize, that elusive gem small-town journalists mostly only dreamed about. One of his trips to the swamp led to a chance encounter with a one-armed Seminole alligator wrestler named Eldridge Drake, a kindred soul, who was vacationing in a glass-bottomed boat. The two struck up a conversation and soon they were off in search of Haller's allegory.

They are rumored to have found it, but Drake, after realizing the thing's magnitude, balked at the prospect of a one-on-one match. "Too many implications," he said. "I don't want to be the one who drags it to the light of day."

"What about heavy equipment?" Haller pleaded. "Lift the great story."

"Let it be. It's a job for future generations, archeologists, historians, literary critics. Let them sort it out." He was the first to talk some sense to Haller, although his words took a little time to sink in.

Haller, bearded and gaunt, slumped down in the boat, a week's worth of swamp stuff clinging to his clothes, and wept. So this is what it comes down to, he thought. After all these years, no newsroom pals to shoot the shit with, just loneliness, an old man clinging to the dream of landing one last story, the big one. Have I become pathetic? No, he thought. Just the same stubborn bastard I've always been.

He had a few intermittent sightings, once on a remote beach, where it lounged like it had all the time in the world, not a serious story, but a joke in many ways. Not the kind of story you'd like to have following you around if you were a serious person, or a candidate for political office, for instance. A playboy kind of story. He once saw it at play, alone, spinning its tail in the air, apparently just for fun.

The last time he saw it he got a good look at it. He knew the facts. It was true—that much was clear—but it would take another reporter to make that judgment, to vindicate him from the slander heaped upon his name and reputation, after the water had cleared, after the frenzy of peripheral criticism that ignored the undeniable facts. There was no telling where it would end up. Haller made one last report, as a correspondent, but it passed with no fanfare: a night editor placed it deep in the paper and it got no attention.

Eventually, it became clear to him that nobody cared about the story anymore. The politician it followed for all those years had drifted out of the public sphere, retired. Good riddance. Nobody wanted to hear anything about him. Such was the nature of a story, even a really big one. Everything had its day. Perhaps it would return one day. Haller knew this but it didn't make it any easier on him. He shaved for the first time in months, bought himself some new clothes and sat down to watch the television news. He was left with the sense of greatness passing him by while the allegory remained out there, somewhere in the swamp, submerged just below the surface, sunlight refracting around it, switching its tail to maintain its stability in the nebulous waters.

THE PRISONERS OF GRAVELY ROCK

Jenean McBrearty

D r. Hollings George read Government Protocol Directive T-4 for the third time. In response to his request for clarification, the IRS had simply sent another copy of the directive and underlined the sentence he questioned: Sonograms revealing any condition covered by Sec. N(39) indicate termination. "But what is Section N(39)?" he asked Health and Human Services Director Chad Velasquez. "That's what I need to know if I'm going to be in compliance with the new protocol. I damn sure don't want to lose my job just because nobody in D.C. will answer my questions."

Chad gave him a reassuring smile. "Trust me, no one in Congress or the IRS has read all 2029 pages of the National Health Bill. They don't have a fuckin' clue if anyone is in compliance or not." Hollings watched him on the monitor as he searched his bookshelf's bound volumes of government regulations.

"That puts me out on a shaky limb, Velasquez. I've reached my quota of new enrollees for the year and it's just March. I've got six women entering their second trimesters next week, and if I'm gonn'a have to abort the bastards, I want to do it before five months—that's all I'm saying."

Chad pulled volume 13 and flipped through the pages. "Okay. Okay. Let me look this over and I'll get back with you on this." Hollings saw Chad's eyebrows raise as he skimmed the text. "Yeah, I'll get back to you." The screen went black.

"Ah, shit," Hollings mumbled. A blackout meant classified information. No record of transmittal allowed. Someone was covering his butt. Whatever the directive meant, he wasn't going to find out anytime soon.

"Any luck, Doc?" Connie said as she put cartons from the Wok-n-Go Chinese take-out on her boss's desk. Hollings shook his head no. She handed him a plastic fork and emptied the cashew chicken onto a paper plate. "Fill out a C-17 and be done with it," she advised.

"And let some bureaucrat know he wrote an order I can't understand? I want my promotion." He tugged at her hand and she gave him a kiss on the cheek. "I want us to retire well, Connie."

"Okay. Then just abort them all. They don't know each other. Show them all the same picture of the Memphis Monster in utero and they'll be beggin' you to scrape their innards. You'll be at quota and no harm done."

Hollings sighed. "I want to be under quota. That's the way to score points. Will you call the mothers for me while I'm out at the prison?" She used the chopsticks while he stabbed at the rice with the fork.

"Sure. I'll give them my best damn-it-sometimes-things-go-haywire-doctors-aren't-God speech."

Overworked and underpaid. That's what he was, seeing fifty patients a day and rotating with three other doctors two day a week to bring health care to "underserved" areas. This year, the Gravely Rock Federal Prison had been added to the roster. He drove his Mercedes into the sally port and waited in Warden Hank Huber's office while rookie COs searched his car. Huber wasn't here today, they'd told him, and Hollings was glad. He wasn't in the mood to hear other people complain about underfunding. If the government had any money left over after paying public pensions, it damn sure wouldn't send it to a stink hole like Gravely Rock.

"Who's in hospital today?" Hollings asked the rookie, a twenty-two year old girl with a crew cut.

"Prisoners fifty to fifty-four for routine check-ups. The one shank wound we had became a fatality last night," she said. She even walked like a man. Side to side. But her voice was feminine. She led him through sliding gates and then opened a three-inch thick steel door. "After you, Doctor."

Inside five men, all chained to the wall, sat six feet apart on a narrow bench. Hollings put on his stethoscope and checked their vitals, making notations in the files the rookie retrieved from a file cabinet. "Any of you have any complaints other than indigestion and blue balls?" he said, not looking up.

"I need drugs," one man said. The others laughed.

"It was that need that got you in here, asshole," Hollings said.

"What got you here" the man snapped. "Malpractice suits?"

Hollings didn't respond, but the question was a fair one—the prisoners got the kind of care they paid for—and he thought about it as he and the rookie walked to the first gate. "Baylar dead yet?" he said, pushing the prisoner's challenge to the back of his mind.

"Uh-uh. You gonn'a check on him?"

"Every week," he said, and they turned down a hall that led to the west wing where the Persons Deemed Dangerous—PDDs—were housed. "You gott'a wonder what's keepin' the old man alive," he said softly as they walked past barred jail cells to a row of solitary confinement solid cell doors.

The rookie shrugged her shoulders as she opened the door. "Maybe he's waiting for a pardon. Or Perry Mason."

Skylar Baylar didn't look like a dangerous person, but few people do at ninety. Still, he didn't look frail either. His white hair was thick and unruly, his eyes as blue as the veins that snaked under his translucent skin. Though bent over a desk, when he stood up, he was almost six feet tall, and his handshake was as firm as his voice. "Nice to see you, Hollings," he said.

"Senator," Hollings nodded and the rookie left. "How's the prostate?"

"Doctor Grihalva says it's getting smaller. Doctor Lopez says it's getting bigger. How the hell do they know by taking my pulse?"

"I can tell you it's not cancer." Hollings sat at the desk. "You'd be dead by now." The prisoner's question was nagging at him—what brought him here. My failed marriage, he'd almost said. My failed parenting. My failed finances. All true and all a lie he told himself so he wouldn't have to think about the real truth. He was a lousy doctor like Grihalva and Lopez, practicing medicine because it was an easy ticket to early retirement—if you didn't mind unnecessary abortions or assisting suicides. "I'd like to get some background on you—for the file. We don't see many men like you anymore."

Baylar perused his stash of teas and chose an Early Grey. "You mean old men or disgraced Senators?" Baylar filled a kettle with tap water and set it on the one-burner hot plate. "Or people in general unwilling to die because the government wants them to?" Baylar rinsed out two mugs and hunted for the sugar.

It was becoming clear why the government wanted to shut Baylar up. "How did you get here?" Hollings said before he could stop the words.

"By plane. Then by bus." Baylar was unwrapping a package of cookies he took from a box with Amnesty International stenciled on the side.

"That's not what I meant," Hollings said sharply.

Baylar turned around. "I can't read your mind. Fuzzy thinking makes for imprecise words. You're a real Party Man, alright." He put two makeshift saucers, cardboard squares he'd cut from a box and decorated with pen and pencil, on the desk, and laid a napkin and a spoon next to each one. How did Baylar know he would stay for tea and that he'd eat cookies. Did he look hungry or thirsty?

"I mean, what did you do that put you in prison—and this prison in particular?" The question sounded precise, but Baylar's eyes told him otherwise. The old man sat down, and folded his arthritic hands in front of his saucer.

"I didn't put myself in prison. The government put me in prison. And because the government wanted to make sure no one of consequence would hear or understand anything I have to say, the government chose a prison in the Mojave Desert. Now, do you want to know why the government sentenced me to prison?" The kettle whistled, and Baylar drowned the tea bags in bubbling water. Did he expect an answer?

"Yeah, I want to know," Hollings said. Baylar was stirring his tea slowly as he added each of two sugar cubes to it. Hollings was riveted. Watching someone think was a new experience.

"T-4."

"What?" Hollings put an uneasy hand on his medical bag though he knew it contained no government papers. He looked around the cell for a computer screen, a cell phone, any device through which Baylar might have been able to access government records.

"I'm in prison for T-4."

"Impossible. T-4 was just issued two weeks ago." Baylar hadn't moved.

However he found out about the government medical protocol, he was speaking the truth—he knew about it.

"Oh, no. T-4 was issued eighty-one years ago. Well, a form of it anyway.

The United States government pretended it was an innocuous addition to the national health program, but Hitler implemented it in Germany in 1939—a euthanasia program to eliminate life unworthy of life. Some history buff policy namer's idea of a joke, I suppose."

Hollings examined a chocolate cookie. He'd heard about 20th Century Oreos, but had never seen one except in an old magazine Connie had found in an antique store. All cookies had green or pink soy centers now. "Euthanasia is only allowed in certain extreme circumstances—terminal illness, retardation or physical deformities—and then only if accompanied by documentation and parental consent before birth," Hollings explained.

"T-4 started the same way. Midwives and doctors registered newborns and children that displayed symptoms of retardation or were impaired. Three doctors read these reports and marked either red or blue crosses on the forms. Those with unanimous red crosses were sent to the Children's Specialty Department and euthanized." Hollings was doodling on his napkin, tracing and retracing the form of a fish, then switched to a sideways figure eight.

"You have to admit, Senator, women are better off having access to abortion. An unwanted child is an unhappy child. It's better to prevent miserable lives than to force children and parents to suffer," Hollings said, hoping Baylar couldn't detect his distress. Connie would have made those calls by now. He'd spend the next two days persuading healthy women they needed to abort.

"As long as it's the woman who's making the decision," Baylar said.

That's why he's dangerous. He knows about the abortion guidelines the government denies. Had Baylar seen the standard sonogram photo shown to mothers to scare them into consent?

"The Nazi program was expanded to older children and adults. With his own signature, Hitler designated medical experts who would make decisions about all kinds of patients—schizophrenics, epileptics, paralytics and those who had syphilitic diseases, encephalitis, Huntington's chorea—then those who had been institutionalized for at least 5 years. The program was expanded again to include those without

German citizenship or who were not of German blood, and then finally Jews, Negroes, and Gypsies."

Hollings let out a deep sigh of relief. Baylar was a Holocaust Militant, one of the Congressional Protestants who demonstrated on the capitol steps against every expansion of the national health. He'd seen them on television when he was a kid, and asked his high school history teacher about Hitler's killing machine. Nothing but distorted mythology repeated by racists to discredit Congress' landmark legislation, she told him. Still, if the Protestants were just misguided crazies, why did they keep getting reelected? "You believe all that ancient history shit?"

"Oh yes. My father took me to the Hadamar psychiatric hospital when he was stationed in Germany. That's where the holocaust really started—hospitals. A picture of the savage Christian hung in the foyer," Baylar said.

The moniker intrigued him. "Who was that?"

"Christian Wirth. Spearheaded the euthanasia program. It might have continued openly if Bishop von Galen hadn't preached his anti-euthanasia sermon. Hitler suspended the program in 1941 in favor of a less public approach, but by then the SS was well schooled, and the concentration camps were operating in full force under people like Wirth, Stangl and Reichleiter."

Baylar was lost in thought again, having crumpled the napkin with the doodles in his fist and thrown it into the wastebasket. "Are there others still alive who believe as you do?" Hollings asked, knowing it wasn't likely Baylar would know or admit it if he did.

"You'll know sooner than I," Baylar said. "I assume you're here to administer my good death." Baylar nodded towards Hollings' right hand, and then looked at his watch. "I'll bet you have the death certificate in your bag with a time of death already noted."

Hollings brought his black bag to the desktop and opened it. "Go ahead. Check it yourself." Baylar went through the bag, piling its contents on the desk: stethoscope, head scan thermometer, blood pressure gauge and cuff, aspirin, bandages, antibiotics—pills and ointment—tongue depressors, prescription pad and blood and urine sample collection vials. He stuffed the paraphernalia back in the bag and gave Hollings a weak smile.

"Guess they don't think you've got the right stuff," he said.

"The government has let you live all these years, why would it kill you now? You're no threat to anyone as far as I can see." The government wasn't perfect, but it was entitled to a defense when people, even crazy ones, got irrational about it.

"It's been twenty years. Societies will be generous, even merciful when they can afford to be, but now all those kids born after passage of the national health want the good life they were denied growing up. They're tired of paying for people like me—multiply me by a few million and I'm as expendable as they are. T-4 kicks in when the money runs out," Baylar said. "Economic collapse. That was the real reason for the Holocaust. America thought it couldn't happen here."

His reference to T-4 again made Hollings shiver. Baylar was staring at him. He was dangerous. "Not everybody on the Titanic could be saved."

"No one tried to pretend the captain could save everybody. But he only had fourteen minutes. Congress had sixty-five years to get ready for us Boomers."

"That only proves people are human and have no crystal balls," Hollings said. That was the trouble with old people. They knew too much and remembered too much to argue with them. They didn't understand what it meant to care about people.

"It proves people who aren't smart enough to have a little foresight and don't have any balls at all shouldn't be put in charge of the most private relationship two strangers can have—that's what Roe v Wade argued isn't it? No government interference with a woman and her doctor? Now the government is her doctor and she's a one-too-many taxpayer patient. Do the math."

"I'm no good at math," Hollings said.

"Then try poetry. The one that goes—they came for the Jews but I said nothing because I wasn't a Jew. They came for the Communists and I said nothing because I wasn't a Communist. Add Lutherans and Catholics, trade unionists, the crippled, the old and insane—I said nothing—then they came for me and there was no one left to save me."

Hollings jammed Baylar's file into his medical bag and snapped the clasp. "I think Lopez is up next week. See you in three weeks," he said.

Helen's Hash House was empty except for the trucker couple wearing matching Old Dominion t-shirts. Hollings walked past them and slid into the last booth at the rear of the diner. His extended visit with Baylar made him miss the lunch special, but Helen had saved him a double ration of red meat and brewed fresh coffee for the dinner crowd.

"Thought maybe the paperwork on that shank death held you up," Helen said. She was usually too busy for small talk.

"News travels fast," he said.

"The graveyard COs were talkin' about it." She punched his red meat ration ticket, and left the coffee pot along with the hamburger in a yellow plastic basket on the table. Talk. That's all people did these days. There was a time when he would have been expected to answer an emergency call from the prison. Now the California Supreme Court had ruled first-aid was the only medical care inmates had a right to. Violence was neither cruel nor unusual for incarcerated people and the State had no duty to protect inmates from themselves or others like them. On-site medical facilities were closed in prisons throughout the Ninth Circuit when the federal court upheld the rulings, saving the State billions of dollars in medical costs.

Hollings opened his bag and found the aspirins, swallowing two with a sip of coffee. He'd pay for that no-no later with a good case of diarrhea. "Son-of-a-bitch," he said when he saw Baylar's wrinkled file. It meant a half-hour trip back to the prison. "Fuck it." Huber wouldn't notice it was gone. The rookie didn't.

He attacked the hamburger. Connie would have a fit if she knew he was backsliding on his diet. She was the food cop. The career coach. The power behind his shingle—the professional wife role his first wife didn't know how to play. Was Baylar ever married? If he'd had a Connie by his side, he'd be a free man. Hollings cracked open the file. Maybe it was time he got to know his patient.

"I talked to Chad Velasquez this afternoon," Connie said. They were having a dinner of vegetarian chili. He'd been home five hours.

"And?"

"He's flying in this week-end to see you—and Gravely Rock prison."

Thank God for Xanax and Prilosec. "What's to see? Big ugly gray buildings full of big ugly criminals and a couple hundred PDDs."

Connie wrapped well-manicured, slender fingers around the stem of a wine glass, part of a set they'd received as a wedding gift. "He says you're in line for a promotion. He wants you to run the facility."

"Me a warden? Talk about adding responsibility. Lopez and Grihalva turn it down so he piles on the black guy? Not a chance."

"Lopez and Grihalva have exceeded enrollments quotas the last three years. You haven't."

Maybe she was angling for a compliment. "Thanks to you. You made it easy," he said. She smiled. They'd have sex tonight. "You get the sonograms taken care of?"

"Five calls. Four faxed consent forms."

He contemplated a second helping of chili. "Shit, who's the Mother Mary hold-out?"

"Jennie Corcoran." Her smile disappeared.

"Isn't that an Irish name?

Connie rolled her eyes and nodded. "That's the trouble with on-line medicine. We don't get to see the patients until they come in for procedures."

"I thought the Irish preferred to stay in Boston. That's their place, right?"

"She's married to a CO at Gravely Rock—a brother named McKinley Corcoran."

Hollings let out a disgusted, "Humph," and tossed his napkin into the air. "Now what? Do I protect the half-black kid or come in at quota?"

"Chad says it's your call."

Hollings smiled. Connie was good at running interference. "Did he clarify T-4's N-39?"

Connie started clearing the table, stacking their plates and then bowls. Maybe she hadn't heard the question. "Connie, did he say anything about the Protocol Directive?"

She stopped moving and rested motionless hand in her lap. "It was sent by mistake—no, too early. Gravely Rock is going to be a Detention Center for PDDs. You know, put all the rotten apples in a basket and watch the basket."

"What about the prisoners and the PDDs there now?" Hollings said.

"They'll have to be euthanized." She didn't look at him. Her eyes were aimed at the tureen of chili that rested on a platter decorated with crowing cocks.

"All fifteen hundred of them?" Hollings took a pen from his shirt pocket and scrawled the numbers of his napkin. A human being averaged two feet wide, five feet long. That's ten square feet times fifteen hundred—he'd need fifteen thousand square feet to bury them—or one big fuckin' pit. Unless the bodies were burned. His hand went limp—he was doing the math.

"They're criminals, Holly, the worst of the worst. That's what Chad said."

Hollings brought Baylar's file to the table. "This guy ain't a criminal. He's not even dangerous—if you ignore his senile babblings. And he's a doctor. A damn good one, from what I can tell. Did Chad say he had to be killed too?"

"Yes. Lopez was supposed to go out there last night, to certify his death, but Lopez was drunk from his daughter's Quincenera."

Hollings sank into his chair. "Fuck." Baylar was smart enough to know a set-up when he saw it. Shanking, my ass. The graveyard COs killed the wrong inmate—some poor bastard instead of Baylar. Fuckin' bureaucrats. Or maybe not. "Why not transfer the prisoners to a Rent-a-Con company? They can earn their own fuckin' keep."

Connie looked up at him, finally. He saw coldness there, empty icy holes in a face he loved and caressed and vowed he'd do anything for the soul who wore it. "Baylar's white, Holly. They're all white. They're a minority but a dangerous minority. Burdens to society who exploit and oppress decent dark folk. They're the enemy. Slave owners. Race defilers. Idol worshipers, Capitalists, nationalists. You have a duty, Holly."

Hollings moved his chair beside her and opened Baylar's file. "Look at him, Connie. He's an old man now, but ninety-nine other Senators once called him "the Gladiator." He was a cardiologist at John Hopkins. He knew all about the conversations people have with their doctors about their bodies and their minds and maybe their souls, if there is such a thing as a soul."

Connie pushed him away and took the dishes to the kitchen. "I'm just saying I don't want to kill this guy," Hollings said towards the kitchen. "That's all. Let him live out his life drinking his hot-plate tea and eating cookies out of care packages."

She appeared at the doorway. "How does he get a hotplate inside a prison anyway?" He knew why he loved her. She was sleek, strong, sexy.

"I suppose the Amnesty International people sent it along with the cookies."

"Well, that answers that question," Connie said.

"What question?"

"Why he's still alive. It's that crazy organization that monitors high-value prisoners."

"You mean the one that kept Mandela alive in South Africa? That crazy organization? The one Senator Baylar fought to keep funding?" He pointed to the open file. "It's all in there. The whole list of his crimes that reads like a Nobel Prize nomination. What the fuck, Connie. Why murder a bunch of white people?"

He didn't see her open-palmed hand swing at his face, but the blow sent him tumbling over the table. "Murder! It isn't murder when you kill your enemies. It's self-defense. And it isn't murder when the State protects you from hate mongers and genocide, it's execution," Connie yelled.

It was the first time she'd struck him in two months. He'd hoped the anger management counseling had worked its miracle and the abuse was over, but she was again an uncontrollable monster. "I'm going for a ride," he said. He grabbed his keys and Baylar's file. Leave before she gets going full throttle. That's what the counselors told him. He left for his office, stopping only once to drive through the parking lot of the boarded up Winchell's Doughnut shop. He could use drugs, but couldn't eat empty calories. It didn't make any sense from a medical point of view. Baylar ate contraband—yes, he saw the pop-tarts and potato chips in the box along with two other packages of cookies—and the old cracker was in great shape. Hollings looked in the mirror and saw Connie's handprint on his face. Maybe she'd knocked some sense into him after all. If he followed Velasquez's orders, she might have some respect for him, but after that it wouldn't matter. He still wouldn't be able to eat cookies. Baylar was a freer man than he was.

"I'm here to see Huber," Hollings said. A swing shift CO waved him into the sally port, and another escorted him to a small cottage where Huber stayed during the week. Huber answered the door with a hearty hello, and told the CO it was all right.

"You're here about my not sending in my blood pressure readings, right? I'll get them in, Hollings. I promise—it's the construction going on. The powers that be are finally getting around to redoing the facilities. We're expanding. New showers, new stoves, new ovens—all environmentally friendly. No emissions. Not that anyone could smell burnt toast in this god-forsaken place."

Huber was white. His 2010 P.T. Cruiser sported an "I heart Germany" bumper sticker. What do Irish and German people know about living in a desert where the heat can reach a hundred and twenty-five in the shade? "It's okay. I'm here to get some information about the shanking last night and to return this," Hollings said, handing him Baylar's file. "I accidentally took it this afternoon."

Huber hesitated. "I'm sure there's no harm done. Just put it on the end table."

He doesn't want to touch it. No fingerprints. "What was the name of the man who was killed?" Hollings said.

"Ah...I don't know. Jenkins. Anderson. Does it matter?" Huber's face had sobered.

"For the record. Was it Gerald? Gary? Galen?"

"I'll check into it and get back with you."

Huber's evasion was as good as a blackened screen. All bureaucrats knew how to delay, deny, and divert. He'd have to risk being direct. "Chad Velasquez...?" Hollings began. Huber's mouth quivered. He raised his index finger to his lips and his head shook a no. "Is a stickler for record keeping," Hollings finished. Huber was writing on pad, and shoved it towards him. Surveillance—was all it said.

"On second thought, I think the record's on file. Come with me," Huber said, and led him through the yard where gaunt, uniformed men lolled about in the evening heat under canopies made of green mesh. He should be afraid of men as white as these. He was a dark beetle crawling in snow. A chessboard and a deck of cards rested on a picnic table. No one was playing.

Huber led him to an oddly shaped building. A sign reading STORAGE was hung above a set of double doors. "It's our chapel," Huber said as they entered the cool dark room filled with rows of pews in front of a podium.

"You had an illegal funeral service," Hollings said as the door closed behind them.

"There was no service because there was no body," Huber said. "No one was killed." He moved the podium aside, knelt down, and pulled up three floorboards. Underneath was a stash of rifles and ammunition. Huber looked up at Hollings. "Lopez told me Velasquez activated T-4 N-39—the American version of the final solution. We've been smuggling out prisoners for the last two weeks. A hundred a night."

"Lopez is in on this? Fuck! What the hell is going on?" Hollings picked up a rifle. It was real. He returned the rifle to the floor.

"Most of the people in here know how to shoot. Baylar taught me." Huber slowly loaded one of the guns. "Calipatria. Atescadero. Sacramento. Every prison in California is being retrofitted as a detention center. I know I won't be spared."

"What about the COs? They have to be in on this," Hollings said.

"The desert swallows the dead. The only difference between prisoners and guards are uniforms. You couldn't tell the difference this afternoon."

Hollings heard a loud click. Baylar and the rookie stepped out of the shadows. Baylar came close—so close Hollings could see the silver chain and a silver fish charm hanging around his neck, and the silver Glock Baylar had pointed at his forehead. "Are you going to shoot me?" It was a stupid question. Huber had been telling him why they had to kill him since they left the cottage.

"You're one unlucky dedicated public servant, Dr. George. Put the cuffs on him Corcoran," Baylar said.

The rookie locked Hollings' hands in steel and he held them in front of his face. "I take it you're Jennie Corcoran and Mr. Corcoran is rotting in the desert," Hollings said. Some doctor he was. He didn't know a pregnant gait when he saw it.

"He's loading supplies, " she said. "Let's get this over with."

Hollings tugged at the cuffs. "Okay. Kill me. But what about the two thousand white faces on their way? And the next two thousand, and the next? White people aren't the only ones that have a history—you ever heard of the Underground Railroad? You got Lopez on your side to operate transport. All you need is a black warden to keep excellent fake records of the dead." Baylar lowered his pistol "And a few more buses," Hollings said.

"I wish I could let you live. But you're the most dangerous kind of person there is—a man without the courage to stand by your convictions because you don't have any," Baylar said.

Hollings frantically fumbled around his inside coat pocket and withdrew a legal-sized envelope. "Are you sure? Before you pull the trigger, read this."

Baylar looked at the contents—a sonogram printout and a letter addressed to Jennie Corcoran. "Dear Mrs. Corcoran," Baylar read:

A terrible mistake has been made regarding your child. Here is the accurate result of your self-administered sonogram you e-mailed this office March 23, 2040. Your pregnancy is normal, healthy and with proper prenatal care should produce a normal, healthy child. I also feel that the desert air is detrimental to your asthma and will recommend an immediate transfer for your husband to warden Huber. We apologize for any distress our mistake may have caused you. Sincerely, Doctor Hollings George."

Jennie ran her fingers over the fuzzy print Baylar handed her, and tears sneaked down her face. "I don't have asthma, Dr. George."

"I couldn't think of any other way to get you out of here safely." He turned to Baylar. "There are four other letters in my car. Make sure they're mailed," he whispered.

Baylar nodded. "Get everyone on the bus and take off, Hank," he said to Huber.

"You're not going?" Huber said.

"If he's on the level, we can save a lot of people before they're on to us. If not...well, I'm old. I can afford to trust him. Maybe Doc George and I can start a beautiful friendship."

The two men watched the bus disappear into the blue desert night under confetti stars. "What'll I tell Velasquez?" Hollings said when they were in Baylar's cell, dunking Oreos in large glasses of milk. This was joy.

"If I know my Nuremberg history, Velasquez isn't going to want his fingerprints on any of this. You think he's really gonn'a to come to the desert in the middle of summer?" Baylar said.

Hollings looked at the thermometer that hung above Baylar's sink. It was almost midnight and it was a hundred and four. "Hell no. He'll believe anything I tell him."

"Then tell him the truth. The prisoners of Gravely Rock are gone."

THAT BUSINESS WITH THE HOLE

Mark Rigney

The second morning dawned colder, and the air smelled sharply of impending change. A blustery wind sent copper-colored leaves whizzing through the air. Some of these landed next to the hole, on the lawn, and scattered like frightened mice. Others fell directly into the hole and disappeared.

"Ollie!" yelled Mike. "Can you see those leaves coming in?"

Ollie's reply came from some undefined, almost reluctant distance, and Mike could just make it out. "Got a few, yeah. Tulip, mostly. Tulip and red maple. Always liked them red maples."

Mike shook his head. The matter-of-factness of the exchange would have been hilarious if it hadn't been for—well, if things weren't the way they were. He cupped his hands, kneeling where the lawn gave way, the very edge of the rift, and called again. "Ollie, I know you're going to think this is crazy, but CNN's coming. Fox News, everybody. There's a station from Japan, they're at the airport right now. Your back yard is about to become world famous."

Behind Mike, Melissa Hogan slapped a hand to her forehead; strands of disheveled gray hair blew round her temple. "Oh, my goodness," she said. "I need to mow. I need to mow this yard."

"Is Melissa there?" Ollie's voice sounded like an echo of an echo of an echo, a faraway horn section lost in a mine shaft.

"She's right here."

"Mike," said Melissa, fingering the cross at her throat, "tell him—Lord above, you know I can't talk to him like this. No wife could talk to her husband like this. So please, Mike. You just tell him to find a way back outta there!"

Without waiting for a response, Melissa hurried toward the back door at a trot and banged the screen hard on her way in. Mike hoped she wouldn't glance out the picture window, facing the street. So many strangers watching on the front lawn. Hundreds, and more gathering by the hour. He knew Melissa wouldn't like that.

Turning back to the hole, Mike said, "Ollie, you know Melissa wants you to come back up."

"Holy Christ, Mike, don't you think I would if I could?"

Mike could almost picture suspender-clad Ollie sitting hands on knees, puffing out his jowly sixty-year-old cheeks in frustration. Of course, Mike couldn't form a very accurate picture of his long-time neighbor or of how he might be sitting—if indeed he was sitting—because he couldn't be sure where exactly Ollie was. And Ollie—salt of the earth Ollie—was no more sure than he.

"Mike?"

"Yeah, Ollie. Still here."

"You don't see nothin', do ya'? A ladder or somethin' that maybe we missed?"

"No. Sorry."

He and Lindy had tried lowering a ladder the day before, in the morning, right after Melissa, frantic, had called and reported Ollie's accidental tumble into the hole. The ladder, twelve feet of rugged fiberglass, never hit bottom, and when they lost their grip and the ladder rattled and bumped into the hole, bouncing once off the edges of the soft, yielding turf, it had disappeared entirely. Ollie claimed he had neither seen nor heard it go by. Where, then, had it gone? And where precisely was Ollie, other than stuck down in a hole, somewhere beneath—beyond—his otherwise normal suburban back yard?

"Well," Ollie said, his voice resigned, glum. "I'll just hang around, then. I guess. 'Til you all up there think of somethin'."

"Ollie, don't worry. What goes up must come down, right? So what goes down..."

"...must come up?"

Mike stood, checked to make sure no one else—no reporters—had found a way into the back yard, and dialed Lindy on the land line. She picked up immediately, already talking on her cell. "—I was saying, yes! It's chaos!"

"Lindy?" Mike ran a hand back through his thick sandy hair, newly dyed. "Lindy, can we do one call at a time?"

"Sorry, Boo, but everybody wants to hear what's up, y'know?"

Mike nodded. He y'knowed. "Lindy, honey, listen. The story is definitely out, and if I want to keep hold of this turf, I have to be way on the ball."

On the other end of the line, Lindy hopped up and down, giddy like a schoolgirl. He didn't have to see her to know what she was doing. He knew his wife backwards and forwards. Of course, he'd thought he'd known his next-door-neighbor's back yard, too, until yesterday, when the hole had appeared, more or less where the Hogans normally put the grill for their everyone's-invited weekend barbecues, and good old Ollie, distracted by a migrating wood warbler, had fallen clean in.

It was an odd-looking hole, not properly a hole at all but more of a gap, an absence, roughly oval in shape, no more than five feet across at its longest axis. It had neither scent nor consistency. From most angles, it looked grayish, like very dark soap-scum, but when you leaned over and stared straight down, it took on an oily appearance, faintly iridescent. Mike didn't like to look at it for long, not even with Ollie's homely voice emanating from inside. That intrusive, unfathomable gray gave him the willies.

It had also made him an overnight, international sensation. Now the denizens of seven continents knew affable Mike Przewalski of Channel Sixteen, Springfield, Illinois. Mike Przewalski, with his Ken-doll looks and his easy smile. Mike Przewalski, with the story of the century.

"Boo?" said Lindy, still hopping, this time because she needed to pee. Five months pregnant and over the moon about becoming a first-time mom at thirty-two, peeing was something she'd been doing a lot of lately. "Boo?" she said again. "What if we can't get him out?"

"We will," Mike assured her. "But until we do, I'm telling you, sweetie, this is our ship, and our ship has come in."

More breathless hopping on Lindy's end of the line, then quick good-byes.

Defense, Mike figured, that was the thing. D-fence! He'd done a fair job the day before at keeping the entire thing under wraps until he could ensure that no other news agency even had permission to be in Melissa and Ollie Hogans' yard. The Hogans' yard was already ringed by a seven-foot privacy fence, and now the only way into the rear yard was either through the house or around the sides, and Mike had blocked the side yards with hastily employed hurricane fencing and fifteen NO TRESPASSING signs tacked up on tomato stakes by Lindy and Melissa.

He'd worried at first that Melissa might be an obstacle—she was nearing sixty and increasingly nervous with age—but as soon as the fire and police crews had given up, scratching their heads, she'd handed Mike the keys to the kingdom. "Mike," she'd said, "I don't fancy the idea of my house and yard turning into some kind of circus. That's my husband down there, and I don't want just anybody gawking. But you're here, I know you, I trust you. Everybody else? To heck with 'em. You get this yard sealed up tight, you hear me? Tight!"

An hour later, Mike and Hayes Millard, his regular cameraman, had sent back footage that had turned Channel Sixteen upside down. When Mike requested help with cordoning off the yard, the station sent three entire news crews and every intern the building had to offer—which was a good thing, because by then, a host of crackpots had shown up, rubber-neckers of every stripe, evangelists and doomsayers and everything in between, and of course the other local news outlets hadn't been too slow on the uptake. They ran lead stories about the Hogans' "Fabulous Hole to Forever!" and hollered for equal access. National attention had followed on the heels of the six o'clock news, and by nine, Hayes's footage and Mike's face were all over YouTube, with so many hits that the story took down two of YouTube's server farms.

Just as Mike was dialing the station, a competing news crew appeared from atop the Hogans' side yard fence, leaning over the pickets by means of hastily erected scaffolding in the Corbetts' neighboring yard. A camera just like Hayes's was suddenly aimed straight at his cash cow, the hole.

"Hey!" he called. "You get down from there!"

"Not going to happen!" responded a scarf-wearing blonde, clearly a fellow reporter. "We paid a thousand bucks for access to this yard, and since we're not on the Hogans' property, we're not trespassing. Now if you could step a little to the left so we can get a clear shot...?"

Mike swore under his breath. So the Corbetts were renting their yard at a thousand bucks a pop? Where were his thousand bucks an hour?

At least no one was about to appear over the other side yard fence, since that was his, and Lindy would never let a competing crew in, not for any money. But what about the rear fence, on the north side?

Mike trotted over to Ollie's shed, rust-blotched corrugated sheet metal, hauled open the doors and gave the shed's dim mustiness a quick once-over—yes! Large and filthy and blue like a child's plastic swimming pool, there was a tarp, easily twelve-by-twelve. It took Mike only minutes to unfurl it, stake down the corners, and cover the hole. The Corbett-yard news crews cursed him to the skies, but he tuned it out, smiling at his own success. Greedy little bastards.

Damn, but there was a lot to do.

He called Lindy again, told her to start renting out the use of their bathrooms for twenty bucks a shot, and not a penny less. He gave her a whole laundry list of jobs, half of them leaping into his head as he went along. Get Melissa a lawyer, the best, big shots who knew property law and criminal trespass and maybe had a connection to the entertainment business. Call a contractor, maybe Gerry, tell him to start putting up the highest fence they've ever built. And call Subway, order sandwiches—no, never mind. Call Ted at the station, get them to pop for sandwiches...

As he swept on, he avoided eye contact with the belligerent, heckling news crews from the Corbetts' and a second gaggle of reporters who were popping their heads over the rear fence—Who even lived over there, anyway? Five years in the neighborhood and he still knew no one on the next street over—and then Hayes stepped into view, big-boned slouch-shouldered Hayes, his rumpled cargo pants and untucked shirt conspiring to announce that once again, he had something to complain about.

Mike snapped his phone shut and rounded on Hayes. "What?" he demanded.

"They put milk in my coffee," Hayes sighed. "Sons of bitches."

"Hayes," said Mike, adopting the same tone he used when Lindy wanted to move furniture, "we are in the middle—the midst—of experiencing the single most incredible event in the history of the world, and you're worried about the quality of your fast food coffee?"

Hayes downed another wincing sip of coffee and cast a dubious eye at the yard. The unkempt flowerbeds had finished blooming months ago, and the shrubs were gangly and untended. The tarp billowed like a live thing as a fresh breeze shook it.

"I don't know, Mike. We've got a five billion-year-old planet, right? Maybe this is normal and we just haven't been around long enough to notice."

Mike stared, momentarily dumbfounded. "Hayes," he said, "there were no TV cameras for the first four point nine nine nine billion years of this planet's history, which makes this"—and he jabbed a finger down at the tarp—"a major earth-shattering event! Okay?"

Hayes shrugged. "Just so long as the Buckeyes win on Saturday."

For the rest of the day, Mike and Hayes broadcast virtually non-stop. For a precious handful of hours, and largely by resorting to clandestine peeks under the tarp that no other crew could provide, they held the entire world in a rapture of breaking-news suspense. And, thanks to surcharges on bathroom use, a tactic that every last home on the block was employing by noon, those suddenly prime-time hours provided Mike and Lindy with several thousand dollars. Cash.

Then Gayle Norland showed up, all five-foot three of her, buttoned snugly into a gray woman's business suit the exact color of class and prestige.

"NSA," she announced as she marched toward the cordon of police ringing the Przewalskis' front yard, and she flashed her badge. A chevron of aides assembled behind her, a squadron of jet-black sunglasses and obvious earpieces.

The lieutenant in charge of crowd control hesitated.

"National Security Agency," Gayle prompted. "Which I run. I'm going in."

She found Mike and Hayes in the back yard, and she swept toward them with efficient strides. Melissa appeared from under the tarp, where she'd been trying to deliver Ollie a ham and Swiss on rye; she'd brought five sandwiches initially, and lowered each on a rope in half-quart Ziplocks, attached by clothespins. Ollie claimed never to have seen a single sandwich trail past, but Melissa's rope kept coming back empty. Only one sandwich remained, and she held it aloft as she scrambled back out from under the tarp, her hair flying.

"Who's that?" Melissa said, pointing with the ham and Swiss, and a world's worth of television viewers got a glimpse first of flustered Melissa, the frantic but stalwart wife, and then, as Hayes swung around to pick out the intruder, a rare viewing of the secretive Gayle Norland, her infamous frown, her sharp chin, her legendary broken nose—broken, said those in a position to know, during an alleyway fistfight in occupied Kuwait.

"Get that camera out of this yard," Gayle snapped, addressing her aides more than Hayes, and that was accomplished so efficiently that in seconds, only Gayle and Mike and Melissa remained, Melissa with a sandwich, Mike with a now-useless Channel Sixteen microphone, and Gayle with a handful of expressionless aides. With a practiced eye, she took in the flapping blue tarp, the ill-kept yard, and the ring of over-the-fence onlookers, most of them armed with cameras and cell phones, every last one aimed at her.

"Move those people out," she said, softly this time. "Don't take no for an answer."

All but one of the aides disappeared, intent on making her wishes an instantaneous reality.

Mike found his voice. "Who are you?" he demanded, and once more, the badge came up; the department name dropped like a gauntlet.

Melissa hurried forward. "Thank God. You're gonna get my husband out of there, right?"

"I wouldn't count on it," replied the NSA chief. "But if we deem the threat level to be acceptable, we'll give it our best shot."

"Excuse me," said Mike, "this is private property."

"Listen to me, Mr. Whoever You Are—"

"Mike Przewalski—"

"—either you're dumb as an ox or you're greedy beyond all belief. That hole there, if it's for real, is a matter of national security. For the entire United States. Now, you've had your fifteen minutes. But it's over. I'm in charge and the circus is closed. Now show me what we're dealing with."

Under the tarp she went, led by Melissa. From below, Ollie made his case for rescue, for the reality of his predicament, and Gayle dipped her I.D. badge briefly into the upper limits of the hole, only to pull it out again as if it might catch fire. It was unchanged. She rose to her feet and abruptly pushed her way awkwardly out from under the tarp.

"I mean, what the hell?" she said, eyes darting around the yard as if she were a songbird all too aware of a lurking Cooper's hawk. "What kind of color is that? What kind of—where did it come from?"

"You know I've got no idea, ma'am," said Mike. "The key, the only thing that matters, is getting Ollie out."

"No," she said, and her voice dropped half a register. "The key is sealing this thing up. So it can't spread. So it isn't here. So it never was here. The key is making this go away."

Melissa's eyes grew as round as saucers, but when she tried to say Ollie's name, her mouth opened, and no sound came out.

The Army arrived first, a brigade up from Fort Campbell. Then came the Corps of Engineers, diverted for once from their endless plans to shackle the Mississippi, and by week's end, they'd erected a steel-and-concrete hood over the hole, a construct that looked, from above, remarkably like a segmented turtle's shell fifty feet in diameter. It allowed no view whatsoever of the hole. At a further remove of two hundred yards, the Corps built a second wall, very stout, with guard towers and a single gate, through which no one was allowed to pass without NSA clearance, or the home address of Melissa and Ollie Hogan. The only outside visitors allowed were Mike and Lindy—Melissa had insisted and Gayle, in a moment of weakness, had relented—but even they were forbidden to enter the back yard.

Mike, conflicted over the loss of Ollie and more than a little sick at losing control of the goldmine to end all goldmines, got Hayes to outfit his bill cap with a tiny camera. "A little pixilation in return for a major exclusive," Hayes said, when they first tested it out. "Not a bad trade."

It took the NSA only minutes to figure out who was broadcasting forbidden images from inside the Hogan Quarantine Zone, and then they hauled Mike, handcuffed, to a military detention center, while three burly guards restrained Lindy. Only Melissa's abject pleas for mercy averted federal prosecution, and two weeks later, Mike Przewalski was quietly released back into the wilds of metro Springfield. He was not permitted within half a mile of his former home.

On the first day of December, the last leaves tore free of their branches in a cruel, bitter windstorm. Sleet banged off rooftops and clattered across roadways. Flurries of snow skittered and danced over the metal skin of the dome ensconcing the Hogan's yard, but not a single snowflake, not a single errant leaf, reached the imprisoned hole.

Reluctantly, and only out of a pang of compassion for Melissa, the Corps of Engineers had added a door into the shell that covered the hole. It had four different locks, two of them on a timing system that allowed entrance only at six o'clock in the evening. Melissa made the pilgrimage without fail for fifty-seven days, and did her best to keep her husband company, but on the fifty-eighth day, a bleak mid-winter's Christmas, she entered but did not exit the shell. On Boxing Day, a team of nervous specialists entered in search of her. They had a brief conversation with Ollie, who was sobbing somewhere below them. His wife, he said, had thrown herself into the hole in an attempt to join him, but as soon as she'd jumped, he'd lost track of her voice. It was as if she'd gone sailing past, a train on a separate track.

"I think she's maybe lost," Ollie said, sniffling. "I don't know what to do."

They asked if he was hungry. He said no, he didn't get hungry any more. He just wanted to see Melissa.

Since the Hogans' house was not covered in any sort of shell, it didn't take long for the remaining news teams to realize that Melissa had vanished. No more overhead feeds of Melissa raking up the maple leaves; no more aerial shots of her lonely forays out beyond the wall, bound for the bank or the grocery store. Mike Przewalski covered the story along with the rest, but then he called up the NSA and demanded to speak to Gayle Norland. She took the call. Mike begged to be allowed back into the quarantine zone, for Ollie's sake.

"They don't have kids, they don't have family," he told the NSA chief. "I know he's thirty years my senior, but we were friends. Honest to God, I think I'm the best friend Ollie's got."

Gayle Norland flew both Przewalskis to Washington, so they wouldn't splash their appeal all over the news. The decision was, she knew, a sign of weakness, one that might undo her politically. She did it anyway.

The NSA staff room where they eventually met was faceless, putty-colored, and smelled faintly of lavender air-freshener. The view out the window revealed not a single D.C. landmark. A lone aide stood by the door, stoic and stern, a man who happened to look like a younger version of Ollie. His presence so flustered Mike that by the time he was done making his case for being allowed to visit Ollie, he was rambling, all but incoherent. Gayle Norland raised a hand to stop him, and she gazed out the window, sad-eyed, somber.

"You're a journalist," she said at last. "A journalist."

"A man can be more than one thing."

Gayle fingered her badge and fixed him with a questioning stare. "For most people, I agree," she said. "But for myself? For you?"

Mike, his hands hanging dejectedly at his sides, didn't bother to defend himself.

"Boo," said Lindy, "I'll go. I don't have a job, I'm harmless. Let me go."

The NSA chief frowned at her. "You're pregnant."

Lindy, ever impish, stuck out her tongue. "I was pregnant before. You just didn't notice."

"We don't know anything about the dangers of exposure. You'd risk that? You'd risk your child?"

Lindy nodded. She took Mike's hand.

Three days later, under guard, Lindy once again entered the Hogan's back yard. It was already well past dark. The soldiers left her at the privacy fence with instructions for how to open the locks; they did not show any eagerness to accompany her further.

"If you need help," said one, but his sentiments trailed away with a vapor of breath in the frosty December air.

Powdery snow dusted the yard, showing bare chunks of earth thrown up by long-gone swarms of construction machinery. In the distance, Lindy heard a truck's engine rev, but except for that, there was not a single sound to indicate that somewhere beyond the fences and walls lay the mechanized modern world, the orderly, sensible world she knew, the world from which she'd just accepted temporary exile. Seeking reassurance, she put a hand across her stretched, swelling tummy, and removed a pack of baby carrots from a belt pouch strapped to her waist. She checked the clock on her cell phone and nibbled a carrot, waiting for six.

When the time came, the locks tumbled open just as they were supposed to, and Lindy, armed with a battery-powered lantern, entered the otherwise total darkness of the shell. There was the hole, same color, same slightly irregular shape. Next to it, Melissa had placed a farm chair from the kitchen. Under the chair lay a Bible, with a red leather bookmark sticking out from the top; it looked to Lindy like a red leather tongue.

The door swung shut behind her. Lindy went to the chair. She sat, knees together. She picked up the Bible and opened it to the marked page. The Book of Amos. Someone—Melissa or Ollie, presumably— had circled a short passage:

Let justice roll down like waters, and righteousness like an ever-flowing stream.

Lindy had never been a church-goer, and the words meant little to her. Still, the passage did give a certain comfort. That this hole was neither just nor righteous, of that she was certain. It was just there, it had happened, it had manifested itself. Surely attempting to comfort Ollie was both just and righteous—the right thing to do.

"Ollie?" she called, tentatively at first. "Ollie, are you there? It's me, Lindy."

"Lindy! Is that really you?"

"It's me. Are you okay?"

"Well, can't complain. I mean, I could. I do. I cry sometimes, y'know? 'Cos there's nothing here. There's me, I guess, but what's the use of me without anything else? And I don't change, I'm just—I'm kinda continual, you know what I mean? I don't get hungry. I don't need to use the head. I can see myself, and that's good, I guess, but the last time I saw anything else was when those leaves blew in way back at the beginning. So I don't know. Most of the time, I feel like I just keep movin' farther off. And that's a kind of cruelty. A real lonesome way to live."

Lindy swore to Ollie that she'd return the next day, and again after that whenever she could, but she told him, also, that the NSA hadn't made any promises. Ollie thanked her, said she was a good girl and a good neighbor, good people to know. He told her she'd be a good mother for sure. Lindy sang "Take Me Out to the Ballgame," and Ollie cried again.

The next day, she brought a backpack with four of Ollie's favorite books, taken straight off the shelves in his living room. She read aloud, not hurrying, taking the time to feel and massage each word, but on the third day, she left the books behind. She said she would be back, but she knew she was lying. Ollie knew it, too.

"Lindy," he said. "I forgive you."

She fled into the snow-powdered night, sobbing and swearing, while inside her, the tiny feet of her unborn child clenched and kicked, insisting on the future.

A few days later, in January, a new administration took command of the Oval Office, and Gayle Norland was put out to pasture. The new NSA chief, at the behest of the President, built a second protective dome over the first, bigger this time, a dome that engulfed the Hogan's house and everything around it. The crew in charge did not install a door.

Mike Przewalski's best-selling book, "Standing st the Edge of Forever," provided Mike and Lindy and their three children with enough money to live comfortably for the rest of their lives, but they abandoned Springfield not long after the second dome went up. The extra distance only cheered them in spurts. Lindy still dreamed of open Bibles splayed atop lonely moonlit chairs and appointments she could never keep. Mike's nightmares were no better: leaves chased him down unknown streets, and he always woke to the sensation of falling, of scrabbling helplessly for a purchase, and as he dropped away into nothingness, he heard Ollie calling his name.

The dome remained, and the site became a Mecca for tourists, many of whom thought the entire affair was a hoax, a chicanery hatched by the government to distract from a world of drought and food shortages, of rising oceans and geopolitical turmoil. The good times, said the pundits, were gone. Several hole-inspired religions sprang up—apocalyptic, stringent—and concurrent with their rise, the famines and regional wars finally frayed the knots of civilization to the breaking point. Enlightenment shuddered. Reason gave way. Technology, time-like, ran backwards.

For those who survived, the rains came in springtime and the snow flew in winter. Heat waves blistered the summers and in autumn, dead leaves fell like souls from the treetops.

Centuries passed.

Where Springfield had been, a single redoubtable dome still stood, but it was cracked now, tipping heavily to one side, the result of a massive tectonic quake that had shaken the continent from sea to shining sea. That same quake burst the inner dome's door wide open, and in time, a few timorous locals dared to enter the outer shell, where they found the remnants of a 1954 ranch house and most of its contents: photo albums and vacuum cleaners, magic markers and blue plastic bins marked "Recyclables." It was like a magician's chest, a treasure trove of lost technology, fresh wonders at every turn.

After a few days, the invaders ventured into the inner dome, and there they found bare earth, dim light, and what they took to be an altar, the likes of which they had never seen. It consisted of an old wooden chair, somewhat chewed by insects, together with a lot of desiccated leaves, four perfectly fresh ham and Swiss sandwiches in plastic baggies, a decrepit backpack containing four books, and a fifth book, a Bible, on top of the chair. The other books, once translated, turned out to be *Tuesdays With Morrie, Into Thin Air, Peterson's Field Guide To Eastern Birds*, and *Reader's Digest: Mysteries of the Ancient World*.

All of this would have been amazing enough—revelatory—but it was nothing compared to what awaited just beyond what had been a hole but was now nothing more remarkable than a surprisingly healthy oval of lawn. For there they lay, their heads resting on the edge of a spotless fiberglass extension ladder: A man and a woman, fully clothed but in decidedly antique finery, asleep and breathing, in and out, in and out, regular as old-fashioned clockwork, and holding hands like perfect summer sweethearts.

The intruders argued vehemently about whether to wake the sleepers, but of course curiosity won out (as it has throughout history), and thus did the Male Oracle rise, or at least sit up, and speak for the first time.

"Good Lord," he said, blinking at the raggedy assemblage before him. "What did you all do to your clothes?"

So from the ashes—from a man and a woman and a house and a small heap of books and a hole of unknown provenance—did civilization once more yawn, stretch itself, and struggle toward some semblance of divinity.

It was, as Melissa said, a real peculiar sort of miracle.

Only kind worth having, said Ollie. Only kind there is.

MY MANTLE

Emily Doak

After the disaster all physical items aboveground were to be discarded in good faith because of their potential radioactivity. This has proven difficult for most—some have joined The Movement, but Tessa will not. Her old friend Renu keeps trying to recruit her: "Give to The Movement. Listen to The Movement. We will all remember." Renu has accepted The Pirate Movement wholeheartedly since she moved out of her and Tessa's post-college apartment and got married. But Tessa doesn't believe in the collective memory project of the pirates. She feels her memories are hers, only hers.

And she moves them in three cardboard brown boxes to her new basement apartment in the West Village close to the Path station, where she can quickly commute to the Soap's soundstages in Jersey City across the river. She's been designing for the soaps for years, starting in piecework for the daytime dramas building white models of sets in preproduction. With her promotion to Assistant Art Director and aided by the voucher to abandon her and Renu's old neighborhood upriver, which had started recording high radiation levels, she is able to afford the basement studio in the West Village where she's been living for six months avoiding Renu and her phone calls, until Renu herself is waiting for Tessa one evening when she arrives home.

"You don't answer your phone," Renu says, rolling down the tinted window of her big black SUV, a wedding gift from her in-laws. She'd moved to a hastily erected estate out in cow country where this was the vehicle of choice. She turns down the baseball on the radio. "This is a long-ass drive just to find out you're okay."

Tessa knows this was no hardship for her. Renu drives around all night in the black SUV listening to baseball games on a pirate AM set she had installed in the car. There's a whole pirate community of listeners out there like her.

"Come on, it's the '98 World Series. It'll be fun. I know you remember it." Renu unlocks her car doors.

"I don't," Tessa says. "I can't. You'll have to come inside."

"A little late, but a housewarming gift," Renu says, handing Tessa a box as she walks into her apartment. The place is bare. "I guess I'm not too late. You could at least hang a picture."

Tessa has lived there for half a year and yet the apartment doesn't feel unpacked. This is surprising since she's an Art Director who dresses and arranges space for a living. "It's the fireplace," Tessa says. "I love it, but I don't know where to put the furniture."

The mantel is elaborately carved. The marble looks like fabric draped in delicate folds. It is hard to look at anything else and when Tessa first saw the fireplace, she knew this had to be her apartment, but the mantel and hearth extend two times the width of the firebox, with very little wall space left open on either side. The other walls are a clutter of doors and windows and the kitchen, so Tessa's furniture floats like a raft in the middle of the room, her three cardboard boxes hiding under the bed.

Renu goes right to the fireplace and runs her hands along the marble. Tessa knows it is cool to the touch. "This will be perfect," Renu says. "Open the box."

The present is a new clock, a mantel clock, but Tessa only leaves it on the mantel while Renu is there. She considers keeping the clock on the mantel, but it looks lonely. She'd be too tempted to open the cardboard boxes under her bed and put up mementos and pictures alongside it. She could lie and tell visitors that her family's home survived and the pictures were luckily saved in a vault in a basement, or that the young man, her college boyfriend, Dean, slightly squinting, slightly pixelated, is actually a current boyfriend—it's a new picture, completely safe, completely cold. But with personal Geiger counters built into wristwatches, it is likely she'd be caught with the hot items, so the mantel remains empty. And Tessa already has an alarm clock in the main room—she knows what time it is—so she puts Renu's clock back in its box.

Tessa's been with the soaps so long that her clock is off but not in a fifteen minutes late for work way. She looks for poinsettias at back-to-school time and pumpkins in July. She has contacts in the southern hemisphere in order to procure goods for a production schedule which tapes anywhere from three to six months ahead of the actual calendar. And even getting used to that, there is the oddity that a year in soap terms is but a couple dozen days. Each day can take weeks to get through whereupon the season has changed. There is no transition; there is no slow ebb. Love happens in an instant; hate happens in an instant. There are only the extremes: the day of a murder, a wedding, Christmas, a kidnapping, a birthday, a birth. Nothing connects these days, and Tessa's life has started to resemble them. All high and low events. She goes out for occasions: Renu's wedding, the annual mock-evacuation, Indian Point React/Remember Day, a first date, a last date, which are mostly the same date. She can barely remember anything mundane, coming home each night and trying to arrange the furniture, calling in massaman beef now not chicken—bird flu is more likely than mad cow.

At work Tessa has become obsessed with her favorite character Brooke's storyline and getting an exterior shoot at Yankee Stadium okayed by Production. When the chipper young interns come asking her for jobs, begging her for experience, she ignores them. When Renu calls, she says, there's an intern at my desk and I must give him my full attention. When she hangs up, she tells the intern to go ask Yuri if he has something for him. Yuri's been picking up her slack and she knows it and he knows it and the interns know it.

"Tessa, they can build these models in a second on CAD," Yuri yells across the design studio.

"I don't care," Tessa says, "I want white models. I want to be able to touch them. That's the way it's always been done!"

Tessa knows they don't know how to make white models. They've never held a razorblade in their life. Everything's gone digital, and since the disaster, digital information's lack of a physical presence, and thus the chance of contamination, is incredibly desirable. But she wants to ask these interns if they think the actors would like to act in front of nothing and they can just CAD the sets in later. She wants to ask what kind of a parent would let you come here to this city? Why would you want to work for the soaps? The lousy soaps aren't worth it, but the lousy soaps are big time, government grant big time recently. They are the most popular thing on television as more and more people are unemployed and more and more hours of daytime sets burn into the ratings. She can tell some of the interns have read the blogs, maybe even come to the Art Department because of them. They think there are codes in not just the dialogue, but the sets, the pictures on the walls, the cushions on the couch, which is ridiculous. It's just Yuri and her, the boss and some carpenters. She tells the closest intern to find her Don Mattingly's number and get it over to wardrobe ASAP for Brooke's Rodrigo flashback—Rodrigo is Brooke's long lost dead love. The intern returns to her desk a minute later.

"I asked Yuri, but we don't know what you're talking about."

"He was a Yankee, retired in '95. I was trying to give you something to do. Go to Alicia in wardrobe and tell her 23. You think you can do that?"

The interns' blind ambition to get to their future depresses Tessa. Stay where you are, she wants to tell them, but just stay away from me. She idealizes her past as a place where every single moment seemed to count. It's slow and it's safe and it's unchanging. Everything else seems to sit upon it. Everything else, for ever, is sampled from it.

Tessa's analog years: her freshman year of college she was just learning about sound, analog sound recording. The waves oscillating on the white board in the dimly lit studio classroom lulled her with their gentle, steady curves. She picked up her class allotment from the equipment cage in the basement. The supplies were physical, tangible, bulky. You could touch sound. There were cassettes, tape—the quarter inch kind to record with and the sticky kind to splice with, a dozen reel-to-reel plastic cores, yellow grease pencils and white ones. And to physically cut edits, you needed razorblades. Carefully wrapped in cardboard sleeves, they were dealt to you one by one like playing cards, like fate, by the work-study in the equipment cage. Tessa signed the waiver that she would not hold the school responsible for personal injury incurred with her supplies. There was a rumor that the ghost on the 11th floor was a student from the Seventies who went in to edit all fucked up on acid and slit himself to ribbons with his razorblade allotment. The Film School wouldn't have to worry about that much longer—they were going digital. Tessa would be in the last class to be fully analog.

Tessa decides the fireplace would be a good headboard for her bed, so she pushes the small twin mattress on its metal rollers till it's centered under the mantel. The chimney which she assumed was sealed—the landlord told her the fireplace hadn't worked for years—is not sealed and there is a draft she hadn't felt before. She stays up for hours staring at the underside of the mantel above her, trying not to think of how cold she is. The mantel starts to pulse to the ticking of her alarm clock. Hinged into a small red leather case and needing no batteries, the clock had been her father's travel alarm, and she should've discarded it but did not. She winds the clock fresh every night and is surprised she's never noticed before how loud its fully mechanical inner workings are.

She tries to hear the rhythm in the silence between the ticks instead of the ticks. She tries to hear the silence. It can't be silent. There must still be sound. A half of a second isn't long enough for the sound to disappear. She tries to see the steady curve of the noise rising and falling in its analog wave, continuous and flowing. But all she can see are staccato beats like it is digital, sampled, recording only 1s and 0s as markers for the highs and lows, asking her to fill in the rest.

She can't take it. She doesn't care how cold it is. She gets up, grabs the alarm clock, and shuts it in her refrigerator next to the weeks' leftovers of massaman. Her eyes temporarily blinded by the refrigerator bulb, she tries to look around her apartment for something to stop the draft from the fireplace.

There is the small grouping of cardboard boxes that had been hidden under her bed. They sit in the middle of the floor now, calling too much attention to themselves. She takes the three small brown boxes and stacks them in the fireplace. The last one just reaches the top and she must fight to get it into the flue to act as a makeshift damper. Tessa thinks of what's in the boxes and considers taking them out of the fireplace and opening them, but they are in there tight now. She falls asleep thinking: of their warmth, of how appropriate it is that her hot boxes are in the fireplace stopping the cold draft, of a game she played in bed with Dean. The game was Hot or Cold? He whispered the clues: cool, warm, warmer. The goal was to find him at hot.

Tessa's been fighting in Art Direction meetings for the past month for the rare out-of-studio exterior at Yankee Stadium, and it is time to make a decision. Someone still knows how to build white models because one appears on the conference table. The scale model built entirely of white Bristol board is a ball field set they could erect in the studio. Home plate, including half a dugout and two rows of stands, is directly beside the pitcher's mound, so the cameras won't need to turn around, but can simply be intercut to present the illusion of distance. The boss AD is all for this set-up, and Tessa suspects he built the model himself—it is quite good—but she decides to challenge it regardless. She insists the mock-up looks more like a little league field than anything major league. "Brooke wasn't engaged to a minor leaguer!"

"And we never fool anyone with our fake exteriors," Tessa says, "Fake grass, fake wind, fake trees, painted skies, always soft lit, always medium close up. It's ridiculous. No one thinks we're really outside. But we could be."

She must have been convincing because the AD agrees to take it to Production. Yuri agrees to come on board and do any of the digital work needed.

"My biggest concern is that the grass might not be green anymore," Tessa says.

Yuri convinces her he can fix this easily enough, but his enthusiasm is clearly for the boss. He's shown no interest in her exterior before. Now that she's won in the Art Department, she must get it past the Sweeps Production Meeting. She decides she will:

1) argue the location's importance for the integrity of the story as a whole;

Dominic has promised Brooke that he would honor her dead love, Rodrigo, knowing he can never replace him but he can love her all the same, and so he will propose to Brooke on the pitcher's mound of "Metropolis Stadium" where Rodrigo Fuentes of the "Metro Yorkers" had been struck with a line drive on the eve of Brooke's first wedding night and the sixth game of the "National Series." Brooke doesn't know, although all those with the story bible for the year do know, that Dominic is actually "Ron Holiday," the man that swung the lethal hit and who Brooke has vowed to avenge with her life. This is serious stuff and getting the Stadium right is the right thing to do. Yankee Stadium, the old sort of stadium, is the type that Rodrigo would have played in. If we respect our characters, what we are doing here, it must be done.

2) appeal to their competitive spirit:

No other soaps will have exteriors. It will instantly elevate our production quality and create buzz. Advertisers will assume we are the best, and they'll pay accordingly. And since Sweeps stretches a soap opera day out for even longer than usual, the network will get a whole month out of the exterior. One day of shooting, a month of rewards. And if we promo the Stadium front and center, we can probably even get some men out of the deal. They'll want to see how the old girl is doing. No one has really warmed up to that new Staten Island stadium. And where the men go, the advertisers always want to know.

3) appeal to their patriotism, i.e. the government money:

There's been a rumor the government will take over if the content doesn't stabilize. There've been big fights in the story sessions. Mass catastrophe cannot hit this world, but we've already succumbed to a subplot in which the matriarch's son goes off to war. Try finding a Humvee when all the civilian ones have been commandeered by the National Guard. Or sand when all landscaping and playground sand has been dyed red to assure parents and consumers it isn't contaminated. We can find Yankee Stadium and it can be a gesture of our compliance. It will be old style baseball, pure American nostalgia.

What Tessa will not let them know is:

1) She simply wants to go to Yankee Stadium which is in a restricted area, but has not been demolished. Supposedly the stadium itself sits on a patch of stable rock that records fairly low levels, but the surrounding area is blight meets flight and levels high enough that there were no vouchers, just mandatory evacuation. A new stadium is open on Staten Island, but it never took off. Baseball has actually changed, although the government will not admit it. They still send dignitaries for opening day pitches. But the real fans, the old fans, are people like Renu. They would never watch the current games. Tessa will need to downplay The Pirate Movement that some baseball has grown to be associated with. This shoot will have no hidden agenda. There are no clues, no codes. She isn't hiding anything.

Tessa once hid her sound equipment in a backpack and snuck it into Yankee Stadium during a freshman class outing. She had a sound project due and didn't know it was Mattingly's last season, and trying to make the playoffs, the crowd could think of nothing but their Mattingly leaving them. She didn't know who Mattingly was, and she was certainly not thinking of anything ending.

The one thing Tessa knew about baseball was she loved the dizzy thrill she felt whenever she came to a game and first emerged from one of the tunnels into the stands and the dazzling green of the field simply seemed to suck a part of her away. She'd been to Yankee Stadium a surprising amount for a girl who knew nothing in particular about baseball. In fact, you could chart a certain trajectory of her life if you had snapshots of her in the stadium. When she was a kid, her dad would bring her down for games. They always had nosebleed seats and one summer they came on hat day and it rained and the navy bill of her cap bled a brilliant royal blue stain into the white pinstripe top. She'd keep that hat and wear it to what would be, unknown to her, Mattingly's last game. The boy next to her would share his Cracker Jack with her and their arms would brush, unknown to her. Dean would notice, but Tessa was inside her headphones, riding the levels on the broadcast quality cassette deck in her lap. She wished she had noticed. They had wasted time. It would be two years before Dean and Tessa would go to a game together, back up in the nosebleed section of her youth, two innings late because they couldn't keep their hands off one another earlier at his apartment, and he'd go to the concession stand and miss the only four runs of the game. She would cry. She'd wanted him to be there. She couldn't believe someone was missing a game to get her food. It was such a man thing to do and she'd never felt so loved, so she cried.

Tessa keeps checking the extended forecast. Production has okayed the exterior, and the one thing it can't do is snow. But in case it does, she stockpiles plastic snow that can be used in the studio for "exteriors" occurring in other storylines on the same "day." She knows it's going to tick everyone off that because of one day of real snow, they've got to shoot in plastic snow for a month. But for continuity, if it's snowing at the stadium, which can't be stopped, then it will simply have to snow everywhere.

It seems to be getting colder in Tessa's apartment. The boxes that had blocked the draft are no longer working. It might be getting colder outside, but Tessa thinks it is the boxes themselves that are changing. They seem to be letting more heat escape every night. Exponentially it's getting colder. She shivers, pulled out of and into sleep where she moves towards Dean. He whispers, warm, not so warm, room temperature. He must be playing a trick. Cold, colder, absolute zero.

Spliced. In analog everything was physically cut, physically put back together again. And everything took time, lots of time. Transfer time, edit time, screening time, rewind table time, synch table time, double splice time. So even after Dean left her—their time run out—the footage on the table in front of Tessa was still all about him. She saw every little hint of him: every snippet of conversation they'd had that made the script, every casting choice he'd weighed in on, props that were borrowed from his room, his favorite camera angle. She started to think she understood that razorblade-using ghost. He probably wasn't on acid at all. He was just stuck in an analog edit booth like the rest of them.

She surrendered nothing to the trim bins for fear of losing any speck of Dean. In fact, she started collecting other people's trims left like trash in the canvas carts. And she searched further back through her own reels. She came to the raw audio of Mattingly's last game. She was convinced Dean was in there somewhere, too. If she listened hard enough, she'd find him in the noise. If she'd only noticed him that first day, everything might be different. She played the audio over and over again, but she couldn't find him.

Tessa enrolled in Production Design because she thought it would be fairly safe. Sconces, crown molding, Queen Anne chairs, balusters, pilasters: they couldn't remind her of Dean. There were still razorblades, exacto knifes to be precise, but here you didn't splice. It was about making perfect scores, ones that were just deep enough to produce crisp seams at corners, but that didn't cut all the way through.

And she was really good at white models. She was best at the detail work: the miniature furniture, the delicate window panes, the paneled doors, all of it in the thick white Bristol board paper. She got hired to build them for the Soap. She got supplies and twenty dollars an hour, and white models could take a good twenty hours to make, depending. And she got in the habit of listening to sports, because you had to look down too much to actually follow a TV program, so she'd keep the pennant race and then the Series on in the background. Baseball, football, anything honestly that she thought Dean might be listening to as well. It made her feel connected and not just to him, but to this vast swatch of people that all must be keeping company with the same noise. She got to know all the players, and she realized other people did too. Renu was a real sports nut and it was in this time that their friendship became close.

Now Tessa doesn't even recognize the players. So many have been traded, retired, moved around. Renu doesn't know them either. She is so fully involved in The Movement's broadcasts that she would never watch the highlight to highlight coverage of the current teams. For those with pirate analog receivers, listening has become a sort of religion. It's a sort of remembrance cult, but one that's safe. Renu keeps trying to get Tessa to listen, but Tessa doesn't think she'll find anything there she needs. She knows exactly where her memories, the real ones, the tangible ones, are stored. But The Pirate Movement is convinced that personal memory, since the disaster, has been shown to be ineffective. They believe it is too disjointed, too selective. They aspire to give the whole experience, broadcasting complete sporting events, complete festivals with mics left open on stage between acts, complete recordings of trials, town councils, complete databases of Verizon voicemail computers, raw audio of oral histories from local libraries. As long as it hasn't been cut, they send out from their secret bunkers whatever they can amass—donated, bought, and it is rumored even stolen. But baseball is definitely their favorite. Baseball, in all its slow, complete nine inning glory, has become a symbol of the "whole experience" which is the basis of The Movement. They accuse society of collective amnesia or at least revisionism.

But when people get amnesia in the soaps, Tessa knows it really isn't that big a deal. After all, they are only forgetting like twenty days or something, and maybe only half of those even included their own storyline.

The night before the exterior at Yankee Stadium, and the cold from the fireplace is unbearable. Tessa moves the bed by the windows which is a surprisingly warm spot for being only half a studio apartment away from the fireplace. She lies in bed and looks at the boxes in the fireplace. In her mind she's gone through them hundreds of times while she lay in bed at night too cold to sleep. She has unpacked each item, turning it over in her hands, touching it. She can remember each one and exactly where she packed it, exactly what it looks like, so what would be the difference if she lit up a match. The chimney must work. She does need to get rid of the boxes. They are not safe.

It is snowing at Yankee Stadium. She feels the old master cassette tape in her pocket which she fished out of a box in her fireplace before she left that morning. She'd thought of it all night and couldn't resist any longer. She didn't unpack anything, she just snaked her hand up into the flue and felt inside the top box for what she knew would be there. As she steps out of one of the tunnels into the stands at the Stadium, it is like the tape explodes, a bright flash in her pocket. The place roars. "Mattingly's my Mantle," the crowd shouts, chants in unison. Tessa can hear the tape in her hand without playing it. She'd heard the raw footage so many times after Dean left trying to find his voice. He had been there, right beside her, and she'd wasted time. She wants to have noticed this first moment, Dean and Tessa side by side. Is there the crunch of popcorn? A caramel-coated peanut cracked between his teeth? If only he hadn't been so quiet. She tries to hear his "Mattingly" cloaked in the storm of voices.

She looks around the Stadium and she can't remember exactly where they sat that first day—Mattingly's last. She can't remember their second game if they both had hotdogs when he went to get her food and missed the grand slam or if he'd just been getting one for her. She can't remember if maybe he didn't shout at ballgames at all.

Yuri is walking around on the snow-covered field. There is no green grass. Everything is white. Nothing can be done now except digital work in post. Tessa's skills are useless here. The stadium is too big to dress. That will be for Yuri in post. Push a button, change the world. With no consequences, everything can be tried, fiddled, and returned to normal. There are few effects that can't be reversed and quick. It's all digital: the tape, the editing, the air signal even. The old analog waves are abandoned.

They knew this would happen when she was in school. They were told it would happen. She passed a note to Dean in Screenwriting. Pitch: Pump Up the Volume meets A Boy and His Dog. Pirates take over the analog waves. Followers pillage Goodwills for analog TV sets to tune into the revolution.

Funny how stuff happens. It had snowed after all. Yuri thinks he can get the snow off the seats by running an algorithm to replace white with the blue plastic that should be there. But the field as well, and the sky? It might be too much. Snow. That was the way fallout was explained when she was in grade school and everyone still had a Russian penpal and Chernobyl was their mistake.

"I knew this was a bad idea," Yuri says as Tessa joins him down on the field by the pitcher's mound.

"I guess there were easier ways," Tessa says, digging her hands in her pockets for warmth and rubbing the tape as if she could get some actual heat from it.

The Geiger alarm on Yuri's wristwatch lets out a piercing ring. "This place must not be as stable as they claim," he says, "batting off the alarm."

Tessa steps back from him, clutching the hot tape unseen in her pocket. She pretends to assess the situation with the stadium. "I've made plans for it to snow in all the other scenes," she says.

"But what month are we supposed to be in?" Yuri asks. "I think it's early summer."

Tessa looks up at the stands, at all the places she used to sit. It is a wet, sticky snow and everything is perfectly coated. The stadium looks like a giant white model.

"We'll color it in," Yuri says. "We have to." He digs his heal into the mantle of snow on the field. Tessa leans in to look at the grass, a Technicolor emerald, unearthed beneath.

Yuri's alarm goes off again. Tessa jumps back.

"Let's just get this done," he says. "I'm not dying for this job."

"I'm going to go," Tessa says. "I'll be at the studios."

She'd never really had a chance. When she'd done this before at school, the equipment had been all analog. It could work here, though, and she pulls out an old cassette deck from a back closet. She patches it into the digital board and she waits. She is not sure she actually wants to do this. It is cued up to the part she always used to search.

"We got your Stadium," Yuri says coming into the booth. "I beamed it onto the F drive. It should be in here."

He sees the cassette deck out of place. The Geiger alarm on his watch goes off again. "What's going on?"

"I need to isolate a voice," Tessa says.

"What're you doing with that?" Yuri says. "It's hot, isn't it?"

"It won't hurt you for a couple hours."

"How about you? You've had that all day, haven't you?"

"I just need to prove someone was here. Then I'll get rid of it."

Tessa sits back and watches Yuri work. The voices are peeled back one by one. He asks, Is this him? Is that him? Him? until Tessa can't take it anymore. "Please stop," she says. "I've changed my mind. Really, thanks."

She wants to remember less important things. She wants to remember it all. All the voices, all the moments. Because that is how it really was.

She is desperate for Dean not to become all soap opera days, all highs and lows, all samples. She wants the complete picture, the slow ebb, the graceful dive, nine excruciatingly long innings with crowd noise.

"Really?" Yuri asks.

"Yes, I think I heard him. I did."

"So we're done?"

Tessa doesn't answer.

"You know you could sell this for a bundle?" he says. "I might just know where if you're interested."

"I know where, thank you."

When she gets home there is a message from Renu asking her to come out driving with her. "I know you'd like listening," she says. "Tomorrow night, I'll pick you up."

Tessa looks at the boxes in the fireplace. When she lies down at night, she imagines she can feel them sucking away at her. But lots of people have stuff. It's where the pirates got their idea. And even if she'd felt ready that afternoon, she isn't quite ready for their solution: to listen to collective memories at a distance, safely. They insist the personal is imbedded in them. Clues, signals you can pick up. Everything isn't lost. It is everything that they don't want to lose. But she still needs the physical objects there with her. She isn't as strong as Renu and the rest of them. She doesn't trust her memory to be satisfied in the way theirs is. If she is found out, she'll be arrested. If her neighbors find out, they'll probably lynch her. It's selfish. It's destructive to have kept even these few hot items. They are dangerous, shortening her life every moment she keeps them.

As she moves the boxes out of the fireplace, a picture of Dean falls out. She'd cut the picture to fit a square frame she's since discarded following the appropriate protocol. He is exactly the way she's been picturing him, except the photo is in black and white and she often sees him in color. There are a few other photos, some letters, but the bulk of the boxes are filled with white models. There is a replica of her childhood home. There is Renu and Tessa's first apartment. There is the first project she did in her first design class after Dean left, which is actually his apartment if anyone were to see it who knew. Then there is the living room that she simply imagined would be theirs, because there was always some small chance of reconciliation. You heard about it all the time. Meeting after years apart. But there is no chance now. It is an impossibility and yet her mind can't understand such large things. She spreads the models around her on the empty floor in front of the fireplace. She lies down so she can look into the rooms at eye level, and she sees them furnished in rich woods, sees the blue comforter on Dean's bed and the yellow walls of her father's study.

She pushes the skeletal white rooms closer to the hearth and then closer again. She could always rebuild them. But the pictures, the letters, the alarm clock, the cassettes, she simply must keep. She needs to be able to touch them. She'll risk it.

She calculates how many fewer days she'll have than her parents ever did. What's left is limited like soap time, like dog years, or maybe its infinite like radioactive decay—the time in front of her halved and then halved again all dating back to that one moment before it happened when people chanted Mattingly's my Mantle, Mattingly's my Mantle, my Mantle, Mantle, Man.

On Family

NOW IN CHARGE

Lou Fisher

Harry held tight to the arms of his desk chair. In front of him the phone was ringing, but he couldn't bring himself to answer it. Someone else, he was sure, had run out of fuel oil. Some other sobbing lady, some other cursing man, some other stuttering, whimpering, suddenly orphaned teenager, had dialed the company's service number, probably with frozen fingers … as if Harry Odom were some kind of miracle worker instead of just a person himself, a human person himself. He gritted his teeth. Well, what about it, though? What could be his answer to the stream of phone calls? Where exactly were those promised, regular, dependable, well-known, automatic home deliveries from Odom Oil?

"I'll lose my customers," he said.

In the side chair, Nadine crossed her legs. "Oh? Who do you think will take them? Allied is closed."

Until this week the notion of no more Allied would have brought Harry a smile, a victory smile, but now it only made his heart beat faster. He twisted his jaw, pouting. "Then how about that rotten crook Fryer? Remember when he went to all my customers, offered to cut their grass in the summer if they'd buy his oil in the winter? A chiseler who'd take any opportunity—"

"Not anymore," Nadine said. "Fryer called here earlier, for help."

"Me help Fryer? Fat chance." Harry cleared his throat. "All right, Nadine, how do we stand? Tell me the worst."

She tilted her head. Besides the pencil in her hair, Nadine had taken lately to wearing contacts. He thought the lenses added a strange, steely, reckless gleam to her eyes, as if they came with batteries. Yes, he imagined a pair of tiny transparent batteries, alkaline and highly juiced, with invisible wires traced to each cornea ... God, what the aliens had done to his mind! Still, aliens or not, he planned to tell Nadine—if he could ever work up the nerve—that he preferred the more familiar look, the oval face with the round pink-framed glasses set an inch down on the bridge of her nose.

"We've managed to get two trucks on the road," she was informing him now in a snappy voice. "So maybe we can handle the emergencies. But it's nineteen degrees out there, and that's supposed to be the high for today."

Harry sighed. "Pipes are freezing."

"Yes," she said.

"They'll burst overnight."

"Yes, probably."

As if in verification, the phone lit up, rang again. Harry motioned for Nadine to stay seated. Together they watched a second button light, then a third.

Only when he returned his gaze to Nadine did he feel any comfort, any gratitude, any ease in the hollow aching pit of his stomach. She had been with him for almost as long as Willie. So many years. And every workday she glided through the outer office doing billing and payroll, coffee and jokes, even covering for him on the computers, which he always fouled up at first touch. He liked her crossed legs, her shoulders too. He had never attempted anything romantic with Nadine—as he got older he'd become a lazy lover even at home with his wife Beth—but on days like today when Nadine's hair seemed the color of sand on the beach in the sun ... well, he imagined raking his hands through her hair.

But instead he put them under his chin. His fingers felt big and rough, and on his chin the bristles had conquered the morning's careful shave. He could picture himself sitting there, a middle-aged, dark-jowled, downcast man.

"Harry ..." Her voice barely came through.

"What?"

"I've got things to do," Nadine said.

"I suppose."

"There's only me."

"Yeah, go," he replied. "I'll handle the phones."

But instead he let them ring on and on till they became like background music. Meanwhile, he had swivelled around to face the window, hoping, even expecting, to see Willie's truck pull into the yard, to hear above the angry telephones a spit of gravel followed by the jolly double-honk of Willie's resounding bass horn; and then of course Willie himself would jump down from the cab whistling some just-heard country song, and if the day had been extra good—say, quick and sunny—he might toss a salute over to the office window, or on other days settle for just a wink. But no. Of course not. Maybe never again. Harry turned back, rubbing his head, his eyes, the under part of his nose. Hadn't he tried everything to find Willie? Chased those aliens down the street. Called the police. Listened every hour to the news. He'd even gone so far as to scout around the ships, really close, under the shadow of their rims, but when the aliens spotted him he ran off, and now he was afraid to go back.

Harry and Beth resided on the fourth floor of a co-op building, a nifty place by the lake, and there every night at seven o'clock they started their dinner. But tonight Harry was sunk in the recliner chair, sipping scotch, watching CNN, and Beth, as far as he knew, had not cooked a thing.

"Think the aliens care?" he said. "They make lists, that's all. You should see how they do it."

"How?" Beth asked. In the next chair she had taken up her knitting. A familiar sound, the clicking of her needles, but Harry had a feeling that the rhythm was off. He looked to her, saw the sloped shoulders, the gray in her hair.

"Well, I just told you. They make lists."

"In what language, Harry? Did you see?"

"Sure I saw. I was right there, wasn't I? A couple dozen of them stomped through the yard, swarmed over the trucks, pushed right into the office, stood inches from my face." Harry leaned a bit toward the TV, squinting for details. Two enormous wheel-shaped ships were parked on the grass in front of where the White House used to be. Between the ships an open tent, floodlit by a TV crew, swayed in the wind; the Secretary of State and the Secretary of Defense huddled there in overcoats. The aliens seemed not conscious of the chill. Harry said, "Grunts. Plenty of grunts. And scratchings on a piece of tin or something. I don't know, Beth, it's crazy." He sipped from the glass, his eyes riveted on the TV, as more aliens came into the picture. "Something about a reduction, that's the term that comes through, but no rhyme or reason to anyone they take. Not that I can figure. I mean, why, for example, would they want Willie?"

So far on the screen nothing much had happened.

The aliens were not offering a cancer cure or a faster-than-light drive. They ignored the star map, refusing to define their home world. Meanwhile, any approach of the U.S. Army was met by a threatening motion of the laserods—one troop, in fact, seemed to vanish, off-camera, it wasn't clear where. All communication was difficult because no one on either side had come forward as a capable interpreter, and grunts alone were not overly expressive. Nor were the hand movements, maybe because the gray gloves contained only two fingers.

"So for all the office work they left me Nadine," Harry explained to Beth. "I'm stuck with one old guy handling the garage, and I've got only a couple of route men." Pausing, he drained the scotch. "Takes that many, over all, just to maintain everyone's furnace, let alone deliver the oil. And what about the bookkeeping? The fax, the phones—and, you know, servicing the trucks. Who's going to do all that?"

On TV Harry looked for the President.

What disturbed him most, he decided, was that the aliens were so tall, taller than even the Secretary of State who himself was a former wide receiver for the Cleveland Browns and by far the most imposing man in the President's cabinet; and, further, that the aliens had perfectly aligned teeth, aluminum-like and pitted, and far too many eyes, if that's what they were, those wedged-in chunks of crystal. And the way the eyes circled the head, you just couldn't tell what the aliens had in sight; or worse, if there was anything they were not aware of. So tall. So many eyes. For the first time Harry noticed that the gloss on the alien skin, on their faces, almost matched the sheen on the uniforms, and then, as he'd always seen, there were those sticks, those long-barreled pipes that they carried in gloved hands—the unassailable laserods.

"Beginning of winter," he went on. "Fine time to shut us down."

"Can they?" asked Beth. Her thin face was pinched over the knitting.

"What? Shut us down? Sure. I suppose. Hell, who cares—they took Willie."

The next morning Nadine waited for him to sit at his desk, then brought him coffee and sat down herself, across from him.

"Look, Harry," she said. "You can drive one of the trucks yourself."

"Me?"

"Yes, you. Sure."

"Been years," he said.

"So? Probably it's only gotten easier."

He thought for a while. "I could do that, you know."

"I know." Nadine stood up. "C'mon."

Lifted mostly by her voice, Harry got to his feet and came around the desk. Together they walked to the office door. On the way she put an arm through his, as if they were on a date, a cozy date, a date full of promise. He remembered a time alone with her, back in deepest part of the garage, taking inventory, when he had leaned forward and she had closed her eyes … Why did he back off? Now Nadine's touch urged him to feel daring again, to climb behind the wheel, to roar down the road, to stretch out the hose, to turn on the meter. How long, really, he wondered, since he drove the route—nine, ten years?

A bit of energy drifted into his head and body but only remained there until he passed through the door and got his first look at the outer office: empty chairs, dark computer screens, no coffee cups, no laughter; and then he felt his chest sink in.

"No, I can't do it."

Nadine kept him walking.

At the window she pointed out to the yard, to the row of tank trucks parked as shiny as any spaceships.

"We'll get number five warmed up for you," she said. "Couple of minutes, that's all. Meanwhile, go get a jacket and a flashlight. You can take Willie's route."

"Willie," he said, under his breath.

The two of them had grown up in the old neighborhood. Inseparable, they even decided to quit high school on the same truant morning at the coffee shop, tough-looking Camel cigarettes in their mouths. "Let's just go make money," Willie had said. Sure, some people thought Harry progressed further, ended up, after all, owning his own business—Odom Oil, "the warmth you deserve"—but he respected Willie's choice to avoid responsibility, to stay on the truck. And of course Harry saw to it that Willie was well-paid. For his driving skills. For his way with customers.

"Cookies from the Jones lady," he would come back saying, his wide face blossomed in a smile, his curly hair undisturbed by the wind. And more. Much more. The shared pastrami lunches, the violent cribbage games, the weekend fishing trips, and most of all the long peaceful walks each night, in any weather, shoulder to shoulder behind Willie's loping brown dog. Yes. And what was it Willie would always say about life's tough moments?—"Hey, buddy, it'll pass." Willie would listen too. Listen to Harry. Nod. Narrow his eyes. Scratch the dog's floppy ears. Shake a fist. Listen.

"Time to go," said Nadine.

She turned Harry away from the window and then she was looking into his eyes. Above all, he didn't want her to see his tears, but what could he do. "Poor Willie," he said, as more tears came. In front of him Nadine's face was a creamy pink mist.

"Don't worry," she replied quietly. "They've got him somewhere, but he's all right."

"Think so?"

"Sure."

Harry shook his head. "I don't think so."

Harry drove home in the icy rain. He was used to such precipitation, here along the lake. What he wasn't used to, what now poured inside him wet and cold, was his awful day on the fuel oil truck.

"Can't tell who's here or gone," he said to Beth, as he shook out of his overcoat. "Get to a house—nobody's there. Doors locked. Shades drawn. So do I fill 'em up, or not?"

"No," Beth said. "Don't."

"What? How can I decide that?"

"You asked me," Beth said. When Harry's coat stopped dripping, she draped the garment on a hanger in the front closet and turned back to him. The bend in her shoulders, it seemed each time he looked, grew deeper and more irreversible, and her once-blue eyes seemed as colorless as smoke. As ashes. In her he recognized his own age. "Well, if everything is such a problem," she said with a slam of the closet door, "go see Larsen."

"Mayor Larsen?" Harry caught his breath. "Can you imagine what the mayor's going through? He won't see me."

"Why not? You've always been one of his big supporters. Just have Nadine call from the office. She'll arrange a meeting for you."

Thinking about it, Harry followed his wife to the living room. There he poured himself a scotch. Glass in hand, he eased into the recliner chair and pushed back, letting his feet rise, settling into the position that always helped him relax; yet he could see in the drink that his fingers were shaking.

"Let's not watch TV," Beth suggested.

"No, turn the damn thing on," he said, and with the remote, and without waiting, he did it himself.

The local newscaster was a black woman with red lipstick. She said that rubbish pick-ups would be limited to once a month. The police force was functioning, sort of, without weapons, but 911 had been discontinued. The status of schools remained a question. At that Harry shook his head. "Oh, Beth, think if we had kids." He closed his eyes. In that darkness he again saw the aliens storming the yard, grappling with Willie, then coming closer, coming in, sifting through the office. Boots. Gloves. Laserods. Surrounded. Sure, he thought, give them Willie, give them any damn thing they want. He opened his eyes. A jovial man came into the TV newsroom to update the weather forecast: snow mixed with rain, to start, to continue. "One thing the aliens can't change," Harry snorted, "is the rotten weather. Serves 'em right." Then the woman came back and interviewed an alien. They sat face to face. She asked questions, some of the very ones that were in Harry's mind. Like how much reduction did they plan? And what exactly happened on their own world?

The alien only rubbed the palms of his gloves together and grunted. After a couple of minutes of that, Harry wanted to throw his scotch glass at the screen. "Fly across the damn galaxy," he complained to Beth, "but learn to talk, hell, no." Every grunt sounded pretty much the same to him. At that moment, though, an attempted translation began to run in white letters across the bottom of the screen, sporadically, as if each word was a major computer accomplishment; and Harry, in spite of his outrage, leaned to the picture, read what came, hoped for help.

BE CALM … BE NICE … COOPERATE.

"It's so confusing," Beth said.

From the lobby on in, City Hall was crowded with aliens. Most of them were standing still, feet apart, just holding a position. Covering each door. Securing the bulletin board. Blocking the vending machine. A few others acted as escorts, accompanying the lawyers or politicians who scurried through. To Harry's surprise, one of them was even running the self-service elevator, and Harry, when he stepped in, drifted to the other side of the box, where from across that short distance he obliquely studied the alien. Pained him to look. And why shouldn't it? Who in his right mind could ever have imagined ... The alien's head, eyes this way and that, reached close to the ceiling. The shoulders were square but not wide, too narrow in fact for all that height. At the waist there was the impression of a belt, but it seemed on second look a permanent elastic part of the glossy uniform. Down at floor level Harry spotted the laserod, behind the alien's boots, leaning in the corner. And up in the two-fingered hand a little beamer activated the lighted board of floor selections; something, Harry assumed as the elevator started to rise, that couldn't be done through the glove.

On the third floor, another alien sat on the desk in front of the mayor's office. With seemingly no hurry, his laserod came up to make a target of Harry's heart.

"I have an appointment," Harry said.

The alien grunted.

"Odom Oil," Harry said.

The alien grunted again.

"Me and the mayor." Harry made each word distinct. "An appointment."

Harry saw himself reflected and multiplied in the ring of crystal eyes. A stare, perhaps. A mind reading. A brain photo. Who knew what these aliens could do? Meanwhile, the teeth slid like saw blades back and forth ...

Finally the alien scratched something onto a rectangle of metal, then stuck out a gloved hand that Harry followed into Mayor Larsen's office.

"You know," Harry told the mayor a minute later, "I don't ask you for many favors." As he talked, he felt ill at ease. Sure, he'd been in the mayor's office before, a couple of times in the past year alone, but who could think straight when hemmed in by aliens. "And I wouldn't ask now, really. It's just that Willie's gone."

"Who's Willie?" asked the mayor.

"Maybe you don't remember him. He drives one of the trucks. And he took care of the beer kegs at your campaign picnic."

"Oh, he's gone, huh?" Larsen, short, pudgy, and going bald, didn't look like the kind of man who required a half-dozen aliens to guard him at his desk. Each one, besides, held a laserod, though in some kind of confidence the weapons were lowered neutrally toward the floor. The mayor, for his part, had only a fountain pen, and the point was capped. "So you want to know what's happening. Take it from me, Harry, the less you know …" The mayor shook his head and his eyebrows came together as further warning. "All right. You're saying these guys took someone away?" "If you could help me find him," Harry said. "If you could do anything about it."

"About what's-his-name." Larsen seemed afraid to move his head again, but his eyes shifted back and forth across the aliens in his sight.

"Yes. Please."

"Somebody who works for you."

"My friend, Willie," Harry said. He swallowed the name, and hoped he wouldn't have to say it again.

The mayor inhaled. Then, with a fluttery nasal wheeze, he let out the breath and brought both elbows up on the desk. Above them he entwined his fingers. "Nice," he said finally. "But not too smart, Harry. You're worried. So you came to me. I'm the mayor, after all. Sure, I can see why you came here." His hands unfolded, and he swept one of them toward the aliens. "But so can they. Look how they're watching you. God, I can't stand it." He shut his eyes briefly; when they reopened they were less sympathetic and much more official. "Harry," he said with that attitude, "you made a big mistake."

The aliens tried to explain reduction. An initial attempt at translation covered the front page of the newspaper, but either the article was censored or no one clearly understood the grunts. A follow-up article was equally vague. For sure it didn't yield to Harry's many readings.

Meanwhile, the arrivals of alien ships were recorded on the stock market page. The graph rose so steadily and acutely that on each successive day it was reduced in type size and extended down the page, already trailing below the middle fold. One day Harry didn't look at the paper, stood instead in the center of the fuel-oil yard gazing up at the sky, the sky filled by the ships, so many of them, whirling by, landing everywhere. Another day, crouched in his desk chair, he followed the newspaper's graph line with his finger. According to the statistics, more and more ships arrived, and none left. Wait just a minute, Harry said to himself. In the whole week none had left. So if what the aliens were doing with people was carting them away, hauling them off somewhere, say, back to their former world … well, how? Or, as Harry put it—when?

And suppose they weren't carting them away.

In their first TV demo of the laserod, the aliens had disintegrated the White House in less than a second, just like that, in a blink of Harry's eyes, and with no residue. Now they were doing the same on other TV spots, to a BMW, to a bridge, and to a horse. A big gray horse. For some reason they left the tail, Harry observed, but nothing else; not a bone, not a hoof, not a shoe. The aliens had not yet shown publicly what a laserod could do to a human. They had not even implied—not in a single grunt—that there was any connection between the laserod that each alien carried and the long-range, low-profile plan they called reduction.

If there was anything that made Harry fidget, it was having his two favorite women in one place. Even though at the office nothing had ever happened between him and Nadine, he still considered her a kind of sweetheart, and he worried that here at his home at dinner she would say something bold or incriminating to Beth, although what that could possibly be was not clear. Beth leaned to her across the table. "Listen, Nadine, the appointment—Harry saw the mayor this morning."

"I was just going to ask." Nadine turned to Harry for information. Returning the gaze, he realized with a little stir in his heart that he'd finally gotten used to the way she looked in contact lenses, but he thought maybe it was too late.

"Tell her, Harry," Beth said.

He shrugged. He didn't feel like going into details. And he didn't want to remember anything Larsen had said. The mayor's words came back to him anyway: a big mistake. Harry twisted the napkin and shrugged again. "A useless trip," he said.

"Mine too," Nadine told him. "I went to Willie's house right after work, with the office key. No sign that he's been there."

"What about the dog?" Harry asked.

Nadine's jaw dropped. "Oh, that cute happy dog. I don't know. Where did he keep him? Maybe I should go back and check."

"Don't—" Beth came half out of her chair.

"No, wait a minute," Harry said. "Better leave the dog to me." He reached over and covered Nadine's hand with his own, more intimately than he'd ever dared at the office. To his surprise, Nadine's hand was quivering. He'd have thought she'd be the last person to be discouraged. Wasn't she the one he relied on to give comfort, to hold her own, to whip the computers, to run his office, to spark and bolster his dreams? If even

Nadine had reached her limit, then who was there now? Just him. Him, and no Willie. He patted her hand. Her smile was grateful but not much more. "You know," he said, "I'd better go to Willie's place now. The dog could starve."

Beth rapped the table with her knuckles. "Then let it starve. Haven't you done enough? The mayor this morning, and all."

"You're really going?" asked Nadine.

He bit his lip. "Willie would do the same for me."

Harry got the house key from Nadine. Then, while both women cleared the dishes, he retrieved his overcoat from the front closet and went, on further thought, to the bedroom dresser to get a scarf. This time of year the wind coming off the lake could blow you over. He shuddered, anticipating the chill, and came back into the living room just as someone knocked at the door.

He turned that way.

The knock came again. It sounded to Harry like a gloved hand.

"Who's that?" Beth shouted from the kitchen.

Harry continued to button his coat. There were times this past week, maybe even up to a minute ago, when he might have become confused or frightened. Collapsed. Run. Complained to Nadine at the office, to Beth at home, about the way the day was working out. He was not like that anymore.

He tossed the scarf around his neck. "I'll get it, Beth," he called back. "I think it's for me."

He opened the door and there were just three of them. From bottom up, six boots, three laserods, and a profusion of eyes not all of which were focused directly on where he stood. For the briefest of moments Harry leaned on the doorknob. Then his breath came back and he stepped forward into their midst, pulling the door closed behind him. Yes, he thought, something very difficult had come along. It was unexpected. It was unbelievable. But it too, in its way, was sure to pass, either by a sudden shaft of light from a laserod ... or else he'd find Willie.

THE BLIND CAT

Mardelle Fortier

Tim's lean body lay still, in his old-fashioned bed, trapped in nightmare. His mother's face frowned down at him. In this dream, Tim sat on a chair far below hers. The wrinkles in her face were etched in as though by iron claws. Her frame was bordered in black. Firmly, enunciating each syllable, she stated: "Be careful. This is the day."

He lurched into wakefulness.

The clock showed 5:59, one minute before the alarm. Quickly his finger shut off the clock, since his nerves were too frazzled for the clanging bell.

Hurriedly, the 46-year-old accountant got ready to go to work, in the autumn chill, pulling on a crisp shirt, brushing his pale, skimpy mustache. He kept trying to block out the awful nightmare. He didn't believe in dreams, seldom had them. Besides, his mother was no longer alive. She had died (he trembled as he realized) one year ago today.

At his desk, Tim tried to concentrate on his accounts. The rows of tiny figures soothed yet did not erase his dismay. His stomach lay like a bird huddled in a nest during a windstorm. He'd had no breakfast.

This is ridiculous, he told himself. What would his mother say?

Her face floated in front of the balance sheet, grim as in his dream. Strange, in his nightmare she'd looked so alive, and resembled her living figure exactly. Mother had always been so much larger than Tim.

The thin accountant started as he sensed an enormous woman behind him. The supervisor! Hurriedly Tim answered a question on Mrs. Bradley's inheritance tax.

Tim forced himself to concentrate until almost noon. Then he went for a quick break in the coffee room. A middle-aged matron (the secretaries' supervisor) looked up from hacking at a gooey brown slab on the table. She peered at Tim over bright, pricey glasses. "Some days I would kill for a brownie," she said.

Tim scurried back to his desk. At lunch he tiptoed back into the coffee room. Warmly he greeted Molly, a blonde receptionist. Tim was drawn to her because she was mature (35), motherly, and kind. Long, narrow fingers gripping his coffee cup, Tim chatted: "I brought an egg salad sandwich." He unwrapped it from a plastic baggy, closed with wire covered in green, and tested the olive with his finger. His lunch looked precisely the way his mother used to fix it. "Do you believe in dreams?" he blurted.

Molly smiled warmly. "Oh ... it depends. Sometimes they seem like scrambling of the previous day. But—"

"Do—so sorry to interrupt—do you think the future is, uh, written in stone?"

"You mean, can we change it? I'm not sure." Molly stared reflectively at the eggshell-hued wall.

Stomach knotting, Tim could barely digest his egg salad sandwich. He felt a strange dread in the pit of his stomach.

After work Tim boarded a train, and endured the long commute home. He still lived in the big old house, which, as the only child, his mother had left him. Isolated from its neighbors, the dilapidated, gabled building sat in the middle of ancient, murmuring woods.

Drained by his long day, Tim trudged up the battered, creaking stairs. The door whined out a thin, high-pitched warning. In the living room, rich shadows greeted him. This dwelling had for so many generations been owned by Lithuanians, that even the shadows seemed Lithuanian. With shaking hands, Tim lighted a fire in the hearth.

Glancing alertly about him, the aging man poured himself a brandy. He sank into a chair, which pulled him down into its pillowy depths, and peeled off socks and shoes, sliding into slippers. The ceiling loomed high over the slight man; shadows watched from corners.

For the millionth time, Tim wished at least one of his parents was still alive. How strong they'd been: large-boned and reliable.

Slowly, he sipped the warm sparkling liquor. Maybe he ought to have married, filled the house with children. But his mother had complained over each of his choices in women. It was not too late— maybe Molly—

Abruptly his nightmare flashed before his eyes. He recalled more: a room choking with lilies, enormous and towering, opening and closing, whispering rumors. What was that? A sign? Some words … yes, a blackboard. Large chalk print ordered him: "DON'T FORGET. I'LL BE BACK TONIGHT." His mother had never been a schoolteacher, but she left notes everywhere. She had prepared for death as much as she had prepared for life.

Drink forgotten, Tim stared at the remembered image. The words seemed indelible. He could not recall an eraser.

Shadows licked at dry wooden walls; rain pattered on panes. Mother had put her will and funeral arrangements in perfect order. Tim sighed. Should he re-examine his will? Yet he had no close relations to leave his possessions to. Tim's clothes were limited to a few tidy, gray suits. He had the heavy, old furnishings, dark and respectable. He had the house.

Restlessly, Tim gulped the remaining drops of brandy. He wandered toward the kitchen, past the black, gleaming piano … past the stained glass of half-moon window in the hallway. In the vacant, echoing kitchen, he stared at cupboards, a big bowl of apples on the old oak table, without appetite.

Dreams meant nothing. He was rarely ill as an adult, looked after each detail of his health as his mother had taught him to. He'd tried to keep the house clean, but was not as perfect as she had—

Something crawled along his bare ankle. Looking down, he noticed his mother's dark, ageless cat. Blind for years, it had by means of high-pitched nerves and cold claws, learned to feel its way through any dim cranny of the house. The animal had never taken to Tim. After winding around his leg like a chill snake, the creature disappeared under the table. Watching for it, the man noticed the whites of eyes gleaming in the shadows. Lightning trembled in the sky like a bluish-green vein. Silently, out of enormous, vacant eyes, the cat studied and judged the man; Tim felt a strong sense of this—though the beast was blind.

Goosebumps rising on cold skin, Tim exited the kitchen. He paced the hall, as lightning lit the sky like a nerve fried on black coals.

He returned to the parlor and sat at the piano. Hesitantly, his hand slid over cool white keys, interspersed with black, like decay setting in. To block out worries, he began to play. The chords, low and sweet, spiraled around his ears like falling apple blossoms, in clear, minty air.

His mother had made him play an hour a day as a child. Yet when he'd confessed to a desire to be a music major in college, she'd squelched the idea. She insisted that he switch to math, in which he showed aptitude. Mother had always loved numbers, once hoped to become a schoolteacher.

The son's fingers searched out the high notes, reawakening his dream of becoming a concert pianist. He'd never breathed his secret to anyone: elegant in a tux, loving the applause. If he did not…waken tomorrow, he'd never—

His wrists pressed hard against low, vibrating keys. Abruptly he shifted into a joyful waltz by Strauss, playing loudly and wildly, thumping against keys as thunder rolled. He banged and hammered, finally storming out his anger against his mother. If this dance on the beautiful chords was vibrant enough, it would push away death.

Thunder crashed. The cat screeched.

Tim's fingers stilled on the white keys. The cat howled from the depths of the basement.

Nibbling his mustache, he edged toward the basement steps, innards clenched. As a pale, ailing child, he'd been repelled by the lower bowels of the house. Tim forced himself down the narrow chill stairwell, listening to his mother's imagined demand: "Don't just sit there, get the cat."

Teeth chattering, he opened the half-shut door, that creaked with aging, nasal protest. "Scared, huh?" He could hear his mother laughing at him, as her dark eyes sparkled. The slinky cat yowled; the accountant's nerves went numb. He hunted for it, as shadows stepped out of the way like gray ghosts of his ancestors. His grandmother's old wind-up victrola, with strange, cracked records, stood in a lost corner. Tim felt horribly guilt-stricken at the buildup of dust, the bad mess.

In deepest darkness, amid smells of mold and decay in clammy bins, potatoes sprouted ghostly white tumors, bulging with life. Green-black things bloomed with roots like old teeth. Red onions grew wriggling worms of mold. Living beings did not easily give up life, Tim thought. How surprised he'd been to see his mother on her bed at the end, screamingly thin, with an eerie grimace of pain. She'd fought cancer for an agonizing nine months. "How can I leave you behind? Who will take care of you?" Then, without warning, she'd quietly given up. He still couldn't believe how her steel will melted away. Sagging bags of bitter fluid drained from her body. In the end, nothing remained but a dry skeleton, most of the flesh devoured.

Leaning against damp cardboard boxes, Tim fought dizziness and nausea. Lightning tingled against high, clouded windows. Thunder blasted, like something getting smashed in the center, and breaking up. Something big breaking.

Tim caught sight of his mother's pet. It was strangely silent. In a waking nightmare, the cat watched Tim in the blackness, with sparkling, gleeful, dark eyes. Shaking violently, pushing, Tim freed its paw from between boxes. A huge box on the next higher shelf rocketed toward the accountant. He jumped out of the way but was caught in the leg. "Mother," he yelled as he skidded, hands striking sharply against frozen cement. He stared as several boxes started sliding from highest shelves. The man rolled over and clapped hands over his head.

With a bang, a thunderous trunk landed by his right ear.

A queer silence. The cat leaped on his back.

Tim twisted to frown up at it—the ancient beast seemed to be laughing.

Despite acute aches, the man began laughing too. In the tomblike stillness, he heard his loud laughter. It sounded nearly like a maniac. His hand was scraped, bleeding; his pants torn.

The accountant took a deep breath and told himself sternly: Calm down. If that didn't kill you—

Slowly he got up and looked around. The cat was nowhere to be seen.

It was a relief to have the claws off his back, to have the bony, slithering body far away.

He listened. No thunder. The rain had dulled to a soothing patter ... He shook off his uneasiness and marched upstairs. The clock struck ten. Time to have a glass of milk, go to bed.

As he entered the kitchen, the cat screeched and scratched at the door. It always got out by itself, feeling its way without seeing. Then the screen door would click shut.

He opened the door. The animal was wailing at the other end of the porch. Groaning, he trudged toward the animal. Feeling his mother's expectations closing in, Tim groped in shadows toward the crawling cat.

Lightning blinded his eyes, electricity scorched his hair, fire began to devour him. "Mother!" he yelped in horror.

THE GLASS CHILD

Alyce Miller

Before the Baby

there were books about babies. There were baby books and book babies. There were baby posters and baby postcards. Magazines with foldouts of babies. There were babies painted on walls, babies dancing on ceilings, babies holding hands and dancing in circles. Holograms of babies, inflatable babies, balloon babies. Bouncing, babbling, dimpled, dazzling, beautiful babies.

Before the Baby, there were babies.

The baby arrives the old-fashioned way, as some babies still do, when they have nostalgic parents.

A gush of water, like the release of a spigot, the subsequent pops and sighs of muscles contracting and expanding, sparks and arcs, unabashed moans and hollers, then like a bale of hay skidding down a chute, emerges from gooey fluids the small slick sack of skin, hair, toes, fingers all accounted for, ungainly genitals the size of its wobbly head, everything red and bawling, a misshapen and slightly mauled piece of meat, but oddly human too, with a face, and nose that look like his, eyes like hers, somebody else's chin (grandma? uncle?) even though parts of the baby are darker than they eventually will be, and other parts are lighter than they eventually will be. The cord still attached, the anxious, triumphant father bearing down like a headlight, the mother a freshly burst ripe peach, her vocabulary diminished to monosyllabic wow's and ooooooh's, the swirl of relatives armed with camcorders—never miss a moment— a conspiracy of marvel.

Just imagine, it's a veritable club out there—4.2 babies born every second, 250 every minute, and 15,008 every hour.

The baby is pronounced: *perfect.*

The miracle.

That they generally turn out as well as they do is a testament to the power of evolution, the triumph of the human spirit, the will to live, the revolutions of the planet, fairy dust, and pure, basic luck. Exhausted, but proud, the mother falls back into a deep slumber. The father repeats how lucky they are it all happened without intervention; no fertility drugs, no donor eggs or sperm, no petry dishes, no invasive surgeries, no cesarian slashing and dashing, no cloning, no cells cooked up in a lab. Just a pop and a plop is how he likes to describe it. The old-fashioned way. They have the DVD to prove it. For friends and family, and eventually for the baby itself.

Much less expensive this way. Money left over for college.

Released from the hospital, or more like jettisoned: *healthy baby goes home now:*
in a container—
with instructions for care:
feed, bathe, feed, enrich, feed, bathe, feed, enrich (lots of Mozart).

The contract

includes an arbitration clause and a one-year warranty for parts and labor. The framed certificate is penned in elegant black calligraphy, and spells out the baby's identification number, dimensions, weight, IQ, sexual orientation, disease risks, and future potential, including occupations.

So there will be no risk of allergies or germs, the father drags the totally unadoptable and aging family pets to the pound where, being complicated and infirm, at least one of them incontinent, they are almost immediately euthanized.

The house disinfected, windows scoured, surfaces made shiny and spotless, counters scrubbed, carpets replaced, walls painted, Mozart quartets emanating softly through the rooms from artfully recessed speakers, selected visitors are asked to wear disposable paper slippers and paper masks. Touching permitted only after temperatures and throat swabs are taken.

Down the road the parents will order the bag of dirt advertised on the city monitors that will introduce the baby slowly to specially prepared "organic germs," necessary to strengthen the immune system. But for just yet. Even the nanny who tends to the infant wears gloves, a smock, and a mask.

The baby cries

and cries and cries
and cries.
The baby wets and poops and cries some more.
The baby feeds. Oh, how the baby feeds! The more progressive books discourage sucking. Too tactile. Can create problems for later life—sexual, psychological, social. The carefully screened wet nurse named Bob disagrees and fills his artificial breast over and over with the balanced formula that guarantees a five-pound weight gain in the first month. Weight is good. Baby happy.
More crying, more pooping. Sleeping. Back to crying.
The parents hover. Hover and worry. The baby's mouth opens very wide. The baby always seems hungry, sad, in pain, mad, jealous, perturbed, distressed, angry—perhaps even upset about being born. In reality, the baby has gas in its gut. Undeveloped gastrointestinal system. Gas! gasp the parents, and fires the wet nurse Bob on the spot for not sticking to the prescribed non-dairy, low-residue diet. They opt instead for subcutaneous feedings that some professionals fear interferes with the complicated process known as hardening, but others feel are cleaner and quicker.
The baby's mouth opens even wider. Pacifiers are verboten.
The baby is saying: *I want I want*

I want I want.

That they have between the two of them, managed to produce such a perfectly formed thing of beauty is enviable indeed. They both take Baby Leave from their reasonably lucrative occupations. In the afterglow of shock and pride, they watch entranced as the incredible little creature flails and wiggles and writhes. They take turns sleeping on the sterilized latex-free mats stacked next to the baby's container.

Darling, they murmur to each other.

It looks like you, each says to the other. *Darling*.

Sometimes they forget to breathe. They order out for food from guaranteed non-contaminant services. They turn off the alarms at the communications center. They sit or lie in silence, watching. Tick-tock. The baby's brow furrows. Tick-tock. The baby's eyes open, one at a time, slowly, as if weighted with sticky tape. Tick-tock. The baby's eyes close again with a little click. Shshshsh. The baby's lower lip buckles. Tick-tock. The baby fidgets. Snap-snap. The baby sucks air. Gurgling noises, the sound of wet suction, air bubbling. The baby—oh, horrors, look, the baby is sucking its thumb. Quick, quick, place the envelopes over the baby's hands. How did this happen? Sucking like that will slow down hardening. But they've caught it in time. Relief! You can't be too careful.

One parent at a time gets up quietly to answer the front door, to read the mail from the Entertainment Screen, to heat up food in the solar oven, to take a bath in the mini-pool. The baby dreams. The baby's eyelids flutter again, this time soft as butterfly wings.

Ooooh, oooooh, baby, baby.

When will the baby be old enough? everyone asks.

Soon, says the pediatrician. *Soon*, says the lactation specialist who is still seething over the firing of the wet nurse Bob. *Soon*, says the curandera who specializes in yerbos and has laid various dried plants around the room. *Soon*, say the experts who write the baby books.

At the first signs that the time is nearing, they begin to prepare the container, by first lighting safe-flame, wick-free candles on either side. A multi-faith priest arrives to bless them all, waving cigar-shaped smoking sage sticks and stalks of lavender incense through the chambers.

It's so much simpler nowadays, everyone says. *Imagine the old days when babies stayed soft for all those years! And all the worry and trouble about their fontanels. ...*

In the computer room, a plan is in motion. The baby software package is being downloaded; soon it will display on the screen the whole future: a top-notch pre-school three blocks away, the social group appropriate to their demographics, reading readiness and computer classes, arts enrichment,... so much to do... email consultations and interviews with teachers, virtual tours of facilities... closed or open facilities... diversity (a mix of hard and soft children), or not?

The baby is ready.

At a precocious three months, the baby allows itself to be lifted from the container for the first time by proud parents, and pressed into place on the little metal pedestal that carries warnings the size of mattress tags not to jar, jostle, or jolt. Some families choose to keep their babies in elegant transparent cases an extra month, some squeeze them into frames, others store the babies in special paper away from light so they won't fade, but this isn't recommended as there have been instances in which babies have failed to harden, and remained soft, with dire consequences.

The parents agree on a compromise—they place the baby on the metal pedestal with a partial UV-ray shield, on the dining room table under the chandelier, like a centerpiece.

We are so lucky when you consider what parents of lesser babies go through.

The baby begins to laugh.
Say dadda, say mamma.
Mamma, murmurs the baby from its perch, *mamma mamma mamma, mammy, ma-me-ma-me——me me.*

Big eyes, big head, cute as a button, chubby, dimpled legs, chubby, dimpled arms, chubby, dimpled cheeks. A baby you can't help loving. Full head of hair. Curls. Perfect complexion. Symmetrical features. The baby likes being upright, a position the maintenance manual says reduces crying and simplifies defecation (laws of gravity), which will eventually be done away with altogether when the tubes are inserted. It will take a full month more for the baby to harden and for bodily functions to be brought under the control of the outtake system the parents have purchased, so in the meantime, the baby is handled only when absolutely necessary. The first two weeks of curing can be difficult, because the baby's protective shell is still forming, and the mother has not yet suppressed the milk-releasing urges in order that at this crucial time, the baby can, if parents agree and sign on the dotted line, partake briefly of "mother's milk" the old-fashioned way. The new lactation specialist helps reassemble the mother's nipples and breasts so they will be more baby-friendly. The mother also dons the polypropalene suit that prevents potentially deleterious skin-to-skin contact. The baby is not allowed to suck. A small device keeps the baby's lips pursed.

The baby is clearly advanced and is really developing fast.

At the sign of the first veneer, the doors and windows are opened, and friends and family are invited to touch the baby. Now is the time to spread around in strategic places some of the organic germs ordered from the only respectable site on the Internet. The dirt doesn't look like dirt, but like ash, and instructions explain the baby should eat about a teaspoon a day. The baby toughens nicely and takes on a healthy, glossy, polished look.

Your baby is weathering so well, everyone remarks.

It must be in the genes, says someone, *because it took our baby almost 6 months to be finished.*

Our child is advanced, the mother agrees proudly.

When the baby is fully coated and the first layer of its outer shell finally hardens—further evidence of a high I.Q.—the parents decide travel will be broadening. They take out baby insurance and purchase air-highway time to several plum spots around the world that involve history, music, ancient ruins, and art.

They wrap the baby in heat-treated linen cloths and nestle it in resilient foam peanuts inside the transparent carrying basket designed for safe and comfortable air transport.

It is difficult to go anywhere in the streets of strange cities without being stopped by total strangers who want to gawk at the unusually beautiful child. The baby's perfection leaves admirers speechless. In several still-undeveloped nations the parents are stunned to see up close and personal that children as old as six and seven are still soft, and running loose in the streets, where they acquire skinned knees and bruised heads and broken noses. They've only seen photos of such barbarisms, but to witness them firsthand leaves them reeling. They donate money to help these children, who are scarred and broken.

On the trip the baby decides to crawl. This isn't supposed to happen yet, but good thing, the father informs friends later, that they were in a "civilized" place where it was possible to purchase an ambulation mat. *Imagine if we'd been stuck in some god-forsaken place where the baby had to touch the ground!*

After the trip, and they're back home again, the parents are exhausted. The nanny, who accompanied them, is also exhausted and asks for a pay raise, a new electric car, and a free trip on the air-highway to see her parents in what used to be Canada. The lactation specialist is replaced by a subdermal therapist who will manipulate the baby's muscles and bones. The baby is now ready to start eating protein-enriched organic mushes made of genetically engineered fruits and vegetables. The baby can be comfortably fed through the tube affixed to its navel (they chose the navel over the option of introducing a new port through the neck).

The baby becomes a toddler.

It toddles—no, teeters—— safely on the ambulation mat, which slowly decreases its range of motion over time. At night, when the parents fasten it back onto its stand, the baby looks pleased with itself, pleased with the growing sea of toys and mobiles and whirly-gigs and gee-gaws that have been showered on it.

More more more more more more, says the baby. More more more more more more more more more more more more more more more more more more more more more more more more more more more more more more more more more more more more more more more more more more more more.

Through the Listen to the Baby Sound Pads placed at intervals around the house, the baby's voice can be heard echoing throughout. *More more more more more more more more more more more more more more more me me me me me me me me me me.*

The mother joins mommy groups and the father joins daddy groups. They all sit on ambulation mats, though less up-to-date parents still carry their babies in containers (and one poor dolt arrived with his baby in a sling, heaven forbid, but was not invited back, thank goodness), and they all sing songs and work on advanced skills.

Our baby isn't ready for a stand, says one mother smugly, still shamelessly clutching her infant to her breast. The rest of the mommies turn toward her with concern and disgust. Flesh on flesh... there's legislation afoot to criminalize it.

What about germs? He hasn't hardened yet? Aren't you worried if you keep this up you'll have to take care of your baby until age eighteen like in some outer province overseas?

No, the book says… .

The book says… .

We need a different book, says the mother anxiously that night to the father. I met a mother today who said her baby wasn't ready for a stand. She was still holding her baby—right in her arms. It was so distressing. She said she wanted to prolong babyhood because it is a precious time, but she was thinking only of herself, and not the baby at all. I mean, the legal implications of keeping a child soft like that… .

What antediluvian thinking; people like that shouldn't be allowed to have babies, the father says shaking his head. It's really time they started prosecuting! Talk about abdicating parental responsibility. Our baby is progressing so nicely, we should maybe stop going to these groups and continue with our plan so as not to be exposed to such influences. Our baby will be way ahead all the other babies—maybe even be the first to have a mold.

I have to say, says the mother, there are moments where I have to resist holding the baby. I mean, don't get me wrong, I'm committed to doing things the right way, but sometimes I get this crazy impulse... .

Ancient limbic brain, says the father with understanding. Some hold-over from our primitive selves. You're not completely done with all that yet. After all, your mother was a holder, and you've never found it easy to criticize her. Look, if you want something to hold, why don't we just get a sibling?

A sibling! says the mother.

We could do a trial sibling, says the father. I can go right online and download one... .

Never! says the mother. That's going too far.

It's all the rage, says the father. Everyone's talking about it at the daddy group. The trial siblings are perfect because there's no commitment. Ship 'em back is the motto. Or if you keep them around long enough they just disintegrate.

Isn't it terribly expensive? asks the mother.

Only if you don't renew the lease, says the father. The contract gives you an out after a year. I mean, it's not the greatest investment, since they don't appreciate, but if we were to get attached, we could just call the accountant and see what she advises. Might be a tax write-off.

At the age of one year, the baby has hardened.

Spectacular baby—shiny, sturdy, I.Q. off the charts.

The baby is the envy of all their friends, both with and without children. The perfect child in every respect.

What about a sibling, family and friends press. Have you considered a sibling?

They mean a real sibling, not a trial sibling, and the father and mother do not say one way or another, because these choices should never be public, and people who ask are rude and nosy.

The sibling's not the only choice we have to make, says the father one night as he and the mother sit in their great room watching the baby asleep on its stand. Time is of the essence. This is our last week to frame the baby if we want, or else we must keep it on the pedestal. The baby should be in a play group now, but we can't proceed till we've resolved this other matter once and for all.

He turns on the application, and the choices blink blue and white in front of them. The mother isn't so sure.

A play group, she says reluctantly. I've heard some real horror stories about the older pedestal kids.

We just have to choose carefully, says the father. I mean, there are play groups and then there are play groups. Happy Holograms is considered top-notch.

You didn't tell me that. I worry about bad influences, even if they are holograms, says the mother. What if the baby picks up bad habits? And germs?

Not our baby, the father assures her. Remember, we've done everything by the book, and all we have to do now is finish this part of the process.

I think maybe this is a good time to look into the trial sibling now, says the mother cautiously. That way we'd have more control, and we wouldn't have to worry about—well, things like exposure to child molestation, television, and irradiated foods. And we could put off the decision about the pedestal or frame... I'm just not ready. I'm sorry, but I'm having second thoughts... .

The father studies her briefly, then says, A trial sibling sounds like the ticket. There's a full range of choices now. And the timing's great what with financing and warranties being really competitive right now— something about it being the first of the year, and they have to clear the shelves. We should be able to get an excellent interest rate, and then there's the consolidation option.

Do you think there will come a time, says the mother, when no more babies will be born the old-fashioned way?

Probably, says the father, but it's been kind of fun doing it this way with the first one. Sort of a nod to the past. Cutting-edge of us, in a way. The neo-traditionalists.

It is an unforgettable experience, says the mother, but not one I'd ever want to repeat. So messy and so invasive.

It's brought us closer together for a time, says the father.

I think we're good parents, says the mother.

Very good, says the father. Some people just have a knack for this, you know.

They watch the baby who has awakened and is now sitting cross-legged in the pedestal prongs like a little Buddha.

Look, says the mother, maybe we won't have to make any decisions. Maybe this will be the position our baby chooses after all. Why don't we wait a bit? It doesn't really have to happen right now.

The father disagrees. You know what could happen if we wait. I'm not willing to take that chance. Destroy everything we've worked for here.

The mother tries to explain. I was just thinking maybe it's best to have it framed in a few weeks, if we really have to decide. I've seen some awfully cute framed babies lately, and their life expectancies have gone way up with the new advances.

Wow, says the father, I'm shocked. This is such a departure from our plans. I mean, we discussed how waiting could cause problems down the road. And we already took a chance with the old-fashioned birth... .

Well, I've been thinking—with talk of a sibling and all, says the mother, it might be safest to explore a more permanent sibling, and then we could talk about whether we want to frame number one and pedestal number two.

You're worrying me, says the father, with an edge to his voice. I mean, the selected pre-school focuses on the pedestal kids. I'm afraid a framed kid might not get the same attention... . framing can still cause complications.

How about home schooling? asks the mother. If we have two babies, they'll help each other learn.

That depends on the kind of sibling we choose, says the father. And of course we could cross ethnicities this time, if you like, just for variety's sake.

Ethnicity's so passe, says the mother, but if it's important to you, I would consider it. We should check with our attorney first, though, since I heard of a family who went for the permanent sibling right after the first one was born, and it turned out the sibling's papers had been switched and it was full of genetic flaws, but by the time they discovered the deceit, it was too late. It was a terrible tragedy, really, when the baby just got interrupted... ."

Try not to be negative, says the father. We have so much to be grateful for. Just look at our perfect baby. Let's not press our luck. We don't want to tempt fate. Maybe we should just stick with what we have right now, and count our blessings.

The baby opens its eyes and looks out at the parents with complete devotion. Baby eyes all misty with vulnerability, darling dimples appearing along the jaw line.

The heat and savage need of infant love.

Look, look! cries the mother. Our baby loves us. Maybe we shouldn't frame it or put it on a pedestal. Maybe we should just run off to another place where babies are kept the old-fashioned way and let it soften. We can still encourage flesh. It can play in the grass, get muddy, touch animals! It's not too late... .

Quick, says the father, who is terrified the mother is losing it, and grabs up the large glass bell from the overhead shelf and drops it down neatly over the baby in one swift movement. A moment later, the baby trembles, gasps, stiffens, then goes rigid. There is no turning back. What's done is done.

Oh, my God, says the mother, bursting into tears, I wasn't ready for this.

I know, I know, says the father. But one of us had to make the choice. It really is better this way.

ONCE I WAS A GRAVEDIGGER

Joanne Seltzer

Comfortable with my career, I joked about death until dirt walls collapsed on me. Face down I could not speak, could not move the leg that was hit by a toppled monument. My non-life passed before me like some television rerun, until a headstone engraver near at hand denied me free burial by responding to the surprise rush of air.

When the hospital dismissed me, leg incarcerated in plaster, I telephoned my brother. Ivan hated me, always he had hated me, because Mother hated me. Already she had a boy, Ivan the Magnificent, and often told of how she cried upon unpinning my diaper the first time to authenticate my sex. Still, she would have named me Rosemary. But the nurse wrote Ross on the birth-certificate application, father blank, and sent us home by taxi to Ivan. I was an ill-chosen gift, wrapped in Rosemary's pink nightgown, held at arm's distance until deposited in my brother's lap.

Every family is dysfunctional, yet most children grow into apparent adults. I waited for my bone to knit, and Ivan controlled my destiny. He installed me in the darkest corner of his roach-infected apartment that soon reeked of overripe death flowers my former employer sent. After two days of neglect, my brother turned compassionate, brought my pain pills on a handpainted tray, emptied my urinal on demand, serenaded me with his drums. I became so focused on my boom boom headache I forgot about my boom boom leg.

On the seventh day of captivity a new kind of pill, baby pink, appeared on the handpainted tray alongside the white pain pill. He shrugged when I asked, Why the pink? He shrugged again before revealing his wish to make Mother happy. Which would be difficult, I reminded him, because Mother drowned in the bathtub years ago while changing into a dolphin. Ivan cited heaven. I reminded him of Mother's earthly estate. Yes, my caregiver said, she wanted the female issue that modern technology can provide. Mother, he continued, will do dolphin leaps upon learning that Rosemary inhabits the body once inhabited by Ross.

I like myself the way I am, I said.

And, concluded Ivan, your sex-change operation will offer stability; no longer will you stumble into whoreholes. It was a gravehole, I reminded him. But to Ivan the two are the same, he cares not for women. His longtime lover, Lionel, a self-employed pharmacist, provided the female hormone pills. No pink pill, no white pill, teased my brother, knowing my acute sensitivity to pain. Since a single dose of estrogen seemed fairly benign, I obeyed. Day turned into night. Night turned into day. Pink pills kept company with white pills. The moon began to put on weight

The full moon brought a nightgown, baby pink, in a bag from Victoria's Secret. Try it on, said the tormenter, it reminds me of the nightgown you wore, newborn, the first time I saw you. Soon I will buy you a bra, he added, you are developing nicely, almost ready for surgery.

I remembered that last grim day at the cemetery. Having transcended an unsealed grave, the rest of my life seemed redundant. A minor operation, my brother said, like removing a clump of warts. Then you should have your warts removed first, I said, grasping him with eagle eyes. Never fond of taking risks, Ivan required a canary to investigate the air in the cave he planned to enter.

Time heals what it cannot kill. Quite beautiful without my warts, a self-proclaimed sex-object, I am leather-lined Rosemary now, Lionel's new mate. We postponed our wedding, Lionel and I, until my brother was healed enough to stand as maid of honor. Ivan became Vanessa. No longer interested in drums, Vanessa bought herself a piccolo and plays high-pitched music to the roaches in her life. As for the scars that represent progress, I will someday show them off to mother.

MOTHERLY PARTS

Jennifer Tomscha

I was just eight, and we were mired in the Lenten season, with church on Wednesday nights and fish sticks at school on Fridays, when my grandmother told me she was disappearing. So far, she had lost her right pinky toe, her right middle toe, her left heel, and half of her "motherly parts." The body was still a mystery to me—a temple, we were told—but my own mother had not long before had another baby, and I could guess that by "motherly parts" my grandmother meant either the maroon flower upon which babies sucked or perhaps the secret internal coves in which babies grew (a hot, damp location near the stomach). All these parts of Grandma Vi were dissolved away, dissipated, disintegrated, into white crystal, into a luminous sand. Gone now for good, she said, her jaw tight with the loss. The left heel in the garden, mixed in with the bulbs. The middle toe fizzled away in the bathtub, with just a few grains left near the drain, all the rest of it swept through the old copper pipes to wherever it was the soiled water went.

"The water treatment plant," I offered. We had been there for a field trip.

Just a few minutes before, my Grandma Vi said, as she was taking down her hair in the dark, her left pinky toe had begun to tingle, and then, swiftly, the little thing—her favorite toe—had become a tiny pile of white sand that she would sweep up in the morning.

I began to cry. Tears came easily then, like dime-store candy and skinned knees. "Are you dying?" I asked.

"No, of course not. Don't be silly. Only God knows what will happen next. I'm just going to need some help around the house. And you can't tell a soul."

That night the moon was full, and its light illuminated Grandma Vi's white hair spread out over her pillow. We had already said our prayers to the moon—not to it—prayers were to God, but my grandmother Vivian, being Catholic, was open to the possibility of icons, weeping statues, saints, and relics and virgin births, and she said we could think about the man on the moon as the Face of God, and so I often did, when I thought about God, which was not so often then as it is now. Then I thought the man on the moon looked like a fat curmudgeon who mocked you. A God with His own private jokes. "Exactly right," Grandma Vi had said when I told her this. "God often laughs at us."

"But are you dying?" I asked again. I had not yet learned to manage my grandmother.

"I said no," Grandma Vi said sharply. "No one dies anyway," she continued, turning on her side so we were face to face in the dark. "Remember there's heaven, and Jesus is there. And your grandfather, who would like to meet you. And those little baby rabbits that Goldie-cat killed last spring." With this she touched my head.

"What if you disappear completely?"

"Don't you worry about that, my little night creature." She called me this because I had nocturnal eyes. I didn't know what that meant—nocturnal eyes—but she wouldn't tell me. She said one day I would know. I do know now, I think. Men fall all around me like ill-made houses of cards.

Hot tears rolled down the side of my nose. I sniffed. A tear shot up my nostril and the surprise of this made me choke.

Grandma Vi reached around to my back and gave it a couple of hard pats. "Now's the time to stop that nonsense," she said. My grandmother's patience was known to be the length of a spider's leg.

I tried to breathe through my mouth.

We lay quietly in the moonlight. My grandmother moved onto her back. Past her, the open closet loomed in the dark. I shut my eyes against it.

"You owe me, Gretta," she said finally. "I had to have thirteen children for you to be born. Thirteen children. My body was little more than a vessel for newborn babies. An entrance point for thirteen souls. I know I've said your father just flopped out like a slippery little fish"—I didn't remember her saying this—"but I was just trying to make you laugh. It was a tough pregnancy. I was so old by the time I had him. Forty-two and with child. My thirteenth. The way people talked. All of it for you, so God would give me you and Ginny and now little Gregory."

I knew even then that I could never be grateful enough for the happenstance of my existence.

"Now," she said. "You have to swear to me that you will not tell a single living soul."

"Not even my mom?"

My Grandma Vi's eyes opened wide. In the dark, they were colorless. "Especially not your mom. And not your dad."

"But why not?"

Grandma Vi grabbed my arm. Her hands were cold and dry, but soft with her age.

"Do you want me to get sent away to the home?" She began to speak in a higher register. "To the Home? Your mom and dad would send me there, Gretta, you don't understand, they've been trying to for years now and I would die there for sure."

Even then, so young, I was becoming suspicious of her stories of my father. My mother graded stacks of papers and in between pages muttered occasionally about my grandmother. About how she exaggerated and schemed and instigated and plotted and other verbs I didn't understand.

"I don't think they would do that," I said. "Not if you don't want to go."

"No, they would. You don't understand adults. Listen here, Margaret. You can't say anything because even if your father doesn't incarcerate me, which he probably will, he'll tell your uncle Thomas and then Thomas will come here and force me. If you tell this, and they come and take me away, then I will die. I will die of sadness. It will be like a candle that gets wet and snuffed out and then it will be your fault. Do you want to be responsible for that? For killing me? Allowing me to be taken by Thomas, to shrivel up in that cockroach-infested hole? "

Uncle Tom was the fifth child, Grandma's oldest son. He taught tango lessons and preached from a book called The Power of the Will. He ate only salami and saltines, the saltines being part of his execution of will power. Crumbs sometimes got caught in his moustache. He came once or twice a year and he and Grandma Vi fought so much that some inevitable midnight, Uncle Tom would ring the doorbell at our house because Grandma Vi had cast him out. My father didn't like Ginny and I to talk with him. Tom—some fifteen years older—had sometimes shoved my father's head down the toilet until he choked and heaved great gulps of toilet water up his nose and one January afternoon, while the rest of the family attended five o'clock Mass, had locked my father out of the house with no shoes on, my father banging on the door and hopping up and down on the icy step until he finally gave up and curled under the porch. My father kept his feet in the fur of the stray mutt that sometimes made its home there. When I recalled this, I understood that my grandma was right, that Tom would make her go.

"But maybe you're sick and the doctor can help you," I suggested.

"Doctors only want to take my money." She raised her hand to her forehead and rubbed it as if she had a headache. Then she turned on her side again and put her hand underneath my chin, holding my face up toward hers. Her cheekbones—the high cheekbones I am said to have—made a hard, curved line in the dark and the skin underneath her chin sagged, a little flap that moved back and forth when she talked. "You better help me or I'll haunt you." Her nostrils flared at this, this my grandmother's one true threat. "I'll haunt your dreams every night."

Grandma Vi in my dreams, her long white hair swirling about in the dream-wind, her crochet needles clipping away a delightful trot, her happy voice combating the green-haired man who came to me and sometimes sat at the edge of my bed. I wanted that.

"But what if I wanted you to be in my dreams?" I asked her.

She was quick in her answer. "It won't look like me. You won't ever know if it is me or some eternal demon, and I won't be able to tell you. This would be terrible for me too, you know."

An overwhelming despair came over me. I covered my eyes and began to cry again.

Grandma Vi made no motion to comfort me.

The world is a terrible heap of worthwhile fears. Mine is being caught lost, alone, in the emptiness of a South Dakota blizzard. My grandmother had her own—the shiny tile, the steel railings, the stiff bleached sheets. In this way our fears were the same—the white against the white. All the horrors behind it.

"Okay," I said finally, "I won't say anything."

"Good. You are a good granddaughter to me. Now you might be tempted to tell your mother or your father or Ginny, or you might even want to whisper into little Gregory's ear, because you think that he can't understand you, but walls have ears, Gretta, and you cannot even tell the baby. Remember, Jesus was tempted in the wilderness. The way your mother keeps her plants, I'd nearly say your house was the wilderness too."

"I won't tell. I promise."

Grandma Vi tapped my nose with her finger. "Now go to sleep. Do some hard multiplication problems." She preferred this to counting sheep.

After a few minutes, I turned away from her and faced the wall.

"Which problem are you working out?" she demanded.

"Ninety-seven times forty-seven." Ninety-seven times forty-seven was a favorite of mine, and I got so in medical school I had to chose another one, because I could do it so fast in my head: forty-nine carry the four sixty three plus four six hundred seventy nine and place the zero and so on until four-thousand five-hundred and fifty-nine.

"The Sandman will come fast with that one." She approved.

Some nights Grandma Vi would sing "Mr. Sandman, bring me a dream, make him the cutest I've ever seen." But tonight I could not ask her to and she did not offer.

I have no recollection of having slept, but know that I must have, because next there was the very early morning, earlier than even the birds.

Grandma Vi had already pinned up her hair. She was sweeping the floor.

"Let's make some breakfast and then get you home to enjoy your Saturday," she said.

We ate one-eyed sandwiches with salt and pepper, Grandma's runny and mine cooked through. We did not speak of her dissolution, it was not mentioned over breakfast how she had brushed the tinkling sand into the dustpan and then siphoned it into one of the old pickle jars, how she came down heavily on her right foot when she walked, a limp I hadn't noticed before, but when Grandma Vi dropped me off, she said, "Don't say a word, Gretta."

"I won't."

"And come and see me on Monday after school."

"I will."

The weekend went by slowly. My mother said I was being mopey and forced me outside. It was a damp March. Little tulip buds were nearly ready to bloom, and I could see their colors now breaking out through their folds, red and yellow. I poked around in the dirt for awhile, then I walked across the street to Ann-Marie's house. No one was home, and secretly, I was relieved. I could think only of the body dissolving away. I imagined each cell separating from its neighbor, because who knew what held us together, really. We had just learned of cells in science class, and the nastier boys would rub their hands up and down their arms and then shove them in our faces, the white flakes of their skin floating up in front of us; these boys would then proclaim that we were breathing them in, sucking up their bodies onto our tongues, the way we did when we tongued the Host. "Cannibal" was a new playground insult. If dead skin cells could float off our arms and circulate through the air, couldn't live ones as well? At night, I willed myself together. Stay, I thought to all my parts, Stay.

On Monday, Grandma Vi greeted me at the door.

"Are you okay?" I asked her.

"Of course," she said. "Come in and let's play some War. And you know what? I am going to teach you gin rummy—you're about old enough for that."

I stayed with Grandma Vi until supper time, and she didn't say a word about her disintegrating. She talked instead about my father, how he had been her favorite, her little baby boy, with his midnight black hair. She always called him that—her favorite child—and I wondered if she was simply being diplomatic. I sometimes imagined my older cousins, cousins who had moved away to Texas and Oregon and other places far from the prairie, sitting here at her dining room table, flipping cards over with a snap and listening to my grandma claim their mother or their father as her favorite. "Yes, my Victoria," she would have said, "my seventh child, my favorite little girl, with eyes the gray of a robin's wing."

While Grandma Vi shuffled the cards, I searched her body for clues, for missing pieces. Maybe her left earlobe was a little shorter than the right, as though she had taken her index finger and thumb and pinched it off. Perhaps there was a certain smoothness to her skin. But if there were more parts of her lost, she didn't mention them.

"Remember, don't say a word, Gretta," she said as I hopped out of the cab of her pickup truck.

"I won't."

"And come and see me on Wednesday after school."

"I will."

In mathematics, we began to practice long division. To pull out the answer correctly, to come out right on the top, you had to know what had gone into the denominator. You had to know how the number was built, what patterns it contained, before you ever came at it with your pencil. I was terrible at this.

In the weeks that followed, the pickle jar filled slowly with white sand. My visits to Grandma Vi's became increasingly frequent and increasingly long. She lived only three blocks from school, so I stopped in to see her on my way home, and I let Ann-Marie walk ahead.

"What's wrong with your grandma that you have to see her all the time?" she asked.

"Nothing," I said. I've never been a good liar.

"Well, you've been acting like a freak," she said. Being a freak was almost as bad as being a cannibal.

"Maybe you're not being a good friend."

"You're the one letting me walk by myself," she said and kicked the last bit of dirty snow that had been the winter pile next to the playground.

With that, Ann-Marie stopped waiting for me by the old burr oak, and she began to walk home with a horse-faced girl from the grade above us.

This did not go unnoticed by my sister.

"You and Grandma are best friends now," Ginny taunted. "What happened to Ann-Marie and the rest of your nerds? Did they reject you?"

"Be quiet," I said. Ginny always seemed to have her finger on my pulse, and this worried me.

Ginny had stopped staying Friday nights at Grandma Vi's the autumn she turned ten, after she had gone to see Grandma Vi one afternoon without me. There had been a fight, and Ginny—her tongue like an unleashed hawk—had said something terrible to Grandma Vi, but Grandma Vi had said something worse in return. Ginny had run all the way home, sobbing. Over dinner, with Ginny still lying with her face hidden in her pillow, my mother had said to my father in a small voice, "With her granddaughter, too?" although this was only half a question. I was sent to Grandma Vi's alone after that. I didn't mind though, having Grandma Vi to myself.

Iasked permission from Mrs. Johnson to spend my recesses inside the library, researching. She said yes without even asking what I was reading about, as she had her hands busied by dirty boys with dry skin on their arms and shrieking girls who had recently relearned the power of their voices. Also, according to Ginny, she was getting a divorce.

The small science section in the elementary school library was not enough for me. The thin-spined, dog-eared books, with their pleasant sketches of dissected young children, who smiled while pointing to their livers, their kidneys, told me nothing I needed to know. I requested an interlibrary loan. A week later, my books arrived from the college where my parents worked: picture-less textbooks indexing every known disease; Henry Gray's Anatomy of the Human Body, with its black and red sketches; Molecular Cell Biology, in color, outdated by an edition or two.

Slowly, the human body revealed itself to me. I studied the metacarpus, the flexor brevius, and the navicular, the lunate (without your palm, the hand is little more than a claw). I began to know the lumpy pancreas, how it rests lazily between the kidneys. I read of the battles between the rolly white bloodcells, rough with defenses, and the invading germs.

"You're an ambitious one," the librarian said. She was accustomed to having the library to herself. It was where she wrote her romance novels, according to Ginny. "Wouldn't you rather read something you can understand better?"

"I'm going to be a doctor," I said, my voice so cogent I knew then I wasn't lying.

I left the books in the library, but often came back to class late. Mrs. Johnson didn't notice when I would slip into my desk in the back. She usually had her face in her hands, as though she'd rather be sleeping or crying and not listening to twenty-five students chanting their spelling words aloud. "Melancholy," we said. "M-E-L-A-N-C-H-O-L-Y."

"Gretta, I'm in trouble," Grandma Vi announced when I walked in the door the Monday before Easter. She sat in the armchair in the corner of the living room. The previous Friday, I had noticed her limping even more than usual, and she had been missing both her ring and pinkie fingers on her left hand.

"I lost both feet over the weekend," she continued. Her legs hung above the ground, unfinished, a couplet without the final rhyme. "My right foot disintegrated in the kitchen, but my left—what remained of it—disappeared before I could even notice it was gone. I even shook out the bedsheets, but not a grain of me fell out."

"Grandma—"

"Maybe we should say a prayer to St. Anthony and he could help us find them," she said. I couldn't tell if she was kidding or not. We often said prayers to St. Anthony, for keys, for the remote, for lonely socks. "I'm really fine, Gretta." She eased herself down to the floor and showed me how she could crawl around her house. "It's actually easier to scoot around on the floor without your feet in the way." For a second, her pants crowded up above where her ankles should have been, and I glimpsed what remained, round, smooth stumps. A lack.

I began to cry again.

Grandma Vi turned around in the dining room and craned her head up at me. "That's enough of that from you," she snapped.

"But maybe we should call somebody. Maybe someone should come and help you."

"No, no, no. You promised me. You're the one who's going to help me. Now stop snibbling. We need to get some supplies before the kids get here."

My father's older sister was coming up from Sioux Falls for Easter—and Tom, Tom would be there too.

"I need to run a few errands," she said.

We took her truck. We waited until the coast was clear—no ten-year-old boy biker gangs on their way to the creek, no neighbors poking about with their garage doors open—and then Grandma Vi leaned on my back and I carried her, bending forward at my stomach and with her arms around my neck, her weight pushing me quickly and unexpectedly.

"Open the door, open the door," she squealed, choking me with her grip around my neck. As I pulled the handle, I nearly fell over backwards, but I clung to the door and got Grandma Vi leaned up against the seat and she hoisted herself into the cab of the truck. She had been small to begin with, but now she could no longer reach the pedals.

Grandma Vi's truck smelled of a man, all musk and smoke—the scent of my grandfather, she said, the Ford had been his truck first, and he, like all men, left parts of himself behind, carelessly. One of his smoking pipes still clamored in the cup holder when we drove across the railroad tracks, and hanging from the rearview mirror by a red ribbon was the desiccated claw of a pheasant my grandfather had shot. The talons had curled up into eerie spirals, its scales some primordial color between green and gold.

"How are we going to go anywhere?" I asked. My heart jumped. "I can't drive."

"Of course you can't. You're not driving. Crouch underneath the dash here. You're going to do the pedals and I'll be the eyes and the steering wheel."

The floor was littered with dead leaves and little stones. I tried not to get too close to the ends of Grandma Vi's legs, where her feet should have been. In the library, I'd been reading of contagious disease. But Grandma Vi settled her stumps on my back.

We practiced first. "Gas, gas, gas!" Grandma Vi shouted, and I pressed the big oblong pedal on the right. Now brake, slower, and I pushed the horizontal square.

Grandma put the car in reverse, and we lurched out the driveway.

"Not so hard, or we're going to hit someone," she shouted. "Now the gas again, slowly. Thank the Lord your grandfather got a deal on an automatic or there's no way we could do this. No time to teach you a clutch."

From the floor, I could feel the rumbling of the engine beneath me, like a great beast. My neck hurt from crouching.

"Woohoo," my grandmother yelled, "You're driving, Gret. You're driving!" She clapped her hands. "Hit the brake a bit now. Easy. We're passing Officer McMilligan, and I'm waving at him. Hi there, Officer McMilligan."

After we had pulled in safely to the hardware store parking lot, Grandma Vi let me pop up from the floor and gave me my instructions. "Get four plungers, a skein of rope, and a bottle of wood glue," she instructed. She wouldn't tell me why.

When I returned to the truck, a bouquet of plungers in my arms, Grandma Vi had her elbow hanging out of the driver's side window and she was chatting with a woman in the car beside her. Grandma Vi knew every white-haired lady in the whole town, and if you asked her about one, she could tell you all about her husband and her children and the time she accidently set the house of her husband's mistress on fire or how supposedly she had gone to visit her cousins for seven months but really lived at the home for unwed mothers in Minneapolis.

I hopped into the passenger's side of the cab.

"What's your little one got four plungers for?" the woman asked.

"Well, first of all, you're forgiven for being nosy, Darlene. It's that Lambertson coming out in you again. But you know I've got three toilets and one of them's in a heck of a lot of trouble."

The woman laughed. "Vivi, tact has never been your strong point."

"No, it hasn't," my grandma said, turning to me and giving a wink. "Don't you think I have the most beautiful granddaughter in town?"

"She is a pretty one," the white-haired woman said. She started her car. "Well, I'll see you at Holy Week services."

"No," Grandma Vi said quickly. "You won't. I think I've been to enough church for now. Not sure I'll go this year."

"Really?" The woman's penciled-on eyebrows rose to meet her fluffy hair. "That doesn't seem like you."

"Well, we're all new in the Lord," my grandma retorted, rolling up her window.

After the woman had driven away, Grandma Vi grinned. "Darlene had a thing for your grandfather," she said. "Of course, a lot of the girls did back then. But your grandpa Frank noticed me dancing at the Olswings' barn raising, and he was all mine. Whatever that meant for us."

"Was it love at first sight?" I asked.

"No, not that. But lucky for you that he saw me in the corner there, in my organdy with black high heels and my hair done just so. Pearl hair clips. I had pearl hair clips, and my hair was just your color, like the color of molasses against the snow, and not just the color of snow. Yes," she sighed. "You're a lucky one, Margaret. Thirteen had to come before you could squeak into the world. Now press that gas pedal. Gently now."

With that, we made our way home.

G randma Vi called my parents and let them know I'd be staying for supper.

We made her new feet with the plungers. I retrieved a saw from the musty garage, and we cut the wooden handles to the right length, so she wouldn't look too tall. "Better if I've shrunk a bit," she said. "They're used to that." Then she pulled off the rubber tops of the other set of plungers and worried them onto the free end of the handles. She tied the rope to either handle of the new double-sided plungers and then around her waist.

"We used to wear a contraption like this with our pantyhose," she said. "It was called a garter, although I think they've gone out of fashion. Except among ladies of the night."

"That's me!" I shouted, thinking of how she had said I had nocturnal eyes.

Grandma Vi laughed and nestled her leg in the suction cup of the plunger. "No, that's certainly not you, Gretta. Unless you marry for money, then you are not much better than a high-class prostitute. Marry for love, I'd say, but who knows where that will get you. Maybe where it got me. So many hungry stomachs to fill. And it's funny, every time I asked God for help, He sent me another baby."

For supper, we had beans and wieners and bread with butter. Grandma was quiet. In the past, she had been a great entertainer, and we would laugh until my spleen hurt. But that night she sat with her hands in her lap, and she appeared inanimate, tired. For the first time, I wondered if she might be lonely, living for so many years as a widow, her children spread out across the world in a chosen exile.

"Well, it's time for you to go home now," Grandma Vi said, when I had squashed the last bean underneath my fork, in an exaggerated way to try to make her laugh. "You know I'm not going to be able to drive you anymore."

"But it's dark," I said, trying to hide my panic.

It was a full mile to my parent's home, the road winding along the creek. Tall oak trees clawed at the sky—no leaves had yet budded— and there were few streetlights, for who walked those kinds of roads at night?

"You'll be fine. Just steel your courage." She touched my head. "Steel your courage, my night creature."

"Maybe we can call my mother and she can come and get me," I suggested.

"No," Grandma Vi said. "She'll be suspicious."

"You could tell her that the truck is broken," I offered.

"Absolutely not. Your parents cannot be involved here. Remember your promise to me."

"But my parents won't like me walking home alone at night."

"So don't tell them." Her eyes were unrelenting.

"But what if they ask? It's lying."

"It's not lying if your mother doesn't find out, because it is true in her mind."

I understand now why Grandma Vi was dangerous in the world, why my mother sometimes muttered about her, why my father avoided the house and hired someone to mow her lawn. Why her children had scattered. Because she spun things. Because what she wanted, she made true.

"We just have to get past the weekend, and then we're in the clear."

Halfway home, I felt a warm breath on my neck and burst into a sprint. The trees watched along the creek, and the feeling followed me all the way. I couldn't look back or then it seemed this banshee, with its hot breath, would be true.

My mother was busy, as always, juggling the baby and dozens of composition papers, and my father was up for tenure and analyzing lake core samples late into the night, so no one but Ginny noticed when I burst through the door, my breath heavy and sweat soaking my shirt.

I spent the week helping Grandma Vi practice her walk. We made a cane for her from a tall birch stick I had found near the creek. We took out the hems of all her pants and ironed them flat so they hung down to the floor and covered the plungers.

Friday afternoon, she put on some old Count Basie records and we danced around the living room. By then, she was pretty good with her plunger feet.

"Grandma, your skin looks tighter than it used to, shinier," I shouted over the trumpets.

"I know!" she exclaimed. "I'm un-aging. All those useless folds are falling away and making a sandy mess on my floor."

"But what will you say to everyone?" I asked.

"No one actually looks at an old woman. You spend your whole life being looked at—by men, by other women—and then you hit seventy-five, and poof, just like that, you're invisible. You'll see," Grandma Vi said. "Plus I've got some tricks anyway."

She was right. When Pamela and Tom arrived, Grandma Vi sat in the armchair in the corner and conjured up all the old quarrels.

"You look good, Mom," Pamela said as she bent down to kiss Grandma Vi's cheek.

"Oh, do I?" said Grandma Vi. "Do you think you could help me find a married man to steal away from his wife? I know you know how to do that."

My aunt Pamela was married to a lawyer with an ex-wife and a son around Ginny's age.

"Oh, don't even start with that," Pamela said. "You know that Bob was already divorced when I met him. I've told you that."

Grandma Vi shook her head as though in profound disappointment. "Did I raise you Catholic or not? In the eyes of God, marriage is a permanent and unbreakable bond. Bob and—what is his wife's name? Oh yes, Sheri—Bob and Sheri are joined together forever. That means that you're an adulterer. My little Pamela. I wouldn't have wanted that for you."

Aunt Pam made a growling noise from the back of her throat. "Jesus, Mom. This is why I don't bring Bob up to see you," she said and disappeared into the kitchen.

"So you're the same as ever, huh Mom?" Tom said from the doorway.

"Of course," Grandma Vi replied.

"Tom." My father nodded, just barely, at his older brother.

"Hey, little buddy," he said in return.

"William, you had better get your shoes on, just in case," Grandma Vi said, grinning at my father. "You might end up under the porch again." Then she looked at me and her right eye closed slowly, softly, in a subdued wink.

All week we had been working so Grandma Vi could have the Easter dinner without exposing the stumpy parts of her hands where her fingers should have been. I had mashed up yolks for deviled eggs and glazed the ham and chopped up fruit for the marshmallow Jello salads, all under strict instruction from Grandma Vi, who mainly watched from a chair we had brought the kitchen. She could no longer guide the knife in her good right hand. I had even peeled all the potatoes and slivered the onions for Grandma's famous Easter onion and potato soup. We had laughed, Grandma Vi and I, at the uncontrollable tears seeping from my eyes as I sliced the fat white onions. We had laughed until both of us were crying.

That Easter afternoon, the table had been set, the ham laid out, and the deviled eggs mostly eaten when Grandma Vi called me over to the stove.

"My hand fell into the soup," she hissed.

I peered into the pot, searching, I guess, for a remaining bit of the hand to spoon out.

"Oh, that's no use," Grandma Vi said. She waved the ladle in front of my face with her remaining hand, and then bent down close to my ear. "We've got to cover this up fast. Go get my heavier cardigan from the closet. The red one." A little blob of spit landed cold in my ear.

I went to get the cardigan, passing my family in the living room. "Grandma's cold," I said, although no one seemed to notice. My father and his brother were snarling at each other, some old hateful words, my mother and my aunt looking over old photo albums at the dining room table. The baby had been placed on a blanket on the floor and he was chewing on something indistinguishable and green. Ginny had disappeared to the attic.

When I returned to the kitchen, Grandma Vi had the ceramic bowls set in two rows on the counter and she was pouring out the first ladle of stew.

"Grandma, we can't eat that! Not with," I paused and then whispered hard. "Not with you in it."

"Nonsense. Every person in that room has eaten of me in some way or another. It won't do them any harm to do it again." Some odd revenge curled in her smile.

"But that would make everyone—"

"Cannibals? Of course not. Cannibals cook the flesh, and this is more like a seasoning. No need, anyway, to throw away a perfectly good soup." A couple more of her teeth had fallen out, and those that remained were dull gray, like unpolished river stones. If I hadn't known better, I might have thought I had been descended from a witch.

I thought of Ginny lapping up some of Grandma Vi, turning the spoon over in her mouth in that way she did that irritated my mother. My father, chomping on the meatballs, with Grandma Vi adding a saltiness that he would like. Baby Gregory slurping on a soupy Grandma Vi potato.

"Let me dish out the soup," I said. I took the ladle from her and opened up the sweater so she could put her arms through. "You should go sit down in the dining room and tuck your arm underneath the table before someone notices what's missing from it."

She hesitated.

"I'll get the soup and I'll bring out the salads too. Ginny will help me. Just tell them that we wanted to play waitress."

I heard her hobbling into the dining room. Sometimes the plungers that cupped her legs made a suction noise, but no one else seemed to notice.

The pot steamed. Shaking, I took my index finger and stuck it as far down my throat as I could. Ann-Marie said her older sister did this when she wanted to lose weight. After several tries I expelled a spew of chocolate Easter bunnies and egg whites. The vomit floated on the top.

Then I walked into the dining room. My eyes were watery from the force of my gut.

"I threw up in the soup," I declared. I couldn't look at Grandma Vi.

"You what?" my mother said.

"I'm so sorry. I threw up in the soup."

Uncle Tom let out a great howl from the living room.

"Oh, Gretta." My mother drew me to her and put the back of her hand on my forehead.

"Looks like nobody will want to take any of my saltines then," Tom called.

"You mean you vomited in my Easter soup," my grandma said, ending on a shrill pitch.

I couldn't look at her. I kept my head down and nodded.

"In the soup. My special Easter soup. How did you manage that?"

"I don't know. It just happened."

"Well, it's official," Grandma Vi said. "Thanks to Gretta, we won't have enough to eat. And I am sure the grocery isn't open."

"That's not true," Pamela said. "We have an entire roast of ham."

"Vivian, it is hardly the girl's fault for getting sick," my mom said.

"And it's hardly my fault that your daughters are as spoiled as rotten meat," Grandma Vi said. "All Virginia does is hunt up in that attic for things to take from me. And now this from her." Her lips puckered with distaste, as though she couldn't even bear to speak my name.

"Now, that's ridiculous," my mother said. "Gretta has been really good about coming to see you. And why would she have chosen to ruin your soup?"

"Yeah, Grandma Vi," I said, lifting my head and meeting her eyes. "Why would I want to ruin your soup?" I sounded like a brat.

Grandma Vi and I stared at each other. Her eyes seemed bigger than usual and a long strand of white hair had fallen from the nest on her head and hung all the way down her back. I wanted to tell, but I knew if I told she would never speak to me again. Instead I ran past the table and past Tom and my father in the living room.

"Someone a little upset?" Tom asked

"Let her go," I heard my mother say as I opened the door to the porch, "She's a preteen now. That phase of life starts earlier with every generation. "

Two weeks passed before I returned to Grandma Vi's. I walked the long way home from school, down Washington, where there were no sidewalks, big hunting trucks splattering mud on my clothes.

I continued my studies in the library, although I had found nothing yet. No textbook mentioned a tightening of the skin, a dissolution of the cells, a disintegrating of all the parts of the body. I ordered more books, from other colleges. I have never found anything, not in all my training. In science class, we were divided up by gender. The boys went outside to play kickball, and the nurse came to talk to the girls about our blossoming bodies, the ripening of motherly parts, our journeys into womanhood, how our bodies would change, even if we willed them not to, as this changing was the will of God. Nothing was said about the monthly bloodletting, the pearl-colored ovaries, or the ostium abdominale spreading outwards like many-fingered hands, or how the moon would pull us in some unknown way, as it pulled the tides.

Once or twice I rode by Grandma Vi's on my bike. The bungalow was still. A shiver played along my spine, but I turned my head and rode straight ahead, wondering if Grandma Vi had seen me through the window.

On May Day, Ann-Marie had left a plastic cup with chocolate pudding mud and little gummy worms on my doorstep, which I took to be a good sign, even if she wasn't yet talking with me at school. We would have the summer to patch things up, and the spring had already exploded in a loud green.

"So you finally learned what a bitch Grandma is," Ginny said one afternoon.

"No. That's not it. You shouldn't use that word."

"Why haven't you been to see her?" Ginny swung her long legs over the arm of the couch. "Don't you miss her? You must have known you wouldn't always be her special pet."

"I'm no one's pet."

"Well, I'm sorry Grandma turned on you," Ginny said. "But it's good for you to learn."

"Jesus Christ, Ginny," I said, unable to contain myself.

"You shouldn't take the name of our Lord and Savior in vain."

"And you don't know everything," I said. "As a matter of fact, I was actually going to see Grandma right now."

"Yeah, right," she said. "You're hilarious." She gave a fake hoot. Her mouth was purple from a leftover May Day sucker.

I rang the doorbell first and then knocked. For many minutes, I heard only the sound of the robins newly returned. At the neighbor's house, the telephone rang.

"Grandma," I finally shouted, pushing the door open. "It's me. Gretta."

The voice came from the corner chair. "You are my granddaughter. But obviously not entirely. You're not as stubborn as Frank and I were. That's from your mother's side, I think. We wouldn't have returned at all. But you are here." The voice was higher than hers was, as though it had been wound up.

"Grandma?"

"Here you are, back to visit me."

"Grandma?" I couldn't see her. The light in the room was dusky and yellowed.

Her long white hair spread out along the seat of the armchair.

I didn't come any closer.

"I'm on the armchair. I'm not quite myself right now."

"Are you okay?" I asked.

"Oh, I'm fine," she said. "I just need you to do something. Take me outside."

"But—" I inched closer, slowly. The wooden floorboards creaked with my approach. I caught a glimmer of light in front of my feet, and noticed then the white sand trailing all over the floor, along the davenport and continuing into the dining room.

"Margaret, just do this. This thing for me."

I came up upon her. She was little more than a sack of potatoes, a jumble of fleshy parts that I didn't recognize and a crevice for a mouth and two big eyes at the top.

"I don't know how," I said, my voice rising up to a kind of scream, my hands clenched.

"Calm down," she said with a squeak. "I haven't been outside in weeks now and I want to go out. I'm sitting on this blanket. Just pick me up, the way you would a little baby."

"I can't."

"Yes, you can."

"But why?" I could hear the trembling in my voice. "I'm going to call someone to help us."

"No. Don't call anyone. Don't you dare." Then she was softer. "We should go outside because I want to see the sun again. And because you are my granddaughter and we should have a picnic."

I waited a minute, shaking, and then I held my breath and picked up the blanket as gently as I could.

Bits of luminous sand fell out everywhere, scattering on the wooden floor.

I screamed.

"Calm down," Grandma Vi said from my arms.

"I'm dropping you all over the floor," I shrieked.

"Don't worry about that. We'll get that later. Just get me outside."

She felt lighter already. Keeping my arms as still as I could, I used my shoulder to open the latch of the screen door and walked down the porch stairs. I had to be careful not to trip over her hair, which came down in front of me and dragged on the ground along my feet.

"To the back," Grandma Vi said, more quietly.

The skies were the blue of a vein and a warm prairie wind had broken from the south. The afternoon moon watched us.

When we got to the backyard, I noticed she was siphoning out of the cracks on either side of the blanket, the parts where the blanket had been folded.

"Grandma Vi. Grandma, I'm losing you all over."

"How does the garden look?" she asked.

"Good," I lied. It was too early in the season to be much more than a bare patch of earth. "It's turning green. The daises are starting to—"

"Gretta. Hey," Grandma interrupted, no more than a tiny squeak. "Never mind, just, when you tell it, when you tell about me, don't you tell about this."

The wind picked up and caught her long hair. Pieces soared into the air, breaking apart and lifting higher. A few little birds came and picked at the flying strands.

The blanket blew open. Her eyes fell out and rolled like two stones down the small hill to the garden.

Perhaps I was screaming then; I cannot remember.

She was spilling out from my hands, slipping through the cracks in my fingers and the smallness of my palms. Not knowing what else to do, how else to keep her safe, protected from the wind, I brought my right palm to my mouth.

We have very little to offer one another, but we have our bodies. At the Mass it is said to take and eat, do this for the remembrance of me. Although not one of us has asked for the feast, we are given and partake of it.

My grandma Vi was not sand, after all, but sugar. And salt.

On Romance

PARIS STREET

Susan Sterling

Elaine is such a good friend that when I meet her one afternoon in late summer, walking along a dusty road, I don't pause to think of my own destination. I forget where I am going, that I am going anywhere, in fact.

She twists a plume of goldenrod in her hands and tosses back her long dark hair, hair men tend to fall in love with. Her green eyes are troubled. "Do you have time to look at something?" she asks.

"Sure," I say, and we walk back together along the road, taking a turn where it bends back into town. There on the outskirts the small wood houses are all crammed together, tumbling on top of each other so that you can practically lean out your window and hang your damp clothes on a neighbor's clothesline. They are all in need of repair, these houses—peeling paint, broken porches. Still, they have an erratic charm. Children linger in the doorways. Purple asters bloom around the woodpiles. People are poor here, but they don't think so much of that in August. They forget the unpaid fuel bills, the lack of winter boots. All that comes later, maybe never. While the evenings are balmy, it makes sense to sit out on the front stoop, drinking a few beers and listening to the quarreling songs of the cicadas.

This afternoon, though, the neighborhood is strangely silent. There is no one in the yards, not even a stray cat.

"I didn't know you'd been here," I say to Elaine.

"Well, yes," she says and takes me down an alley I've never noticed before, into a street—Paris Street, reads the sign—that I've never seen on maps. At the end two small houses squat close together, finding shelter in each other's shadows.

We peer through a window of one house, into a living room where a tall man with thin yellow hair sits on a sofa reading a book. Or pretending to read, because from the angle of the window I see that he is gazing at a letter concealed in the book's pages. His hands tremble. Then he sighs and kisses the letter. I worry that we're intruding on his sorrow, and I'm about to suggest that we leave when Elaine steps back into the shadow of the other house.

"He's fallen in love with me," she confides. "That's my letter he's reading."

"Well, what's wrong with that?"

"He's married. He has a wife and children. I don't know what to do!"

The fragrant aroma of rosemary and roast chicken drifts from the back of the house. Inside a woman begins singing "Three Blind Mice" in a wobbly soprano. Then she stops. "Get me a tomato, Love, then wash your hands."

"Don't get involved with him!" I say, feeling cross. As if someone had given me a cup of tea leaves to read in which I see nothing but abandonment and disaster for my friend.

"Ah," says Elaine unhappily. "But if you knew..." She glances at the neighboring house. "He wants me to move in here. Then he could slip over afternoons when she's at work and the children are in school. It wouldn't be permanent. But for a while ... until I feel better ..." Her voice falters.

"But you'd hear her singing in the mornings!" I say. "You'd see his children riding their trikes on the sidewalk! Maybe they'd play with your children. So many lives could be ruined!"

"I know" she says. "I lie awake nights and think about it."

We walk back down Paris Street and through a patch of woods. We come to the river and stand on the bank, watching the current drift along. A school of black fish darts past. Just beyond where the river bends, we come upon a yellow house. At first it looks as if it's about to tumble down the bank into the water, but as we approach I see that it's sturdier than it first appears. The green shutters look vaguely familiar. I take a step up the walk.

Elaine grabs my arm. "Don't go up there!"

"Why not?"

"There's a hole in the floor. You might fall through!"

"You've been inside?"

"I live here. I've made curtains and tried to make it homey. But it doesn't feel like home. And there's no bottom to that hole." She takes a deep breath. "Now you understand. And I'm sure there's no hole in the house next to his. I've been inside."

For a moment I don't know what Elaine is talking about. "But Elaine," I say. "This isn't your house. There are geraniums by your front porch, and it's painted cream, not yellow, and there certainly isn't a hole in your floor. You have an Oriental rug in the hall. Your house isn't even near a river!"

Then I look more closely at the shutters. One of Elaine's filmy nightgowns flaps on the clothesline. Her son's red bike is leaning against a tree. A pathetic looking rosebush grows by the cellar door.

We are silent for a moment, listening to the crickets chirping in the field.

I take a deep breath, deciding to humor her, go along with her fantasy about the hole. "Okay, Elaine, even if there is a hole. You can fix it! You don't have to leave it the way it is!"

Elaine rests her hand on my arm. "Maybe you're right." Her green eyes brim with relief. "What would I do without you?"

"You don't need him, Elaine," I say.

She gazes at the pine woods on the far side of the river, lost again in her thoughts. "Perhaps we could still meet for afternoon picnics. I wouldn't have to sleep with him again. He's been so kind."

"He isn't kind at all," I protest. "A man who would abandon his own family? I can tell he's no good."

By this time it's way past closing at the library. I will have to forego the novel I wanted to borrow for another week. But it doesn't matter. How can I concentrate on a novel, seeing nothing but black clouds on the horizon for my friend? I cut a few asters from Elaine's garden, remembering a similar conversation we had years ago. Then she had fallen in love with a man who was so afraid of losing her that she felt as if he'd tied her to him with a rope. She mostly sensed it when she tried to go off by herself. When they sat together in the evening and talked, she wasn't troubled at all. Nor when they made love. It appeared the rope even enhanced their lovemaking, though she never could explain exactly how. She confided in me for a year, then decided to marry him. "He has a wonderful mind," she explained.

"Elaine," I'd urged her then. "What about the rope!" For months she'd been bringing me pieces of frayed hemp, showing me the marks on her wrists. I made her herbal teas to increase her strength. I begged her not to marry him. Though in the end she disregarded my advice, Elaine was always grateful. She does not take affection for granted; that's one thing that makes her a wonderful friend.

Now, standing on the porch, I assure Elaine that life holds more for her than this tawdry affair. Then I go home, make spaghetti for my husband and children, and feed the dog. We read *Goodnight Moon* and look at the stars through the telescope. After the children fall asleep, my husband and I make love. The weight of his body burns against mine, but when he tenderly kisses the nape of my neck, I feel only half there because I am thinking about Elaine.

The next morning I find a large piece of white paper in the attic and make a sketch of this man who claims to love my friend. Then I tape the picture up on the closet door and toss darts at it until the face is full of pinpricks. This is satisfying, but after an hour of dart throwing, I see that the eyes I've sketched are sad and full of yearning. Who knows what sorrows have drawn him to Elaine? Perhaps he will be better for her than the man with the rope, who disappeared, leaving her with two small children to raise. Do I want to deprive her of the consolation of their picnics? I imagine the two of them, lying on the bank, eating strawberries. Cows meander through the grasses, regarding them with soulful eyes. Perhaps Elaine and the man can just be friends?

(No, I decide, crumbling up my drawing. How can you go back to being friends, once you've indulged adulterous love?)

Every afternoon then, for the next few weeks, Elaine and I take a walk in the woods near the river. We talk about her lover: he wants Elaine but is afraid to leave his wife unless Elaine promises to love him forever. We talk about other things as well: the changes in Eastern Europe, our children, recent movies we've seen. We've always been drawn to the same romantic novels. We love obscure treatises by herb-growing monks, the letters of missionary balloonists, nineteenth century prints. As we tramp through the fallen leaves, we recite lines from Shakespearean plays, whole scenes we once memorized in school. We collect richly flavored mushrooms. We carry umbrellas in the rain.

This has been my plan: I've decided that if I keep Elaine busy every afternoon she won't be tempted to do something foolish. But after a few weeks I become restless. I want to spend those hours reading, or talking to the friends I've been neglecting during Elaine's crisis. I still haven't been to the library. But if I leave Elaine on her own, even for a few afternoons, will she believe again that her house has a hole plunging through its floor? Will she seek comfort in the arms of another woman's husband, another family's father?

And then, one September afternoon I fall under a spell myself. I go to a matinee at the local movie theater and catch a glimpse of the projectionist bent over the reels of film up in his tiny booth. His eyes, reflected in the faint glow of the projector bulb, are dark blue, like the sea. As he holds a reel up to the light to thread it, his mouth takes on an intense set, as if he were holding the mysteries of the universe in his hands. I recall then a couple I saw on a cruise ship before I was married. It was a moonlit night and they were dancing alone at the far end of the deck while a jazz band played bright tunes. The woman was wearing a white dress, and the man had a low, tender voice that wove in and out of the ragged notes of the saxophone.

Then the lights of the theater dim, and the movie begins—an adventure story about Africa. When it is over, I turn in my seat, pretending to look for my program. The projectionist is leaning over the projector, watching the reel click backward. He smiles to himself, and I believe that he has been inhabiting his booth forever, indifferent to weather and the rise and fall of political fortunes.

That night I lie next to my husband, obsessed with strange yearnings. I rest my hand on his shoulder as he drifts away into his own dreams. I believe in marriage; I love my husband. And yet it seems cruel to me that I will never find happiness with the projectionist.

After that I find myself at the theater nearly every afternoon, taking the same rickety seat near a poster for Olivier's Henry V. From this vantage I can turn and see the projection booth without bringing attention to myself. I watch as the projectionist runs a hand through his dark beard. I worry about a jagged scar I glimpse over his left eye. He moves about the booth decisively, a man who has never been caught in the currents of self-doubt.

All that autumn, I see the same films over and over, with all the old stars—Humphrey Bogart, Bette Davis, Fred Astaire. I am transported to exotic places where I feel the pain of unrequited love, of romances that are doomed. And throughout these afternoons the intense, brooding features of the projectionist are projected in my mind over the rugged faces of the screen heroes. He smiles passionately. A man who is devoted to me. Who brings me yellow roses, tells me I have changed his life.

One afternoon just after Thanksgiving I meet Elaine at a cafe downtown. We sit at a table overlooking the street. I apologize for not having seen her for so long, but she assures me she did not feel abandoned.

"How are things?" I ask.

She stares at the water in her glass. For the first time I'm aware of her resemblance to the delicately wan women in the pre-Raphaelite paintings we both love. Knights in silvery armor. Lush green woods. Damsels in brocaded gowns.

"Not so good," she says. "He left his wife and children for me. Actually she found out about our afternoons in the house and asked him to leave, though she still loves him. Because she still loves him. I still can hear her singing in the kitchen, do you remember? We both feel so guilty."

This strikes me as an indulgent sort of guilt, but Elaine looks so stricken that I refrain from saying anything. She sighs. "He truly wants me. He tells me I have changed his life. He brings me yellow roses."

"But that's lovely!" I feel a reluctant envy, remembering my dreams of the projectionist. "What's wrong with that?"

"I'm tired of roses." Her eyes are warm and searching. "I need your advice. I don't know if I want him. What should I do?" A faint line deepens in her forehead, and she takes a bite of poppy seed cake.

I run my finger along the fronds of a potted fern and stare out the window at the empty street. Once I saw Elaine's life so clearly. Much more clearly than my own. It was as if I had the privilege of looking down on it from a great height. Her choices seemed to lie spread out like labeled roads on a map, their consequences obvious to me, if not to her. But that vantage is no longer mine, if in fact I ever had it. Besides, Elaine has never followed my advice. Things must look different to her than they do to me; otherwise she wouldn't take the turns she does.

I lean my elbows on the table, trying not to be dissuaded by her hopeful smile. "You're my oldest friend, Elaine. And I love being with you. But I can't tell you what you should do."

"You've always known before!" she protests.

"I haven't. I only thought I did."

"I can't believe that."

"It's true."

Outside, someone begins whistling "The Days of Wine and Roses." The front door opens, and the air in the cafe suddenly smells of snow.

I glance at Elaine, and her face seems to be drifting away, like a ghost image on a film.

Then I have a sudden inspiration. "Look," I say. "There's a matinee of *Gone with the Wind* this afternoon. Why don't we go?"

The theater is dark when we walk in. I lead Elaine to my usual place, near the poster of Lawrence Olivier. At the end of the movie we both weep when Rhett Butler tells Scarlet he doesn't give a damn.

"Did you see the projectionist?" I ask hesitantly as we are walking away under the marquee. In a few days it will be December; the theater lights are already twinkling in the early twilight. "Did you see how tenderly he threads the reel?" But Elaine shakes her head. She hasn't noticed him at all.

The next afternoon I arrive at the theater early for *A Farewell to Arms*. I walk into the lobby and I'm startled to see the projectionist selling candy and soda behind the counter. Perhaps the concessions girl is sick? I slip into the theater without buying my usual popcorn. I don't dare to risk hearing his voice, as if it might disappoint me—a silent screen hero who should never risk the change to talking movies.

After a few minutes, the theater doors close. When I turn around the projectionist is just entering his booth. He glances out over the theater, and in that moment his blue eyes appear so ordinary, his smile lacking in mystery. He looks like anyone you could pass on the street without thinking much about him. I escape as Ingrid Bergman tells Gary Cooper she's never kissed a man before. I'm tired of spending my afternoons in the dark eating popcorn. I've fallen out of love with popcorn as well.

This is, clearly, a story to share with Elaine. What can I tell her about disenchantment? The streetlights turn on as I walk out of the theater. Though I haven't been back to Paris Street since Elaine took me there,

I find my way without difficulty. The two houses lean—even more uneasily it seems to me tonight—into each other's shadows.

A wind rises in the trees. A faint light emanates from one of the houses. I walk up to it and, standing on my tiptoes, peer in through a window. The front room is empty, but I can see into the room beyond where Elaine and the man with yellow hair are seated at a card table. The man holds Elaine's hand and gazes fervently into her eyes. She, however, looks very far away, as if she were barely inhabiting her own body. They don't see me. A candle flickers on the table. I follow Elaine's glance to a red poinsettia on the mantel, then down to a broken place in the floorboards, dark and jagged, like an ink stain.

My heart goes out to Elaine. I try to call to her, but the wind muffles my voice, or perhaps the windowpanes are too thick, or I simply can't speak. The man gets up and stacks three logs on the fireplace, then struggles to get a fire going with some newspaper. Elaine puts her head in her hands. Down the street a dog barks, a bottle shatters. It's turning cold, but still I can't bring myself to leave. I stand in the shadows, keeping watch, while the stars come out above the shabby roof.

BECOMING

Ivy Rutledge

Delilah had been trying to get Henry's full attention all through the evening, to no avail. While they were window shopping, he was looking back out over the street. During dinner he kept glancing at his watch and the other diners. Now, the thing that got his attention was a bird.

The bird was bright and stunningly out of place in the wet gloomy downtown Savannah park. He was perched on a low branch, and his long sapphire blue plumage jutted out among the gray draped beards of Spanish moss.

She gasped at his beauty and completely forgot all about the aloof boy she was with. The bird was blue with streaks of silver like a brilliant night sky lit up by a shower of stars. The slender tendrils of curled plumage extended behind him twice his length, with matching feathers extending from his crown.

She was drawn to the bird the way bored women are drawn to shop windows full of lovely goods. Walking up to the tree, she realized that Henry was by her side, close, touching her elbow with his fingertips.

"Look, Henry!" she whispered.

"Yes, I see. Be careful, don't get too close or you'll scare him."

Delilah heeded his advice and slowed her steps. She took a long look at Henry, who was looking at her. They stood together, closer than they had been all night, as though this was the moment the date had been leading up to. The bird cocked its head and looked down at them, but mostly at her.

"It's looking at me, I think it likes me!"

"Be quiet and still, and hold out your arm. Like a branch."

She did as he said and extended her arm.

"Hold it steady now," said Henry. "Now wait. See what he does, maybe he'll perch there."

Delilah stood holding her breath, afraid to look at the bird in case she scared it away. Her arm started to ache, holding it so level was a challenge her yoga teacher had been trying to prepare her for, but now she regretted her lack of effort.

Then, in a flash, the bird flew down to her arm and landed just below her elbow, gently curling its claws around the flesh of her forearm. It was smaller than she had guessed seeing it so far up in the tree. Just over eight inches, she guessed, taking a good look at it and smiling broadly at Henry.

"Now what?" she asked.

"Just stand quietly, let him get used to you."

"How do you know so much about birds?"

"I grew up with a pet bird, he was special and was my friend. We both grew up though," Henry said, and the story stopped there.

The bird craned his neck up and looked at Delilah expectantly. She gingerly ran the side of her hand down the nape of his neck and he seemed to coo at her.

After more back and forth between Delilah and her new bird friend, it was decided that she would take him home to live with her. He seemed like a magical creature, and she was excited about having a bird with her during lonely days writing in her apartment.

Henry knew just what to do, and Delilah soaked up his sudden attentiveness. They stopped off at a supply store where Henry went in and came back out shortly with a large cage and some food. Her apartment sat silent, and upon crossing the threshold the bird began a throaty hum that sounded almost like a harp. It was angelic, and Delilah believed he felt happy.

She didn't even notice that Henry slipped out at some point. She was so enthralled with her new pet. The days passed, and she didn't hear from him, and she wished she'd said, "Goodbye, Henry, thank you for the bird!" With each passing day her hopes dwindled that he would call her.

With each passing day the bird became more and more accustomed to her routine. She found him waiting for her on her nightstand when she awoke, then on the edge of the sink as she got out of the shower, and he was waiting on the coat rack when she returned from the market.

She named him Streak, for the lucky streak he seemed to have brought her and for the silver streaks in his blue feathers. Since she had brought him home with her, she had sold oodles of stories, and her fortunes were increasing.

Streak listened to her attentively, he chimed while she sat at her desk typing away, and he sang her to sleep at night. He started to sit on her shoulder, her elbow, her lap. He came closer and closer, landing on her foot, resting on her big toe as she lounged on her balcony. There was no fear that Streak would fly away, in fact, quite the contrary. Streak seemed intent on staying near her.

She stopped setting his place at the dinner table, but he'd be there anyway. He'd slowly inch his way to her, sliding his feet on the wood. Shuddering, she'd slide him back; he'd look at her and rumble an apology. But moments later the sliding would begin anew.

She'd wake to find him on her pillow waiting and looking. Occasionally he'd preen her at sunrise, and she felt maddened to be woken so early in the morning by a crazy bird.

"Shoo! Go somewhere else!" she'd say.

"Cheee cheee," he'd chime back at her and nestle into her underarm, which tickled her, but she remained upset. Wherever he could fit himself on her body, he would be. And when she would fling him gently away from her, his body would swipe across the room and spin around, his plumage swishing through the air, then he would meander right back into orbit around her.

Sometimes when she was writing she'd feel him rubbing her legs, back and forth, back and forth. The petty motion made it hard for her to work, but she tried to forge ahead and write her stories. Her stories grew darker, with few threads of hope in them.

She had taken to closing the bathroom door at times, for privacy, but the relentless pecking would begin immediately. She'd turn on the radio while she bathed, in an attempt to drown out the sound, but she could hear him, pecking and hurling his body against the door in harmony with the song she was playing.

She left her apartment and went to the park to write, and enjoyed herself for a little while. But, she always had to return home, for she was new in town and had nowhere else to go. And there he would be, waiting to climb underneath into the folds of her long skirt and make her dance.

After a month of this she began to seethe. The bird had become a ball and chain. Finally boiling over, her anger turned to shock when she shook her fist at the bird and felt a pop, heard a pling and watched in horror as a silver feather sprang from her shoulder.

"You did this!" she raged at Streak, who sat perched on her other shoulder with his eyes wide. He tried to sing her his most soothing song, but she would have none of it. Within the hour, she had grown feathers across her shoulders and on the back of her neck. They were mostly silver, and they matched his streaks. As her anger melted into fear and sadness and the daylight faded, she curled up on the couch and cried.

Her tears brought smaller, lighter feathers on her belly and forehead. She lay motionless for days, weeping. Then she got up, brushed herself off and stood up straight. Pulling her shoulders back she took a good long look in the mirror.

The anger feathers were silver, and the sadness ones were pale blue. She had to admit that they were lovely feathers. Streak nodded. Out of her head sprouted a delicate fernlike green plume, barely three inches long. Yes, the green feather was becoming.

After several days away from her desk, she had lots of writing to do. She sat and typed for hours, but as she typed her hands began to tighten up, and her fingers began to slide on the keys as sharp claws sprouted from her fingertips.

Despair brought on a flurry of silvery blue feathers along her arms.

She sent off her last article, then walked away from her desk. As she walked, her legs shortened and became hardened and strong, her feet spread out and clicked on the floor. She glared at Streak.

"Why is this happening?"

"Because you needed me, you wanted me."

"Not like this!"

"But consider this, open up to it," he said.

Her continued fuming mixed with occasional feelings of lightness. Eventually her pride softened, though, and she allowed herself to feel more free. She even took a test glide across her living room while Streak watched and flapped his wings in approval. She liked the attention, and noted that the true love feathers were sprouting a brilliant jade green.

Bit by bit, Delilah learned to love being a bird. It took a few more weeks to completely embrace her birdness, but with each passing day she grew smaller and lighter and prettier. Soon she couldn't reach her desk or stove. And with each passing day she loved Streak for this surprising gift to her.

Eventually they realized that they didn't need to stay in her apartment any longer. Streak suggested they fly to the park where they first met, and she fluttered her wings in agreement.

It was her first long flight, and she started on the wall of her balcony, took a deep breath, then plunged. Air swirled around her and lifted her wings, and she glided and circled with delight leaving a sparkling trail of air in her wake. Streak and Delilah raced, dove and spun their way to the park, that square of trees and benches with a fountain in the middle and couples walking hand in hand.

They perched high in a magnolia and watched the lovers and families. By then, Delilah's feathers were mostly green, with streaks of silver and blue. Then Delilah saw Henry, and her face flushed as she remembered that night, her longing for him.

"That's Henry, that's the man I was with when I met you."

"Yes, I know. Henry didn't think he'd ever be able to find someone for me."

Shannon Gibney

What he wanted was not so unusual. To live a life full of meaning, yet not bereft of comfort. To come to the end of a hallway, detect a door, open it, and then finally, walk through.

He, a mass of bubbling neurons that no one could isolate into matter or even anti-matter. He, whose entire center fluctuated daily, traveling in and out of biospheres and worm holes, past amber atmospheres of sulfur. He who had no shape.

He who had never witnessed a triangle, could never dream of a hexagon. He whose first word was rupture, when what he had wanted to say was rapture.

He who saw the star bomb itself into bits just by chance, taking NGC 4414 by the corners, anxious to elide the peculiar gravitational pull of its neighboring, whirring galaxy, when Boom! All silence amassed in the space that wasn't space within and without him, and he could almost hear for the first time...And what it said was * * * * *.

He saw her then, the eulogy for the nothing at the center of all those spinning stars, the dark matter, the silence, the silence, and he wanted to be her. * * * * *. Hungry, grabbing hands that took even light and stretched it into more nothing. He could feel the peace of it, her emptiness everywhere. If only he were the same, he could bear the loneliness, knowing that he had become something that already was, and would never end. He could finally let go of his him-ness.

But he could not find her. She turned herself into a parsec, and then became a circle circumnavigating itself. He became a parsec, and tried to circumnavigate her, but she had already devolved into dust. Still moving, she transpired into clouds of violet, and he conjured himself the same, but the tint was not as brilliant, the shape not as seamless, and he knew, disdainfully, that he was still him. He brooded there for millennia, building a hyperspectral eye to watch her with, but the eye was not curious, and chose to simply stare at him. It had no desire to move. Unlike him, it had no desire to be her, so he had to abandon it.

In the planets, the gravitational fields, he fell, allowing his disappointment to fester and spread. Where were the galaxies he had once pinned to his lapel? Where were her solar eyelashes, burning the soot of spacetime? Without her, he had no idea how to move, or even how to feel. His thoughts were slowly freezing in the vacuum of darkness, until they cracked and were gone. Where is my * * * * *? he shouted...but the shout was more like a caught breath in the outline of his half-formed trachea.

And then, finally, she snapped before him, a quantum particle of indescribable dimensions. She was the interaction, the particle, and the system, to be exact. She generated her own energy, and was too complex for elementary excitations such as his. Her smallness amplified everything the world had ever lost, her nimbleness the possibilities of cross-dimensional touch. He tried to collapse himself, or whatever he thought he was, into her, before she could move, or even detect his presence, but he had miscalculated: She wasn't actually a particle, but a quasi-particle, behaving for just a moment like a particle before disappearing into the vagaries of the system.

His thoughts became long, hairy fingernails, and his disappointment mutated into a muscular, taught torso. He grew legs before he could pry open his enormous ears, and the first breath of his incipient lungs almost annihilated him. In panic, he turned toward where she had been an instant before, but she was already gone. He roared his animate body, and flung it towards Jupiter's unknown brother, the planet Keqwi, in the Elbriap System.

THE DIVIDED STATES OF AMERICA

Lucille Gang Shulklapper

"In the year 2052, the second civil war, fought between the wealthy and the poor, divided The United States," Jeremy Shader told his students.

"Where were you?" asked Harley Whitehead, scratching a patch of baldness on his close-shaved scalp. The teenagers settled themselves in their rotating seats. Some wore shoes this morning as the cold started to settle through the rotting window frames. The newest fad was to wear shoes that had cut out holes in the toes. The bigger the hole, the stronger you were. The toe had become a symbol of power.

"I was living in what used to be known as the inner city in New York State. Before New York and the other states became separate countries. I made a map last night to show you what the United States looked like thirty years ago."

"My father said you're cool for an old man, Mr. Shader. Iced. He said you were in your twenties and you fought for the poor people even though you were rich. That true?"

"Yes."

Jeremy stared at the dying branches of an apple tree from the windowed wall and continued the lesson.

Later, as he picked his way up six flights of stairs to his studio apartment, he watched the slanted light fall upon the children playing on the stairs. He could smell urine and he took a deep breath when he reached the fourth landing, hoping to inhale the cooking odors from behind Mavis Smith's closed door.

He sensed her waiting, could almost see her full-hipped body tense in the narrow kitchen. The door opened. Inside, the pungent odor of the stew, the cloves of peeled garlic, assailed his nostrils. "Looks and smells like the galley of my father's yacht," he told her, and she laughed.

"Well, I'm much too young to remember anything like that." She moved between the counters, sliding the drawers open, rummaging through mismatched cooking utensils, until at last she held up the slotted spoon she used to stir the vegetable stew. They both sensed the moment when he could see the rounded outline of her breasts push against her red sweater as she raised her arm and waved the spoon in the air.

She undressed quickly and pulled him toward her. "I'm sterile," she told him. "I can never marry. Have you fathered a child?"

"Yes. He would have been a few years older than you."

"Then…. you…"

"Yes. The government decreed limited breeding powers to survivors."

She paused and searched his eyes. Then she reached up and pointed the camera toward the wall and Jeremy forgot about the technicians who listened to sound waves when voices were inaudible. He lost himself in her flesh, heard her moan, and felt remembered joy.

The red light on the camera blinked and three short bells rang in their ears.

Covering themselves with bedsheets, Jeremy and Mavis aimed the camera toward themselves and punched separate codes into the transformer. "Permission granted," boomed a voice from the overhead speakers and those located in the flooring. "Your merger will be approved."

Mavis was one of fifty queens cloned with sterile eggs. Despite their differences in age and race, the government approved, and proclaimed their marriage over loudspeakers through the streets. No longer forbidden to marry, Mavis promised the government full disclosure of her new life in exchange. "Merger of War Hero with Queen," traveled by sound waves into the lake and forest regions of the domed country.

"Congrats," Harley later said, slapping Jeremy on the back. "Can I have your apartment?" Which meant that Harley was his official watchdog.

Mavis kept all of her computer chips in the right places. She came from a long line of genetic food engineers. There was her photograph on the interspace; the toothy smile, the yellow-streaked green hair falling into her round hazel eyes. The cutting board loaded with diced hothouse vegetables, pureed melons, and exotic tea leaves.

And he had fallen hard. Wanting her consumed him. The microphone in his brain chip echoed in his body. The government followed his brain waves and allowed him pleasure.

Only at night, the demons awakened him from sleep, speaking in the foreign English language of his past. "What's wrong?" Mavis inquired, and then covered her mouth, knowing that Harley and all the technicians could listen if they chose. And he thrust himself upon her, leaving the camera turned toward them, hoping they preferred to watch, than listen. He whispered in Old English, and as he did, she opened herself and took him in.

The next day, Harley demanded to know what Jeremy whispered to Mavis. His monitor had recorded nothing. "Of course, I'll tell you," Jeremy replied. "I'm not certain if Mavis is a true clone or if she has flaws and will turn against me to further her needs. She weakens me at night as you well may know."

Harley's slitted eyes narrowed as they traveled over Jeremy's tall, slim-waisted frame. He stuck his big toe in Jeremy's face. "Tell me what she wants from you and I'll look after it," he declared.

"She wants a baby," Jeremy said.

The technicians came and took Mavis to Center while Jeremy was at school. Waves of music surged through Jeremy's head. Mavis had been altered.

"My brain waves have been reset," she told Jeremy. "I endured the pain because I want to stay with you."

Jeremy knew about Center. Could still hear his son Blake's dying screams. And those of his wife, Kendra, who tried to protect Blake. He recalled the vaporized faces of family and friends, marked x for enemy on their foreheads, whenever a low moaning sound filled his head. Mind chatter, the government called it.

The demons shrilled in his ears until one night an iron arm glided out from the wall and operated on him. He now found relief by rubbing the patch of skin on his forehead where a computer chip had been embedded.

Mavis had a collection of knives for cooking. Her cleaver, a paring knife, and bread knife, with serrated or sharp pointed edges were always on hand. "Let me help you," Jeremy insisted. "Of course," Mavis complied, gazing into the camera.

"Now you can teach us to prepare our own food," Harley said, biting into a luscious pear that Mavis had peeled, solar-baked, and covered with raspberry sauce. I want to try this myself tonight."

Harley asked if he could borrow the paring knife and Mavis sent it through a tube that expanded and contracted in every apartment.

"Where's the paring knife?" Jeremy asked later that night.

Mavis patted her greasy face and stuffed some grapes into her mouth. "Harley has it. I'll go see how he's getting along."

In the morning, Jeremy reached for Mavis. "Why are you crying?" he asked, aching to comfort her without a glance toward the camera over their bed. He had become inured to Harley who witnessed their lovemaking and made the requisite reports to the authorities.

A limited amount of fear intruded into Jeremy's libido-stroking chip. Mavis was not lying next to him. The crying came from the hallway. Jeremy followed the sound down the iron stairway, until he saw the baby, an interbred with Harley's Humanoid, and Mavis' Clone features.

Harley was right behind him, holding Mavis' paring knife between his rotting teeth.

"Where's Mavis?" Jeremy cried.

"At Station … she has to be purified…inspected."

Jeremy took a deep breath, held it, slowly released it. "Why?" he asked. "How did this… ?"

"The government granted Mavis her wish and I got mine. Got my share of the riches! Private breeding room, chemical-permeation mattress, hothouse fruit … And Mavis."

"Merger of War Hero with Queen Annulled," the speaker in the camera boomed.

"Merger of Harley Whitehead and Mavis Smith Shader Approved."

Mavis opened the front door. It swung back and forth. She picked up the baby, breast-fed him from her cream patch, then handed him to Harley. "I reported Blake's birth. We've been approved to make another child."

"Has Station properly restored you?" Harley asked.

"Yes," Mavis replied. "My reproductive papers are stamped. I'll run upstairs and pack my suprasack."

"You lied to me," Jeremy cried. "You said you endured the pain because you wanted to stay with me. And I believed…"

"Careful," Mavis whispered in Old English. "I believed you, too." The cameras whirred. Jeremy paused. Furiously, he rubbed the patch of skin on his forehead until he composed himself. Slowly, he turned around and faced the swinging door, stopping when a sudden sharp pain penetrated his mind chip. History, he thought. Something about history. In a sudden burst of a memoblast, it was gone.

Outside, rain began to fall on the stunted trees. Jeremy closed the door with his big toe, watching it grow to an enormous size. As big as Harley's, he thought. As big as Harley's, he repeated. He would have to enlarge the hole in his work shoes.

THE WEIGHT

Esther K. Willison

She told Anna she had a weight inside her body.

"It's a weight, Anna, a real weight. I know it is." Anna was almost relieved to hear Calli say that. She had noticed that Calli's body had begun to tilt to the left. She thought it started about three months ago, after Calli's son, Jordan, tried to kill himself. Anna herself had not yet recovered from her mother's death a year earlier. She had lived with her mother, Grace, in the same house her whole life, except for the two years in Paris when she was an art student. Anna still expected to hear Grace calling her name when she came home from work. Her long illness had occupied much of Anna's time and she was not yet comfortable with her new freedom.

Anna had always wanted to know Calli better—a woman bringing up her son alone (she had heard the husband had left when the boy was only three), a poet who wore long cotton skirts year round and kept her garden going all winter enclosed in glass boxes—but never had the time. She would see her arriving home, sometimes, her body bouncing to the music coming from her car, her long golden red hair falling on her slight shoulders. Hair like the sunrise, Anna thought. Something about Calli's pensive face always made Anna smile and turn away from the window, as if Calli might catch her looking. Catch her at what, was the question. Calli came by a week after Anna's mother had died, bringing coffee cake. She knew when she couldn't move her eyes from Calli's incredibly long light (were they white or light tan?), eyelashes she was in love—again.

Catch her at falling in love was the answer. She had not felt this way since living with Veronique, in Paris.

Then, shortly after Jordan's suicide attempt, Anna noticed the slight tilt in Calli's body. Her sunrise hair shone longer over her left arm. Anna had stared in amazement, silent, waiting to make sure. A month later, when the tilt was still there, they talked about it and Anna persuaded Calli to go to Karen Ferris, her own doctor. Karen had cared for Anna's mother and had become more like a friend to them both. Anna knew she made time for, and listened carefully to, each patient. She would do her best to understand, and treat, Calli's problem.

Now Anna and Calli sat at the white wooden table in the tidy kitchen of Calli's small house. The table was separated from the rest of the kitchen by a high counter. On the counter sat an old wooden bowl with fresh vegetables; yellow peppers, green cucumbers and deep purple eggplants. Beyond the counter, against the far wall, was Calli's refrigerator and to the right her stove. Over the stove bundles of drying herbs hung from a cabinet knob. And, against the other wall, at right angles to the refrigerator, was the sink and more herb bundles hanging against the large window over the sink.

Calli began to tell Anna of her visit to Dr. Farris.

"I told her that I can feel the weight inside my body, on my left side, and I told her I can't straighten up when I walk. But she couldn't find anything wrong with me, Anna. Isn't that strange?"

"Well, did she give you any medication?"

"No, she didn't. But she did give me the name of a psychiatrist. Do you think I need a shrink?"

"I don't know, Calli. I don't know." Anna put her coffee cup down and looked at her friend carefully. Calli's clear blue-green eyes reflected the sunlight blinking in from the side window. Anna tried to study those eyes quickly; with the light in them they might reveal more. The day of Calli's first visit, a "condolence call" Anna had named it so she wouldn't get her hopes up, they had an exchange of confidences that had brought them closer and they started to visit each other more often, seeking, and finding, the comfort they both needed. Calli told Anna that she never understood why her husband had left but that she had never missed him.

"Maybe that's why," she had added, smiling at Anna. She had never heard from him again. Calli had supported herself and Jason by editing the town's only newspaper. She had her own poetry section, and encouraged contributions from other poets. With a large gift from one of their benefactors she had recently hired Anna, who knew about computers, to install them in the paper's offices. Anna lived alone in her big old ivy covered house and was glad to share her practical skills and to have the company of another writer. Freelance work had left Anna on her own much of the time. She liked independence but not isolation.

"You look tired," Anna said, noticing that Calli's face was pale and her eyes were in their looking, but not seeing, mode.

"I'm okay," Calli answered, keeping her head down. Anna liked sitting in Calli's small kitchen. It seemed safer than her own. Anna watched Calli pick up the coffee pot from the stove. Calli had to keep her wrist turned to the right, to counteract her body tilt. If she didn't, the coffee would spill. Pouring it was even more difficult for her.

"Here, let me help," Anna offered, reaching for the pot.

"No, no, I can do it," Calli answered curtly. She looked up at Anna's frightened eyes. "I know you just want to help, but I need to learn to adjust to this thing, whatever it is."

"But maybe you don't, Calli. Maybe you do need to see a shrink. Maybe it is because of Jordan." Anna was sorry as soon as she said it. She put her hand over her mouth. Calli hated to talk about Jordan.

"Jordan has just had a temporary breakdown. I mean, my God, his bride was killed on the day of their wedding. Who wouldn't go crazy? You know that, Anna! He'll be okay in a few months. He needs time to recover. Disa was his first love—it's a terrible loss for him. He's not the cause of this."

"Sorry, Calli, I just thought there might be ..."

"My lean is caused by a weight, a real weight, Anna, inside my body. I know it is. I can feel it, damn it. I don't know why it doesn't show up on an x-ray. The left side of my body is heavier than the right. If they would just open me up and take out this damn weight, I'd be okay!" Calli's face was flushed. When she put the coffee pot back on the stove she forgot to to compensate for her tilt, and hot coffee splattered to the wooden floor. Anna jumped up, tore off some paper towel from the roll over the sink, and wiped it up.

Calli sat down at the kitchen table, with her elbows pressing on the cold, formica surface, her head in her hands.

"Thank you, Anna, for cleaning up." Calli paused and looked up at Anna. "I don't want to talk about Jordan," she added, quietly, "okay, Anna?"

"Okay," Anna replied, reaching across the table to lay her hand gently on Calli's arm. "Hey, want to go to Crawford's with me? They have a lot of new herbs."

"Sure," Calli smiled at Anna. "Let's go. I'll just change my blouse." Anna washed the few dishes in the sink while Calli was in the bedroom. She had been self-conscious, at first, going out with Calli; so many people stared at Calli's tilted body. And each week the weight seemed to get heavier, the lean more pronounced. But now, six months later, Anna was used to it and she ignored the stares. As she rinsed the cups in hot water she wondered if Calli noticed the stares.

Calli came back into the room wearing a clean white blouse and a cheerful smile.

"OK. All ready. Lead me to those herbs."

The ride to the herb garden was a pleasant one. They drove along the river, slowing down to watch a barge enter one of the old locks. The water rose slowly against the worn stone walls, lapping at the corners, like a large cat's tongue. The huge flat boat stood patiently outside the iron gates, waiting its turn to be transported across the water.

"I used to love to take the bike trail down to the river here and watch the boats," Calli told Anna. "So many of my poems are about the river. Jordan and I would picnic along these banks when he was little and I taught him to skip stones. He got quite good at it but he became more interested in the stones than the skipping. He always went home with his pockets full of stones, all shapes, sizes and colors; he liked the reddish ones best. I still have some of them. He left his collection with me when he moved out." Calli hesitated a moment, looking down at her hands, as if the stones lay huddled inside her palms. "I went to the river, almost every day, after Jordan shot himself. But now, with this weight, I can't ride. I try but the bike keeps falling. The last time I tried I scraped my knee."

"That's terrible, Calli. Really. I wish they could figure out why..." Calli interrupted Anna and said, leaning forward with one hand on the dashboard, "If only I could do something to take my mind off it."

"What about the paper, Calli?" Anna asked as they turned off from the main road and entered the countryside. "They knew your leave was temporary. I'm sure they want you back. Have you talked to them about working part time?"

"No, I haven't. And I don't know if that's such a good idea. You know, Jordan might need me and I want to be there for him."

"Well," Anna continued, glancing sideways at Calli's face, "I mentioned it because I was also thinking that this herb house might be a good place for you for part-time work if you can't work full time now. It's pleasant and..."

"Listen, Anna," Calli interrupted her again, "I know you mean well, and I know in a way I brought it up, but I really don't want to talk about working, okay?"

"Sure, of course."

A few minutes later Calli put her hand over Anna's on the steering wheel and said softly, "Anna, I really appreciate all you're doing and have done for me. You know that, don't you?"

"Yes, of course," Anna answered. Anna felt Calli's hand on hers long after it was gone. Every time Calli touched her, even a playful poke, she could feel the touch throughout her whole body, a kind of tingling that took a long time to subside. She would never became used to it and knew instinctively it was not yet time, and maybe never would be, to tell Calli of her feelings. She often had the image of herself, in relation to Jordan and Calli, as a kid trying to sneak in between two adults in order to see what's going on. Maybe that's why Calli's husband left.

They were both silent for some time. Calli put her head back on the seat and closed her eyes. Anna noticed the deepening lines between Calli's eyes at the base of her forehead. One short, one long, they diagonaled towards each other like a rooftop, almost meeting, leaving a space between them for unanswered questions.

"I see the same image, over and over again, Anna. Jordan's bedside, almost a year ago, where he lay shaking, still so pale from having his stomach pumped. I see myself sitting in a large chair close to the bed, my hand holding his cold fingers. He doesn't move his head but looks at me sideways with his scared dark brown eyes. I guess this was a mistake, he says, more like a question than a statement."

Anna wanted to stop the car and put her arms around Calli. Instead she said, "It was such a shock, Calli. It's no wonder you keep thinking about it."

"Part of me didn't even believe it when I was there, by the bed. It's not me I kept thinking. This is not my child. I must be somewhere else, watching from a distance. This couldn't have happened. This is not my son, I kept thinking. This didn't really happen."

"It is unbelievable. I don't know how you stand it."

"Jordan said he didn't know what he was doing. He said he had gone to look for Disa. He said he felt now like he'd come back empty-handed from hell, like Orpheus when he returned from Hades without Euridice. I sat with him until he fell asleep. When he closed his eyes I watched a small tear form in one corner. You know what I wanted to do, Anna, do you know? I wanted to pick him up, I wanted to carry him in my arms, up with me, up through the hospital ceiling, up past the trees, up into the sky to the warm sun where we could look down and smile and laugh and I where I could take him into the spheres with me, where I could carry him in my strong arms, away from himself, away from danger. He would be light as music and we would fly upward, both of us, weightless."

Anna turned down the Herb Garden road with her eyes filled. She pulled into the parking lot, turned off the car motor and shifted toward Calli, touching the sleeve of her coat. "We're here. Are you okay, Calli? We don't have to get out. We can sit and talk, or go somewhere else."

"Oh, no. I'm fine. Really." Calli smiled at Anna and looked out into the garden. "Let's just wander around on our own for a while, okay?"

"Sure," Anna answered, getting out of the car. She smiled. "I'm going to look for some Rosemary. It cures everything."

As Anna started up the S-shaped path of the garden she could smell the herbs. She was always amazed at their tenacity. They appeared to survive the relentless unpredictability of the elements. Maybe Calli would do the same. Maybe she would be okay. Maybe I should tell her how I feel, Anna thought. Maybe what she needs is to know she can have her own life and... or is that selfish of me... selfish and presumptuous? Is it just so I can fill my own need to love her and protect her? Would she even welcome this kind of love? Anna looked across at Calli who was bent over a crowded section of herbs. She had her hand on the plants but her face looked upwards. A woman with a stroller was trying to get by but Calli blocked the path. The woman appeared to be trying to get Calli's attention. Anna walked back up the path quickly, holding a plant she had picked out for her.

She heard the woman speaking to Calli. "Excuse me, Miss, Miss ... can I get by?" but Calli made no response. Anna knelt down along side of her and put her hand on her shoulder.

"Calli. Hi. How're you doing? This woman would like to get by." Calli looked up into the face of a young woman with the stroller.

"Oh, I'm sorry." She stepped out of the way.

"Are you okay?" Anna asked.

"Oh, yes, I'm fine. I was daydreaming, as usual. You know me. Sorry." Anna held out the plant. "This is for your garden." Calli took the plant from Anna and put her other arm around her shoulder.

"Anna, thank you. You are such an amazing friend. I'd never make it without you."

On the way home Anna looked at Calli's profile in the car for a long time. Her high forehead and strong straight nose gave off a radiance even her "weight" couldn't diminish. Sometimes, in spite of her small size, Calli was as large as a tree. "Tell me about your daydream in the garden," Anna said. Not a request, not a command, almost a kind of continuation of their conversation on the way to the garden.

"Well, okay, but don't think I'm too strange, all right? It happened when I bent down and ran the palm of my hand over the tops of the plants. I could feel them grow under my hand; I could feel them rise up slowly from the ground and I entered into their world of stems and leaves and roots. The plants became as tall as myself; they enveloped me and wrapped my body in their own scents, filling my nostrils and my head, making my eyes water." Calli shifted the plant on her lap and pulled the visor down to block the late afternoon sun.

"That's wild, Calli. And sensuous." Anna glanced at Calli for more.

"I rose up with the herb plants, clinging to their branches and their roots parted gently from the sweet earth. I flew across the hills, the sharp smells changing at every dip and turn. I ran my hand along the tops of the hills, lifting it over the jagged edges so I wouldn't scrape myself. I laughed with the herbs, freeing my arms long enough to pick a leaf and rub it between my fingers and smell it and roll it around in my mouth. Then I washed my hands in the leaves, I washed my whole body in them, turning round and round, my face, my arms and legs and feet until I was as pungent as the plants themselves."

"Wow! No wonder you didn't notice the woman trying to get by. I love it! I wish I could do that." Anna smiled admiringly at Calli whose face showed her surprise and pleasure.

They were quiet again and Anna thought about Jordan. Calli had visited him in the hospital every day for a while. The beginning of the second week Anna had asked if she could come along. Calli seemed delighted to have her company. Anna and Jordan had often talked with each other about Greek Mythology, a topic of interest to them both. Calli didn't share Jordan's interest in mythology and she was glad he had someone else to exchange thoughts with on this topic. They had brought him his guitar that day, thinking it would make him feel better but he had no urge to play. Jordan had slumped in the large lounge chair in his hospital room. He had held his guitar in his limp hands.

"I'm lost," he had said to his mother and Anna. "Adrift—without Disa I have no place to rest." He sat up straight in the chair. "I've had such bad luck and now, no matter what I do, I can't seem to change. All that poetry and music! How am I supposed to survive on those?" Jordan struck the guitar strings with the back of his fingers—a loud, dissonant chord blasted the room. Anna watched Calli flinch at the ugly sound.

"What does the doctor say?" Calli asked gently, sitting down on the corner of Jordan's bed.

"Nothing. He keeps asking me about my feelings before I...before I took the pills. I've told him over and over again. Why does he keep asking?" Calli was quiet.

"No matter how many times I tell him," Jordan continued, "he doesn't understand that it was my way of getting her back, that it's my fault she didn't make it. I didn't go far enough. You see, I knew she was dead and I knew the only way I could reach her was if I was dead too, or at least near death. I knew it was taking a chance but I'm not alive without her so what do I have to lose?"

Jordan stood up and walked to the window. "All the doctor cares about is that I might try it again. He doesn't even listen to me."

Calli was not able to comfort her son, no matter how she tried. Anna stayed quiet sitting in a small chair in the background—there was no space for her to nestle between, or even along side of, mother and son. She and Calli left with their heads bowed, quiet in the hospital elevator. On the way home, in the car, Anna glanced at Calli's pensive face and asked, "What?" Calli looked at Anna and smiled, enjoying the ease of that one word between them.

"It's hard for me to watch his pale face and sad eyes," Calli answered. "His hair is so limp now across his forehead. I remember how playful he was as a child and how his tight black curls used to bounce against his shoulders when he ran. You know, Anna, sometimes I feel like I'm carrying his childhood around with me like an overcoat, waiting for him to slip it on again, anticipating that feeling of relief when the second arm goes through the sleeve, and I can let go and the weight of the coat is gone."

"He must have been a delightful child, Calli, but..." Anna took her right hand off the wheel and touched Calli's arm. Calli, not listening, continued.

"Sometimes, when he sleeps in that narrow hospital bed, I search his face for that young healthy boy with the strong voice. But the sound of his voice is bitter now and his rosy cheeks are gone. I can't find him." Calli reached under the front of the car seat, pushed a lever and moved the seat further back. She brought her right leg up, squared it across her left knee and shifted the weight strapped to her ankle. "Maybe it's my fault, my crazy fantasies. He gets them from me. Flights, chasing the fantastic. Only he really does it while I stay grounded. His attempt to reach Disa is incredible. Maybe he's more courageous than I...maybe..." Anna heard the tear in her, the split between guilt and envy.

During the next few weeks, after the visit to the herb garden, Anna watched Calli get more and more discouraged. She suggested she start to write again, told her to "free write," like she used to, but Calli explained why she couldn't even do that.

"My poetry had always been a celebration of life, you know, of what I think of as 'ordinary heroes.' But now there's nothing to celebrate."

Anna was glad Calli still sang in her Madrigal group, but even that became harder and harder. Calli had to remain sitting, at least part of the time, when they stood to perform for local groups. Anna had asked her about using a walker, to help keep her balance. Calli, who usually became angry at those suggestions, grew silent.

"Well, Caloo, what do you think?"

"I don't know. You really think it would help?"

"Maybe. It's worth a try."

"I'll call Dr. Farris," Calli had said, but she didn't. Anna figured she didn't want to hear again that she should call a therapist. She was disappointed in Karen Farris. "I know there's a real weight in me," Calli insisted. "I don't need a shrink."

Anna swam twice a week at a nearby pool and she asked Calli if she'd like to go with her. Calli agreed.

"I used to be on my high school swim team," she told Anna, and I love the water." Anna started picking her up every Tuesday and Thursday evening for a swim. Calli seemed elated after each swim and told Anna that it was a relief to be in the water; it was the only time her weight wasn't dragging her down.

"The water seems to balance my body," she explained once when they were getting dressed in the locker room "and I'm able to swim almost as easily as I did when I was younger."

"That's great, Calli." Anna watched her friend lean against the locker and take off her suit.

"I can stay under the water and be me again. I love it when the bubbles kind of caress my cheeks when I let the air out of my mouth. The rhythm of breathing brings me a peace I don't have on dry land." Somehow the words "dry land" made them both laugh and in that moment of connection Anna felt a vicarious joy through Calli's pleasure. Her cheeks flushed despite the cold air in the locker room.

"The other day, under water, I even imagined myself returning to—well, the womb," Calli continued. "I lay curled inside my mother's belly. It was like I wasn't breathing yet and the fluids swarmed in and out of my mouth in a natural flow, filling each space and splashing off my gums. I folded my legs into my body and pretended to drift inside those walls listening to the slow heartbeat of the outside world against the quickening rhythm of my own. It was so soothing, Anna, and I would have kept my eyes closed, welcoming that black place forever, if I hadn't bumped into another swimmer." Calli ruffled her long blond hair with her towel and took out her brush. Anna was trying to make sense of her words.

"What black place, Calli?"

"You know, just a place, a place that's safe." Calli took the towel off her head and looked directly at Anna.

"Oh, don't worry, Anna. I just mean I like to swim, that's all!"

"Well, Caloo. It's an amazing thought. The womb. I'll have to try it. Do you think one person can float into another person's fantasy?"

"I think so if the two people are close." Calli's green eyes narrowed playfully. Anna turned away from her, and started rummaging in her swimming bag.

"I'm always sorry when our time is up at the pool," Calli said. "I know there are people waiting to get into the lanes. But I hate leaving. As soon as I come up the steps, leaning on that silver railing, I'm off kilter again and I hate that long, cold walk back to the locker. I hate this... the inability to stand up." Calli tried to walk with her small duffel and fell back on the bench. Anna took the bag from her. This time Anna met Calli's eyes but neither one smiled.

One month later, Jordan was released from the hospital, given medication, and judged well enough to live on his own again. Calli and Anna helped him clean up his apartment and make a list of places to contact where he might perform. Some of the places he had all ready been to, some were new. Mother and son even sang one of their old songs together, and, although Jordan' voice was much sweeter than Calli's, they complimented each other. Anna applauded loudly, clapping over her bursting love for Calli, afraid her feelings might be heard.

"Jordan's been writing songs since he was six years old. I know every word of every song he's ever written," Calli proudly announced. When they left his apartment the two friends were hopeful; Jordan was on the mend. He hadn't mentioned Disa once.

A few weeks later Anna received a call form Calli early in the morning.

"Anna, I'm sorry to call so early, but I'm in bad shape. I woke up when it was still dark and couldn't sit up. I keep falling over to the left side. I tried to wait until the sun came up—I hate to wake you so early. And I thought maybe my strength would come back."

"Calli, my God, how terrible. I'm sorry you waited. Are you still in bed?"

"No, I'm by the front door. After I waited a while I called Jordan. You know he's in a rock group now and he's sometimes comes home early in the morning. But there was no answer. So I called you."

"I'll be right over. Stay where you are." Anna was already out of bed, looking for her jeans.

When Anna arrived Calli was sitting by the front door, not dressed but smiling. In a second Anna took in her whole body, the thin white cotton night shirt with the high collar unbuttoned, her knees protruding underneath, as she hugged them to her body, and her golden hair in tangles around her tight shoulders. "My God, Caloo, how did you get here?

"Easy. I rolled myself out of bed onto the floor. Then I rolled over to the corner of the room. I braced myself against the two walls in the corner and gradually shifted myself up into a standing position, my weight mostly against the left wall." Anna squatted down facing Calli at eye level. It was cold along the floor.

"Why didn't you wait for me?"

"Well, I didn't know what to do. Besides it was kind of an adventure. I had to move slowly from the corner to the closet door, leaning heavily on the wall. I was almost to the closet when my arm slipped against the wall and I fell on my side. God, what a loud thud that made. Even scared me. Jordan asked me the other day, 'does your weight hurt, Mom?' I told him no but this morning I would have said Oh, yes, Jordan, yes it does. Then I managed to crawl to this door." Anna knelt staring at her friend's quizzical expression, wanting so much to sit down next to her and enfold her in her arms, yet afraid to create the slightest crack in Calli's cavalier outlook.

On the way to the hospital Anna was amazed at Calli's acceptance of her condition.

"You know, Anna, I had to laugh when you said 'Stay where you are, I'll be right over.' Kind of a sick joke, don't you think?" Anna couldn't share the joke with Calli. She was afraid of what was to come. Why couldn't the doctors find anything wrong with her? Maybe she should take Calli to a specialist in New York. Maybe she should have done that a long time ago.

Anna went to see Calli every day the two weeks she was in the hospital; not one of the specialists could identify the cause of her imbalance and none of the medications helped. Anna took care of Calli's plants and brought her herb mixtures to drink.

Jordan came to visit her once, when Anna was there, but he seemed distant, staring past his mother, his responses slightly off, as if he were an actor in a movie in which the sound track had skipped a beat. After he left Calli seemed pleased. "He's looking good, don't you think, Anna?"

Anna answered yes, uncomfortable with her dishonesty and knowing Calli would argue with her if she said no, he's not. Jordan would always be between them. Maybe it's because I don't have children that I resent him, Anna thought, watching Calli arrange the flowers he had brought. Maybe it's not. Nothing can come between them, yet everything has. Shall I leave her eventually, like her husband? Or will she leave me, like Veronique?

Anna sat in her chair and watched Calli sleeping, her head turned toward the older woman in the other bed. Anna fidgeted with her pocketbook and shifted her legs a dozen times in the chair. Her neck ached and her eyes stung. The two sleeping women looked so peaceful she began to think maybe she was the patient and they the visitors, dozing off in deference to her own discomfort.

When Calli awoke her roommate was gone, wheeled downstairs for tests, Anna told her.

"You know she's eighty-three?" Calli told Anna. "Burned in a fire in her kitchen. Did you see her face? Those open blisters? My God."

"I wonder how well those things heal," Anna replied.

"You know how crazy I am, Anna. I had a kind of fantasy of healing her myself." Calli looked at Anna a long time, smiling. "When she first got here I stared at her while she slept, and I imagined touching her face with my fingertips and the wounds healed. I watched the skin slowly lose its dark color and return to normal. Then I stretched my hands further and healed the patients in the room next to ours and then…" Calli hesitated,"Do you really want to hear this?" Anna nodded, "Of course, you can't stop now."

"And then I healed the patients in the room on the other side of us. Then I connected myself to all the patients in this hospital and healed them all, wherever they were. People began getting out of bed who hadn't been up for weeks, everyone began talking to each other in amazement. The nurses stood in the halls, astonished, some ran to call the doctors. I went from room to room listening happily to the sounds of recovery. Jordan, still here, among the healed of course, came to me running down the hall." Anna was picturing Calli's fantasy and having such a good time with it it took her a moment to respond. "Ah, there was a method in your madness. I love your fantasies, Calli. Don't ever hesitate to tell them to me. Have you ever had any about me?" What in God's name made me ask that question, Anna thought as she got up from her chair and stood by Calli's bed. "Don't bother answering that. I don't know why I asked." She began to straighten Calli's sheets. Calli was about to speak when Dr. Farris came into the room.

"You can leave tomorrow," she said, taking Calli and Anna away from fantasies.

"We still don't know what the problem is but we have some more tests to analyze. I'll call you as soon as that's done." Karen Farris glanced over at Anna as if she knew how closely connected to the pain she was. Then she spoke to Calli again: "I know how difficult this has been for you and I'm sorry."

Anna was happy to drive Calli home. She looked at Calli's worn face and said, "You are amazing, Caloo. You look great. How did you manage that, after all you've been through?"

"That's what friends are for. To make the impossible possible. Thanks, Anna. I love you." Calli reached over and put her hand on the back of Anna's head and ruffled her short curly hair. Anna jumped slightly in the seat and tried to concentrate on the road ahead of her, her hands tightening on the wheel. She wanted to say the obvious, I love you too, Calli, but the words, as if caught up in one of Calli's fantasies, grew heavy and, instead of coming out of her mouth, sunk down into her toes.

"I'm grateful to the doctors for one thing, even though they can't figure out what's wrong with me I learned to walk with a walker. See this ankle strap?" Calli lifted her pant leg and Anna glanced at a thin leather strap around her ankle. She noticed how strong Calli's leg looked in spite of her problems.

"They strapped a small weight to my right side to counterbalance the lean to the left. At least I won't fall now." Calli let out a deep sigh. "I'm ready to go home."

The long warm fall finally ended and winter put in a sudden appearance, forcing Anna to put her gloves on when she filled the bird feeder. She had persuaded Calli to return to the paper as Literary Editor so they worked together almost every day. They still went swimming twice a week. Calli told Anna she looked forward to those moments of freedom, when her body no longer crushed her spirits and she said she had begun to write poems again, in her mind, as she swam.

"How's Jordan doing?" Anna asked Calli one day.

"Oh, I see little of Jordan these days; the group he joined is his whole life now, and when he does visit he always asks for money. I told him I can't figure out why he needs so much money so often but he insists he has expenses. He tells me that sometimes it takes a long time to get paid for a gig. What can I do? I don't want him to be thrown out of his apartment. So I give it to him." Calli got up from the computer and limped over to the window without her walker, one hand on the row of file cabinets for balance. Her back was to Anna as she spoke. "He's so grumpy these days. I don't know what's wrong with him. He never used to be like that." She turned towards Anna, the light from outside framing her bent body. "And when I try to talk to him about it he..." Calli put her hand up to her mouth, as if forgetting something, or maybe trying to forget something. "...he says things like how could you understand me when all you do is daydream and you've never really been there for me. He's so angry." Calli put her head down, her hands over her face. Anna got up, walked quickly over and put her arms around her.

"Don't be afraid to cry, Caloo. Let it out. Let yourself go." Anna planted her feet firmly as she felt Calli's full weight on her own body.

Calli lifted her head and looked at Anna through the light, her eyes sharp with the intensity.

"Maybe I shouldn't give him the money. Maybe I should try to find someone to talk to him. Every time he closes the door behind him there's a greater distance between us. The last time he left I wrote this river poem." Calli let go of Anna and sat down in her desk chair, reciting slowly.

"'Your tenacious curve along the banks, / echoes the ins and outs of rocks and moss / Who would have thought / a soft flowing body / could cut so deeply?' When I wrote the poem I felt myself stand on tip-toe and dance lightly over the letters in tenacious." Calli stood up and began to dance across the floor, catching herself momentarily on a piece of furniture. "I felt like a stone skipping across the water, one foot on top of the t, then a slide along the e, over the n, a jump to the a, a turn on the c..."

Calli started to fall and Anna ran to catch her. As soon as she was upright she continued. "...over the i but under its dot, my head down, across the o to the bottom of the u, up the u to the top of, then around the end of, the s, lying on a slant with my feet up..." Calli fell gently to the floor, "and my head tucked in the curve of the s, to catch my breath."

A few weeks later Anna's phone rang at four o'clock in the morning. She was hoping it was a crank call but her heart beat wildly in anticipation of the possibility that it wasn't.

"Anna?'

"Calli?"

"A policeman called me. He told me there'd been an accident." Anna could hear Calli's shallow breathing, as if she were gasping for air. She pictured her sitting up in bed, leaning against her pillows. "He said Jordan was found, a few minutes ago, in a friend's apartment. He said it looked like ... looked like a drug overdose

... but they're not sure."

Anna waited a moment before she asked, "Where, Calli, where is he?"

"He's at the hospital. But he's...he's gone, Anna. Gone."

"Oh, my God." Anna put the phone on her shoulder and leaned back on her pillow. She took a deep breath. "I'll come over and we'll go to the hospital."

Anna hung up and got dressed. When she got to Calli's house Calli was waiting for her but moving slowly, in jerking motions. Anna had a sense of dragging Calli along with her to her car, a feeling they were both under water, being pulled by the undertow, scraped and bruised along the bottom, fighting for breath, salt water burning their eyes, sand and stones stinging their skin.

For the next few days Anna walked along beside Calli, helping her slowly move through the motions of death and its formalities, one hand on her arm, her face searching her friend's eyes for some hope. But something had changed for Calli, her weight in her thoughts as well as in her body. She drifted between pain and numbness, floating, in her mind, over and over again, in a space just out of hearing.

"The voices around me echo," she told Anna, "as if I hear them through a glass, the words are rounded, blurred at the edges." Anna noticed that Calli's neglected herb plants, unable to sustain their determination, died. Time, Anna kept saying, time was a healer. Believe in time. Let it pass.

"But is there any time left now?" Calli asked. "Was there any time between the phone call and now? Had any time passed between the closing of the door when Jordan left and the closing of his breath when he left again? Was there any time when I could have intervened, could I have run into the room and yelled wait? Time is anything you want it to be, Anna. But it cannot pass now. It stands still forever." Anna looked at Calli quizzically. "But forever moves, doesn't it? Doesn't it?"

For many months Calli did nothing but sit and stare and then slowly she began to function. Anna persuaded her to take a part time job at the herb garden and they began to swim again.

"My thoughts, Anna, always of Jordan, begin to take shape while I swim. I make up my...well, I guess they're death poems, in my head and write them down when I get home. Want to hear one?"

"Of course," Anna said, always glad of a confidence from Calli but afraid of the poem.

"I know it sounds morbid, Anna, but they make me feel better. Listen:

"The joy of that
slip-turn birth
making me with child forever, the agony of that slumber back in,
a different forever now mine.
Coming and going are no match,
shall I search for you

(as you did for her)
and find what, beginning or end?"

Anna looked carefully at Calli's sad face. She dared to hold her hand against her cheek and look into her somber eyes.

"What do you mean 'Shall I search for you as you did for her?'"

"Oh, don't get so maternal, Anna. I'm not suicidal. It's a poem. You know me. I'm a survivor. I'll find a way out, or a way out will find me when I'm not looking. I'm still dragging this old body around, askew as it is, aren't I?"

"You're amazing, Caloo. Really."

"What do you mean? If I am amazing it's because of you! You realize that, don't you?" The two friends moved into each other's arms and held each other a long time. Anna put the palm of her hand against the back of Calli's head and felt her warm soft hair. Calli let go of the walker and allowed her body, weight and all, to rest on Anna's small frame. Anna stood firm, never moving. Her heartbeat coursed through both of them, countering Calli's weight for a moment, holding them together, upright and calm.

"There's no one else who could share the weight of my..." Calli couldn't finish her sentence. She hopped back up to a standing position and grabbed the walker.

"Hey," Anna said, "let's go swimming."

"Great idea. Come back in fifteen minutes, I'll be ready."

Anna picked up Calli and they went to the pool. It was late in the afternoon and there was free swimming instead of lane swimming. Anna made sure Calli got to the deep end (she liked to dive in) and she went down to the shallow end. She was not a good swimmer and preferred shallow water. Anna stood at the top of the steps and watched Calli at the other end of the pool. She saw her leave her walker by the side of the diving board, saw her press her back against the board, set the palms of her hands down on the board's surface and lift herself onto the board.

Anna smiled as she started down the steps to the water, still keeping an eye on Calli who now sat on her behind and inched her way to the end of the board. Calli stopped and looked up for a moment. Anna waved.

Calli waved back. Anna watched as Calli slowly lifted herself up into a crouching position. Then, leaning as far as she could to the right, she gradually stood up. Anna, now standing in the water, was surprised and pleased to see her standing alone. Calli looked around, almost proudly it seemed to Anna, brought her arms back behind her back, then forward once to practice, still standing. Then Anna, watching intently, saw Calli once again bring her arms back, this time quickly, then forward raising them high above her head. She pushed off her body with her right foot and leapt into the air. How Anna wished she could fly with her as she watched Calli look out over the pool, high above the water, weightless, Anna thought, freed from matter, from substance. Just before Calli's head bent down and her fingertips broke the surface of the water, Anna thought she saw on her face an expression of absolute ecstasy.

Anna ducked her head underwater and swam a few strokes. She popped her head up for a gasp of air and went under again, staying as long as she could. She was jealous of this amorphous liquid and wanted to understand its ability to lure away her love. When she emerged it took her a few minutes to connect the commotion down at the deep end with Calli. Then, when she saw a few people lift a body out of the pool, she screamed, "Calli! Calli!" She ran to the side, up the steps and down to the end. Calli lay on a towel and the lifeguard was beginning to give her CPR. Everyone was out of the pool by now, standing silently, some with their hands over their mouths, some not daring to look.

"I couldn't believe it when I saw her body at the bottom of the pool," an older woman whispered to her companion. Anna knelt by Calli's still form. Calli's face was white but serene. The young man breathing into her mouth was working hard. Someone had called an ambulance. But Anna knew Calli was gone, gone by plan, to search for Jordan, or gone by mistake, when she wasn't looking. She would never know and she would always wonder.

Everyone knew Calli was a good swimmer. Dr. Farris, at the Hospital, ordered an autopsy. She knew from Calli's records that she had no family, at least none she knew about, so she called Anna and asked her to come in to discuss her findings.

"It's the damnedest thing," she said. "We found a fairly large stone, I mean a real stone, uncommonly heavy, on the left side of her heart, can you believe that?"

"Yes, I can," Anna answered. She turned away, remembering Calli's words. *It's a weight, Anna. A real weight. I know it is.*

"And look," Karen continued, "the side facing down was polished, as if worn down by water." Anna held the rock in her hand and looked at its shiny reddish grain. She turned it over. Staring out at her was Calli's miniature face, her features unclear but the smile absolute.

MY POLISH WIDOWER

Karen Kovacik

The cliché about your life passing before your eyes at the moment of death is only partially true. I had just sped across four lanes of traffic on Warsaw's notorious Wisłostrada, when a beer truck cut me off. One minute I was braking hard behind a four-foot bottle of Okocim Porter, rumored to be the Pope's favorite brew, and the next I was sailing through the windshield of my husband's tiny Daewoo. I had time for only a few scenes from my life—an autobiographical greatest hits—before I found myself in the proverbial tunnel of light. Oddly, one of those scenes was Driver's Ed in Hammond, Indiana, taught by Mr. Krebs, the eternally patient woodshop teacher, as if death by car crash had rendered null and void my hard-earned C in the subject decades before. Had I been driving that '75 Monte Carlo instead of Tomek's fiberglass breadbox, I might well have survived. Instead, I began acquainting myself with the rights and privileges of the newly deceased. I could now spy on my husband any time I wanted.

My first glimpse of heaven's gate reminded me of Warsaw itself, specifically the Central Train Station, with its fluorescent lighting, platforms of waiting passengers, and staticky loudspeakers announcing arrivals and departures. The officiating angel, who resembled an auto mechanic in his glowing striped jumpsuit, explained that while the omnipresence would kick in immediately, omniscience would be granted more gradually. "Trust me," he said. "Sometimes it's better not to know."

I always hoped that if I preceded Tomek in death, I'd be admitted into the labyrinth of his mind. You can perceive a lot about a spouse—his appetite for jellied carp or fondness for solitary reading or devotion to friends—and still be awed by the extent to which he remains unknown. Add to the mix our linguistic and cultural differences and the fact that Tomek had spent considerable time alone before he met me. Solitude made him a watcher, not a talker. Had it not been for my garrulous, semi-coherent Polish, which propelled him to fits of extroversion, we would never have fallen in love.

The fact is, husbands and wives never love each other equally. And in my marriage to Tomek, I was the one who loved more. I with my lisping American accent, big soft ass, and dyed blonde hair that frizzed in the rain. Ever since I made him smile during our first English lesson some 13 years ago, he had been my elegant boulevard, and I his tornado.

For that first meeting, we had agreed on Warsaw's Constitution Square, a post-Communist hybrid of massive sandstone steelworkers and the neon logos of a global marketplace. The Café Hortex located there was itself a throwback to the former centralized economy, each miniature bistro table topped by a cheap porcelain sugar bowl and a drinking glass filled with a cone of worthless tissue napkins. While waiting for Tomek to arrive, I stared at my wedge of strawberry gelatin cake, attempting with all my power to resist it. Impatient waitresses swished past in their apple-green uniforms, and some grandpa at the next table hummed along with the radio. I had ample time to review the grammar and vocabulary lesson I'd prepared.

I was dressed in the wool skirt and high-necked cotton blouse that I always wore for first lessons because they minimized my ridiculous curves. My tall black boots remained home in the closet, and on my feet were flats so sensible I felt embarrassed to wear them in public.

On the phone Tomek had told me he was an architect, 33 years old, and gave his height in centimeters, which led me to expect a fairly tall man. In person, however, he was no more than five feet, in a blue raincoat and corduroys, with one of those small Polish shoulder bags, a kind of purse for men. I must have outweighed him by 20 pounds. That day's lesson was to be on verbs of motion—a refresher since Tomek had already studied English for five years. I poured him some jasmine tea from my pot, slopping a little onto his purse in the process, and started talking about coming and going. Maybe it was the radio's Chopin sonata unspooling its vehement silk or Tomek's blue-eyed amusement at my careful lesson, but I suddenly knew we would be good in bed together. "To come has another meaning in English," I found myself explaining, then offered examples: "She was never able to come with him" and "He made me come five times in one night." That's when Tomek smiled.

Tomek was in the tea aisle at the Hala Kopińska when the call came from the city police. He'd just bypassed all the fruity herbals, the wild strawberry and blueberry I loved, in favor of the dense black grains that inspired him to flights of architectural fancy. I watched Tomek flip open the tiny mobilnik and answer with his typical subdued "Tak, słucham." Literally: "Yes, I'm listening." He stiffened when the policeman identified himself, a predictable reaction among Poles of Tomek's age. Then a look of wonder crossed his face, the same perplexed curiosity he exhibited when I mixed up two unrelated but similar-sounding Polish nouns. "Yes, Carla's American. 44 years old." He didn't cry or make a scene, but looked so pale and shaky that security didn't stop him when he walked off with a tin of premier Darjeeling.

The sight of my petite Tomek straining against the November wind made me wish I had proceeded with greater caution into those four lanes of Wisłostrada traffic. I longed to wrap his muffler around his neck—one of those motherly gestures he despised.

It was only in the elevator to our ninth-floor flat—the narrow, mirror-adorned lift where we hauled up groceries and argued about French cinema and once almost made love—that my Polish husband, now my widower, permitted himself a couple of tears. I had seen him cry on two occasions in our marriage: the death of his favorite aunt and the time I drank one Wyborowa too many on New Year's Eve and French-kissed a lecherous poet in the buffet line. Of course, Tomek was not one to sniffle at a party. He drove us home in silence, forcing me to endure the avalanche of his disapproval and hurt, and averted his eyes during the interminable elevator ride. It was only in the bedroom, after I stripped off my low-backed jade dress and attempted to convert everything I couldn't say into a no-holds-barred seduction that I was stunned to see him cry. A reddening of the nose, a quick shamestruck covering of the eyes. We were in bed, he seated with his back to the wall, and when I noticed his tears, I pulled him on top of me in a fierce American hug. I called him by name, I called him beloved, I stroked his hair and neck and back and butt and hissed in his ear, "I want to make love to show you how sorry I am."

He arched up on his elbows as if taking my measure. In his coldest, most official-sounding Polish, he said, "You're not capable of that."

"Let me show you." I knew that mind games always aroused him. His blue-gray eyes were already dry and alert.

"Nie." The monosyllable of refusal resounded with arctic finality, though his penis seemed of a different persuasion. In the end, Tomek let me know the terms my apology would have to take: he would thrust me very slowly sixty times. With each stroke, I was to tell him I was sorry for kissing that horny idiot, Waldemar. I was not to have an orgasm until or after this sixtieth stroke despite the fact that he knew very well— we had been married three years—how to bring me to the brink. The legalistic precision of his terms amused me, nudged me from abject to ironic. Mercy fresh from the freezer was better than no mercy at all.

"Jak chcesz," I said. "As you wish."

And so it began, so we began, the first ten superficial as a blueprint, my faint I'm sorrys rote with defiance. Around 20, I started to feel the architectonics of him, the subtle buttressing of his pride, his fear of losing me. At 35, I began to cry myself, so I could scarcely whisper the thick phrase of apology: przepraszam. 38, 39, random images of my love for him: the care he took when defrosting our tiny fridge, tilting it back on an orthographic dictionary, or our evening walks through the Park of Happiness, the willows and poplars cascading toward the ground. 45, 46, his nuanced finger on my clitoris; 50, 52, the choirloft shrieking with sopranos; 53, his blue eyes dark with lust; 57, the counterpoint of our breathing; 58, fighting the aria inside me, and finally, 60, 60, 60.

In the tiny, mustard-tiled kitchen, Tomek plugged in the electric kettle, pried open the tea tin with a spoon, and covered the bottom of a glass with dense black leaves. The kitchen looked much as I had left it. The same windowpane dishtowel hung on its hook, and a heel of rye rested on the table, cut side down. How odd to spy on one's own life, one's own husband. I felt like a member of the secret police, a tajnik, watching him this way, for my Polish husband valued privacy above everything.

Tomek called one of his friends, an artist with a century-old apartment in the Mokotów district, to cancel their afternoon meeting. They were supposed to have been planning the new kolorystyka of the flat—a bolder look with ultramarine cushions and citron-colored walls. I didn't need even limited omniscience to predict that the artist, Grzegorz P., would invite Tomek over for a drink, would even pick him up since my widower, thanks to me, no longer had a car. Nor was I surprised when Tomek, surrounded by my headbands, hats, and scarves, confronted by my breakfast dishes in the drainer, accepted the invitation with gratitude.

My husband had always liked working with artists because they had feasible intuitions, and typically they bartered a painting for a design. He dreaded the dithery clients who had no sense they were ruining a teak Saarinen coffee table by cluttering it with a souvenir ashtray, week-old newspapers, and TV remote. I approached that category myself with my fondness for kiosk kitsch such as the little felt rooster that I used to display on the moderne étagère until Tomek could bear it no longer and threw it in our building's incinerator.

It happened that Grzegorz grew up in the southern mountain resort town of Zakopane, the only place in Poland where cognac was the primary drink instead of vodka or beer. So in Grzegorz's high-ceilinged flat, adorned with elaborate sconces shaped like lilies, the brandy snifters appeared immediately, along with a bottle of some high-octane Armagnac. Had I not been dead, I would have enjoyed handling one of those glassy bells, twirling the rich brown liquor within, and taking its plummy woodsmoke into my mouth. Which is what my widower was doing, seated in the straight-backed chair that his host had provided for him so he wouldn't disappear into the sofa. Grzegorz, too, was cradling a swollen snifter, his long legs in blue jeans stretched beneath the table, the beginnings of a belly spilling over his belt.

In their circle of friends Grzegorz threw the best parties and had the most women. And while he typically favored Art Academy brunettes—if the young things hanging on him at gallery openings were any indication— I more than once caught him staring at my ass. He had a surveyor's gaze, an instinct for declivity and rise. Regardless of how intelligently I managed to talk about twentieth-century painting, including his own geometrized portraits, I was always aware of that narrowing of the eyes, that sense of appraisal.

With Tomek, Grzegorz displayed none of that judicious weighing. It pleased me to watch how skillfully he maneuvered the conversation to put my widower at ease, starting out with recent Warsaw buildings. And Tomek, though he never swore in my presence because of some old-fashioned notion of courtliness, used even the most notorious Polish words for describing Roman Z.'s green monstrosity of a supermarket.

Eventually, however, Grzegorz brought up the subject of my abrupt demise.

"Co zrobisz teraz bez Carli?" No American would ever ask a bereaved friend straight out how he'd manage now that his wife was gone, but the question seemed unremarkable to Tomek.

"God knows." Tomek swirled the brandy around in his glass. "Even though a dozen times she almost drove me to divorce."

Were I not dead, I would have grabbed that beautiful glass from his hand and flung the drink in his lap. Sure we fought, operatically even, Tomek locking himself in his room, and I swearing at him through the door in English. He was the sort of person who would measure an entire wall before hanging a single picture on it, while I would use every dish in the kitchen when preparing a three-course meal. The Polish equivalents of "Quiet down" and "Get a grip on yourself" were Tomek's favorite and absolutely enraging rejoinders to me.

"While I myself don't believe in marriage," Grzegorz said, "I must say you and she seemed content enough."

I recognized that appraising gleam. Grzegorz wanted to find out something about me, something he never dared ask while I was alive, I could feel it.

"It's just that Carla was, in many ways, a child," Tomek said. "You know what Americans are like. They're served the wrong dish at a restaurant, and it's cause for war." He sipped his drink for dramatic emphasis. "On the other hand, they can't wait to see what the Christmas Angel will bring." Grzegorz laughed at this ridiculous national stereotype which I allegedly fit. For the record, I have to say that during our entire marriage, I threw precisely one tantrum at the Restauracja Staropolska, when the waiter not only brought me a dried out schnitzel instead of the Kotlet de Volaille, but also dribbled gravy on my purple wool suit. And as for the Christmas Angel, the Polish counterpart of Santa Claus, I admit I did look forward to my annual gift, but that's only because Tomek chose so well. A red silk peignoir one year, a book of idioms the next.

Grzegorz assumed that insinuating posture once again. "But certainly, Carla jako kobieta loved you very much." The phrase "as a woman" dripped with innuendo.

Tomek, slouching in his chair, looked bereft. I had always wondered if the dead found comfort in the grief of the living. The answer in my case was clearly yes. Without looking up, my widower muttered, "I never knew a woman who liked it so much."

Grzegorz seized his chance. "I suppose she wanted it all the time."

Tomek nodded. "In the car, or at the movies. Even at the Filharmonia once during intermission." My widower always sweated when drunk, and he was sweating now, poor thing, a hand clamped over his eyes. His voice didn't rise above a mumble. "She was wearing that ginger perfume I loved," he said, "and some huge vulgar pearls, obviously fake. We'd gone to hear Schubert and Schumann, and by the break, Carla was so pent up she couldn't sit still." Truth is, I moaned so extravagantly in Tomek's ear that he draped his coat over our laps and slid an expert hand up my velvet skirt. It was like whole notes followed by thirty-second notes. More scherzo than lieder.

"We pretend to miss the soul or the mind," Grzegorz said, softer now. "When it's the body we can't live without."

My widower stared into his empty glass as if to confirm the truth of this remark. I thought how every night I enfolded his slender back into me, blanketing him with my scent and softness and warmth. We'd fall asleep with my nose in his hair, my hands tight around his waist. His tongue often tasted like tea. The prospect of never sleeping with him again seemed unbearable. Was this how haunting began?

While playing with one of the sconces in Grzegorz's flat, I managed to ring the bell at the reception desk in heaven. Behind the desk a window opened onto a frenetic scene. The newly arrived, pale and travel-worn, carried twine-bound parcels and dented valises up interminable escalators. But a pitcher of lilies rested on the desk itself, as did an enormous box of chocolates. That grease monkey of an angel in his glowing, striped jumpsuit was chewing on a cloud-colored pen. "Yeah?" he said.

"Sorry," I told him, "but I'm not cut out for this place."

"Says who?"

"Me," I said. "I miss living too much. Heretical as this might sound, I'd give it all up, even the eternal bliss, for one more night of bed with Tomek."

"Hold on, you're getting ahead of yourself." The angel looked at his fat silver donut of a watch, marked with an infinity of years instead of hours. "You'll be having relations again with your husband in 31.5 years."

Without asking for permission, I helped myself to a truffle filled with persimmon and spice. "You've got to be kidding. I want him now."

"Tough. Your old man's not due to give up the ghost till he's 75."

"How will he die?" I figured I might as well use the angel's ESP to my advantage.

"Cancer of the liver. Awful way to go, but his wife will be by his side the whole time."

"His what?"

"Lady, you heard me. Can't expect the guy to live like a priest for thirty years."

I didn't feel like being schooled in sexual mores by an angel. Jealousy hit me worse than a thousand windshields. I grabbed another chocolate, this one flavored with violets and champagne. How could Tomek marry again?

"So who's the lucky bride?" I sneered.

"Girl named Beata S., twenty years his junior. They'll meet next year at the opening of her sculpture show." He gazed again into the crystal ball of his wristwatch. "And they'll marry three months later."

I pictured one of Grzegorz's Art Academy brunettes wearing only a bridal veil, straddling Tomek on our narrow bed. To comfort myself, I imagined that she had flunked out of French and had only minimal English, though of course she'd prattle on in Polish with a native's flair.

"Will they be happy together?"

The angel shrugged. "What marriage is completely happy? Tomek will be lonely without you. He'll be impressed with Beata's sculptures, which in my opinion are a little weird, though the Holy Spirit likes them—they're these huge black and purple gourds wrapped in fabric. She'll chat with him, make him feel appreciated, and to be honest, she's not unattractive." The angel paused to see how I'd absorbed his prophecy. I rolled my eyes.

"But soon enough," he continued, "she'll consider him an old man. Someone to be coddled and sheltered from the truth. She'll take other lovers, and Tomek will again miss you and your passion."

Hearing about my widower in this way, I felt like an audience member in some upper balcony at an opera. The story reached me from such a distance it inspired only pity and not a lightning of the soul. So now Tomek would be the one to love more.

I glared at the angel. "So I'm supposed to park myself on a cloud till he gets ready to die?"

"Truth is," he said, "you're slated for purgatory." I wasn't eligible for heaven, the angel informed me, because in life I had neglected to cultivate patience. In purgatory, I'd be obliged to wait and then wait some more. They'd assign me a narrow cell with five ticking clocks all set for eternity. I would pray rosaries, endless white beads slipping through my fingers, and meditate till my mind stilled. Regular field trips to earth would be mandatory. I'd have to watch as Tomek brewed countless pots of tea, walked alone in the Park of Happiness, and made love with Beata S.

"You'll learn," said the angel, "that you can get through desire without giving in to it." He looked me in the eye to drive his point home.

I reached once more into the box of chocolates. My hand closed over what looked like a petit-four adorned with a buttercup. But this time I glanced at the angel for permission. When he nodded assent, I popped the confection in my mouth and let it dissolve slowly. It was a chocolate of final things, more bitter than espresso, dashed with the salt of regret, and dense as the densest loam of the earth.

On the Body

IF YOU MUST KNOW

Nicole Louise Reid

These are the early cicadas, four years ahead of schedule, chirping, shrilling, blistering through their skins. Thirteen years ago the night was electric with their noise, and one burrowed right into me—that little flab of skin beneath the arm socket. Thinking me a tree because I lay so still at the thought of what we'd just done beneath the water oak, Wallace and me. It broke through my skin and climbed deep within, planning to live there for its next seventeen years, sucking and sapping what it can from me. And so there must be something in people akin to the marrow of a tree's sweet pulp, because my locust is alive and waiting.

We went to all the doctors, of course—each grabbing hold of one of my corners, like an old shrunken fitted sheet that pops off just when you thought you had it. They were wanting to slice me open to extract the thing. But I was fifteen and big enough to put up a genuine fuss. You see, I felt romantic about it. Everything was sacred that day: the sky such a blue as kittens' eyes, the grass beneath us so plush with summer, the oak perfectly leaning for shading us, the creek moving slower than breeze, the absolute shrieking of the cicadas waking in the bark.

And yes, the one locust burrowing into my armpit.

I never even noticed it. Wallace held me afterward counting out the ways I was the sun, and for a while his fingers just ran back and forth over the lump, caressing me. Finally he took away his hand and there was the slimmest trace of blood across his ring finger.

What it felt like it still feels like: no hole at all, a completely enveloped thing three quarters of an inch long and half an inch wide, hard and slightly humming.

Any other day I'm sure I would have been the first to grab a knife. But I just cozied back down into Wallace's arms and the day was perfection. Once home, Mama whisked me off to the emergency room knowing if they wouldn't do it she would. And the doctors all agreed with her: there was no telling what damage this thing may do, no telling. Couldn't you feel it wriggling? they wanted to know. How'd it get all the way in when didn't you feel it gnawing at you? I kicked and bit them and refused everything; so finally they let me go, insisting all the while that at the first sign of necrosis it must come out. I even saw someone slip Mama a scalpel for moontime surgery.

I don't think it bit me. I lay on my back, Mama's girlhood silver mirror—tarnished as a dead granny's sugar spoon—angled just so, looking at my bug all that night and there was not one trace of how it got in me. Mama crying through the wall, Father clueless and sleeping one off on his raggedy houseboat. No slit, no hole, nothing. It sounds silly but I've ever since just believed I was chosen. I was the happiest thing on earth at the moment my cicada burrowed, and I have always liked to think that's just what it was looking for.

I feel a certain duty to my bug, and because Wallace didn't pan out, I used to always try to recreate that day. I reclined beneath the water oak, waiting on Wallace to come back and the gangly boys from school lined up, a sort of carnival of people watching. That first year, I was true to him, it was always Wallace. But after he left for training at Lackland, and I still had three more years of high school, well, I just needed to find myself back by the creek, and who I was with seemed to matter a tiny bit less each time. Thereafter it could be almost anyone. But now it's been a few years since I've truly had any chance at recreating that day, and I can tell my cicada's wishing he'd done better for himself.

He hardly ever chirps now, and I can't blame him.

I live with Mama, and though some may say I'm too old or too far gone or whatever else it is they're saying behind us in my little runt of a Kroger, I haven't any need or desire to go elsewhere. And while there is Father in the pontoon houseboat with Lerlene Gessum, teased red hair— truly a deep, deep shade of pink, and not one strand of it real—coming out past the width of her shoulders and hitting me in the side of the head when I'm over for supper on Tuesdays (Mama's night at painting class)—he's of no help.

So everything here was skating along just mediocre when last week, I saw him. Him, you know exactly who-him I mean. Wallace. The same mossy green eyes racing with blue dots and golden flecking. The same cinnamon hair grown into a more businesslike buzz cut, but still high around the tops of his ears, no bangs tangling up in his eyebrows. Same Wallace who spun the moon and held my cicada all night, the three of us burrowing, sighing, moaning, and chirping.

If you must know, I did almost faint. Truly. The thing that saved me was that he saw me and came right over, like he'd come to the grocer's to find me on a shelf next to the cans of Slim Jims. He came right over to checkout #2, and I was near a swoon but breathed real deep and gripped hold of the cash tray and managed not to tumble to the floor—even if the quarters did a little dance in their bin with me tugging to stay up.

He was all the same—seemed high school again, me working after school, him dropping in for sticks of butter, an egg, just to be near to me. He had a head of iceberg lettuce, one cherry tomato, and a roll.

"Pearl," he said, grinning. "It's you."

"Oh Wallace," I said, trembling.

You can laugh, but this is exactly what we said.

"You still got that old bug up there?" he asked, pointing to my underarm.

I've got to hand it to Mr. Smoothy. I can't say how many times I wanted to dip his words in Vaseline before opening my ears.

"Mmm-hmm, and you know he's not just an 'old bug.'"

"Well, sure," he said, tugging at some little bit of eyelash wanting to pull free.

Goddammit, my stomach hit the floor. I'd forgotten him doing this, him tugging his lashes making sure no loose ones hung about, seeming to be a boy needed loving. Heartless, he was.

"How you been?"

"Fine," I said. "Real good. Things are good."

"You still living at your mama's?"

"Well, course. She needs me, you know. With Father floating the Pea with that woman. Of course I'm still with her."

"Yeah," he said, bruising his tomato rolling it around on my carousel conveyer belt. "I'm just back now for a bit. Thought I'd come see how you turned out."

"How'd I do?"

He looked me once over. "Just fine, girl. Just fine."

I chewed at my lip. "Wallace?" Couldn't help but tilt my head clear to my shoulder, looking down at the pockets of my blue smock. "You ever think of that night, Wallace?" Dammit to hell, didn't I have one drop of self-restraint?

"Sure," he said, looking up. Shit-Jesus, those eyes again. "Nobody believed me at Lackland. Keesler neither."

"You told people?" I tried to sound hurt, abused. But frankly, I ate it up.

"Well sure," he said, looking up at the exit sign. "It's not every day your girlfriend's infested."

Girlfriend.

It didn't quite matter what he said after that because I don't recall a single word of it. Just that he picked me up off Mama's porch near dusk and held my elbow crossing the street, one or two fingers trying to slide upwards 'til I clamped my arm to my side; nothing's for free anymore. Still, I could swear I felt my little locust start buzzing about, just to be back near him.

There's hardly a thing fancy in Eunola—just Martha's Home-Cook, which I suppose is out of the question—so Wallace took me to the Pizza Inn over in Geneva. Well, there are worse things than Diet Pepsi in dimpled, amber plastic.

"I've been thinking about you a lot, Pearl."

"You have?" The words came out like a breath.

"Sure. Wonder what you've been up to."

Didn't know what he was getting at, but pretty certain it was me so I thought I'd give him a hard time. A bit. "You could have called and asked. Or written. Lacey gets all sorts of letters from boys she's... hmm."

"You don't want to finish that sentence?"

Blushing would be nice. I've never blushed. It would be nice. "I think I'll just leave that where it is," I said.

"You always could rev me up, girl."

"Wallace McCabe, shame on you."

Oh, the way a boy knows how to look at a girl, the way he knows how to send his fingers through his hair, or wink at her when he's complaining over the green peppers being on her side of the pizza. How he can glance at her bosoms without being obvious enough that she might be duty-bound to slap him. There's a great deal a boy knows about subtlety more than I know. If he asked, I'd pull off my clothes right here in the ripped vinyl booth and climb right on top of him. That's exactly what I'd do.

"I've been thinking, Wallace, that maybe he's just been waiting for such a night to come on out. It's almost time, you know. And maybe he's on a different schedule. Maybe he'll be early." He was holding me again just like that first time. We'd gone a little berserk that night, me straddling him—my knees scuffing up on the oak's shallow roots. Wallace was looking at me and sucking at me, and I about ripped his dick right off him rocking so fast.

"You're just as crazy as ever, aren't you?"

"Tell me things, Wallace," I sort of slurped into his ear in that breathy way a girl talks when she knows she's got him close to giving her the world, let alone a little bit of air like need or love.

He was gripping one of my hips hard, letting his other hand climb up the front of my blouse, letting himself rumple the rayon and tug at the buttons, letting himself pull down one of the cups of my bra.

"Wallace," I said again, "what do you want?" Now I was well aware that my phrasing was dangerous. Any boy's more than likely going to opt for the I'd like you to suck me silly interpretation, versus I want you always and forever, you're my girl and I want you with me something bad. But I wasn't sure how forward I could be with him: we hadn't set eyes or tongues on each other for twelve years after all.

Sure enough: "This is wonderful, Pearl," he said, and didn't even open his eyes.

"I been thinking," said Wallace later on at the tree while collecting ourselves. He stuffed one hand deep down in his pocket like he'd put something there just for me, but then left it right where it was. "If I could take a couple pictures, maybe write a little something about it." He touched a finger to my side, all careful like he thought the lump might burn him. "That's what I'm doing now. Got a few stories in the Biloxi Daily."

"We talking about my li'l ol' bug?"

"It's amazing, Pearl. Nobody's ever seen such a thing. It's like it's out of the Bible or something. People would think you're incredible."

"Me?"

"You."

"That why you're back here?"

"Don't pout, baby. I wanted to see you."

"Is that why you're back?"

"Course not."

"Which one?"

"You've got me all confused," he said.

I put maybe a centimeter between us where we were leaning now against our tree. I pulled my knees to my chest and felt all the things a girl feels after giving it up for what she thought was something but really only amounts to free. All that heaviness in the belly, all that dread of coming across a mirror one of these days. And I'd felt all that before, of course, but this was Wallace and so I 'bout could have gnawed through my wrists to slit them, for I had no knife.

"Pearl," he said, craning his neck to see up into my face. "Pearly."

"What?"

"What you think about the story, maybe a picture or two—else they just won't believe it." He touched my arm, and I could swear to you that I came again right then and there, though I know you'll be calling me a liar, so I won't tell you that. (Even though it's true.) What I'll say is that he touched my arm and then gave it a little squeeze, and I thought: So, he wants pictures. He wants pictures of you, Pearl. He wants to take home pictures of you and your bug because maybe he's having trouble remembering you and is planning on coming back, and there are things you could do to encourage him returning or even taking you with. He could take you with him. That's not beyond the realm, of course. Just smile all puckery and maybe a little pout and let him touch you almost as much as he wants.

He had a camera in the Dodge. Film loaded, flash hooked up. A big jobby with swirly lens and all.

"Now lean up right here, Pearl." He walked me backwards up against the hood of his car. Me in no shirt, just my bra—which he said wouldn't show much 'cause he was going for close-ups, but I was sort of hoping it would.

"You don't think we need better lighting?" I asked him, but he just shook his head and went on about fiddling with the various switches and dials on the camera 'til he was ready.

"Now," he said, "put your left arm up over your head. Maybe put your right hand on the skin there, kind of showing right where to look for the little fucker."

He started snapping shots all over the place, walking around me for every possible angle, my eyes going completely starry for the flashing.

"Wallace?" I said.

"Pearl."

"I'm starting to get cold over here."

"Just a couple more."

"Wallace."

"Pearl."

"I'm starting to feel cheap."

He took me home a little after that—after three more angles, even one bird's-eye view. Mama was in bed. I crept in. I avoided all mirrors and any sheet of glass. I went to bed, tucking my right hand around my left side, hoping to feel the buzzing, but there wasn't an ounce of delight going on in there.

Weeks later there I was in clippings Wallace sent back: BIZARRE BEAST BURROWS IN 'BAMA BEAUTY. And then our Eunola Weekly picked up his story, too: LOCUST NESTS IN LOCAL LADY, BOTH SAID TO BE DOING FINE, with his same picture of my armpit and the swelling beneath my skin—really just a flash of white and then the shadowy outline where my other hand was pointing. You can just imagine the stares I got in checkout lane #2. You can just imagine. All those girls from school, the ones never wanted their boys to look crosswise at me. All those boys begging. Now here I was becoming a sort of celebrity, and so all those boys who'd ever laid a hand were back in lane #2 saying:

"Strange as all, Pearl. That damn bug is strange as all."

"Didn't feel like no bug I ever squashed." That was Darryl, whose head was busted in all those years ago in our homecoming game.

"You boys just stop, now," I cooed and dimpled.

"Wouldn't mind seeing it in the flesh again, Pearl."

"Buddy LaDette, Cherry's just over there in lane #3, buying her groceries separate from your little can of ham. You don't think you ought to get back over there with her, do you? Before she decides you're on the porch swing tonight?"

Darryl hooted.

This is how it was the first week. After that, I started getting mail. All from the same somebody, but I didn't have a clue who that somebody was. Always the thinnest paper—those AirMail sheets Father sent on home to Mama talking about the caves in Marble Mountain at DaNang, back when there was something between them. And always just a few words in my letters: "SLOW DOWN CRAZY-THING" or "TOO SWEET FOR HONEY BEES." Clearly a crackpot dipshit like Buddy LaDette. But any day there wasn't a letter, I changed my clothes after work and slipped right into bed, just taking a Yodel cake in there with me and waking in the morning to the crinkling of its wrapper stuck to my cheek. You'd have done the same, I'm sure.

Mama was beginning to take up with her art teacher, a thin man with a ponytail and only black clothing. Having passed through seventh-grade ceramics under him at Mercy Walker Junior High, we'd all been sure he was gay, but I can assure you, as one who tried and failed at sleeping next door to whatever it was they're doing, it wasn't anything like gay. Nevertheless, there are some pretty big closets in the world, and maybe Timothy Ray just crammed his whole life into one and is seeing how it plays out.

It was a Wednesday night when I checked the mailbox and found it. All day long I'd been double-pricing and double-billing every third or fourth item and being yelled at here and there by the wives who couldn't keep their husbands home—we all know those types, little shriveled-up things who're so tight they wrinkle 'round their mouths in starburst puckers like dog butts. There'd been nothing in the mail for several days, and I was beginning to feel passed over. Old news. I almost didn't open the mailbox; our red flag on the side had been broken since Father left— that very day when he backed the Mercury into the pole and grabbed hold the flag to hoist it back up on the cinders again. Well, so I did check just because I figured there might be a bill or something, trying as I was not to think of the secret letters.

And there, in the center of the otherwise empty mailbox, woven through with red ribbon, was the strangest little wooden box I'd ever seen. It was only about five inches in every direction, and looked like a small prison with its bamboo cell bars and a front door that slid up and back down to keep something in or out. And this ribbon. The prettiest grosgrain you ever saw. Wide as three full inches. A cranberry red. And a strip of rice paper tucked inside said nothing more than SOON.

Well, you know I 'bout shit a brick at this. You know I didn't sleep, but just turned this box in my hands all night like Mama when Rubik's Cube first came out and she had a whole passel of them tossed off the bed, screwed up beyond unpuzzlement. The next day I was triple-pricing and triple-billing.

There wasn't much more to say about the week. There wasn't much more to say than to impress upon you how rattly I was those days. How everywhere I went I could still smell Wallace on me. Wasn't true, of course; it'd been many soaks since him. But the smell of boy was with me, was a little like soured milk—just the start of milk souring, nothing frightful or gloppy. Just that little nibble at the nose. Just that little bit of boy. And the wispy-papered letters—no postmarks or any way to know who it was. They frightened me.

A little.

Like having my legs up over Wallace's shoulders. Feeling… things. Like frightened. Because it was happening. He'd been back but I'd known he wasn't staying. And if we were still just smooching and breathing hard, his hand up my blouse begging, well then there'd be hope. But once you give it, even at the moment of giving it—it's gone.

"Pearl." Mama came in for lunch, and we sat in the workroom on orange crates with the oranges still in them, the fruit under Mama sinking so low a trickle of juice seeped right on out the corner of her crate. "I think it's time you find a place."

"What?"

"Don't you think?"

"No, I most certainly do not!"

"It's not as though you're a girl needs anybody's help. And you got your wages steady."

There was some fleck of leaf on my pants cuff. Oak leaf. I let it be.

"Look, Pearl. I'm not gonna beat around this bush much longer." She took another bite of her egg-salad sandwich that gummed up her whole mouth, so I was dreading her starting back up again, for a number of reasons. I dropped my eyes to her left hand all puffed and swollen tight. "I feel a little hemmed in."

"Go to hell, Mama."

She went on chewing, maybe shifted her eyebrows up at me a touch saying, "Well, all right."

I stopped being able to look at Mama's face, I mean really study it, when I was nine. Ever since, all I see's that left hand, the recessing slick white groove of empty skin at the base of her ring finger.

The Saturday Father left us, she flipped her ring off the kitchen sink backsplash right down through the drain. Mama and Father'd been stuck in a low-grade fight a few nights running, and the last thing he'd said before passing out that Friday night under the paper in his favorite sitting chair was, "Damned if that ain't a mess of dishes in there, Lois." We all three looked up and in through the kitchen's pass-through window right at the teetering stacks of morning, noon, and night grazing and her pitiful attempt at providing us meals not out of cellophane.

Come Saturday morning, she was making about as much noise as she could with the water and the clanging, and every few minutes she looked over her shoulder just confirming his absolute no-goodness, his snorting, drip-jawed, easy-smile sleeping. She handed me the last fork, and I set to wiping it dry in the now soppity flour-sack towel she hadn't washed long enough that Hormel chili and tinned pumpkin pie filling (meals at least one season apart) were mingling together there on the fraying hem. She went to him, stood before him, leaned into the chair—her big old bosoms knocking around loose in a plaid housedress and coming to rest just over his face. Still he went on sleeping, went on snorting and growling up the spit collecting at the back of his throat. I thought maybe she'd start in yelling—I'd seen it in her before, the very same pressure-cooker buildup and explosion—and I crossed every finger I had against it 'cause he looked tired, and what else did she have to do, and he was my father and somehow being near him didn't make me stand up straight and breathe all rigid the way being near her did.

That time, though, she was quiet. She stood up and let her knees creak-crack walking back to the sink—didn't even look one eye at me. She just flicked that sliver of gold from the soap gully, sending it spiraling once, twice, hard on the enamel and right down the drain with a good swallow. Then came laundry, mostly Father's short-sleeved line shirts—faded and soft blue cuffs for the rolling 'cause he used to smoke some back then (before Lerlene spewed her little Chihuahua coughs his way). So Mama went about the house quiet and stealthy as a cow can be in a chute built for calves.

It wasn't until near lunch Father was up and about. I heard them in the kitchen: him opening the cupboard doors 'neath the sink, hitting the pipes hard and metal so they rang, and throwing his elbows into Mama's stand of soap bottles and abrasives and polishes which she hoarded in bulk, just like they were snack cakes, for days when she had industrious intention (if not industrious action). She stood behind him, blocking his light—couldn't help it—her arms crossed over her chest best they could reach.

"Did you run water?" he was asking her.

"I don't know," she told him, not betraying the least little bit of sorrow.

"Least you could do is remember that."

"Well I don't, and that's a fact for you."

"You think a tone's what you need here with me, darlin'?"

"You wanna ask your chair what tone I oughta take instead of my sweet, calm, genteel—"

"My chair," he repeated, sounding puzzled.

"I've had it," she said, throwing up her hands and shooting out a leg from what, somewhere in all that cloth and skin, was a hip meaning to sass him. But she stood right where she was. Truth was, she wanted it back. Needed it back. But even more, she wanted him to do the retrieving.

Father was on his side now, his torso folding in on itself almost fetally, making him seem small and helpless. He was fitting the wrench to the nut holding the S of pipe to the drain. His elbows were stiff, his twisting of the wrench exaggerated. He saw me in the doorway. "You know how this happened, baby?" he asked me. "You tell me if she meant it."

"I was drying," I said, meaning I hadn't seen, though this deception wasn't at all something I wanted to do for Mama—it just came out; I'd been siding with Father all these years and always figured to go on doing so. Until what he did next.

Wrench in hand 'cause he wasn't getting anywhere with that old rusted nut, he poked his head out from the cupboard, ducking to avoid the hanging dishtowel and making a big show of not wanting it to touch him. "Worthless," he said looking at her, and I admit I smiled. "Two peas in a fucking pod," he said, and looked those fierce blue eyes right at me.

I went to the sink then, stood to the right of his bowlegged knee-proppings, and I spun the COLD handle and let that water wash through. We could hear the ring push off the catch of loop to the S pipe, and then all we heard was water.

Mama stood there looking strangely peaceful, breathing deep and slow. I regretted it then, my careless choosing and her pleasure for it. Father ducked out of the cupboard and went to the Mercury. And that's the day he did a number on the mailbox backing up onto it. Didn't once come back.

It's the bruises get you stuck somewhere. The little thumb-sized spot of brown on a shoulder. The swell of raspberry turning to plum on the left inner thigh because his hips are bony and he favors leaning on his right. The little aches of breaking beneath the skin. Those are what get you stuck somewhere.

And so you let yourself feel it—the truth of who you are and how little you're keeping to yourself after so much giving away. Would I change things? Someone might. But I don't think I'm capable of not taking the easy route, the quick route. The one leads straight to my water oak, and straight to hell. I don't mean fire-and-furnace-hell. I mean that gully of thinking it through and knowing when something's finished because of something I did. Some days I can get through without feeling the weight of such a thing as personal ruination by choice, by lack of proper choosing. But then there are the days after: of bruises and of knowing that given a thumb line-up, you couldn't match up the imprinted spot on your shoulder—that little spot of tugging that remains on your crest of bone—to its right and proper hand.

And so you get stuck. Eating Yodel cakes in bed. Waking in the crumbs. Touching your fingers to the lump on your side to wake it up, but there's nothing, not one damn shimmy. Sniffing at a dusty bottle of Dry Sack sherry Father forgot in the bath cabinet, loving that it smells like soy sauce, and you used to think he'd maybe come on back for it. You used to think maybe you'd get him to stick around if you offered to pour it for him. But he doesn't even drink that stuff—just some damn workroom gift 'round Christmas instead of a raise. Still, you sometimes think about him sipping it with you. You even dream it sometimes, though he's often a number of people, men-people, in that dream, shape-shifting in and out of focus.

I'm getting sidetracked here. Let's say it was a rough patch. Let's just say that and drop it.

Now Wallace may be back in Biloxi, making squadron first sergeant and getting all sorts and sundry wing awards, and I might be starting not to feel that divide anymore. I might be. What I'm feeling instead is that I'm split down the middle into two girls and neither one likes the other.

I've started seeing a lot of one boy. One I've never known before 'cause he's new, a city boy come down from Montgomery to a cousin's car-parts shop. Someone real quiet and kind of nerve-wracking the way he couldn't bring himself even to kiss me our first night. That afternoon, he came in the Kroger in an orange button-up shirt. He was drifting my way with his basket looped to his left hand. Standing his boxes in grid formation, taking away his hand after each one, waiting to see would it fall when the belt started up conveying the circle again. He nodded hello, all shy-like. He's starting to bald at the front of his head, his bangs thinning through his middle part—just barely, and I pretended not to notice; it's nothing. He was in tight blue jeans. His cheeks full of color like a drunk half a bottle shy. His fingernails short, almost painful.

"Pearl," he said, like it was a question he was reading off my embroidered smock, pulling it apart into sound without meaning, just lovely, lovely sound.

It'd been eons since I heard my name come out some new mouth, so I was caught chewing my cud when what I should've been doing was bagging his rice mixes.

"Bet you don't need a mix."

"No, 'course not," I said.

Then my hand was somewhere it shouldn't have been and he was tugging it up off of him to hold in the air out between us, but holding on to it nonetheless. Letting me think there could be something more to me. Letting me breathe.

He waited for me to get off work and we walked, just walked 'round the town, me trying to give him a tour that didn't amount to naming each boy I'd been with at each corner or park bench. And when dusk was on us and I'd had near enough of waiting on him and leaned in real close when he was saying something, who knows what, he told me, "You won't believe this, but I've never done such a thing so soon."

Well, shit-Jesus, knock me clear unconscious! I slid right into his arms and kissed on him like there was no tomorrow. And then? Well, slow as molasses on a February sidewalk in Memphis and quick as spit in a can, depending on if you're asking me or if you're asking him: three days 'til the water oak and that night when I found Lacey's key under the mat and slipped in without waking her shit of a brother who likes to squeeze through whatever doorway I'm standing in, I started feeling it.

That low ache through the middle. That deep wanting to crawl inside a boy. I won't give you his name. I won't think on him or spend a lick of Yodel cake on fretting this one out.

(Wishful thinking.)

Give me some time to feel this through and I'll tell you. Give me a chance to ask the bug. I will say he told me I'm smart. I will say that, because it's fair. That you should know he thinks about me. It's fair you should know that.

But tell me this. How does a girl know one solid thing, one big old rock formation of not going anywhere when there's a breeze? You understand: I mean, how can a person be certain she's the one when the leaves are falling around her and the current's speeding up? I'm not beating around any bush—Mama's or otherwise—this is an all too unwieldy thing to put to words. This fear of becoming what Father would call tedious and Mama would only know to say is dull.

He told me he'd seen the article but didn't read it. The picture, but didn't snip it out of the paper and tack it to his wall. A curiosity, he called it, my bug. And he didn't try much to touch it or look at it, though on the other hand, the few times his arm was about me and slipped down my side and over the hard lump of it, he didn't cringe or wince or pull away in the least. And then he started talking about it.

"They're not like other bugs," he told me one time we were sitting out front on his porch.

"No?" I said. He'd poured us lemonade so pulpy I had to keep pretending to sneeze and then wipe my teeth under the cover of my hair falling over my face.

"They're like crickets sort of, but they don't jump. Just fly or crawl. Real slow, up the trunks of trees, you know?"

"Yeah. I remember. They were everywhere that night. Everywhere."

"They've got beaks for sucking."

"Beaks!"

"Beaks," he said, and then real quiet. "They don't always have to mate, you know—sexually."

We sat there a minute, his hand on mine. Me pretending I wasn't thinking of jumping up on top of him. Me pretending I wasn't thinking to find me a good spot on his neck.

"But you've got it all wrong, Pearl," he spoke urgently all of a sudden, needing me to know this.

I stopped wiping at my teeth and put my hair back over my shoulder to see him.

"Your bug—well, it just doesn't make sense: I mean, an adult wouldn't go into you. And it's impossible that just one egg would be laid. It just can't happen like that."

I reached my arm around to my side, pressed at the little thing, felt it give a little reply. I held it. "I know what I know," I said, sitting back on the step.

"I didn't mean anything by it," he said, putting an arm around me. "There's all sorts of strange phenomena out there we just don't understand. All sorts."

I kissed his cheek, sipped some more pulp, sneezed.

He squeezed my shoulder once, a sort of wordless bless you. "It's the boys make all the sound."

"Isn't it always?" I said, feeling entirely, transparently dumb.

He squeezed my hand. "Girls spread the honeydew," he said and he kissed me.

So if I tell you he buys dirty rice mixes three times a week, always checkout lane #2, and smiles at me and pays cash and says, "It's lovely to see you this evening," even though it's five in the afternoon—if I tell you all that, what can you make of it for me?

And tell me, where is he now? Isn't that the crux right there? Says he wants solitude sometimes, says he needs quiet. And I walk through this world shaking for how still it is to me, how little it seems to see me.

Sometimes I hold my breath, wait to see if he'll notice how quiet I can be.

Along came Tuesday back around, and from Lacey's front window, I saw Mama strolling the sidewalk in her big floral number, looking like a squared-off sofa bed on its way to being pulled out. She had her portfolio under her arm, a big sketchpad filled with penises pointing every whichaway, some charcoal sticks and gum erasers.

I tried phoning him but it just rang. Off the hook or unplugged 'cause sometimes he says he just can't face it. I called the shop but his cousin said he was off all day. I phoned his place again and sat there so long with the cord wrapped around my waist and up my arm that I forgot what I was doing and where I was, and when of a sudden there was his voice, I hadn't any breath and couldn't have told you my name or his name to save my life.

"Hello?" he said once more.

"It's me," I said.

"Oh. Pearl," he said, and that little bit of falling in his voice knocked me clear to the floor. "Like I said last night, sometimes I just need some time to myself."

"I know," I said. I didn't but thought it would please him to be known, to be fully comprehended. "Just a bit?"

"Just a bit."

My hand needed to hang up the phone. My heart needed other things. "You missing me, darlin'?" I said it as sweet as I knew how, sweet and quiet, just like someone not asking one thing in return. Though, of course, that was exactly what I was doing.

"Pearl," he said, low and near cold.

"Yes?"

"Some time, okay?"

"I'm in over my head, I think." I didn't mean to say it out loud. Shit-Jesus, I didn't mean to say it.

"I'll find you," he said. "By the honeydew." A click. Then the hush of nothing on the other end.

Sitting there, I gathered my skirt and found it. The bruise was black, if you know what I mean. I mean black-muddy. I mean done and over with being on fire and now turned all the way to ugly and alone.

So I went to Father and Lerlene's. Right about now you're thinking, Girl needs a good sock to the head, a good shaking. Yeah, well. Lacey says I have father issues. But I been wanting to be petted since the day I was born. Got not one thing to do with Father or his going from us.

Okay, so I braced myself for stepping onto the shifting Astroturf deck of the houseboat, braced for having to look at Lerlene Gessum putting her fingers through what may or may not qualify as Father's hair—just long, droopy strands plucking out of the top of his head every inch or so. Braced myself for Father asking me what's doing these days. Never did know what to say to that; surely he'd been off the boat and into town enough times to hear some things, and really, I had Mama, I had checkout lane #2, I had my water oak up at the school, I had or didn't have some strange new boy, and I had my bug. And I never really thought he wanted to hear about any of these.

He poured us gin in low blue glasses. These were Lerlene's glasses and I never trusted a woman so weak of core she thought more of colorful glass than seeing what was in the cup. Still, I drank it, though I don't drink ordinarily but tonight I was feeling some fog might be nice.

"I'm thinking to float on up to Elba next month," Father said. "Hear Jackson's got some good work for me there. You won't miss me too much, darlin', will ya?"

"I'm gonna take up floral arranging with Diane. His wife." Lerlene wasn't saying this to me, just reciting the plan they must have already cooked up to avoid thinking about living here in Eunola too much longer, and meaning to cut me off. I knew she'd been pushing for them to pick up and go a long time—not too thrilled still to be the other woman as far as the law and I were concerned.

I poured myself some more Gilbey's.

"Pearl, you tell me now what you're doing with your life. You got yourself any plans, girl?"

I grabbed for the Apple Jack, too.

"She's hitting it kind of hard, isn't she, Juice?" She didn't even bother to whisper to him. Called him Juice.

Father patted her hand on his thigh, then looked at me with some faith in my coming through with something spectacular to keep him tethered at this dock 'cause he had not one bit of desire to leave Eunola. His forehead scrunched up with how high his eyebrows were. Hopes too.

In me. His girl-baby, his once-upon-a-time doll. His darlin' who's got not one thing in this world to make him proud, and each of us on this floating house knows it.

What else could I do?

I stood up.

I lifted my skirt to my waist.

I pointed.

"I have a bruise of a hipbone on my inner thigh," I began kinda slow. "My plan is to see if I can't make something work in my life. If I can't convince this certain hipbone that I'd like to talk to him, that I'd like to sit near him and wake finding him watching me, his fingers unsnagging my hair. If I can't close my legs for once in my life and sit still beside a boy who thinks I'm smart and clever and charming, and just be quiet. Just still and quiet and charmingly, motionlessly perfect. I'm not quite sure what my plan amounts to, how I mean to set about at it, but that's my plan." I dropped my skirt and then sat back down with my blue glass of brandy cupped in my lap.

Father's eyes ran up and down me, quick, darty.

"Well, that's fine, Pearl," said Lerlene, picking up our glasses from the table and whisking them away. I understood: we were done.

Father and I sat facing each other but watching the grain of the tabletop inch this way and that. 'Course Father is a drinker, so he was probably steady as can be on a houseboat.

He rubbed at the top of his head, and smoothed down the hairs. "You make me sick," he said.

I was slugged. But sat there. Couldn't think to move because then there wasn't ever any hope for him taking it back. He stood up and went down the narrow hallway, beyond the teensy kitchen and the red drape across their "room." Must have been crazy, but I thought he was getting me something, wanting to show me something. A little gem of inspiration maybe. A little tenderness he kept hidden from Lerlene. An old photo he'd squirreled away in his undies drawer of Mama and him dancing or kissing or holding sweet baby me between them, him in vertical-striped pants and a brown suede vest. The kind of picture makes you believe in things, in spite of this world. I thought he was coming back to me. Lerlene was at the sink, rinsing out the blue glasses, setting them in the drainer to dry right next to a lilac bud vase and a red milk glass.

I was very, very small then. Almost nothing.

"He says I'm smart," I called out to neither one of them. And then I left, feeling how deep-in the ache of my bruise was now that it was leaving my skin.

At the end of my shift tonight, I start back to Lacey's place alone. She's off with so-and-so straight from work. Dreading her brother in a door jamb, I take as many loops in my walking as I can. I flip Mama's mailbox open in passing just to be sure. Nothing. Go over by the high school and see kids get frantic, start stuffing bottles around the base of a rock been spray-painted over every year by seniors on the verge of graduating (to what, God only knows in this place)—and I have to wonder then, do I really look so old I might nark? I suppose I do.

I walk to the end of the field by them, need a bit of creek and to sit at my water oak. Feel a kind of heaviness in the air, a kind of heat seems to be the earth feeling clever. Makes it hard to breathe some. These early cicadas shaking the world with such a rattly peeling-free of their skins.

I wake without knowing I've arms and legs. Numb without the needles, true numb. Just my lips I can feel, and the tip of my nose. He's with me. Near me. One hand slipped between my legs, the other inside my top but feeling for my heart. Sitting right here beside me. Him-who? Does it matter? His arm's around me, his face nuzzling into my neck and shoulder, saying my name, saying, Please, Pearl.

There's a loud pop of tire, some hoodlum driving doughnuts in the school lot. I've my arms and feet back. No one's here but me.

It was Wallace because, I figure, it'll always—to some degree—be Wallace. No matter the dirty rice mixes. No matter my wanting to tug down my skirt; I'll always tug it back up for him.

I'm tempted to fabricate. Tell you words of his he's setting just inside my ear. Tell you where his hands are, his heart too. Tell you I can feel the rumbling end to hibernation going on in my skin, the waking of life brought on for hearing the other cicadas cluttering up the air, banging away at my ears, the waking of life for fooling us both into thinking Wallace is here.

Do you ever think your life's shaping up with so many clues you need an Easter basket for the hunt-and-gather? And with so many angles to see something, with so many true signs, you're just fooling yourself to think there's no end point coming? That's how it is this very moment sitting here at my water oak: pictures of me taken by someone I know never loved me more than a fish in a tank who'll swim through the plastic tunnel and kiss the vinyl seaweed for a flake of TetraMin, a mama gone plumb wacko, a Father living on a pontoon barge of a house being sucked on by a maroon-haired nothing-or-other, a tenderhearted stalker who somehow knows me and is sending all sorts of things cause a commotion in me, a bruise sunken too deep to doubt, a boy seems both to love me and want nothing of me, and a bug. If you were to grant me wishes—just pretending there were such things and such possibilities—I wouldn't know what to ask for; I think I've never really known what I want at all.

Not even Wallace.

So here, under my water oak, coming back to the breathing world—the kids sip and titter, pointing at one another after a good joke—I can't help but feel so much I've wasted. It's hitting me hard, the finity of time. The end always approaching. I've a good mind to find some water deeper than this here creek, deeper even than the Pea, and sacrifice the suspense.

I'm not prepared to offer any happiness.

"Hey," I call out to them 'cause they're the only ones around. "Hey, you got yourself a Swiss army on you?"

They're laughing that sort of laugh you do when you're a kid and somehow the tables turn and some old thing's wanting something from you instead of your hand always out begging.

"Yeah." He's the shortest of them, and I notice the way he stands with his legs apart, a sort of low castle, and I wonder if it ever leaves his mind—that he's beneath his friends, always. A crinkly blue windbreaker tied 'round his waist, his cutoff jeans shorts dragging low off his hips anyhow.

"Sharp?" I ask.

"Damn straight."

"Well bring it on over," I tell him.

And he does. This freckle-nosed, mole-armed blond boy. He stands over me, and I can smell what it is they've got: beer and whiskey both, some pot a couple hours back. The sun's low behind him, giving the curls at his temples a nice glow. I wrap my left arm up over my shoulder, pull a little at my tank top. I lay two fingers over it to be sure. Nothing. Utter stillness. Complete remorse.

I run my thumbnail along the groove of a few of the blades. Decide on one somewhere in between big and small, with a fine point at the tip. "If you're fixin' to watch, best step aside of the light."

Then I do it.

I lay the point alongside the lump and then push it in and under. No sawing. Just clean sweeps of the sharpness, careful to err on the side of flesh rather than beast. The boy holds out a bottle to me I hadn't seen before; must have come from his waistband. "I'm good," I tell him. There's hardly any blood and that surprises me. Once I've a half-moon drawn around the head, I set the knife in the grass and feel with my fingertips. It's all sorts of knitted into me. I run the knife along the flap of skin, cut as I can to free it, to let it go. I set the knife down again and check it.

Nearly free. I'm bleeding now. More of it. Down my side. Feels like sweat slipping beneath my breast.

"You sure?" says the boy, not even certain he's making sound.

I grab hold of it; one more cut and it's out. It's in my fingers. This small, very small gray thing not a bug at all. Just a mottled and stringy bit of something. I push at it in my fingertips and smash one end of it with my thumb. This is body. Body gone wrong, but only body. A bit of me, really. That's all it's ever been.

"You cryin'?" asks the boy.

"No."

"Don't cry." He's come forward, is leaning over me. His hand letting itself touch me, my arm. Then my cheek, just like a lover wanting to soothe something, send it away. Like in a movie.

"Take your fucking knife."

He moves closer, for the knife, I think, but then squats in the grass. Lays his hand on my arm again, and I can feel the boniness of his fingers gripping me—not so much asking to stop this for my sake but for his own; he's frightened.

"Tommy," calls one of them.

He doesn't answer.

Then, "Give psycho a kiss."

"Shut the fuck up," he hollers over a shoulder. "Y'ought to set your hand to that," he tells me.

I look again at my side and see what I've done. Look again at my palm and see what I've believed in. I grab my side and feel it hot as hellfire.

Don't know how, but I wind up in a hospital room and there are beige railings on the bed, a beige water pitcher and a beige cup nearby. Mama's in the hall but won't come in; I know those are her flowered muumuu knees jutting out into the corridor.

"Thought you'd sleep the day away," says Lerlene, and then shuts her mouth for good. Finally.

Father comes stand right at my side, looks at me saying, "Damned if you weren't always a little off, girl."

Lerlene hides there behind him wishing she had her blue glasses to rinse, forcing herself to be in the same room 'cause she knows I came first and even though I'm one big fuck-up to him, she knows I'll always have come first.

He pats the edge of the bed, by my hip. And to have his hand there—well, mine moves to his without even thinking, without even knowing it.

"You let them take care of you now, you hear?" He's turning, catches a glance at the ceiling TV.

"Father, please don't go—" I start to give in to that same hunger always gets me in trouble. I start to, but he saves us both from it.

"Just lie back and be good," he says. And then they're both gone.

Lacey's next. She squashes her lips in her fingers, pushes them over to the left, the right. "I think you'd be best off back home again, if your mama will hear of it."

"Sure," I tell her, "sure."

That's it, just them. The hallway empties except for Mama's knees and what I can see of Timothy Ray's left hand patting her thigh.

Someone's left a pleated page from the Biloxi Daily, another clipping from Wallace: Bug-Girl a Sham. And my little locust cage, red grosgrain strung through, sits empty on the bedside table telling the world he never really knew me at all, not the boy or the bug—its new slip of paper the very last lie: FREE. It says: FREE.

SHADOWS

Adeline Carrie Koscher

They started to show up again.

She remembered each and every one, but never expected to see them, again.

The thumbprint under her right ear was the first one she noticed, a deep indigo pressed there so firmly that she wondered at not being able to see the detailed swirls, only the mark of pressure.

After a shower on a warm spring afternoon, the window open, birdsong and salt air slipping through the gauzy curtain, she breathed the day deep into her lungs and exhaled a note of freedom. She turned her head to get a look at herself in the mirror. Her hair piled in a towel revealed four distinct blue punctuation marks around the back of each shoulder. She blinked. Upon closer examination she ascertained that they were indeed there, under the surface of her skin. She touched them to see if they hurt, but there was no sensation, none, only a numbness.

The weather grew warmer day by day, and she found it more and more difficult to hide the marks. Certainly she'd had practice with that, but the shame and humiliation was not fresh, no absence of explanation filled her mouth.

Colorful bangles encircled her wrists, bluegreen, purple, almost black in spots, tattooed. So much for the yellow, linen sundress she found at the thrift store and planned to wear on this first summer she felt alive again in her body. It hung on the curtain rod. Sometimes, a breeze filled it with form, and it danced a little fox trot, inviting her with the promise of its mirth.

She became increasingly creative in her fashion. Make up, concealer and cakes of powder, did nothing to hide the circles and stripes that began to cover her like evidence of a tribal ritual. Long sleeves gave way to light scarves and shawls over tank tops and tee shirts. She considered a fuchsia sari in a store window, admiring its dual attraction of gauzy lightness and complete body coverage.

Some of the shadows were easier to conceal—hipbones and ribcage, waist and back—but she remembered them all and knew more would come. Some surfaced beneath others creating Rorschach inkblot tests. She wondered what her therapist would make of these. Many in the same locations darkened as each shadow surfaced.

It became difficult to disguise.

The discoloration contained no pain, no shame, no denial. She wore her history like age spots, a recollection of a life past. She hid them only to avoid causing discomfort in others, a memory fresh in her mind. Often people visibly wished she'd concealed the marks more effectively.

She began to notice the shadows revealed themselves in the order in which she had acquired them and knew that there would come a time when no attempt to conceal them would be effective. That day came one steamy morning late in July.

The previous night, in just a pair of cotton panties she stretched herself across the giant bed, smiling at the moon and enveloped by the gentle pressure of the cool sheet against her skin.

In the darkness she could not see them and slipped into a dream of a body—flush, softly worn, gently wrinkled, vital. In her dream she wore the yellow dress and walked alone along the shoreline. A breeze stirred her hair, the sun illuminated her shoulders, and the earth shifted under her feet. Eventually, even the weight of the feather-light dress was too much to bear. She slipped out of the puddle of sunshine. Newly able to breathe, her body responded to the air; her pores opened, and her nipples hardened. From the very last knuckle of the jetty she dove into the cool water. Empowered by the force of her dive and the freedom of her nudity, she felt the water envelop her, and she slowly became aware of its pressure against her skin. She resisted, but it was all around her. The thrashing led to a need for air and a heavier pressure on her chest. A watery hand clutched at her face forcing her below the surface. She thrashed and pulled at it, choked and woke to her own hand crushing her mouth and nose, pressing long blue lines along her cheekbones. Her other hand—red, clutching—tore at the smothering hand.

Release, a gasp, a blink into the hot July sun, fully risen in the sky, and she sat at the edge of her bed looking down at her hands. A wash of freedom without frustration rushed through her as she saw the anemones burst on her hands, tiny fireworks of blue, red, yellow, green erupted across the backs and down the fingers.

He had crushed them many times. He never hit. There was never a black eye or a welt. He did not slap her or punch her or even fling her across the room. A grasping, a clutching, a pulling tighter—she knew a constant and ever-increasing confinement that had enclosed her.

"Honey, if he's hitting you …"

"If I ever see him slap you …"

"We cannot do a thing if you do not report the battery."

Voices of threats and warnings swirled in her memory.

There was no "battery," per se. No one could remove the hand from over her mouth but herself.

She stood, stretched catlike to the sun, and walked to the full-length mirror. Her naked, technicolor body stood, a totem, a story, one that must be told. She walked out the front door into town.

TRANSFORMED, THE OFFICE NARCISSUS

P. Kobylarz

It was the day he no longer recognized his foot that, really, everything changed. And foot, not feet, because the other one was the same as usual. Long toes, a half-moon hung in the big nail, a pinkie toe curled as a quietly sleeping fetus, nearly as long as its cousin finger, eek!

That foot, the right one, was fine. Same bald man's head heel, too.

But the other one, the left one, was somehow different. Was it from a mis-step in a tidal pool the day he thought he might have clipped an urchin? Or was it the day she got him so mad that he kicked the wall? Twice. Or was it a genetic snafu made apparent only by time's slow fuse, not noticed until now?

Who's to know these things. How was it, um, different? Well, the imprint it made on wooden floors after a shower was more—pointed. The hair on its smooth lady-like skin carapace began reddening. The toenails altogether stopped growing. A definitely higher ankle, a more profound arch. The weirdest thing was, after a long day contained in the prison of sock, it even kinda smelled different. Like it wasn't, well, his foot.

Eight thirty-seven a.m. Generic coffee a-brewing. At the office the workers began piddling in. There were three women who were definite "definites." That's to say, they are in my book, definite definites, and only in mine. I have no idea what the other teachers think for they are, number one, professionals, and two, professors, and thus their minds must remain closed-book mysteries. Everyone knows they really don't have personalities. And that is why they are teachers. They know nothing.

From time to time, perhaps in the lunchroom or in the elevator, even in the echo chamber that is the stairwell, one of them might mention a student by name. Just the name, the moniker. Never even a hint of a glance, nor a gesture, that might reveal a subtext of a reference or a splinter of meaning, and if they do reveal something it is to those who have already figured them out. Or a human, soul-inspired line might be offered to a fellow teacher or student of a youngish nature who is/are however non-ironically also, of an extremely beautiful nature, and well, all in all, nothing is ever really said.

Back to the matter at hand. There are three very definite definites.

Some simple questions are just that. Take for instance how some people stay extremely fit. They eat a lot of fish. Perhaps mainly from a sushi-based diet. Or, say, fish cooked in the oven, or salmon smoked, the occasional oyster, mussel, abalone, and as much raw shrimp as possible. To make the mind sharp or to keep the fat off the important places. The places others need to grab and hold on to. But forgive me. I'm doing what I am paid to do. I am endlessly digressing.

Having a different foot is not a crisis in itself. At least not publicly. Shoes conceal many things. Including hygiene. What one considers sexy and how they take care if it leads to this thing we call appeal. Maybe it's in the fact of knowing a part of you, of your anatomy, is all of a sudden one day, changed. Revelations the shower brings. But how to appeal a change?

Everything changes. Food begins to be a particularly picky affair. No longer can your mouth sink into a perfectly grilled t-bone, rainbow red in the middle, in a pool of its own sanguine juices, on an extra large plate heaped with the cuttings of grilled vegetables. Not when you are trying to, like the Japanese, stay extremely fit.

Nothing tastes the same. Not even the basics. The cool, sweet draw of a glass of creamy vitamin D milk. Not even the crisp retort of a baguette bitten into fresh from a bakery. Not even the elixir of a glass of artesian tap water. Not when your foot has changed into that of another's.

What else does one need than definite definites? Of course it sounds bad. Most propositions do at first. But taken into context, it begins to make sense. Sense in the way one absolutely has to look at life. Life and its options. And the options on the options.

Sheree is just that type of person. You know, the type that dresses, or shall we be frank and say overdresses, as the classy kind of woman she reveres and not so secretly wants to be. Right down, or up to the hippest Italian made frames and lenses, the most stylish little ensembles she can pick up at the outlet (nobody knows), and the latest of the latest shoes that grace her manicured feet like perfectly fitting leather rickshaws. At least some people's parts never change.

Sheree the sprite of the photocopier where she always is, cheerfully. Perusing through a book, mentioning the weather, not saying much to anyone although greeting and chatting with an equal degree of sincerity and kindness. She wears lip gloss, her hair up or down, both as devastatingly seductive as she herself knows it to be, and a perfume that will only allow itself to be described as honeysuckle in the rain.

There aren't enough windows in any building anytime when a looking-out-of-the-window-feeling comes. No groovy tree-shaded grove with an Akita tied to one of its trunks. A bus psssshhhhhtttiinnnnggg by and dropping off four black ladies wearing similar hats on a day that just about everybody's car is broken down, probably a dead battery, and a long, long crack in the window, fifty-pound sack of birdseed in the trunk. Windows to the outside which clouds form in for moments in time asking for someone—anyone—to think of them and their shapes as giant, cottony genitals.

How come nobody wonders if ghosts get hungry?

Reenita was the sun rising anywhere but the tropics, unless from under needles of palm trees. She was nothing that words can in anyway describe so why not then try? It's like this—cat or mouse—we're either after fur or bait. She was a teacher of the Romantics, the Victorians, the Elizabethans, literary anyones who were literally anyones. She was a Queen of lineage purely intellectual, a pure-blooded Yale-ian, Oxfordian, Sorbonnianne and this is how she carried herself wearing the requisite facial expression. A dreid Jack-O-Lantern.

This is what Reenita expects: be nice to her or leave the room. Hold open the door if she is leaving or entering. Offer to make her a cup of coffee or tea. Instruct her patiently and clearly, and lovingly, on how to send a fax. Do not attempt to get to know her deep enough that you'll be able to guess one of her favorite wines. Do not attempt to learn what she, herself, living human flesh and blood, really thinks of Shelley's tear-stained letter or why she wears like clockwork sheer panty hose with the line down the back.

Camera pans in from the Superstition Mountains of all places Arizona, fast time, over the yellow blooming bushy heads of a forest of palo verdes, like a cruise missile misfired. Towards a city, first a white-line on the horizon, then some rooftop, then the microchipped, electronic card design of a planned suburb to crash and crash just over spouts of water shot into the air by a group of mating whales in the cold Pacific Ocean. Smart bomb camera tv out. A flicker. Then, blackness.

Finally one day a decision will have to be made. A commitment. You will have to sit down and accept the fact that the place that surrounds you is where you live and where you, geographically and mentally, are. You have willingly chosen a certain package of clichés, a locality with certain options and lack of them, a story book setting from a best-seller only you will read. A river city with a slow moving swell, big shade trees, young people bicycling by, false bistros, a walkway made for promenading that no one uses, a city in which the food's so good everybody eats out. Lifestyles built around buffets.

Or it'll be a small mountain town with great water. Ski resorts surrounding, a mix of wealthy inhabitants and not rich locals mostly deriving from Scandinavian midwestern stock, great shopping and a brick-paved outdoor mall where people get together to eat and drink and get drunk and even watch performances of themselves provided by street actors.

Or it'll be the anonymity of a gigantic city where everything is believed in, sampled, used and reused, phone numbers written on shirtsleeves or bar tabs. One great big park where everyone brings their pet, acting as gauchos without style or pinache or a reckoning of the slave/master relationship. Who's the boss of the boss? And designer leashes hold who in check, willingly.

When the city that is just right even down to the stylized decal on police cars, the mortgage cleansed, and the white fence boldly painted blue or magenta, the indoor/outdoor lighting and flower beds complimentarized, you disappear. Once and forever. It's called the endless highway with no rest stops.

Well, luckily, she would never leave the opportunity to view the renewing, slowly changing "We." She indeed would never see my, and I beg your pardon, lint-free innie gradually extend to a little fleshy tower of babel further extended. When hair begins to grow on your body, thicker, more wiry and in places and in patterns never before experienced by the angles of your particularly under-regarded but never steady best pal of a skeleton. Sometimes one says things that are not meant to be meant.

Today, nothing much different. I feel, maybe, it's the teeth. Maybe my teeth are changing. A tighter bite. More yellowed, probably from smoking after lunch break, which I apparently do not do. Not until tomorrow's craving. A wider expanse of arse, but firmer. A smaller stomach that has a taste for vegetable dishes and exotic cheeses. One of the lungs is still the same. Thicker nipples. Unrecognizable forearms and hands that dry easier with one of them sporting two rings that have nothing to do with marriage. The same throat and voice but the tongue seems stuck always with the bad aftertaste of chicken gizzards or cheap white wine. It is changing over. My eyes, well I've never been able to recognize them anyway so who's to say? Hair, face, lips, earlobes, chin—all are broadening. The mind. One always changes her mind.

I, you see by now, am the third office woman. Jaquelaine. Yes, definitely a Jackie.

FALLING SIDEWAYS

T. Shontelle MacQueen

U p until she'd walked through the Supplicant's Door, checking one last time to be certain her sash was tied properly, she'd been prepared to feel afraid, nervous, uncertain, embarrassed. She'd been prepared for many emotions, but it hadn't occurred to her to prepare for the lack of them. She wore a white robe intended to preserve her modesty until the screens came up at the end, and it struck her suddenly as an odd sort of conceit to protect something from view that was about to disappear forever anyway. She stood barefoot on the pale flagstones of the cavernous hall, but she was not cold.

Rays of light fell through the high stained glass windows, dappling clergy and congregation alike in hazy splotches of color. At the center of the hall Christ loomed over her, looking down from where he hung limned in a psychedelic halo of shifting shades. If she closed her eyes and listened she was aware of feet shuffling in the bleachers, parents hushing their children, the preparatory clearing of the minister's throat, a susurrus of background voices, but God did not speak to her. She stood in His shadow and watched the dust motes floating lazily past her eyes. She found herself leaning towards one, as if she could follow it on its careless journey through space. As if she could just let go and fall sideways into another world where she would be content to drift along, unhurried, continually alighting and then moving on. She heard the click of a camera.

The press was here today, of course, documenting the ongoing battle between the Millennium Church of Christ and the State of North Carolina. The state had made very simple, very reasonable arguments. The technology was not ready for distribution, sufficient research had not been conducted, long term side effects were unknown, it had not been approved for human transportation, it might or might not constitute murder. The church's argument had been even simpler. This is a religious issue—stay out of it. The church was not breaking any laws, mostly because the laws had not yet been made. It had happened much too fast.

In June of 2004 came the announcement that a subatomic particle had been successfully teleported. Despite good arguments against the possibility, the original particle was destroyed at point A, and an exact replica materialized at point B. Scientists predicted that in a few years, maybe ten, an entire atom might be teleported. Instead it happened only a few months later. Scientists suggested that by the end of the century, groups of atoms could be teleported, potentially revolutionizing the world of computing. In 2006 a lab in the United States teleported a very small group of atoms.

The understanding in the field was that it would be virtually impossible to teleport a human simply because of the staggering number of atoms involved. The calculations would be too astronomical to compute. When a human was successfully teleported (luckily it appeared to be an all or nothing event) the discovery shook the world. For reasons she didn't understand, and didn't really care about, the teleportation only seemed to work for a few feet. Perhaps due to equipment or computing issues, that was the maximum distance so far. Not particularly useful for world travel, but it did have its potential applications. And the Millennium Church of Christ had leapt on it.

It was certainly paying off. The Church boasted over 2,000 members, and, thanks to all the publicity, the numbers were growing every day. The Church had struck a chord with people who were looking for something new, and the idea of being physically destroyed and reborn at baptism had turned out to be very powerful.

There were even some recent studies showing a negligible weight loss following teleportation. Although only in the neighborhood of an ounce, the loss was consistent. The woman had joked about it with her friend on the phone. They had imagined weight loss clinics devoted to running around in circles to teleport over and over again, women getting more exercise in one afternoon than they had in the last 6 months on the newest diet gimmick. She had laughed at the idea with her friend, but, in her mind, she still saw the women going around and around, their lives circling the drain while they got smaller and smaller. It was an image she couldn't seem to shake.

The woman became aware of an expectant silence. The minister had stepped forward. "We are gathered here today to celebrate the rebirth of our sister in Christ. Let us pray."

After the murmured "Amen" the minister turned to her. "Have you come here today of your own will?"

"I have."

"And do you accept Christ as your Savior and promise to worship Him, following Him in faith from this day forward?"

"I do."

"Do you freely confess your sins against God?"

"I do."

"The congregation will now join the Supplicant in the confession of sin."

The woman let the words of the ceremony wash over her. The preparation for this day had been extensive, and she knew every word by heart. This part of the ceremony had gained some extra emphasis lately as the change in weight following teleportation had been interpreted by the Church as the absence of sin—it having been washed away by the rite of baptism. The fact that there was not one shred of evidence for this didn't bother them. It was symbolically perfect, and the doctrine had done nothing but boost membership. Imagine, having the weight of your sins literally lifted from your soul. It was the reason that brought so many to the Church despite the controversy. But it was not why she came. The woman had not decided to be baptized in order to have her sins forgiven. She did not believe in God.

As the woman said the words, moving from one declaration to the next, she yearned for the moment when she would step, dripping wet and naked, onto the teleporter. She had waited so long, attending one class after another, mouthing beliefs that seemed more ridiculous every day until they poured from her without effort. A river of passionate nonsense falling from her lips until she felt that her words did not belong to her at all. They took on a life of their own, dancing around her. She took her entourage of words everywhere with her, but they were entirely separate from her thoughts.

Her thoughts were always and entirely on this moment. The moment when she would step out of the shadow of God and end the struggle. God did not speak to her, but she felt Him all the time. She did not believe in Him, but something inside her was always aware of Him. He would not leave her alone. She fought to ignore Him, but her experience refused to align itself with reality. She could not stand it anymore. It was almost over.

The congregation flipped through their Bibles, following along with the minister. "A reading from Acts chapter 8, verses 36 to 40.

"'As they traveled along the road, they came to some water and the eunuch said, "Look, here is water. Why shouldn't I be baptized?" And he gave orders to stop the chariot. Then both Philip and the eunuch went down into the water and Philip baptized him. When they came up out of the water, the Spirit of the Lord suddenly took Philip away, and the eunuch did not see him again, but went on his way rejoicing. Philip, however, appeared at Azotus and traveled about, preaching the gospel in all the towns until he reached Caesarea.'"

The minister reached for the jug and filled it from the baptismal font. "By the power vested in me by God and the Millennium Church of Christ, I baptize you in the name of the Father, the Son, and the Holy Spirit." Cool water dripped into her eyes, and she blinked.

The woman had joined the Church because of the weight loss data. She was surfing the net when the data formed itself into the key to her freedom and dropped into her hand. She understood that the weight loss was not due to the loss of sin. That was intuitively absurd. To start with, everyone's weight loss was almost exactly the same. Scientists were at a loss to explain the data, but the woman knew what it was.

"Are you ready to be born again?" asked the minister. His kind eyes supported her, and she felt a moment of guilt at deceiving him so thoroughly. But she felt the key like a heaviness in her hand. She felt her first moment of fear.

"I am."

The God that did not exist would not be able to pester her anymore. The part of her that called to Him would be gone. He would have to leave her in peace.

She took a deep breath, letting the air fill her lungs and calm her nerves. She was ready. When the screens came up, the woman dropped her robe and stepped into the light.

AFLOAT

J. Weintraub

L et me be very clear about this. I did not agree to participate for my own sake. After twenty years of service as Chief Scientific Officer, I had much to offer to our government and to future generations, and although the expense was considerable, my experience, my technical expertise, my abilities to innovate and process information would certainly produce value far beyond the initial investment and the custodial costs. By tenfold, at least.

After all, genius—and that is not my own characterization but that of the media and my colleagues—is not a commodity that is easily obtained, but a gift to be appreciated and nurtured when it so infrequently appears.

Nor do I take personal credit for having defied—or at least temporarily deferred—death. As with most technological advances, this was the product of years of development, thousands of hours of work by hundreds of technicians, a series of timely synergies, and—since our stated objectives were of another sort altogether—not a little bit of serendipity and luck.

Let me explain. For many years it had been the charge of my division to develop an AI capacity that would equal the cognitive power of the human brain. Naturally, we modeled our efforts on the thing itself, although it was generally believed by most of our biotechnicians that any attempt to replicate the full functioning of the brain—with its hundred billion neurons connected by ten trillion synapses—was an exercise in futility. And who knows, perhaps they were right, since we never managed to achieve more than a crude imitation of the higher powers of cognition.

But along the way we were remarkably effective in converting visual and aural signals into electronic configurations, and it was those same skeptical biotechnicians who decided to apply these digital conversions to organic neural receptors—an essential component to the success of what was to follow. If we could, they argued, enable machines to "see" and "hear," then why not the blind and the deaf, too, and before long we had patented devices destined to enrich the lives of millions of disabled persons. Advances like these gave our group a solid reputation for biomedical innovation, and before long, the Saratoga Project was assigned to my division.

I had been monitoring Saratoga for some time, and I was impressed by its progress in preserving organs—hearts, livers, lungs, and the like—in isolation. But when the team came under my direction, I was astonished to learn that they had reached a stage where the health and viability of an isolated organ could be maintained, in a controlled environment, almost indefinitely. Of course, their goal was inventorying these organs for eventual transplantation, and until Saratoga became a part of my division, no one had seriously considered experimenting with the human brain. Just as we had failed to replicate artificially its almost infinite complexity, transplanting the brain would have required an equally advanced technology, far beyond our capacities at that time.

But simply preserving the brain in isolation seemed to be an attainable goal, and since, as any reputable philosopher would argue, personal identity resides in that organ, transferring a healthy brain into a secure, artificial environment would simplify the task of prolonging individual existence long after other organic functions had failed. Certainly, it was an experiment worth attempting, and the fact that my own cancer had by then been diagnosed and declared inoperable had little to do with this change in direction, although I don't deny that it may have hastened the process.

Trained as an engineer, I supervised the construction of the environment myself. Of course, it was far more complex than the devices that sustained hearts and lungs. But once the nutrient mix, the varying concentrations of proteins and enzymes, and the daily modifications in ionization levels were determined, the problem became one of implementation rather than content, and I saw to it that the resources were made available to create not only a functioning environment but one that would operate for at least as long as our civilization endured. The plutonium generator, for instance, would provide sufficient energy to keep the mechanism functioning for dozens of millennia. Huge, sealed vats were constructed to store the components for the supplies of glycogen, phosphates, lipids, and enzymes, the contents to be dispensed drop-by-drop into the solution where all the chemical reactions would occur. With much of the waste matter being recycled back into the system, healthy organic life could be sustained for almost as long as the generator produced the energy to keep the systems in operation. Heat displacement would eventually bring the whole apparatus to a halt, but my chief mathematician assured me that even without maintenance, stasis would not occur, theoretically, until long after the planet spun from its orbit and fell into the sun.

Of course, without the ability to communicate—to receive stimulation and respond in kind—I would neither have authorized nor participated in such a venture. But by then our digital conversion biotechnologies had reached such a degree of sophistication that the most complex information could be easily communicated directly to the relevant centers of the brain. If my mental ability could be sustained and enriched by a continuous flow of intellectual stimulation and if communications, in return, could be sent from this superior and continually expanding intelligence—contributing to the betterment of all posterity—then such an experiment would surely be worth the effort, regardless of the cost and the considerable sacrifice. On the other hand, if such communications were not successfully received or if my own observations were not being transmitted, or if either of these activities became dysfunctional in the future, the experiment was to be immediately terminated and I would be accorded the memorial rites due to an official of my standing and accomplishment.

Ordinarily, the surgery itself would have been a fearful thing to contemplate. But by then, my body had withered away before my eyes, an ugly, painful encumbrance requiring larger and larger dosages of analgesics, resulting in longer and longer periods of drugged stupor. Success or annihilation—I was prepared for either one, and even though all of the systems had not been fully tested, I signed the releases, endowed all my worldly goods to the financing of the project, and instructed the Surgical Division to proceed with the intervention a month ahead of schedule.

The procedure took three days, and even though life support was a minor concern in comparison with the tedious implantation of the thousands of microelectrodes, I was later informed that I had been twice pronounced clinically dead, for periods of twenty seconds each.

Of course, I have no recollection of this, no more than a patient under anesthesia remembers the removal of an appendix. But when I awoke, it was to a field of golden sunflowers—the test pattern I had chosen for the occasion—and when I received confirmation of my first transmission ("Mr. Watson, come here, I want you!") I would have cried for joy if I'd had the eyes to do so.

I remained awake for several days, exploring my new environment. I had been born into another world, and like an infant I could first only crawl about, as it were, and take a few awkward steps. Tests had been arranged in advance, but they were far more rigorous than I'd anticipated, and when they were finally completed, I fell into a long hallucinatory sleep. I awoke, still exhausted, and I immediately induced another period of deep sleep, something I could accomplish with relative ease.

Before the operation and with the help of electrochemical stimuli, I had become adept at initiating trancelike states of sleep, full of pleasurable images and experiences. The most effective of these stimulants had been introduced into my environment, and I was gratified to discover that I not only could descend into these trances whenever I wished, but that I could usually manipulate the visions, acting as a director, more or less, of my own dreams. They were illusions, of course, but it was nevertheless a consolation to be able to experience the pleasures of the body—taste, touch, smell, even sex—as if I had been grafted back into the youthful and vigorous self that I'd thought had been lost to me forever. Even on those occasions when my visions would darken, as dreams often do, I could usually dispel the threatening shadows and escape back into a dream that was, if not ecstatic, at least safe.

But although I could manipulate these trances, I was often slow to wake from them, and my team was given strict instructions to arouse me after every eight-hour period of sleep. The schedule that I then adopted was similar to the one I'd followed before the operation. Upon awakening, I would be supplied with the latest scientific and technical findings and research in my field, the most significant symposium papers and refereed articles, and also the general news of the day. Free of the conflicting diversions and interruptions of the body, I found that I could assimilate and retain a remarkable amount of data, but for no more than eight hours, after which I began to read the latest books, listen to the best music, attend the most prominent cultural events—movies, concerts, video presentations—whatever could be digitized and fed directly into my neural receptors. This second eight-hour period was primarily a time for relaxation and reflection, but it also contributed to the store of memories and images that I drew upon for my dreams, which filled the final third of my day.

Whenever convenient I communicated my own thoughts and observations, and over the years I collaborated on a multitude of projects, appearing as co-author of some fifty papers. I've also been credited with participation in several patented techniques, and a good portion of my maintenance costs have been underwritten by the subsequent royalties.

This routine and these activities were continued for approximately thirty-seven years, two months, and six days, and for approximately thirty-seven years, two months, and six days, I contributed to our scientific understanding and the technological progress of our civilization. I say "approximately" because I cannot be sure of the length of that last day, for on that sixth day I was never awakened from my sleep. I could have been dormant for my normal eight hours or for a day or for a month or for a year or even more. I have no way of knowing.

All I know is that after thirty-seven years, two months, and six days—the last day of indeterminate length—I awoke into silence.

After all that time, I had an acute sense of my own physical well-being, and as far as I could tell, all systems were functioning perfectly and my neural receptors were healthy. There was simply no external communication, as if my sensory organs had been disconnected and all that I could perceive was within myself. At first, I was calm and I transmitted one message after another, but if staff were there to receive them, they gave no sign of their presence. Naturally, my communications soon became disjointed and desperate—the digital equivalents of cries for help—and even though I was sure my environment was normal, unchanged, and I was quite healthy, I suddenly felt as if I were suffocating. After a few more urgent appeals for assistance, I concluded that I had entered a nightmare unawares, and I quickly induced another state of pleasurable ecstasy, fully expecting to be awakened into my usual schedule.

Again, I have no idea how long I slept, and when I awoke it was again into silence.

What had happened? All of my support systems were operational. I was properly nourished, ionization levels appeared stable, and despite an occasional suffocating attack of anxiety, I was fully oxygenated. It was as if my entire environment, self-sustaining and functional, had been transported into a closet, locked away and forgotten.

What had happened? I recalled having read reports about foreign insurgencies and new and fiendish weapons of destruction. But there would have been more warning if, say, a global war had erupted, if there had been a threat of mass annihilation. More diplomatic activity, more military maneuvers, more urgency—and I would have been informed. After all, I was still an official, a member in good standing of the ruling government.

I was also aware that there had been increased internal discontent, talk of dismantling technology and a return to a simpler past—code words, of course, for succumbing to our baser instincts and descending into barbarism! Ten years before, in fact, when these same tendencies seemed to be emerging once again, I ordered my environment to be sealed and my supplies to be extended to last through the life of the systems. But even at their height, these were minority movements, and, again, I would have known if they had become serious threats. I would have been warned!

Or perhaps it's something as simple as a budgetary crisis, a loss of government support until funding can be restored. My team has always been loyal and respectful of my needs, even at my most demanding. Perhaps they were simply reluctant or afraid to tell me. Of course, all of the original group are gone, dead or retired by now, and this new generation, this new social climate, with a lack of values I could never understand.... Am I simply being ignored? Is this some kind of sadistic game?... But I've given strict instructions that the project should be terminated immediately if it ceases to be of use. I have no desire to prolong an existence that is no more than a drain on our resources, a freak of technology, like some comatose patient, kept needlessly alive!

But I had every indication that my contributions were still being appreciated and valued, that the experiment was still considered a terrific success. Why, one of the last messages I received had informed me that our team had captured another Masters Prize for breakthroughs in neurological controls, techniques that I personally reviewed and, on occasion, simplified!

Or maybe what I fear most has occurred. Some unexpected planetary catastrophe has suddenly reduced life on earth to a baser level of existence or ended it altogether. My environment is underground, sealed and self-sufficient. It's protected from radiation and severe variations in climate by several layers of lead and earth. Am I to be isolated here in this subterranean chamber to carry on my existence, helpless and alone, until the end of time?

I know this must sound like the hysterical ravings of a frightened old man, but I would not be sending this transmission—assuming my transmitter is still functioning—if again and again I had not awakened from my dreams, each one of indeterminate length, to be confronted by this impenetrable, frozen silence. And now this new, even more imperative concern…

Our ancient Eastern religions spoke of Nirvana as a desired culmination to human existence, and I suppose that when I finally resigned myself to this solitary fate, I sought to achieve a similar sort of transport, if only temporarily, through meditation and dream. The mind contains an inexhaustible store of images and fantasies, and I have no idea how many months, years passed by as I slipped into one trance after another, awakening only long enough to determine whether I was still alone, and then—having received my answer—quickly falling asleep again.

Occasionally, the dreams would darken and become troubling, but I usually managed to turn them into more pleasurable directions, although sometimes they would become sufficiently threatening to awaken me. But the effects of most nightmares quickly diminish, and their content is soon forgotten, and when that uncomfortable burning sensation— as if I had been holding the palm of my hand over a lit candle—first disrupted my sleep, I assumed it to be the result of a fitful dream. When I was awakened again by the same shock of pain, I was sure it was a recurrence of my nightmare. But when it happened a third and fourth time, I suspected that its cause might be elsewhere. Moreover, as it continued to awaken me, the burning intensified by slight degrees and on each occasion persisted for several seconds more, as if the hand were drawing closer to the flame and holding its position for a longer time.

To confirm my suspicions, I remained awake, counting the seconds, minutes, and hours between one of these attacks and the onset of the next. I performed this tedious calculation three times, and each time the interval equaled sixteen hours, give or take a few minutes, and although it had been months, years, maybe decades, since I had followed a routine schedule, I recalled that every sixteen hours the solution in which I was floating would be fortified by an infusion of carbohydrates, enzymes, and phosphates, timed to correspond with my awakenings and my most active period.

In short, something within the system was clearly poisoning it at regular intervals. A corroded valve or joint, an accidental oxidation of some component of my raw supplies, a malfunction in waste removal leading to a surplus of toxins—whatever the cause, something had invaded my environment, and the nutrients and chemical reactions that were preserving my health were now also stimulating my pain receptors at regular intervals and with ever increasing intensity.

Faced with this conclusion, I quickly retreated into another reverie, and sixteen hours later I was again returned to consciousness by a painful seizure, again slightly stronger than the previous and again lasting a few seconds more.

The seizures now persist for about an hour, from the initial searing shock to a gradual alleviation into a throbbing soreness. Afterwards I escape into sleep, but these attacks have the power to remove me from any reverie, no matter how deep. If I were so inclined, I could probably calculate the time left to me before the interval diminishes to nothing, before the concentration of contaminants becomes great enough to prevent me from ever again retreating into the pleasurable quiet of my dreams. All that will remain then to keep my mind alive is the expectation of the constant and certain intensification of each new attack.

Of course the brain, lacking a complex network of nerves, cannot be a source of pain, and there is likely no correlation between what I'm experiencing through these neural receptors and any real damage being done to the organism. But perhaps that's not the case, and I am hopeful that whatever malfunction has precipitated this disastrous sequence of events, will eventually destroy me, too, before sleep is no longer an option and there is no more refuge to be found. Otherwise, unless by some miracle I am heard and the experiment is finally ended, the only solace I can expect is the submersion of my consciousness into madness as I float toward eternity on a sea of fire.

SEA CHANGE

Ellen Prentiss Campbell

Adrienne swam before she walked, snorkeled at six.

"What do you want to be when you grow up?" the grown-ups asked.

"A deep sea diver."

In high school her family called her an amphibious creature crossed with a book worm, more interested in fish and reading than in boys. Not altogether true—she dated the captain of the high school swim team (skinny, hairless tadpole, all shoulders and legs) until outswimming and humiliating him. She discovered you can't cry underwater, swam solitary healing laps, and lay in the sun, reading Jacques Cousteau and Jules Verne.

At New College, Adrienne spent more time in the Sarasota Bay than class. Researching her senior honors thesis—echolocation in dolphins—she met a schooner bum and after graduation sailed the Caribbean with him. In Surinam, returning with groceries from the market, she found him in their bunk with a woman from a cruise ship. Adrienne flew back to the States and graduate school at Berkeley where, in the Department's submersible vessel, she studied clouds of fluffy green phytodetritus, finding even the waste from phytoplankton beautiful. She wrote her dissertation on the *Yolidia* clam's use of a small, mysterious appendage to detect the chemical state of its environment.

Friends married—on beaches and ship decks, in vineyards and redwood circles. She felt wistful but despite a few brief affairs, nothing stuck; she found no one as seductive as the secret world beneath the surface of the water, no late-night assignation satisfying as the midnight lab illuminated by the iridescent green of her aquariums. By the time she received her hood and doctorate, some friends (already on a second child or second marriage) had dropped out of the game to teach high school science, work for pharmaceuticals. Adrienne's clams, plankton, and algae required her full complement of nurture. "My significant other is named *Yolidia*," she said, refusing fix-up dates and introductions.

She turned down a tenure track professorship at San Diego State for the Oceanographic Institute at Woods Hole. The position offered field work on mollusks *in situ*, and housing on the beach. Adrienne bought a sailboat and practically lived in her wetsuit, swimming even in rough winter surf.

The marine snail *Aplysia* captured her attention. Its response to threat—increased heart rate and jets of ink—convinced Adrienne that the primitive mollusk experienced something like fear. The lab chief, Polly, encouraged her to write up the findings and submit a paper for publication.

Shop talk in the lab and the canteen sufficed for company. She skipped lab parties, avoided informal potlucks and the occasional communal "culture runs" to Boston. Evenings, after checking the temperature of her tanks, she wandered through the public display rooms over-run with tourist families and field-tripping children by day. Alone in the aqueous light, she peered in at ancient lobsters and horse-shoe crabs, pitying them, living out their days there instead of on the ocean floor. She felt kin to the captive specimens; even working and living so close to the water, she yearned. Adrienne envied astronauts' lengthy sojourns on space stations in the heavens.

On winter Sundays she made pots of soup big and deep enough to last the week, and read Thoreau's journal of his visit to the cape in 1857, Henry Beston's *Outermost House*. Beston understood: "The world today is sick to its thin blood for lack of elemental things."

One snowy January evening, snug before the fire, catching up on professional journals, a classified ad in *The Review of Experimental Biology* caught her eye. "Seeking adventurous scientist for underwater exploration. Willingness to relocate a prerequisite.*"

Awakening in the middle of the night, she called the number. "You have reached Dr. Jonah Larsen at Massachusetts General Hospital," said the tape. Jonah Larsen, a familiar name, one of the pioneers in work with hormones and sex change surgery. What was he up to now?

The next morning she reached his secretary.

"Would you like a Prospective Subjects Questionnaire?"

"I'd like to know about the project first."

"Due to the highly sensitive nature of the research, Dr. Larsen will only be able to provide a study description to accepted applicants."

"Well, I'm certainly not applying if I don't know what I'm applying for," Adrienne said, crumpling the ad and tossing it in the wastebasket.

But she retrieved the scrap of paper before leaving for work, and tucked it inside the leather cover of her day planner. On her coffee break, she stepped outside. Shivering in the damp cold air, watching a ferry plough through the white caps toward Martha's Vineyard, she flipped open her phone.

The Prospective Subjects Questionnaire arrived; the cover letter confirmed a study description would be provided "only to those applicants selected for in-person interviews." The mystery exerted an irresistible lure. No harm in completing the paperwork, if only to discover what the hush-hush protected.

Documenting her professional background required more space than entering the personal data. Non-smoking, no medications, no chronic health conditions. Single. No children. Pregnant? Prior pregnancies? No. None.

References? The bold print promised no one would be contacted at this preliminary stage but she couldn't risk Polly. Her dissertation advisor would do, warned and prepped before-hand. Probably nothing would come of it anyway. She sealed the envelope and posted it—excited, as though tossing a message in a bottle out to sea.

"I am pleased to invite you for an intake interview. Call to schedule at your earliest convenience." An indecipherable signature scrawled across the heavy cream page. No study prospectus, Larsen still withheld the bait.

"I have to go into Boston," she told Polly, not volunteering any explanation. "Sorry it's such short notice—only for the day."

"Everything OK?"

"Just a personal matter."

Her boss worked long hours across the hall. Like children engaged in parallel play, they shared an unspoken intimacy and protected each other's privacy.

"Leave me instructions by your tanks, for feeding and temperature checks."

Jonah Larsen had likely been handsome once, and still looked distinguished with his patrician bald brow, nose strong and beaked as a Medici's. He interrogated her for over two hours, reviewing her pedigree in marine biology, but spending more time on the personal history. Her open water swimming seemed to impress him more than her research.

He stared at her with pale blue eyes—the color of water in the rocky tide pools of the beaches of the Pacific Northwest. Did she have a boyfriend? Any intention of having children? Illegal questions, if she'd been a job applicant. No and no, she answered, swallowing fury at his trespass.

The fat envelope arrived on Valentine's Day.

"We are pleased to inform you of your selection from a highly competitive pool of applicants. Please read the enclosed protocol. Should you for any reason choose to decline this invitation, you remain bound by the statement of confidentiality executed at your interview. Call to schedule your intake appointment at your earliest convenience."

Adrienne opened the booklet (*Distribution and duplication prohibited*) and began to read.

> *As is often the case in science, a seeming coincidence led to the present inquiry. The serendipity in this instance is my work as an endocrinological consultant at Massachusetts General Hospital, one of the few institutions in the world performing separation surgeries on individuals with the rare congenital condition Sirenomelia, or "Mermaid's Syndrome."*

Sirens, Larsen explained, have fused legs. In most, blood vessels cross from side to side of the circulatory system, precluding separation surgery. Even after successful leg separation, former sirens require extensive hormone therapy in addition to physical therapy to develop the capacity to ambulate more or less normally.

*In addition to serving as consultant to separation surgeons, I have participated in the General's longitudinal follow-up studies of former sirens. A striking, unexpected, and most intriguing qualitative finding is that even years after successful surgery, some former sirens report persistent sensory confusion: a tactile hallucination, a feeling they **still have a tail**—rather like the well-known "phantom limb" syndrome in amputees. These individuals further describe feeling uncomfortable in their bipedal bodies, and many say they feel like "fish out of water." This phenomenon, reminiscent of the dilemma of trans-gendered patients, inspires my present research interest in the novel, highly experimental field of Trans-species Reassignment Therapy. Subjects in the proposed experimental study will receive hormone therapy directed to the goal of affecting a complete reverse metamorphosis. The successful study subject may expect to become fully aquatic, capable of living underwater: to **devolve** from mammal to amphibian and finally, become an Aquanaut.*

The intake appointment required an in-patient stay.

"I need a few days off, just till Wednesday," she told Polly. Adrienne's bi-weekly pay stub showed an astronomical balance of accrued annual and sick days.

"You'll arrange for someone to do the feeding, take the samples for you?" asked Polly. (Not offering, Adrienne noticed, to do it herself.) The world-renowned oceanographer had always treated Adrienne more as peer than subordinate. But now the reed-thin, grey-haired woman pressed her lips together and turned away.

It's science. Nothing frivolous, Adrienne wanted to protest.

Trapped in the stale air of the waiting room, listening to muzak, Adrienne watched goldfish circle a bowl on the reception desk. Her palms sweated, her heart pounded. Just nerves, she told herself. Calm down. Finally, a nurse holding a clipboard appeared.

"Leave your clothes and purse in the locker. Tie the gown so it opens in the front."

She waited another long interval in an examining room, shivering in the flimsy paper robe. "He's hazing me," she thought. But when the room went dark, she panicked and jumped from the table.

The light flicked on. Adrienne caught her breath, embarrassed. Of course, energy efficient lights on a timer, extinguished by stillness, activated by movement.

"Ready?" asked the nurse, opening the door.

Mammogram, EKG, blood work, urinalysis, vitals, reflexes, PET scan, CT scan, MRIs: a thorough going over. During the pelvic exam's routine humiliation (feet spread in useless stirrups, Larsen's gloved hand probing) she imagined fused legs, a neutered state, and flinched. She stared into the fluorescent ceiling tiles and chanted silently *the successful study subject may expect to become fully aquatic, capable of living under water.*

"You may get dressed now," said the nurse.

A battery of psychological tests followed, administered by a young woman with protuberant eyes like a *Pricanthus arenatus* (but excellent legs, very excellent bipedal appendages, in fishnet stockings beneath her short white coat). Adrienne looked down at her own legs—strong and long. Necessary sacrifice, but she'd miss them.

Finally, a five page consent form detailed risks and benefits, possible side effects, probable irreversible change, certain deformity, a chance of death, the possibility of being assigned to the control group on placebo. "The successful study subject may expect to become fully aquatic, capable of living under water," she reminded herself, signing on the dotted line.

Dr. Larsen's severe nurse instructed her in the medication regime and warned against shaving her legs (due to the risk of nicking the anticipated subcutaneous layer of scales).

Adrienne tapped on the fishbowl on the reception counter as the gum-chewing secretary scheduled her follow up appointments. She filled her prescriptions at the hospital's basement pharmacy and drove home on automatic pilot, her copy of the waiver locked in the glove compartment, pills rattling in her handbag. That evening, the last long night of the short month of February, she swallowed her first dose.

By St. Patrick's Day the pussy willows in the sheltered corner by the garage were beginning to swell and fuzz. Like a pre-pubescent girl longing for breasts, Adrienne studied herself daily in the mirror after bathing, looking for changes, for some sign of the hoped for metamorphosis. Nothing. She grew impatient with everyone, everything—the lab, Woods Hole, the scientists and fishermen, the insular community felt stifling. Even her clams and snails ceased to delight her. Every night she walked along the beach and gazed into the dark water.

She requested sick leave for the first monthly follow-up. Polly quivered with curiosity—like an anemone waving suspicious tentacles.

Larsen pinned her X-rays, her scans, to the light board in the examining room: nothing.

She pressed him. When might she expect evidence of the change? What would the first indicator be? Due to the experimental nature of the procedure, he couldn't say, but the first sign might be webbing, between the toes and fingers. Not long after that, visible scales should appear, her legs fuse, and the gills develop.

"Any dreams?" asked the psychologist in the required counseling session.

"No," lied Adrienne.

"None?" insisted the woman, bulging eyes studying her as though reading her mind like a slide in a microscope.

Adrienne confessed the recent nightmare—a flashback to almost drowning once, back in Sarasota. She'd been training for free immersion deep diving, eager to attempt what divers call the most dangerous event in the world, to descend hundreds of feet on one breath. But on her first dive, she blacked out. Afraid to try again, she sold the expensive monofin. Now the aborted exploit felt like an omen.

Anticipatory anxiety, the therapist suggested (dismissive, condescending). Quite a common phenomenon. But if she'd changed her mind, wanted to see if there was any chance of turning back, she must talk to Larsen immediately.

Certainly not, said Adrienne.

She missed a deadline for a grant; couldn't finish the abstract on her findings regarding *Aplysia* and evoked emotion. The heater in one of her tanks failed and plankton floated to the surface, limp and brown. Adrienne filed the required incident report.

Polly summoned her. "NOAA's coming for the accreditation site visit this fall. Your grant is up for renewal. We can't afford sloppy work, any careless mistakes. You know how tight money is under this administration. I'm not formally putting you on probation, but I need two hundred percent from everyone."

"I'm sorry."

"And I want you to join the lab team for the Coney Island Parade this year. We're going as the Global Warming Mermaids."

"I need to stay here, focus on my work."

"You *need* to fully participate in the life of the lab, Adrienne. We *need* esprit de corps, to get through accreditation."

Adrienne, ashamed as though she'd been called to the principal's office, retreated to her lab. The neat columns of data in her log book shimmered through a scrim of angry tears. She needed the escape of metamorphosis. Soon.

Spring advanced: dune grass furred the sand with a haze of olive. Clamorous, northward bound geese filled the sky. Locals stroked fresh paint on shutters, preparing for summer tenants. Adrienne swam morning and night; going in without her wet suit, hoping to discover she'd grown able to tolerate the cold, searching for a sign. Shivering, skin mottled and blue, she crawled out on the beach. *Accept it. You're just a control.*

Parade day, arms linked, Adrienne and the Global Warming Mermaids minced along in tight spandex tails, a chorus line of amphibious Rockettes accompanied by a brass band of pirates blasting *Yellow Submarine.* The sun set and beyond the boardwalk fireworks exploded into dusk. King Neptune, a massive wrestler slathered in silver body paint and festooned with garlands of seaweed, waved from his throne beneath the Ferris wheel. Adrienne broke free, cursing as she tripped over her tail, struggling through a school of little girl jelly fish in gauzy capes and stumbling down the stairs to the beach.

The detritus of the revelers lay scattered on the sand: Mardi Gras beads, plastic tridents, cloth leis. Adrienne unzipped her tail, peeled it off, stashed it under the steps and strode toward the water in her bikini, enjoying the damp sea-spray on her bare legs, celebrating release from the silly costume. An inviting path of moonlight stretched from the shore. She plunged in.

A seal surfaced. No, a man's sleek head, powerful shoulders.

"Hey," he called. "For a moment I thought you were a mermaid."

They swam together, along the shoreline, then waded in and walked back toward the lights. She admired his muscular legs.

"So you are a mermaid," he laughed when Adrienne retrieved her tail from beneath the boardwalk. "What about some dinner?"

"I'm cold, I have to find my friends, get the car keys for my clothes."

"I have sweats and a towel under the next set of stairs. Borrow my stuff. I'll go for carry-out. Sushi OK?"

They took turns with the flimsy chopsticks—he'd only brought back one set. The wasabi stung her nose and she coughed just as he kissed her the first time.

After eating, sitting on his damp towel on sand radiating cold, they kissed again until she pulled away—unsettled by the sensation between her legs. Attraction or—perhaps, finally—metamorphosis beginning? Adrienne tried not to think, tried just to want him. Once, she might have. Her teenage self might have crawled under the boardwalk and just done it, ignoring the grit of the sand, a little turned on by the noise of the crowd above.

"Ever notice how you see the moon in the water first, before the sky?" she asked, apologetic, embarrassed.

"Sure, physics, and Buddhism," he said. Tarn knew about both, he explained, as a physicist and practicing Buddhist, doing a post-doc at MIT.

Timing is everything, she reflected ruefully. He might have been interesting to get to know, if they'd met before.

Curled up in the lab van on the long drive north back to Cape Cod, Adrienne dreamed—not of Tarn, but of diving, alone, effortless and deep. At the bottom, on a shadowed ocean floor, she swam swishing her tail and fins. Waking in the bleached artificial light of a turnpike rest stop, she wondered: if she were a fish, would she dream of land? Always what she couldn't have?

Tarn e-mailed, inviting himself for a visit. Adrienne composed a response, claiming a pressing grant deadline, deferring a visit into some unspecified future moment. Her finger hovered over the "Send" command. Perhaps she should try it, one more time. One last time? Perhaps he was her consolation prize, for being trapped in this body, marooned in the terrestrial world.

Deleting her careful message she wrote: *How about the weekend of the Fourth? There'll be fireworks.* She clicked "send" and regretted it, immediately.

He arrived on the bus from Boston. She'd never seen him by daylight, dry, and fully clothed. He looked shorter, barrel-chested, disproportionate. Hair curled over his collar.

At the fish market, he selected lobster bodies and offered to make bisque. Adrienne didn't confess she'd lost her appetite for rich chowders; she craved miso broth and kelp salad, periwinkles on the side. She bicycled to the farm stand for corn and came back to her own kitchen polluted by clouds of milky, salty steam.

But after dinner, they swam by starlight, fingers trailing reflected phosphorescent constellations, treading water, watching the blinking of the buoys, the purposeful lights of the Vineyard ferry. His curls looked sleek as fur in the water and she could once again imagine him a seal, an otter. They showered together under the rough spray of the outdoor shower and made love in her loft bedroom. The beacon of the lighthouse shone in her window, washing over the bed like water. He fell asleep, anchoring her under a heavy arm. She rolled away and crept out alone to wade on the beach.

The next day after dispatching him on the Peter Pan Bus, Adrienne ran a deep bubble bath and soaked until the water cooled—but her skin did not pucker. Drying off, she discovered a tiny flap of webbing between her toes. Her heart somersaulted. Dialing Larsen's hotline, she quivered with excitement and terror. This must be what her friends described, when a pregnancy test read positive.

Ordered to Boston immediately, Adrienne left her resignation on the soapstone lab bench. She stared into her tanks and tapped a Morse code goodbye on the glass. Halfway down the hall, she turned back, scooped her clams and snails into a bucket, carried them out to the Institute dock, and released the *Yolidia* and *Aplysia* to the sea.

Larsen examined her, his eyes sparkling. On the illuminated x-rays Adrienne saw a ghostly layer of scales beneath her skin.

"Excellent," Larsen said, as she trembled in the paper gown in the air-conditioned cell of the examining room. He froze her with his pale blue gaze—the flat, emotionless glance of the great white shark she'd encountered once, diving off Baja. "You'll be admitted as an in-patient, for the duration."

Adrienne walked along Beacon Street, staring in the dusty windows of the antique shops at relics of earthly domestic life—sherry glasses, porcelain ginger jars. She drank a brandy at the Ritz before calling Tarn.

"I'm in town," she said.

"Great! Come out for dinner. Spend the night."

"No," she said. "I can't stay. Come in. Meet me at the swan boats."

Almost dinner time, the tourists and children and mothers dispersed. One solitary swan boat toiled around the pond. Tarn and Adrienne rode alone on the front bench.

She explained, speaking softly, though the bored young man piloting their swan wore earphones.

Tarn snorted in disbelief. "If you don't want to see me, just say so. Spare me the tall tales."

"No," she said. "It's true." And extended her hand and spread her fingers, revealing the webbing, new since morning, which already reached almost to her first knuckle.

He stared. "There's got to be an antidote."

"It's what I wanted," she said.

"Before," he said, earnest and serious, brown eyes deep and soft as a seal's. "Do you want it still?" He touched her cheek with a hot, dry hand.

She hesitated. Did she want it still? She almost could imagine a future with him, working in a little college along the coast of Maine, teaching their own school of tan, brown-haired water babies to swim (in tiny wetsuits buoyed by fluorescent orange water wings).

Adrienne looked into the shallow murk lapping past the awkward boat. A hopeful duck paddled and quacked in the wake; a crumpled soda cup floated by.

"I'm sorry," she said. "It's too late."

Larsen prescribed bed rest at Mass General. By week's end, a thin layer of glittering green scales girdled her hips and belly. She broke the rules, tried to get up to go to the bathroom by herself, and fell. Her legs had fused. A nurse came running, and called Dr. Larsen.

"Wonderful," he said, rubbing his pale hands together—the fingers long as the stinging tentacles of a jelly fish. He palpated her throat with his chilly fingers, as though checking for swollen glands. "Good, good— that's likely a bit sensitive, isn't it? Your gill ventricles are opening, my dear. Now, I'm putting a tag with a tracking chip in it on your ear."

"A tracking chip?" She didn't recall that, from the consent forms.

"To keep tabs on you. Just a little pinch—there. We'll move you to the Aquarium on the harbor tonight."

"The Aquarium?"

"We're using one of their boats, with a holding tank. If you do O.K., submerged overnight, we'll take you to the Cape and release you tomorrow."

L ying in bed, impatient as a kidnap victim in her strange hybrid body, Adrienne imagined the sea. She yearned for freedom, to swim away. *Is this like dying? Everything left behind, burnt away by readiness?*

That evening, an orderly lifted her from bed to gurney. They rode a freight elevator down and rolled through labyrinthine miles of underground corridors, finally surfacing in a parking garage. The orderly loaded the gurney inside the waiting ambulance.

"Let's go," Dr. Larsen shouted from the driver's seat.

Adrienne gasped; the caustic air seared through her gills.

A cargo net dropped Adrienne into the ship's tank. Water flowed over her gills like cool spring air. Beyond the glass wall, she could see the gleam of Dr. Larsen's white coat. She closed her eyes and sank to the bottom and slept.

In the morning, the boat's engine groaned to life; water in the tank sloshed, rocking Adrienne back and forth. The ship churned out into the harbor, then beyond, into open sea.

Netted, hoisted up out of the tank, she swung out over the edge of the boat in a wild hammock ride. And then, released, she plummeted into the ocean. Down, down, down on a single breath. Free immersion diving at last. She drifted through a forest of seaweed without effort, without fear. Stretching, wriggling what had been her toes, fluttering her tail, she floated to the surface.

Sunbeams refracted by the water above dazzled her with shards of rainbows like a celestial chandelier. She vaulted out of the water and splashed down, exhilarated. A seal surfaced beside her; its smooth, dark head, liquid brown eyes reminded her of something. The faint, indistinct memory slipped away as a school of dolphins nuzzled her, chortling, winking. The mermaid flipped her powerful tail and joined the frolic, leaping up, splashing down into the bottle green sea.

CONTRIBUTORS

Ellen Prentiss Campbell, Rockville, MD.
Ellen Prentiss Campbell's stories have appeared in journals including *The Massachusetts Review, The Potomac Review, The Fourth River, Paper Street,* and *Iron Horse.* An MFA graduate of The Bennington Writing Seminars, she lives near Washington, DC with her husband and retreats to write on her farm in Bedford County, Pennsylvania. She has completed a collection of stories set in the Allegheny Mountains of western Pennsylvania near her paternal grandfather's birthplace and is at work on a novel. As a writer and a social worker, she seeks the story between the lines and behind the words.

Emily Doak, Greencastle, IN.
Emily Doak danced at School of American Ballet and North Carolina School of the Arts before receiving her BFA in film from NYU and her MFA in fiction from Indiana University. Her short stories have appeared in the *Gettysburg Review, Barrelhouse, Inkwell, Yemassee,* and *Isotope* and her poetry in *Spoon River Poetry Review* and *Rhino.* She teaches writing at DePauw University in Greencastle, Indiana and is currently putting the finishing touches on a novel called *Dragon Boys of Indiana.*

Lou Fisher, Hopewell Junction, NY.
Lou Fisher lives with his wife in downstate New York, from where he teaches fiction and nonfiction for the Long Ridge Writers Group. His stories have appeared in every type of magazine and journal, including *The Mississippi Review* and *Other Voices,* and have been selected for numerous anthologies like *The Way We Work* (Vanderbilt University Press 2008), *Hunger and*

Thirst (City Works Press 2009), and *Coming Home* (MSR Short Fiction 2010). He has received the New Letters Literary Award for Fiction as well as a writing fellowship from his county's arts council. His earlier genre novels were published by Dell and Warner.

Mardelle Fortier, Lisle, IL.

Mardelle Fortier has published 15 stories, about 10 essays, and nearly 100 poems. Her stories have appeared in *Bibliophilos, Black Petals, Woman's World, Crime Stalker Casebook,* and other magazines. She writes sci-fi, mystery, horror, and literary stories. Fortier teaches creative writing at College of DuPage and Benedictine University. She has won many prizes in creative writing.

Shannon Gibney, Minneapolis, MN.

Shannon Gibney teaches writing, journalism, and African American topics at Minneapolis Community & Technical College. Her article on Octavia Butler recently appeared in the anthology *Black Imagination, Futurism,* and *the Speculative.*

Tim Goldstone, North Pembrokeshire, Wales, UK.

Backpacked and worked throughout the U.K., Western and Eastern Europe, including the former Yugoslavia. Also travelled in North Africa. Currently writing out of Wales, to where he always returns, despite being born in England. Currently lives in North Pembrokeshire with his wife, child and swamp-dog, in the heart of the marshy landscape between sea and mountains. Studied English and History at Lampeter University, Wales. Currently harvesting material from his memory for *Peach Slices,* a collection of short stories based on the events and characters he was involved with when employed as a mill-hand for a year and a day at Southampton docks.

Terresa Haskew, Greenville, SC.

Terresa Haskew is truly "living the dream" with her appearance in this anthology. This is her first short story to be accepted for publication, and she is grateful for Main Street Rag's warm reception. Terresa is a poet whose work has appeared in journals and anthologies such as *Press 53 Open Awards Anthology* (2010 First Prize for Poetry), *Atlanta Review, Emrys Journal, Kakalak* (2009 Honorable Mention), *Fruit of the Banyan Tree* and *The Main Street Rag*. Terresa was a Top 10 Finalist in the 2011 SC Poetry Initiative's Single Poem Contest, and has work forthcoming in *Pearl*. She and her husband, Ben, have three children and two grandchildren.

Philip Kobylarz, Hayward, CA.

Philip Kobylarz has recent work in *Connecticut Review, Volt, Visions International, New American Writing, Prairie Schooner, Poetry Salzburg Review* and has appeared in Best American Poetry.

Adeline Carrie Koscher, Brewster, MA.

Adeline Carrie Koscher earned her Ph.D. from the University of St. Andrews in Scotland, where she wrote *The New Woman Novelist and the Redefinition of the Female: Marriage, Sexuality and Motherhood* (Dissertation.com 2010). She now lives and writes on Cape Cod, the home of many famous writers—she is not a famous one. Here, she daydreams and grows tomatoes with her partner, James. A high school English teacher, she is working on lots of projects all at once, throwing caution to the wind, to see what the wind will do with it. When not writing letters of recommendation, she writes fiction, poetry, literary criticism, and one-woman shows. The short story published here was written at the Nantucket Soundings Buzzards Bay Writers' Retreat.

Karen Kovacik, Indianapolis, IN.

Karen Kovacik is Director of Creative Writing at Indiana University Purdue University Indianapolis. She is the recipient of a number of awards, including a guest fellowship at the University of Wisconsin's Institute for Creative Writing, an Arts Council of Indianapolis Creative Renewal Fellowship, the Charity Randall Citation from the International Poetry Forum, and a Fulbright Research Grant to Poland. She spent the 2004-05 academic year in Warsaw, translating contemporary Polish women's poetry. Her latest book of poems is *Metropolis Burning* (Cleveland State, 2005). Her poems and stories have appeared in *Salmagundi, Chelsea, Glimmer Train, Massachusetts Review,* and *Indiana Review,* and her translations of contemporary Polish poets in *American Poetry Review, Boston Review, Crazyhorse, Southern Review,* and *West Branch.*

Eva Langston, Washington, DC.

Eva Langston is a native of Roanoke, Virginia and a recent MFA graduate of the University of New Orleans. Her short stories have appeared in *Blood Lotus, Talking River Review,* and *The Normal School,* as well as forthcoming in *The Sand Hill Review.* She also won third place in the 2010 Playboy Fiction Contest, but unfortunately, they do not publish third place. Currently she lives in Capitol Hill and teaches high school math.

Larry Lefkowitz, Modiin, Israel.

His stories, poetry and humor have appeared in many publications in the United States, Israel, and Britain. Among the publications: *Thema, A Cappella Zoo, Third Wednesday Magazine, Yellow Medicine Review, Silver Boomer Book, The Vocabula Review, Runes, The Literary Review, Crimespree*; many online publications; anthologies. Self-published booklet: *Humor for Writers.* Lefkowitz is currently hoping to find a publisher for his novel manuscript *Lieberman.*

Brian Leung, Louisville, KY.

Brian Leung is the author of the historical novel *Take Me Home*, which centers around the historical event of a massacre of Chinese Miners in 1885, Wyoming Territory. He is also the author of the novel *Lost Men* as well as the story collection *World Famous Love Acts*, a winner of the Asian American Literary Award and the Mary McCarthy Prize in Short Fiction. His poetry, creative nonfiction, and short fiction have appeared in numerous journals and anthologies. He was born and raised in San Diego County and is Director of Creative Writing at the University of Louisville.

Amy Locklin, Indianapolis, IN.

Amy Locklin is the editor of Altered States. Her poetry, fiction, and nonfiction have appeared in *Quarter After Eight, Maize,* and *Dots on a Map: Stories from Small Town America.* Poems are forthcoming in *And Know This Place: Poetry of Indiana* and *The Main Street Rag.* Her work has won honors in the Robert J. DeMott short prose contest, the Academy of American Poets Prize, the Associated Writing Program's Intro Journal Project, and the Lois Davidson Ellis Literary Award for fiction. A recipient of Indiana Arts Commission grants and former director of the IU Writers' Conference, she currently teaches literature and writing at IUPUI and DePauw University, and sings jazz around Indianapolis at such venues as the Artsgarden.

T. Shontelle MacQueen, Charlotte, NC.

T. Shontelle MacQueen was born in London, England and lived in Europe, Scandinavia, and an assortment of U.S. states before settling in North Carolina where she is a licensed psychologist. In addition to professional publications, Dr. MacQueen enjoys writing short stories that often defy traditional categorization. She enjoys a variety of interests including music, martial arts, and spending time with her two young children. She is currently at work on her first full length novel.

Jenean McBrearty, Danville, KY.

Jenean McBrearty is a semi-retired political science and sociology community college instructor for military education programs, and an administrative representative/ alternative dispute resolution facilitator. She is currently pursuing an MFA Creative Writing at Eastern Kentucky University, and focuses on creating social science fiction for teaching across the curriculum. She hopes to expand the market for relevant and entertaining higher education materials by demonstrating how effective teaching through the short story is. A native of San Diego, California where she raised two children, she now shares her residence with the most lovable tabby in the world: Mr. Baxter

Adam McOmber, Chicago, IL.

Adam McOmber is the Assistant Director of Creative Nonfiction at Columbia College Chicago. He is the associate editor of the literary magazine *Hotel Amerika*, and his fiction has recently appeared in *Conjunctions, Third Coast, StoryQuarterly* and *Arts and Letters*. His short story collection *This New and Poisonous Air* will be published by BOA Editions Ltd. in June

Contributors

2011. His novel *Empyrean* will be published by Touchstone, an imprint of Simon and Schuster, in August 2012.

Alyce Miller, Bloomington, IN.

Alyce Miller's most recent book is *Water*, winner of the Mary McCarthy Prize. Previous awards include the Flannery O'Connor Award for Short Fiction, Kenyon Review Award for Literary Excellence in Fiction, and the Lawrence Prize. She has published more than 200 stories, poems, essays, and articles, and teaches creative writing, literature, and special topics courses at Indiana University-Bloomington. In addition, she leads a double life as an attorney specializing in animal rights and family law.

Craig O'Hara, Muncie, IN.

Craig O'Hara grew up in Southern Indiana, spending most of his time reading books pilfered from his father's bookshelves. After attending Indiana University, he lived and worked in Vietnam and the Northern Mariana Islands. He later received his MFA from the University of Arizona, and since then his stories have appeared in a number of magazines and journals, including *Confrontation, Spork,* and *The Sonora Review*. He currently lives with his lovely wife in Muncie and teaches writing at Ball State University. The piece appearing here is part of a collection of short fiction about places that no longer exist and probably never did.

Mark Pearson, Pottstown, PA.

Mark Pearson recently moved from Houston, TX, to Pottstown, PA, where he will teach at The Hill School. He earned a Ph.D in English from the University of Georgia and an M.A. in English and creative writing from the University of California, Davis. His fiction and essays have appeared in or are forthcoming in *The*

Best American Sports Writing 2011, Aethlon, Blueline, Broken Bridge Review, Carve, Gray's Sporting Journal, The Main Street Rag Publishing Company Sports Fiction Anthology, 2011, North Dakota Quarterly, Short Story, Sport Literate, and *Stories.*

Vivian Faith Prescott, Kodiak, Alaska

Vivian Faith Prescott was born and raised in Wrangell, Alaska and lives in Sitka and Kodiak, Alaska. She holds a Ph.D. in Cross Cultural Studies and has an MFA from the University of Alaska, Anchorage. Vivian is the co-director of a non-profit called Raven's Blanket based in Wrangell and facilitates adult and teen writers' groups at Air Station Kodiak. She is a Puschart Prize nominee and her poetry has appeared in *Drunken Boat, Permafrost,* and *Turtle Quarterly.* Her first book of poetry The Hide of My Tongue will be published by Plain View Press in the winter of 2011. Vivian's website http://www.vivianfaithprescott.com and she blogs at http://planetalaska.blogspot.com

Nicole Louise Reid, Newburgh, IN.

Nicole Louise Reid is the author of the novel *In the Breeze of Passing Things* (MacAdam/Cage), fiction chapbook *Girls* (RockSaw Press), and forthcoming story collection *So There!* (Stephen Austin University Press). Her stories have appeared in *Sweet, The Southern Review, Quarterly West, Meridian, Black Warrior Review, Confrontation, turnrow,* and *Crab Orchard Review.* Recipient of the Willamette Award in Fiction, she teaches creative writing at the University of Southern Indiana, where she is fiction editor of *Southern Indiana Review* and editor of RopeWalk Press, and directs the RopeWalk Visiting Writers Reading Series.

Mark Rigney, Evansville, IN.

Mark Rigney is the author of the play Acts of God (Playscripts, Inc., 2008) and the non-fiction book *Deaf Side Story: Deaf Sharks, Hearing Jets and a Classic American Musical* (Gallaudet University Press, 2003). His short fiction has been nominated for a Pushcart Prize and appears in *The Best of the Bellevue Literary Review, Realms of Fantasy,* and *Lady Churchill's Rosebud Wristlet,* with upcoming work in *Black Gate, Sleet,* and *Birkensnake.* Two collections of his short stories are now available at Amazon, *Reality Checks* and *Flights of Fantasy.* His website is www.markrigney.net.

Ivy Rutledge, Greensboro, NC.

Originally from Rhode Island, Ivy Rutledge lives and writes in the Piedmont of North Carolina, where she shares her life with her husband and two children. Since earning her BA in English Education and History, she has taught writing in high schools and in home school writing classes. Her work has appeared in *The Sun* and *Home Education,* as well as several local and statewide publications, and she was a semi-finalist in the 2005 NC State Poetry Contest. This is her first published piece of fiction.

Joanne Seltzer, Schenectady, NY.

She earned her B.A. in English from the University of Michigan and her M.A. in English from The College of Saint Rose. Her poems have been published in a variety of journals and anthologies, including *Lilith, The Village Voice, The Minnesota Review, Waterways, The Muse Strikes Back,* and *When I Am an Old Woman I Shall Wear Purple.* Seltzer has also published short fiction, literary essays, translations of French poetry, and three poetry chapbooks. Her most recent poetry book, *Women Born During Tornadoes,* was published in 2009 by Plain View Press. Seltzer has won prizes in competitions sponsored by The World Order of Narrative and Formalist Poets and some of her poems are set to music and used as classroom texts. Her website is www.Joseltzer.com.

Lucille Gang Shulklapper, Coral Springs, FL.

A prize-winning author of fiction and poetry, Lucille's work appears in many publications as well as in four poetry chapbooks: *What You Cannot Have, The Substance of Sunlight, Godd, It's Not Hollywood,* and *In The Tunnel.* Living up to traditional expectations led to work as a salesperson, model, realtor, teacher, and curriculum coordinator throughout schooling, marriage, children, and grandchildren. Her first picture book, *Stuck in Bed, Fred,* was recently accepted for publication.

Susan Sterling, Waterville, ME.

Susan Sterling received her MFA from the Program for Writers at Warren Wilson College and has taught fiction and nonfiction in the creative writing program at Colby College. Her stories and essays have appeared in *The New York Times, the Best American Sports Writing, The North American Review, The Christian Science Monitor, Down East, Crab Orchard Review* and the French journal *Etudes,* and have been anthologized in *The Berkeley Women's Literary Revolution: Essays from Marsha's Salon; The Way Life Should Be: Stories by Contemporary Maine Writers;* and in *A Healing Touch: True Stories of Life, Death, and Hospice* (edited by Richard Russo). She lives in Waterville with her husband, Paul Machlin.

Jennifer Tomscha, Ann Arbor, MI.

Jennifer Tomscha was born and raised in the Great Plains. She has a master of theology from Harvard Divinity School, and an MFA from the University of Michigan, where she has taught composition and creative writing. She is also a 2011-2012 Zell Fellow in Creative Writing. Her work is forthcoming in *Glimmer Train*.

J. Weintraub, Chicago, IL.

J. Weintraub has published fiction, essays, and poetry in *The New Criterion, Massachusetts Review, Michigan Quarterly Review, Crab Orchard Review, Chicago Reader,* and many other reviews and periodicals. He has received awards for writing from the Illinois and Barrington Art Councils, was an Around-the-Coyote poet, and is currently a network playwright at Chicago Dramatists. He has recently performed his "Investigation into the Life of the Screenwriter, Henry Frank" at the Uptown Writer's Space and the Twilight Tales Reading Series at The Mix.

Esther K. Willison, Niskayuna, NY.

Esther K. Willison is one of the founders and teachers of an alternative ungraded public school in Schenectady, New York. She served as the assistant director of a teen theater bringing AIDS education into the public schools in the tri-city area. Her work has appeared in *The Stories We Hold Secret* (The Greenfield Review Press), *Common Lives, Lesbian Lives,* in a collection of essays, *Small Town Gay, 13th Moon, The Litchfield Review, Peeks and Valleys,* and *White Pelican Review,* among other journals. In July, 2010, she received second place, for Memoir, in the Pacific Northwest Writers' Association Annual Literary Contest. She is currently on the staff of The Open Door Bookstore in Schenectady, NY.

Lauren Yaffe, Brooklyn, NY.
Lauren Yaffe holds an MFA from Warren Wilson College. Her stories, poems and essays have appeared in such journals and anthologies as *Alaska Quarterly, Cottonwood Review, Calliope, Frigate, English Journal, Voices from the Spectrum* and others. Her story "The Evolution of Tulips", which appeared in *Fiction Weekly,* was nominated for a 2008 Pushcart Prize. She lives in Brooklyn and is currently working on several screenplays and children's books about worms--the earthy kind.